Katy

*An Irish-American
five generation portrait*

The Attic Was
an Unused Room

Katy King

Waubesa Press
P.O. Box 192
Oregon, WI 53575

© Copyright 1999 by Kathleen Mary King
Published by Waubesa Press,
the quality fiction imprint of Badger Books Inc.

Printed by BookCrafters of Chelsea, Mich.

First Edition
ISBN 1-878569-60-0

This is a work of fiction. Names, characters, places and incidents are either the product of the author's imagination or used fictitiously.

Badger Books Inc.
P.O. Box 192
Oregon, WI 53575
Toll-free phone: (800) 928-2372
Web site: http://www.badgerbooks.com
E-mail: books@badgerbooks.com

Thank you, Maggie, Annie, Cece, Marguerite and Rena for living the stories. I hope I have not stretched these stories beyond what you would like. I appreciate the encouraging words and suggestions from Betty, Leona, Elayne, Chelle, Tony and Ellen. Mariann and Teresa generously helped me with computers and Dave and Helen with photographs. Marv has patiently guided me through the maze of being published.

The attic: where family treasures rest
until the heritage is brought to light

Prologue
Maureen
Northwestern Wisconsin
March 1, 1991

Back and forth. Back and forth. Endless hard work? Sometimes it seemed that way. Boring? No, soothing. Satisfying, to bring in wood for heating. I felt connected with this work, connected to the past, thinking that my ancestors had done this, too, and connected to the future because I was providing heat for myself.

A few years ago, I had started collecting family stories, which led me to realize how much I was like my ancestors. Thirty years ago, when I had become a nun, I thought I was being noble and holy. Later, I recognized the rebellion in my choice: I refused to follow Mom's footsteps into a feisty marriage, into raising a bunch of bratty kids, so I became a teaching nun. Later still, I found out that, going back for four generations of Mom's family, over half the women and some of the men had been teachers. Some rebellion!

After leaving the convent, twenty years ago, I had a modern log cabin built in these Wisconsin woods. Last year I visited the site where my great-great-grandfather John built his log cabin in southern Wisconsin one hundred fifty-five years ago.

I went out to the woodpile, grabbed three chunks, carried them into the walk-in basement, stacked them inside so the snow could melt off them and they could dry and burn well. It was unusual for me to be carrying wood in the winter, but last fall, instead of doing wood, I made all those trips to Florida, to help Dad and be with Mom as she was dying of cancer.

I decided that when I got to my group home that afternoon, I'd have Bob make sugar cookies, Grandma Cece's recipe. We'd send Dad a sweet "care package" and treat ourselves, too.

Back and forth. I wondered how far I would go if I carried a winter's worth of wood myself, instead of having the men from my group home helping me. One, two, three,... it was about fifty paces from outside to inside, about one hundred feet, two hundred feet round trip. The width of the row inside was about three of my "wingspans" (five and a half feet from fingertip to fingertip). I stacked the wood seven and a half feet high. Call it 17' by 7', about one hundred and twenty square feet facing me. In one trip, I carried about half a square foot. So one row would take two hundred forty trips. That would be 48,000 feet of walking for the row, which was about nine miles, call it ten, because I didn't always carry in half a square foot. So I walked about forty miles to bring in all four rows!

This was my thirteenth year of bringing in wood and I finally made the calculations so I could impress myself with how hard I worked, or rather, how hard *we* worked. Mostly the men from my group home helped me; they liked cutting, splitting and carrying wood; the work showed them they were still useful, even though life had knocked them around quite a bit. So why was I doing it by myself that day? Maybe for the peace and quiet of it and to show myself that my cancer-attacked, arthritic fifty-two-year-old body could still carry wood for those three or four hours and only suffer exhaustion that day, and back and shoulder aches the next day, and pains in muscles and joints I forgot I had. Besides, if I didn't use it for bringing in wood, what excuse would I have for keeping my holey old paint-spattered parka, with its warm stuffing all evaporated?

I hadn't done math problems for a while, but I still enjoyed them. So, how much weight was in a winter's worth of wood? A full gallon of milk weighed about ten pounds; a bag of dog food weighed forty pounds. The smaller pieces of wood probably weighed a bit over ten pounds and I probably carried thirty or forty pounds a trip. Thirty pounds times two hundred forty trips was 7,200 pounds, around 30,000 pounds for four rows. Two thousand pounds in a ton meant fifteen tons. I burst into song, using the melody from *Sixteen Tons* with my words about stacking wood. I wondered if Tennessee Ernie Ford ever did enough physical labor to know what he was singing about in that song.

I liked problem-solving and patterns. In school, I had enjoyed solving trigonometry problems and spotting patterns for diagramming sentences in English class. But my interests had shifted: my problems the last ten years were more practical, like which was the best buy in paper towels or how could I nudge the behavior patterns of the guys in my group home toward more constructive actions. But by far the biggest problem I ever had to solve was finding my best self. I realized suddenly that some of my fore-mothers had had to struggle to find their niches, too.

With my mind busy, my back-and-forthing had brought in a sizable bunch of wood. I needed a break.

Sitting in my recliner, I ate a candy bar to revive my energy and noticed my new toy, a VCR on top of the TV. I always liked old movies, but I saw them differently than I used to.

Above the VCR, the photographs of my ancestors drew my eye, especially great-Grandma Annie's portrait. She was a beautiful woman; her eyes told me that she had known great sadness and great joy, too. I hadn't heard so many stories about her, yet looking at her picture, I sensed the great love and strength she wove into the lives of her family and friends. Great-great-Grandma Maggie looked very old, very tired, yet deeply satisfied — the picture of a pioneer woman who succeeded as partner to her husband and as mother to her children. In Grandma Cece and Grandpa Art's wedding picture, both were young and handsome, but even then, she looked the stronger of the two. Mom, Marguerite, in her high school graduation picture, looked so bright and vulnerable, so different from the woman I knew as I grew up. The photographs, the old letters and family stories I have collected from Mom and her cousins helped me to know these splendid women.

I was ready to go back to work. Roy, my alcoholic husband, had started me using wood for heat, bless his cussed hide. Working the wood sometimes seemed like an endless, tedious, backbreaking job. When burning wood, I couldn't just set a thermostat and forget it — I had to fill the stove two, three or four times a day, depending on the weather. And there were side effects: over the years, I had fine-tuned my ability to ignore the need for housework, which meant that whenever I had company, I had to relocate the furniture, buried under a mountain of fine soot. Was Roy up in heaven, laughing at me for working myself so hard, five years after he died?

Back and forth. In October, when I usually brought in wood, I often spotted a late dandelion blooming, its bright, cheerful color lightening my step. Scrunching through dead leaves to get to the wood would bring a grin to my face. But in March, six inches of slushy snow and my heavy boots weighed down my steps. Well, at least I only had to bring in half a row, the easy bottom half. For the bottom half, I just had to drop the wood on the pile; for the top, I had to throw it up into place. And though there were no dandelions in March, the sun sparkled off the snow, melting it away. And soon the pussy willows would be out, the first sign of spring.

When I was doing physical work, I often thought of my ancestors. My great-great-grandparents chose the hard, re-warding life of pioneer farmers. Sometimes I could feel their ties to God, to family, to the land. These bonds passed from generation to generation, so maybe the ultimate reason for me doing this work was that my ancestors led me into it so that I could hear them and get to know them. For it wasn't just in burning wood, teaching and building a log cabin that I followed in their footsteps. It was so much of the person I had struggled into becoming. How my fore-mothers handled tough times, how they reached for their dreams, how they valued education; these and many other family traits had emerged in me. Their strength was in me and *I have needed it!*

Yes. A five-generation portrait, in words spoken by many voices would show the family resemblances which I have in-herited.

1
(Great-Great Grandma) Maggie
On the homestead near Patch Grove, Wisconsin
June 1872

John addressed our daughter and son: "Lizzie and Tom, 'tis a fine rocking chair you have given me this day. Sure and I am thinking I could sit here on the porch and rock the rest o' me life away."

We all laughed. Our four grown children, our daughter-in-law and son-in-law, were gathered together that gentle June evening, while our four dear grandchildren contentedly slept inside. Through her laughter, Lizzie said, "Look at you now! The only time you ever stop working is to tell a story, even if you are seventy years old this very day, and you want us to believe you'd quit working just because you have a rocking chair?"

"Will you tell us a story now?" asked our son, James. "The one about how you and Mother came here."

That one request was enough to get him started. When the others, just as they had when they were small, also clamored for a story, John changed and the tired old man disappeared. Hard and purposefully had he worked, getting here, wresting a prosperous farm from the wilderness, building a school for the children, and a church for us all. But even the wrinkles that bespoke his hard labor couldn't hide the gleam of adventure in his blue eyes or the charm of his smile as he set himself to relive it all again for his eager audience. And I knew, in the telling, his brogue would thicken through that deep rich voice of his, and his correct English would give way to the more colorful Irish version of the language, far better for storytelling.

"Well now, I was after courting your mother, when the English caught up with me. If I hadn't been so smitten, I might have run off, as many another Irish lad did. Seven years I was jailed up on St. Helena's!"

"You were not in prison, Napoleon was, and you were one o' his jailers," I disputed.

"Now Maggie dearest, you know I might as well have been imprisoned, for the only thing I wanted in life was you, and you were far away."

"Go on with you now!" He did enjoy embarrassing me with these wild compliments. And how could I be pleased about being embarrassed? But I was.

"As soon as they let me go," John continued, "I rushed back to County Louth to marry me Irish colleen. While I was gone, she had busied herself teaching the little ones here and there. She had made up her mind that Ireland was getting too crowded and that the penal laws were too harsh. There were laws against Catholics practicing their religion, getting educated, even against owning a horse that was worth more than five pounds. The English stole much o' the best land from the Irish. They decreed that any Irishman who owned land had to divide it among all his sons so every generation the farms got smaller and soon there wouldn't be a living for any o' them. She wanted to come to America, she did, and she wouldn't even marry me until I agreed."

"Listen to that fanciful man, will you!" I protested. "He came back to Ireland full o' stories from English soldiers about America. He barely took time to marry me, he was that driven to go!"

"Sure now, and your mother exaggerates as well as ever I could!" he responded with mock surprise.

John never tells of the boat trip, steerage was that miserable: over a hundred of us crowded into a small space that would have been too close for ten. We had no privacy to tend to our needs. Even the smell of clothes and bodies after seven weeks without a good washing couldn't cover up the odor from chamber pots. We ate wretched food and every quarrel was magnified by our closeness. Then the fever set in, killing the old and the weak, the young and the starving, until it seemed half of us started our new lives in heaven instead of in America.

About a week before we arrived in Philadelphia, John broke

down and cried, telling me how sorry he was he hadn't spent the money to come over in a cabin and not put me through all that. "Nonsense," I had replied. "All those years you were gone, we planned through our letters, saving our money for our farm. We've lived through this and we still have the money, and our grand plan is working so far. We'll just keep going, unless you would rather give up and jump overboard." Startled he was at that; then he laughed, "Sure now and I can't do that and leave the farm all to yourself."

John continued our story: "We stayed a few days at me friend's house in Philadelphia. He helped me find work as a laborer and a place to stay so I could provide for your mother while we figured on what to do next."

His voice turned more serious as he went on: "I would unload ships or clean stables or help put up a building, whatever work there was for that day or week, for ten or twelve hours a day. Then I would go with the other laborers to the Irish pub for a pint or two of ale.

"One Saturday night, I had more than one or two. Your mother didn't seem too welcoming when I finally came in, but she waited 'til we were on our way to Mass the next morning before she spoke of it. 'John, I know you have a fine time drinking with the boys, and sure you deserve it for all you work so hard. But did you ever notice, the more a man drinks, the bigger his dreams get, and the less strength he has for going after them?' She said no more, not even about me battered face.

"I said nothing, being in no condition to think of a right answer. But all that day and the next, her words kept reappearing in me thoughts and so I didn't go to the pub again and that was the right answer." John never told about that before, I was thinking, though 'twas true enough. Our children looked surprised, as was I.

"By the time we realized that local farms cost far too dear for our pocketbook," John continued. "Your mother had discovered a strange sickness in herself, in the mornings, which came to be a daughter, and later, another." His voice quivered a bit, knowing the tragedy that came to them later. "Several years we were there. Sure and we both came to know that we would go west, where land was good, plentiful and cheap. So when our wee ones were old enough and Zachary Taylor came looking for soldiers for Wisconsin, why the good Lord had it all arranged for us."

John always got excited telling about traveling to Wisconsin and sure it was glorious and hard work. "That journey was a fair wondrous one, truly 'twas. Fifty men, two women and three children we were, setting out in wagons to cross Pennsylvania to Lake Erie. The farms we passed were so large and thriving, 'twould make a poor Irishman cry. We would have our farm, too! And the great forests filled our eyes and soothed our hearts, which still ached for the terrible loss the English inflicted on us, those many years ago when they destroyed Ireland's forests, the better to capture Irish rebels and outlaws.

"Bumping up and down on the hard wagon seats day after day was no joy, but the food was grand. There were several soldiers on horseback who would go hunting along the way for deer, fowl, rabbits, whatever they could find. I ate more meat in Pennsylvania than I had all the rest o' me life." He looked at me. "'Tis only a wee bit of an exaggeration, me dear.

"After Pennsylvania, we boarded a ship, sailed down Lake Erie, up Lake Huron, down Lake Michigan to Fort Howard in Wisconsin. Each ship would go to the next land barrier, then we would pack up on wagons or horses and portage to the next lake, just like the old voyageurs, except that they carried their canoes, trade goods and supplies themselves. They had been trading with the Indians for nearly two hundred years, so the route was well established. The fur trade was much diminished by then, as beaver were nearly gone. West went the fur traders and in came the rest of us: farmers, blacksmiths, businessmen.

"To be sure, there were scoundrels aplenty in the settlements where we stopped, drunken whites and Indians brawling in the streets, men selling shares in southern Wisconsin's lead mines, land speculators whose honesty was more than a little suspect. But most of all, we felt a tremendous vitality in the people we met, as if to say, 'I can get what I want out o' life here and there is plenty for everyone.'"

John paused for a moment, then said quietly, "Many's the time I have felt imprisoned, less than meself, by the smallness of opportunity in Ireland, on the harsh rocky island o' St. Helena, by the wretched conditions on the boat coming to America, by the intense poverty in Philadelphia. But the journey to Wisconsin set me free to work hard and have something to show for it, free to give me darling wife a wee bit o' what she deserved."

"Oh," I gasped, a tear in my eye. For all that he showers me with flowery compliments, this came from a spot deep within that he seldom spoke from.

"Aye, and I was thinking the hand o' God was in our coming here; I wouldn't have to kill any Indians, because the wars were over two years earlier, but I was just in time to get first pick o' the choice land, for there were few settlers then."

I wanted to shout, so dear was this man to me, but I could only whisper. "Dearest John, do you know how often I have thanked the Blessed Virgin for such a man as you, who can dream a great tomorrow and then reach out and get it?" I was that close to crying, so I added, "I'll go make some tea."

My heart was full, so I dawdled about the tea. "Can I help you carry it out?" It was John, but instead o' reaching for the wooden tray he had made me, he held out his arms to me and we hugged while our hearts told how happy we were to have each other.

After everyone had enjoyed their cakes and tea, Tom prompted, "So you got to Fort Howard at Green Bay. What was next?"

"Me son, have you not heard enough for one night?"

Tom's great smile dwarfed his bushy moustache. Rare enough that smile, with his health so poor. More's the pity, thought I, for his smile always infected everyone and they smiled, too.

"Never," he said. "If I heard all your stories, one after another, and it took six weeks or sixty in the telling, I would want you right away to start over again. Besides, it won't be dark for hours. You never ended a story before dark."

John grinned. "The Lord loves a good flatterer I hope, for both our sakes. Sure and the trip from Fort Howard to Prairie du Chien was the hardest part of our journey, for we were down to canoes and 'twas ourselves did the paddling. Going up the Fox River, well, I always thought I was strong enough, but there were places where the river was narrow and the water running fast, in the wrong direction, mind you, and with big boulders to steer around, it seemed all we could do to stay in one spot, much less move upstream.

"Our leader kept us close to shore most o' the time, where the current was weaker, but more than one canoe tipped over; no one was hurt, but there were usually a few soggy paddlers; cool the water was, but the warm July air dried the wet ones quickly. The outfitters at Fort Howard, having prepared many a canoe for fur traders, had all our supplies carefully wrapped in oilskins and usually one o' the veterans caught up with supply packs that tried to run away downstream; or if a heavier pack from an overturned canoe sank, someone would dive after it. We portaged around the shorter, faster rapids, carrying the canoes, then going back after the supplies. There was a longer portage, due to rapids, where an enterprising fellow had carts to carry our things for us, at an outrageous price, to be sure.

"Several voyageurs came with us up the Fox, to help out. They paddled along, singing their songs. Sure and I knew the songs were wickedly bawdy, for I had learned a bit o' French from being on St. Helena's. Me darling, I expect she guessed as much, but those rowdy Frenchmen had such fun with their singing we could hardly take offense, could we now, Maggie?"

I laughed. "And how could we fault those boisterous men who did their work well and laughed at the hardships, especially when they were usually the ones who saved our supplies?"

John smiled and said: "Jacques told us that three good men in a canoe could travel from Fort Howard to Fort Winnebago, at Portage, in less than two days. We made it in five days. By the time we got there though, our fur-trading friends saw we could make it down the Wisconsin River well enough, so back they went to Green Bay.

"Even though the fur trade was much diminished, once

winter was well set in and the Indians had time to trap the winter-primed pelts, the traders would head out again with knives, kettles, trinkets, needles, combs and other trade goods; the less scrupulous also traded muskets and whiskey. Beaver were the most prized pelts; they also bartered for sable, otter and ermine. Our voyageurs had worked for the French fur company, but after the War of 1812, the American fur company of John Astor took over, using whatever means necessary to remove competition. Jacques and his friend liked where they were so they took their furs to Astor's men.

"Just after we arrived at Fort Winnebago, three Indians came in, swiftly, silently in their canoe. Strangely, their near nakedness seemed appropriate in this wilderness, civilized only in the small settlement behind us. Having only slightly improved me paddling in five days, I greatly admired their skill and grace and I envied their belonging in this awesome wilderness. Sure and I questioned whether I could make me life here as they did. But then I looked at me Maggie and our babes and I knew I would do it.

"Coming down the Wisconsin River, we hardly had to paddle. We still had to steer around boulders, but now we had more time to admire the scenery: rocky hills, dense forests where crows and jays denounced our intrusion, prairie grass dotted with purple, white and yellow wildflowers all rippling in the wind and swamps where our approach set huge flocks o' ducks, geese and teal squawking into flight. Especially at dusk, we saw deer, bear, raccoon and dozens of smaller animals drinking at the river's edge. By our campfire at night, we heard the eerie howling o' wolves, the lonesome calling o' loons and the hooting of owls.

"Our scouts had finally reported that the renegade Indians they had feared were far away, so the only enemies around were the huge swarms o' mosquitos, gnats and flies, which threatened to devour us down to the very bone. How we welcomed the strong breezes that blew them away.

"Great was our joy in living then, for our dream was near to becoming real in a country that was magnificent beyond all imagining, truly the land o' milk and honey.

"Where the Wisconsin River emptied into the Mississippi,

we came again to hard paddling as we forced our way upriver
to Fort Crawford at Prairie du Chien. When we landed at the
long narrow island, we saw the old wooden fort where the
soldiers lived, many Indian tepees, a few primitive cabins and
one grand house, built by 'King' Rolette for his young wife;
Rolette and his assistant, Hercules Dousman, ran Astor's fur
company in this area.

"Indians wandered between the fur-trading store, the ware-
houses and the taverns, which illegally served the Indians.
They were obstructed by pigs and geese scuttling along the
muddy paths. Across the slough on the mainland, the upper
village reflected the same raw conditions in its cabins, stores
and taverns. And we thought Philadelphia uncivilized! Suddenly the harsh reality o' frontier life smashed into me. What
had I done to me Maggie, bringing her here? Afraid I was as
I looked to her sweet face." John looked thoughtfully at me
and smiled. "Your mother was grinning, all the way from
here to next week!"

Never had I told him what brought on that grin. I would
tell him that night, after the children were gone. The newness
terrified me, for just a moment. Back then I saw the wilderness as raw dough, just waiting for John and I to transform it
— thinking of that brave adventure, I had grinned.

John paused as he thought of the next chapter of our lives.
"Now Fort Crawford was another few years o' misery. The
fort that you know is the one I built." He saw that I was
about to interrupt and he answered my objection before I
spoke it. "Sure, and I had a little help. But when we got to
Prairie du Chien, we lived in the old fort out on the low-lying
island. It always flooded in wet seasons so that sometimes we
had our drills in ankle-deep water. The old fort had been
damaged by the English in the War of 1812 and by Indian
attacks, but mostly 'twas rotten due to recurring high waters.

"So instead o' fighting Indians, we brave soldiers got to
build a new fort, up on the mainland. While some o' the
soldiers quarried rock for the outer wall, which was to be a
quarter mile on each side, I went with others up the Mississippi where we felled the fine oaks and pines and guided them
down the river for housing and other buildings inside the

fort. Fatigue duty we called it and rightly so. Being none too fond o' killing, I was glad enough to build cabins. Oh, there were some renegade Indians yet and we went after them from time to time, capturing or killing them. But mostly, 'twas a time o' building.

"Of course, even at the fort, we had good times," John said. "For balls at the fort, the men and women from the fort and from town came in their best finery. You might see a woman dressed in silk dancing with a private or Colonel Taylor might partner the daughter of a fur trader and an Indian woman. So lively were the fiddles, few could sit by and watch and even they couldn't quiet their feet. And believe you me, your mother danced a lively step in her bright calico dress and her laugh cheered all who heard it. The dances were from many nations, as was the accompanying chatter: English, French, a bit o' Gaelic, Indian and Welsh. After dancing on 'til the wee hours, there would be a sumptuous late supper, for every woman tried to outdo the others in what she brought."

I said, "Aye, and we had good times making maple syrup, too. Early in the spring, before the snow was completely gone, a large group o' women would leave the fort and the town for the maple groves. Some men would go along to protect us and to share the fun and the work. Oh, but 'twas good to get out o' the fort after a long winter! Other men went out hunting, to fill the empty larders and just to get out and about.

"We canoed across the Mississippi with hundreds of wooden buckets and other supplies. While the women set up camp, the men pounded holes in the trees with large iron spikes; then we women curled up pieces o' birch bark to make a spout and hung the buckets, two, three or four on a tree, depending on its size, hanging buckets 'til about noon. After eating we would collect the sap from each tree and replace the buckets, for days, 'til the sap stopped running. We boiled the sap slowly in long shallow pans for many more days 'til the water was all evaporated and it had the rich brown color and the wonderful sweetness came out. The boiling of it kept the men busy getting firewood, I promise you! A hundred trees might produce two hundred quarts o' syrup, for it takes about forty gallons o' sap to make one gallon o' syrup.

"We camped in the woods, cold though 'twas, and after a good day's work, we sat around the fires and sang all our songs and told tall tales. This was welcome work and, in our hearts, we thanked the Indians who taught us how to do it, because everyone knows that you can live without sweets, but how glorious it was to have them to relieve the harshness of our lives! Nowadays, many of us use cane sugar for sweetening, and 'tis a delight what new things we can do with it, but it lacks the sweet memories o' the maple syrup."

John looked at our children, "Aye, her laugh made me heart happy, but her tears near broke me heart when we lost our colleens — how could they have known that the berries they ate were poisonous? There weren't enough Irish for a proper wake, so your mother and I went out into the woods after the funeral. O'Connell, who was a soldier after me own heart, had given us a fine jug o' poteen. The two of us drank and the wild wind of a summer storm keened through our hearts and the thunder roared our anger and the rain cried with us and when the storm was spent, we were quiet. But our brave dream of a fine farm seemed small with no children to work for." John paused, felt again the terrible grief; he shook his head as if that would chase away the pain.

Quietly, I spoke, "When I quickened again with child, we did come alive once more."

John continued our story: "Then that Negro tried to kill Zachary Taylor. The evil in his eye as he walked past warned me and I guessed his intent as he headed toward Taylor. He was only a few feet from Taylor as he pulled out a knife, but quick as you please, I landed on his back, and with a bit o' help, his knife found his own heart instead o' Taylor's.

"Colonel Taylor, excellent man that he was, rewarded me with a land grant, one hundred sixty acres o' me own choosing. I picked out the land I wanted, near where me friend had settled, about fifteen miles from the fort. I chose a long stretch, rather than the usual square, running along a ridge, so the plowing would be somewhat on a level, prairie land mostly, but with a good grove o' trees, and a creek through the dip in the middle o' the land.

"Then I walked to Mineral Point, over sixty miles away, mostly along Indian trails, to buy and record our homestead. I arrived, two days later, in the late afternoon. 'Twas proud I was to lay down our hard-earned two hundred dollars to buy us our dream, this dream o' fourteen years, seven on St. Helena's, seven in Philadelphia and Prairie du Chien."

I commented, "Sure and 'twas like Jacob in the Bible who worked for his Uncle Laban for seven years so he could marry his cousin Rachel. Only Laban tricked Jacob and gave him his daughter Leah. So Jacob worked another seven years and Laban gave him Rachel, too. And the Lord made him prosper for his hard work and patience."

"I never thought o' that," was John's startled response. "'Tis right you are and He has made us prosper, too." But a frown ran across his face. "Now, where was I? Aye, in Mineral Point. Hundreds o' people lived there; some set up shanties, others dug holes into the hillsides, the Cornish built stone cottages. There were several hotels and groceries, many smelting furnaces, churches, a brewery, even six dry goods stores. The lead miners were so busy getting rich they hadn't time to do for themselves; they bought most everything in the stores, even soap, which folks around here still make for themselves."

I interrupted again, "I would rather save the money by making me own soap and, when I get a few pennies by the side, I buy a book. And thinking o' the book to come is how I get through the stink and the mess and the hard work o' making the soap."

John sighed. "If the storytellers in Ireland had as many interruptions as I be having, they would have given up long ago, and what would you be knowing o' the grand history o' her?" He smiled at me. "But I suppose since we made this story together, 'tis well that we tell it together."

He went on: "I watched desperately hard-working men on the hillside beyond Shake Rag Street. They loaded the lead sent up in buckets and scurried it over to the nearest smelter where 'twas molded into rectangular bricks for easier transportation.

"Then I went to the Mansion House, a grandiose name

for a large but simple public house, to find food, a pint and a bed. As I supped, I was joined by three miners, come for relaxing after a hard day, and they told me about their work.

"The miners used shovels, picks, crowbars and blasting powder to get the lead out o' the ground. At the smelter's, they gave over a third o' the lead to pay for the smelting. They would take a bucketful to the grocer or dry goods store, which gave them credit there.

"I asked them how Shake Rag Street had gotten its name. One miner, a burly young man, exceedingly boisterous, perhaps from drinking, explained that the wives and cooks waved a white rag at mealtimes to summon the miners to eat."

John continued: "So I watched the miners, hard-working during the day, spend their evening drinking and gambling; quarrels o' the day, strengthened by liquor, erupted into brawls with fists or knives or pistols.

"These unruly miners, being the vast majority o' Wisconsin's white population at the time, and the richest, grabbed political power. Henry Dodge was one o' the early miners. He settled illegally on Indian lands, gave guns to his men and his neighbors, and defied the army to run him off. The army let him be. His fellow miners so approved o' that, o' his war record from the War of 1812, and o' the infantry charge he led to slaughter Blackhawk and his people, that they got him appointed Governor o' the new Wisconsin Territory in 1836, not long before I got to Mineral Point.

"Dodge's main political rival was James Doty, governor after Dodge's first term and before his second term. As a member o' the territorial legislature in 1836, Doty and his associates bought up thirteen hundred acres o' land at what would later become Madison; that legislature was to choose one o' the dozens o' proposed cities for the permanent capital o' Wisconsin; Doty persuaded other legislators, by gifts o' choice lots in the future Madison, to select Madison as state capital, when there wasn't even a town there yet.

"Another story illustrates how ably the lying, swindling Doty led the territory when he was governor. He appointed Enos Baker as sheriff o' Grant County. At a meeting' o' the territorial council, James Vineyard, a member from Grant

County, opposed the appointment. Charles Arndt o' Brown County spoke in favor o' Baker. Vineyard called one o' his statements a lie. They quarreled; Arndt struck Vineyard, so Vineyard shot and killed Arndt. Vineyard's lawyer got the trial moved to a mining county where the jury acquitted him.

"In 1838, the Wisconsin census showed a white population o' eighteen thousand. Nine years later, the population was two hundred ten thousand. Frontier lawlessness was frowned upon by then and most o' the lead was mined out, so when gold was discovered in California, much o' the riffraff among the miners lit out for the West, the better to continue their wild ways. The lead mines shut down, many mining towns died out and politicians and other lawbreakers became a little more civilized about their misdeeds."

John huffed. "Such a storyteller I'm getting to be. A walk to Mineral Point turns into a dissertation on politics. At any rate, that's how we settled in what became Patch Grove, o' Grant County, in Wisconsin."

Our daughter Margaret asked, "Father, how did Grant County get its name?" as if she, and all of us, didn't know, a hundred times over.

"Oh, 'twas simple enough," John replied. "Grant was a fur trader in the early 1800's. He traded with the Sacs, which made him an enemy to the Winnebagos. Some Winnebagos chased Grant and when they caught him, one brave hit him on the head with a tomahawk, which caused a ringing sound instead of a split skull. After that, all the Indians treated him with respect, thinking him a spirit. All because he wore his cooking kettle under his hat when riding his horse. So the whites respected him, too, and named a county after him."

John played with his audience, "And surely now, 'tis enough of a tale."

"No, no, tell us more!"

"Don't stop now!"

"'Tis not yet dark!"

"Tell us about the early days on the farm!"

"Well, well," he grinned as he looked us all over and his delight in his audience was obvious. "Let me see. Aye, the winter after I bought our land, Colonel Taylor told me to go build a cabin there, so that when I got discharged, me darling and our child and I, God willing, could move right in. So I did and lonely 'twas, being away from your mother. I would walk back to the fort, weather permitting, of a Saturday evening and return to building the cabin Sunday evening. Felling the trees with an axe, cutting them to size, stripping the bark, nipping the ends where they would fit together, dragging them to our homesite, lifting them into place, aye, 'twas hard. I hadn't worked less hard, perchance, in Philadelphia, but here the work made me heart sing, for 'twas our own. And Matthew was born, early was he smiling and his laugh was full o' mischief.

"With only half a dozen settlers here, we had to be largely self-sufficient. Two oxen I bought, and a plow to turn the sod. The roots o' centuries in this untilled prairie were a twisting, twining mass, near a foot deep, that had to be turned over, then plowed this way and that to be broken up enough for planting. Then your mother and I, with a bag o' wheat seed over our shoulders, would walk along, scattering the seed by the handful.

"When it ripened, I cut the wheat with a cradle scythe." John smiled, eager to accept the opportunity to brag, "When I was in good form, I could cut over two acres in a day. The first years, Maggie would follow me scythe and tie the wheat into sheaves and after I had cut for a while, I would help her bind. We used a hand flail to pound the grain from the stalk. Some o' the wheat we traded for salt, tea and other goods. What we wanted o' the wheat for our own flour, we had to load on the wagon and go ten miles to Beetown, the nearest mill for grinding wheat into flour."

Merrily I spoke up. "Never will I forget the look on your father's face the first time I went out with him to bind the sheaves, dressed in a pair o' his pants and one o' his shirts! But he soon got over his surprise and knew I could be a much better help if I wasn't forever tripping over me skirts every time I bent over. Oh, you needn't look so shocked, children. In those days, we did as we had to." I thought a moment. "Aye, hard 'twas, but good, to work with your father, even though we would be dripping wet and the seeds and bits would stick to us, and so hot and dirty we were by the end o' the day, we would go down to our creek and clean up."

If our children were surprised that I wore John's pants, what would they think of all the clothes we didn't wear into the creek? John was smiling, too. I knew he was remembering how we would lie down in the water and roll around and splash each other, reveling in the coolness like two children, even though we were over thirty years old then. Well, and there were some advantages to living in the wilderness.

Looking at me, John teased, "I wonder what old Father O'Brien would have said about such goings-on?"

At that I blushed, embarrassed and angry. Well, it was none of that grouchy old priest's business and were we not just as glad to leave him in Ireland! And if I had confessed it to Father Mazzuchelli, he would have laughed and said our lives were hard enough, we shouldn't waste any thoughts feeling guilty over what few pleasures we could find along the way. And then I laughed. John and I knew that the freedoms we allowed each other would be greatly frowned upon in the Old Country, and though we knew the rightness of our joy, the old ways were planted deep in our hearts and pricked us from time to time in spite of ourselves.

I looked around at six pairs of puzzled eyes, knowing their curiosity at my embarrassment, anger and laughter following each other so closely, me as changeable as the weather in Ireland. I waved my hand and said awkwardly, "Never mind. 'Tis but the joy o' the day."

John, seeing my confusion, brought everyone's attention back to himself. "At first, we didn't keep any stock, other than the oxen, for great was the abundance o' meat running wild, and fish and fowl. And your mother had learned which wild fruits and nuts to gather and preserve. I grew winter feed for the oxen, tended them when they were sick, built their shelter o' logs; I made our bed and table, using planks for the table top. I made chairs from smaller branches, Maggie weaving the seats.

"I shot bear, preserved their meat and cured their hides, which kept us warm of a frigid night. Oh, the Wisconsin cold! I remember being so cold in me bones, that I feared if anyone touched me, I'd break, just like a brittle icicle. 'Twas good we lived first at the fort, for much we learned there about keeping warm. I had filled in between logs with mud plaster and moss, so thick the cabin looked to be made more o' plaster than o' big logs. And when the snow came, I banked it high against the cabin.

"I chopped trees down with an axe, cut them into chunks, split them down to size for firewood for heating and cooking. And the work you children made for me!" But he couldn't be serious with such scolding. "Ah, but 'twas a joy to have children to work for. And by the time you were old enough to help, I had bought meself a threshing machine, the first one in these parts, a treadmill powered by horses. And John Thompson bought a horse-drawn seeder and life was easy. We traded off use o' the machines until our larger crops brought in enough for each to buy his own. Except for the thresher; there are better threshing machines now, but they still go from farm to farm, all the men around going with the thresher to get in each man's harvest.

"And how did your mother while away her time? When she wasn't helping me, she made our clothes, cooked and baked over a wood fire in the fireplace, knitted our socks, caps and mittens, tended the vegetable garden, preserved vegetables and fruit, made our candles and soap, kept the house clean and washed our clothes. But her favorite work was teaching you how to read, write and do your sums."

I broke in, "I read just one o' those fanciful romances. So much foolishness! And where is the pride in a chore well done? I like to see me family all dressed up in clean clothes that I have labored over."

First I made the soap. I boiled all the fat I had collected. The ashes from our fires would be leaching in a barrel o' water. I heated the water from the ashes, poured it over the liquid fat and mixed it with a wooden paddle. After many hours o' cooking, the mixture thickened and I poured it into a wooden box where it hardened into shape. Before it got too hard, I cut it into bars. That always took several days. To wash clothes, I had to haul water up from the creek, boil some of it and pour the rest right into the wash tub your father made. I added the hot water when it boiled, whittled off soap from a bar into the tub, rubbed each piece of clothing over the corrugated washboard, cleanest clothes first, so I could keep using the same water, adding more soap as needed. When they were all washed, I bailed out the soapy water, put in clean water and rinsed each piece, wringing it out with me hands as best I could. At first, the wet clothes went on bushes and rocks to dry, until your father tied a rope between trees.

"Washing clothes hasn't changed, but over the years, much has improved here. Your father built more rooms, put in wood floors, bought a cooking stove, glass windows, factory-made beds and chairs. 'Tis blessed we are, that our hard work has brought us these and many more comforts.

"Blessed, indeed, in many ways, but ..." My heart grew heavy, thinking of yet another tragedy, which I related. "Then Paul was born, and Mary Anne. But the Good Lord wanted Paul and Matthew for Himself, He did. I expect it was diphtheria. The lads were sick first, with sore throats and fever. I tried to cool them, but they died and then Mary Anne got sick. It seemed she couldn't breathe and sure the Blessed Virgin herself told me what to do. I reached down my dear babe's throat and pulled out the awful stuff and threw it into the fire. She could breathe again and her fever went down and she lived and I was glad I had named her after the Virgin Mary and her mother."

I remembered that when I knew she would live, I also knew that she was mine for a short time only. "Mary Anne was ever a comfort, she was so kind and generous. When she grew up, she became a nun in the order that Father Mazzuchelli had started. She had such a vision o' the good she could do as a nun, but she lived less than a year after her Profession."

I had to stop then, remembering the ceremony when she made her vows and was named Sister Mary Catherine. Again the Virgin Mary herself spoke to me, telling me that me time with me daughter was nearly over. I cried there in the chapel, and I couldn't stop. What others except Mary Anne thought o' me outburst mattered not to me. I wanted to explain to her, but I couldn't find the words. How do you tell your beloved daughter that she will die soon? I couldn't. Mary

Anne had boarded with Agnes when she taught school before
she went into the convent and they had become good friends,
so I asked Agnes to write some words of explanation of my
tears, which she did.

Mount Hope, October 6,1858
My Dear Sister Mary Catherine,
Your mother told me she obtained permission for me to
write to you. I am glad, dear Mary Anne, that you have not
forgotten me.
I sincerely congratulate you in your happy choice of a state
of life. Your mother is also happy although she told me she
could not control her feelings when she was with you. She
begs me to write her apology. It was not regret which caused
her tears but the natural outpouring of a mother's love. She
speaks in terms of the highest praise of the institution and of
the great kindness with which she was treated.
Your family is well as is mine and I hope you are enjoying
the same blessing.
Dear Sister M.C., if it is not too worldly I would like to
tell you of our school. At our annual meeting, the lower part
of the ridge, led on by Mr. Coyne, proposed to move the old
schoolhouse a half-mile further down and to levy sixty dollars
for expenses of moving and repairing it. The upper ridge
people did not wish any money expended and did not wish
the school removed as it was in the centre. But the others
carried it by a majority of two.
The next day Michael went over to Mr. Quick and had
the district divided. We have the best part of it including the
schoolhouse. Coyne and the others are very sorry but it was
their own fault. Miss Catherine Dolan has been teaching
here but she is going to marry Michael Cull, so we must get
another teacher.
The children you taught here all remember you with love.
Please pray for me and my family.
I remain, Dear M. C., your warm friend Agnes

I came back to the present and finished what I wanted to
say, "By then, we had you four children, James, Lizzie, Tom

and Margaret. It shouldn't have been so hard to let Mary Anne go, but 'twas."

When the sadness passed, John started talking about his favorite Man o' God: "Father Mazzuchelli, now there was a priest! We Irish didn't like his Italian name too much, so we called him Father Matthew Kelly. Sure and 'tis hard to believe, but even with his terrible accent, he was a better Irishman than some o' the priests nowadays! For years on end, he would go up and down the Mississippi, and off to the east and west of it, wherever there were Catholics, by canoe and horseback and even on foot, to take care o' his flock. And many's the Presbyterian and Lutheran who became Catholic because he was the only Man o' God around then. Later, when the area became more settled, he took to building Churches wherever there were enough Catholics."

John dearly loved to talk about Father Matthew Kelly. "Well do I remember the excitement when we had word o' his coming. In the early days, we had no time for a lot o' lollygagging around, watching a horse-drawn mower and a threshing machine do all the work for us. I hadn't even sons to help me for many years. But when Father Matthew Kelly was coming, the neighbors, Catholic and non-Catholic alike, left their work to gather here from miles around, bringing each their food to pass, and their news, and their babies to be baptized." He looked proudly at his eldest son. "James, you were the first to be baptized here." Then his gaze turned to each of our other children, "Aye, he baptized all o' you, the good father did."

"He would say Mass, preach a fine sermon and bring God's blessing to our hard work. We would all sing the glorious hymns. Then we shared our sorrows and joys and food; thus were we fortified to go on again. Why, I even added a room to the old log cabin, early on, so he could have a separate room for sleeping."

Our son James interrupted eagerly, "I don't remember Mass in our home, but I do remember Father Galtier saying Mass in the log chapel. And I remember dozens of men and women coming here to build the first frame church."

Margaret said: "Before you built that church, you walked

all the way to Milwaukee to see Bishop Henni about giving a
piece of your land for church property, didn't you, father?"

"Aye, that he did," said I, "and if he had waited another
few years, he could have gone by the railroad."

John huffed and grinned, "If I had waited for this and
that, the church would have taken twenty years to build, just
like the railroad." John's face proclaimed his joy. "Great was
me wonder, that I who was persecuted for being a Catholic in
the Old Country, could freely gather friends and build a church
here in our New Country."

Even the memory of that awesome day brought a tear to
his eye, and mine, just as the day itself did. There was another larger church built a few years ago; our Tom and Lizzie
moved into the old one and have taken care of the new one,
just as they took care of the old one.

"Our first log chapel, we built that in the forties," I commented, "and that was only one o' the many changes in those
years. We finally had a house full o' children, even after losing
four. Your father got machines for his farming. Patch Grove
got its first doctor, its first jail and several stores. Patch Grove
organized and elected officials — that's when your father was
appointed fence viewer. *The Grant County Herald,* our first
newspaper, started publication. And Wisconsin became a state
in 1848."

Lizzie begged, "Tell us about being fence viewer, Father."

"Well, now, fence viewers were appointed to settle boundary disputes. There was only one disagreement during my
time in office that threatened great strife. Knowing well the
two hot-tempered farmers, I invited them both to meet with
me over there, under that great pine tree in the cemetery by
the church. I brought along a fourth party, a fine jug.

"So I said to them, 'Such a fine day it is; let's have a nip
before we try to settle things.' Whether the cemetery reminded them o' the shortness o' this life or the church reminded them o' the longness o' the next life, I'll never know,
but by the time we finished the jug, the argument was forgotten."

"John," I protested, "you purely made that up. When
you were a fence viewer, that church wasn't even built yet,

only the log chapel."

"Whether that be or not, 'tis a fine story, is it not?" His attempt at ruffled dignity couldn't hide the mischief in his eye. "And besides fence viewing, I got to take charge o' five miles o' road: pulling a drag along the road to fill in small ruts, filling the larger ruts with gravel from the creek, cutting the brush alongside the road, trying to keep it open during the winter. Usually we worked on the roads in the fall, after the harvest was in, unless they got too terrible in between." John continued rocking, leaning his head back, as if finished telling his tale.

"In the forties," our Lizzie said, "terribly poor harvests devastated Ireland." She even kept her face serious as John's head came forward.

"Aye, me brother Thomas wrote of it from Ireland," John responded, "and the words o' the letter are still in me heart."

Callistown 30th July 1846

My Dear Brother

My reply to your letter has been held back because father was very ill. We did not expect that he would live any time and I deferred writing until I would be able to give you some account of him.

I am sorry to say that poor father is no more. He died after having been confined to his bed for many months; he died without pain, having had every attention in the way of Masses said for him and receiving the Last Sacraments. I let him want for nothing so I have discharged my duty in that regard.

I really cannot say how we will live in this country. The potato crop has failed this year as it did in 1845, with this difference that the distemper or infection set in this year about the end of June before the late crop planted in May had time to form; the early ones are very much infected in places and in other parts not so much but the disease is progressing and we all consider that there will not be a potato to put in at November. We have also had great rains and severe gales of wind, which it is feared has injured the corn crops; so that you see there is a poor look out for the ensuing spring and summer;

should the potato crop fail, as is anticipated, my business falls to the ground.

Your brother James and family (his four sons are as tall as himself) are in good health and send greetings. Our sister Jane, her son and daughter are all well.

Your Maggie's mother desires to say that she is well, but feels unhappy that you and Maggie do not write to her more often. She says Maggie's brother Patrick died last month. Her Aunt Mary gets her health but poorly.

I may perhaps go to America. I cannot yet speak positively because of my wife's health. I might however surprise you by calling to see you before you might be aware of it.

I remain My dear Brother
ever affectionately
Thomas

"When the English introduced the potato from South America," John said, "methinks 'twas about two hundred years ago, it seemed a blessing, because the poor, whom the English were determined to make poorer, could survive with less land by eating mostly potatoes. But during those cruel years o' famine, the great English lords and masters, instead o' helping us out, thanked God for decimating the population, for then they could more easily take over the land for livestock."

John continued, "Aye, 'twas bad in Ireland then, but good here. When the discovery o' gold in California lured a quarter of our Patch Grove men out west to seek their fortunes, I stayed, for I had me fortune already, in two hundred acres o' fertile land, and me own church, me own schoolhouse, me children, and most of all me darling Maggie."

Margaret looked at the old schoolhouse and commented, "The schoolhouse looks neglected, now that others have taken its place."

"So it does, so it does," John answered complacently. "But the seed that was planted there grew into dozens o' schoolhouses, and look at yourselves to see how strong are the roots. If we could count all the books you four have read, why, sure, 'twould be enough to turn the very leprechauns of Ireland green with envy. Back there, Catholics were so poor, they could only dream o' reading. And more's the shame because Catholic Ireland was the great center o' learning while the rest o' Europe didn't even know how to read, for many centuries after the Roman Empire fell apart.

"And you Margaret, and Mary Anne, God rest her soul, were both schoolteachers, passing on what you had learned. I was fair proud o' that, I was, having you teach here, knowing that in Ireland, most Catholics got their learning in hedge-schools, hiding behind hedges that separate the fields so the English wouldn't catch and punish them."

John looked fondly at the school. "You know, do you not, that 'twas herself kept on at me to build the schoolhouse. Sure and she could have taught you in our home, but she was that proud o' teaching', she wanted a fine building just for that purpose. And right she was."

the 25 Dec 1861

Dear Lizzie

I will take the pleasure to write you a few lines. I like my new school very much. Tell me who your teacher is this year and if he is handsome or homely. My teacher is a very kind lady, Miss Shaw. Our school is all girls. I wish we could go to school together again. Do you have as much fun as we did last winter and do you get scolded as much as we did then? I do not get scolded one bit. Don't you think I am a very good girl? Do you still dance as much as we did? Have you had any spelling bees? Do you still like arithmetic? We have vacation now for one week. There has not been any snow until now. Have you been sleigh riding? I went to a festival last night. The only thing I liked was the music. My teacher is a very strong republican, like everybody else. Many people here have seen President Lincoln. I would like to meet him, too. I suppose the soldiers there are all drilling for war. I have told all I can think of. Give my love to Margaret and yourself. I wish you a merry Christmas, also happy New Year.

From your sincere friend
Josephine

I said, "'Tis not only the schools that give us our learning now. For though our first years here were so isolated we near forgot the rest o' the world existed, now the railroads bring us magazines, books and newspapers from everywhere, so we can find information and good reading as much as we like. Sure and 'twas from the newspapers we learned all about the dreadful fires last fall."

"Yes, it was a terrible October," our daughter Lizzie noted. "In fifteen states, drought exploded every spark into a raging blaze, destroying people, homes, businesses and crops. The great Chicago fire alone slew hundreds of people and ravaged millions of dollars worth of property. When I first heard of it, I felt a bit smug; I was glad I didn't live in a crowded city, where such losses were possible."

"A three-month drought in northeastern Wisconsin had aided small fires there," James remarked. "Telegraph lines were down and trains couldn't run, for fear of burnt-out bridges and burning trees across the tracks, so it took many weeks for us to find out that October 8 spawned not only the infamous Chicago fire, but also an even worse one in Wisconsin."

"The Wisconsin fire devastated eight counties and dozens of towns," added Tom, "killed more than a thousand people and destroyed two billion trees. I can't even begin to imagine such losses."

Our daughter-in-law Annie spoke sadly, "I wonder how the survivors are getting past the terrors they lived through. I had frightened dreams from just reading about it, especially what happened in Peshtigo. Residents woke up in the middle of the night to a horrendous roaring. In the panic-stricken streets, people, dogs, deer and livestock tried to run for their lives, through suffocating smoke, flying sparks, screaming people. Some made it to the river, where they spent hours splashing their heads to put out flying embers; burning trees floated downstream; many people were trampled or drowned in the river. And afterward, a million acres of black,: black skeletons of trees, charred carcasses of men and animals, a chimney here and there, a pile of metal that had been a machine, black over every hill and valley, in every stream and river. Survivors lost family, friends, homes, churches and businesses."

Ever the farmer, Joseph said, "When I welcomed the good rain that came on October 9, little did I realize that the same storm would move on and put out those monstrous fires."

"Crops were poor in all the country, because of the drought, but Wisconsin and the rest of the nation came to their aid. We all had to tighten our belts last winter, but better that than let the survivors starve," added Margaret, always the first to help those in need. "So many tragedies, near to us and far away."

After a moment, John commented, "Those fires were awesome. 'Tis also awesome, methinks, to note the changes in our lives and in our country. Think o' the fifty million dollars or so that our government has spent over the last seventy years to purchase the Louisiana Territory, Florida, California, New Mexico, Utah, Arizona, and Alaska. Fifty million dollars, even one million dollars — I can't comprehend so much money, any more than I can comprehend that in a hundred fifty years, this country has changed so drastically, from a few Europeans on the East Coast to an explosion o' whites spreading over four thousand miles to the Pacific Coast. We used to do everything by hand; now there are reapers and threshers and mowers, even tractors, though they may never be practical, as it takes so many men to keep the wood fires going to make the steam that runs them. Just think, Jules Verne, in his adventurous fictions, writes o' traveling to the bottom o' the sea and to the moon. 'Tis far beyond my imagination, but yet..."

Tom responded enthusiastically, "I like to read about scientific discoveries and inventions and seeing them is even better. Like photographs. I look at our pictures; when I'm not thinking: 'Is that really what I look like?' I'm amazed and wonder: 'How can that be?' And Margaret," he asked, "do you not like your new sewing machine?"

She answered, "It was hard enough to learn to use it, but now I find it much faster than sewing by hand. Of course, it won't do all my sewing; I still have to do buttonholes and fancy stitching by hand. But it is a good help."

"I much prefer lighting a fire with a match to using a flint," I remarked. "And do you know, I did enjoy buying me first ready-made dress a few years ago, even if I did take it apart and resew it to make it fit better."

"Of all I read in the newspapers," Lizzie stated, "what impresses me most are the possibilities for doctoring. When smallpox hit Wisconsin in the late 1850s, the whites in the south received Jenner's smallpox vaccine, but the Indians in the north had none. No one who was vaccinated died, but hundreds of Indians and skeptical whites died. And according to a recent article about Pasteur's discoveries, it is bacteria that causes smallpox, typhoid, diphtheria, cholera, puerperal fever and many other diseases."

I blurted out, "Lizzie, how right you are! And if vaccinations would be combined with Florence Nightingale's ideas on cleanliness, perhaps mothers wouldn't cry again for children lost to disease." Then I thought, as I had before, it was a shame that Lizzie hadn't become a teacher, so knowledgeable she was and so happy to share what she knows.

"Me darling Maggie, I agree with you," responded John. "But I find it hard to believe some o' the nonsense the papers print. Sailors on long journeys have proved that eating lemons prevents scurvy, but lemonade as a cure for all stomach diseases, worms, and skin complaints, for jaundice, gravel and liver complaints?"

Margaret noted, "Our newspaper even printed Bishop Henni's official Lenten regulations for fasting and abstaining. I was quite surprised at how detailed they've been getting. We can't have fish and meat at the same meal. We can't even have lard or eggs on Ash Wednesday or Good Friday. The list goes on and on.

"In pioneering times," John commented wryly, "our good bishop would tell us that necessity requires that we eat what we can when we have it. Now, he seems over concerned about particularities. I suppose that comes with old age and civilization."

Annie spoke up, "The knowledge we can get from reading is amazing, fascinating. But sometimes the sheer pleasure of reading makes me sad, thinking of all those who can't or don't read."

"For pure fun," said Tom, "there is no author I know that comes up to Mark Twain, except Shakespeare. In the May issue of *Atlantic Monthly,* Twain wrote about a bad little boy who grew up to be a wicked scoundrel and, as such, was universally respected and elected to the legislature. Which sounds terribly preposterous and all too much like father's stories about Henry Dodge and James Doty."

Here, James interposed, "My favorite author is Bret Harte. I look forward to reading the magazines with his colorful stories of the wild west."

Margaret laughed. "I was visiting Susan last week; she had just gotten her new issue of *Godey's Lady's Book*. In a way, it was fascinating, with fashion plates in color and all; but it also seemed like a lot of folderol over fripperies."

"I agree," said Lizzie. "It would be a good magazine for Jane Austin's women to be reading. Poor Mrs. Bennet in *Pride and Prejudice,* her only concern in life was to get her five daughters well-married. What a narrow, limited world she lived in. And all the misunderstandings! Wouldn't you think people could just say what they mean?"

James spoke up, "True, Mrs. Bennet was rather single-minded, or perhaps simpleminded. But at least her pursuit wouldn't hurt anyone. In *The Talisman,* Sir Walter Scott writes that in the feudal ages, war was considered the most worthy occupation of mankind. No wonder they called those years the Dark Ages! They had no time for building up a prosperous farm, for enjoying songs and laughter, for reading, or for scientific discoveries because they used all their time and energy causing death and destruction." James looked at his father, as if he had a special message for him. "And frankly," our son said, "all the chivalrous rules about battle may have been very polite, but what good are manners to the dead men?"

"Father," Lizzie asked quietly, "why is it you never talk about the Civil War?"

John was that surprised and then pained, it took him a moment to reply, "Oh, Lizzie, methinks that war be the saddest blight on the whole history of our New Country. Slavery is wrong, I doubt it not. Perchance some people fervently wanted to eliminate it; perchance many more just wanted to be at war, like Scott's characters. Think, Lizzie. In the last one hundred years, our countrymen have fought the Revolutionary War, the War of 1812, the Mexican-American War, the Civil War and countless wars against Indians." John sighed. "Our New Country is too much like our Old Country in this: war is more important than resolving differences. For seven hundred years Ireland has been rebelling against English rule and all that ever happened was that the English got harsher and the Irish women always had dead men to weep over. The worst of it all is that if the Irish had ever quit fighting among themselves, any one o' the rebellions might have been successful.

"'A house divided against itself cannot stand,' the Bible tells us. I was that fearful, I was, that our whole New Country would be destroyed by the Civil War. Brother fought against brother, friend killed friend, unspeakable atrocities were committed by both sides. Our northern newspapers wove tales o' heroic courage, wise leaders, great battles won; sure I was that the Southerners wrote the same o' their own men, while on both sides, the blood toll mounted.

"I remember praying that God would open the leaders' eyes, make them figure out a way to stop the killing." John's voice was troubled. "Yet when I read, late in the war, o' Sherman's march to the sea, burning everything, fields, homes, cities, I knew that if he came to me farm like that, I, too would kill. I am mortally ashamed, even yet, o' feeling so murderous, especially after the way I talked to you, James and Tom, four years earlier, when it seemed that war was imminent."

"I remember it well," said James, and Tom nodded in agreement.

"We three, James, twenty-one, Tom, fifteen, and meself went out to the cornfield one afternoon and sat at the edge of it. 'James and Tom,' I told you, 'If war comes, and it surely will, you must not go to fight.' Startled you were, were you not? I reminded you that your mother had lost two sons to diphtheria, two daughters to poison berries and just a bit before, she had lost her daughter Mary Anne to sickness. I couldn't let her lose her last two sons to war. For meself, I couldn't run the farm alone any more, and there would be great need of our wheat when war came.

"I could see clearly that you were both respectfully unconvinced," John continued, "so I reached down inside meself and I told about that fateful drunken brawl your mother never asked about. 'We were all busy about our drinking, and the Good Lord only knows what started it. It never took much for a roomful o' Irishmen to start fighting. A man backed towards me, reeling from a blow; I turned him around and hit him a hard one, all in the fun o' the fight. I hurt him, to be sure, but we recognized each other and his pain was that much greater for being hit by a friend. Taken aback, I was, and didn't see a fist coming at me. I landed flat on me back. There I lay and a worse blow hit me: even as drunk as I was, I couldn't see any sense to it. Why do we hurt our friends? Why do we not stick together and accomplish something instead o' banging each others' hard heads against the walls?'"

Pain filled John's face as he told of this difficult moment. "'So, me James, you are old enough to know your mind,' I told you, 'and Tom, you soon will be. But know that this war of American against American is wrong, no matter what people say to justify it.' And being a prudent man, I asked you not to speak o' me views to others, whether or not you agreed with me, because even me carefully considered opinions were enough to cause strife in those days.

"But you agreed, so when the first call to arms came, I paid two unattached men to go in your places, as was common then. So while many men died, I kept me sons and got rich selling me wheat." John bowed his head, from the weight of those trying years and we were all silent.

Then I spoke quietly, "John dear, you did as you saw best. Not even the Good Lord Himself would fault you for that."

"No, He wouldn't." John grinned awry. "But how can one honestly made decision make a man so miserable for so long? So you see, Lizzie, me opinions about the Civil War, being far from common, I have kept them to meself."

After a moment, I asked, "John, do you think our children be old enough to join us in a nip?" That brought a laugh, since Tom, our youngest, was nearly thirty.

When we were settled again, Annie said, "We could almost be in Longfellow's *Song of Hiawatha* right now. We have everything but the lake and the herons." And she recited,

> *"All the air was white with moonlight*
> *All the water black with shadow,*
> *And around him the Suggema*
> *The mosquito, sang his war-song,*
> *And the fireflies, Wah-wah-taysee*
> *Waved their torches to mislead him;*
> *And the bullfrog, the Dahinda,*
> *Thrust his head into the moonlight,*
> *Fixed his yellow eyes upon him,*
> *Sobbed and sank beneath the surface;*
> *And anon a thousand whistles*
> *Answered over all the fen-lands*
> *And the heron, the Shuh-shuh-gah,*
> *Far off on the reedy margin*
> *Heralded the hero's coming."*

As Annie spoke those beautiful lines, I thought what a rare fine woman she was, who could see the beauty and find words to speak of it. And I knew that she also felt the sadness more deeply than most.

"I enjoyed the *Song of Hiawatha* more than any other book I ever read," Annie said. "Longfellow looked at nature and saw that it was good, from the moon to the mischievous mosquito and the delightful fireflies. There was a rightness in that world he wrote of; Hiawatha was part of nature and nature was part of him."

"But that is so pagan!" Margaret cried out.

Startled we were by her vehemence. James, our peacemaker, replied gently, "Surely God allows even pagans to see the glories of His creation. And didn't St. Francis of Assisi see the goodness of nature when he preached his sermon to the birds and when he called on all creatures, as his brothers and sisters, to praise God."

Joseph, perhaps embarrassed by his wife's outburst, changed the subject, "My favorite books are James Fenimore Cooper's *Deerslayer, Last of the Mohicans* and the rest of the series, where he writes about the whites and the Indians.

Hawkeye, the white scout, has thrilling adventures and his amazing resourcefulness gets him out of one scrape after another."

John laughed. "If I had read that in Philadelphia, I might never have come to Wisconsin, for fear o' what might happen to your mother."

"Nonsense!" I declared. "There is danger anywhere you live. But you wouldn't have missed all your adventuring for the world; and if you think I would have let you have all the fun without me, you have another think coming!"

"I wouldn't have missed it for the world, true, but I would have missed it for you, had it been so." Oh my, this seriousness of his was very unsettling to me.

"Annie," Margaret said quietly, "I didn't mean to be so harsh in what I said. I was just startled by your words."

"It's all right, Margaret. I didn't take it amiss."

We all breathed easier, and Margaret, still a bit embarrassed, said, "It's especially silly, perhaps, when I think that my favorite book is Hawthorne's *Scarlet Letter*. And that is about Puritans. Well, they were Christians, but in the book, they certainly didn't act much like Christians, to my way of thinking. Her townspeople cruelly punished Hester for committing adultery by making her wear a scarlet 'A'. She sewed that 'A' on her dress and on her heart. She sewed for the rich who ostracized her, so she could feed her child and herself and she helped the poor. I admire the strength of such a woman, who can return kindness for cruelty."

I admitted, "Such harshness is not unknown among Catholics, more's the shame. Who among us can tell whether a cruel priest might receive greater punishment than a kind Indian. But methinks 'Judge not lest ye be judged' is good advice the Bible gives us.

John cleared his throat and stated, "'Tis hard for me to admit, such is me strong feeling against all that is English, that we have all read a great many fine books they have written, aye, and magnificent poetry. Worse yet, my favorite book is *The Decline and Fall of the Roman Empire,* written by an Englishman, Gibbon. He was an amazing historian, even if he wasn't Irish. O' course, most Irish history is passed down orally, to safeguard it from English depredations."

I asked, impertinent enough, "Do you believe then, that there be a few good Englishmen, even as there be a few bad Irishmen?" Even as I spoke, my glee at catching him out changed to sadness that I should be mean to him. Surprise flashed across his face, followed quickly by his charming smile as he saw my face change.

Then his smile faded, too. John looked perplexed as he spoke, "Oh family o' mine, you never cease to amaze me!"

"What then?"

"How do we amaze you?"

"What is it?"

He let the questions die, then said, "You know, when I knew you would all be here tonight, I thought 'twould be a good time to speak on a matter that I have been pondering o' late. And you, much as I love you, have been distracting me something fierce, with all your begging to hear the stories. I suppose, just because you know how much I like to talk, that you all thought 'What an excellent way for him to become seventy years old!' Sure and you be right in that. And then you cleverly turned the conversation to reading, which be a topic irresistible to us all. Here 'tis well after dark, and I would speak now about me will!"

Shocked silence was followed by loud squawking about how many years he had yet to live. Finally, he stopped us, "You have made me heart rich. Do not take back your generosity by demanding that I live beyond me time. I'm getting of an age where I have seen what this world has to offer and I'm beginning to wonder about the next life. So, about me will. In England, the oldest son gets everything; in Ireland, all the sons must divide the land. Here, I can pass on me belongings as I see fit. I wish to follow me heart in this matter. Tonight, I have told you a wee bit o' why I esteem your mother so highly. As a token o' me high regard for her, I would leave almost everything o' me worldly possessions to her."

I was that surprised, I only gasped. I tried, "But, John..."

"My dearest Maggie, let me have this."

So he said, without really saying, that he knew, as did I,

how lacking I be sometimes; but he didn't care to think of that just now, and how could I spoil things for him by insisting otherwise?

John continued, "For each o' my beloved children, I would leave a bit o' money, to say that I think well o' you." John looked at James. "James, me fine eldest son, the farm you bought with inheritance money given early provides well for your family; and proud I am of your leadership in church and community affairs. I would ask you to see that me will be carried out." James nodded mutely.

"Dear Margaret, when you and your betrothed came to me to borrow money to buy back his family farm, I refused to loan it to you. I thought 'twould be easier for you not to have to repay it, so I gave it as your inheritance. Well, have you repaid me confidence in your farming, Joseph. 'Twas your father's only mistake that lost it, and he was far from the only one who mortgaged a farm to buy railroad stock, which turned worthless in the bad time before the railroad was going well. So you have received your inheritance, Margaret." Serious was John's voice, but his proud, fond smile went from one grown child to the next.

"Lizzie and Tom, it pleases me greatly that you will stay here to care for your mother and I while we live. When we both have passed on, the farm will go to you, since James and Margaret have already received their inheritance. So, me heart bids me to give most everything to me darling Maggie, while providing for me fine children. I will be pleased indeed if, knowing how highly I think of each o' you, you can understand and agree with what I have done."

In the silence that followed, we all heard the lonely call of a loon for its mate, seldom heard here, away from the lakes, and somehow it was all settled and right. "God's in his heaven, all's right with the world."

2

(Great-Grandma) Annie
On the way to Prairie du Chien, Wisconsin
July 1902

Poor child, Mary. I feel so bad when you're all upset like this. Yes, I'm coming, as fast as this poky old horse will pull the wagon. I know, dear, you're hurting again. I'm coming to soothe you. Oh, my dear sister, I don't know why your mind gets so mean with you and makes you so fearful. I wish I could tear out the rotten part and let you be at peace! Those people at the asylum, they don't even send for me anymore when you get all crazy and terrified; they know I know you're having your troubles and I'm already on the way. I always know, dear child, and I always come. Do you ever laugh at me for calling you "child?" And you fifty-eight years old and me fifty-five, you with four grandchildren, me with six.

Dear sister, you were always afraid, unless you were playing with a pet fox or out in the night talking to the owls. I remember hearing that you brought the first fox kit home when you were only six or seven years old and no one ever figured out where you got it or why the mother let you have it. You took care of it until the next spring, in its cage. Then you let it out and it used to follow you around. It left in the fall and in the spring you found another kit. I remember you telling me, as I grew up, about seeing Long Tail or Bright Eyes or Red Ears in the fields. Was Long Tail an orphan, who later let you have one of her little ones?

And I remember one time I woke up in the middle of the night. I must have been about six years old and you were sneaking out of our bed to go talk to the owls. You let me go with you only after I promised to be very quiet and not tell anyone what we were about. We went into the woods in back of the house and sat on an old fallen tree. You had to help me up. I was cold, even in my coat, but with the moon shining on the few patches of snow and the wind rustling through dead oak leaves, I was too excited to complain. When the owls started their who-who who-whoooo, I heard one right beside me but it was you. It was all so mysterious and beautiful and though I had no idea what was happening, I thought it was very special and wonderful. Years later, I heard a neighbor comment about all the owls we had on our farm and that must be why we never had mice in our grain, and I knew the owls were there because of you.

As we left the woods that night, you told me you wanted to fly away with the owls. Oh, Mary! Why do I suddenly feel like it is time for you to fly away with them? I'm coming, dear. Hold on, I'm coming. If it must be your time, wait for me. I'll hold your hand so you can go easily.

Now, I'm in the woods, Mary. The hills here are too steep and rocky for anything but trees. You know how I love these woods, or any forests. I remember vividly Dad telling us how the English burned down the forests in Ireland. Strangely, it seemed as though he lost more by that outrage than by losing two sons and a daughter to the diseases that followed the potato famine. Or perhaps he could just talk about it more easily. At any rate, I always feel peaceful here, as though I were in church. I dasn't tell that to anyone but you. It sounds very superstitious, yet I always feel stronger after my moments here, at least when it's mid-morning in July.

Driving a wagon through here on a May evening, I've wondered how I have any blood left, for all the mosquitoes take. If that isn't bad enough, they whine around in great swarms, before and after they bite, and the bites itch for days afterwards. But I still hate the ticks more. They not only steal your blood; they're so greedy, they chew their heads under your skin and try to homestead there.

Do you remember, Mary, how we always looked so eagerly for the first pussy willows, the first geese, the first robins as they signaled the coming spring? How we laughed when we finally heard the raucous, croaking frogs! But by the time new leaves knitted their lace on the bare trees, the pesky mosquitoes and ticks did their best to spoil the joy of spring. When we were young, nothing could get the best of us. Now, it sometimes feels as if the bugs outweigh the violets.

I love the green of summer, gardens and fields growing their flowers and food, hot sun, the hard work that helps nature yield her bounty. I love the silence of winter, the evening stories and reading, the beauty of a full moon sparkling on the snow. On a winter's night, I have heard wolves along here. Their howling beckons from someplace. It's not the place, Mary, that you go to when you leave reality. It's more like where you're trying to go. Maybe it's the call of long ago, before original sin, a great yearning for a rightness that just isn't here anymore. Or perhaps it's the lonesomeness of this world calling for the next.

Though I love all the seasons, somehow, now I feel the glories of autumn the most strongly; the brilliant gold and scarlet maple trees, the satisfaction of a good harvest, the approaching winter when all the bugs will be dead. Dear Mary, is that what is happening? Are you about to leave behind all the unpleasantness of this life? My dear, if it is that you're hearing your call to the next life, wait a bit. Wait for me so you can see what I have to show you.

That photographing man brought us our portraits last week, so I'm bringing them for you to see, all wrapped safely in oilskin. Photographs are one invention I like as much as James likes the new farm machinery which has made his work so much easier than it was for his father. I don't know why James insisted on one picture with just me. I look like my heart carries the sorrows of the whole world but my chin is up as if I'm expecting more trouble and I'm going to keep right on going anyway. Now the family picture, James and I with our nine children, all grown up or nearly so, is really splendid. May the Lord forgive me for boasting, but oh my, I have such handsome children!

You know, Mary, Art is the only one of my children that I really worry about. Mary Anne can be a cross-patch, Margaret has been waiting forever for her Tom to get his farm going well enough so they can marry. But Art! Once when he was about seven, I was rushing around getting things organized so I could come and see you through one of your disquiets. Five-year-old Helen asked why I had to go and leave her. Art answered for me: "Aunt Mary is afraid and Mama must go help her." Art understood how you wanted to fly away with the owls, too, but he might have killed them, rather than let them fly away without him. He really understands the heart of the matter, but I think he'd rather strike out against life than cry over it or figure out a way around a problem. Sometimes Mary Anne was angry when I left to see you, because she's the oldest and it fell to her to tend to things while I was gone. So she'd give one of the younger ones a good scolding, do her work, and likely there'd be a cookie later for the one she had berated. I think Art can be much more cruel than that, though he doesn't show it around me. Mary Anne married a good farmer, a man who truly loves his land and his animals. She has never said anything, but I would guess she feels second to the farm in his affections.

Then there is Maureen. She drinks in life like a thirsty thresher! She has always been fascinated by James' stories, like the one about his father saving the life of Zachary Taylor, and that's how he got his land grant and started farming. Well, by the time Maureen heard that story, Taylor had long since died in office, as President of these United States. She got so excited, thinking of how things would be different but for her grandpa! I wonder if James ever regrets that he hasn't such exciting stories about himself to tell our children.

Years ago, Maureen had a friend over one afternoon and, as they shelled peas, Maureen told her, "My grandpa had to cut his grain by hand, with a huge curved knife. And he didn't have horse-drawn seeders or mowers or threshers or anything like that when he first started his farm. And they used candles they made from animal fat instead of lanterns, and mostly winter nights they'd read by candlelight to the children and go to bed soon after dark. When Grandpa read to them, Grandma would knit mittens or darn socks; when Grandma read, Grandpa would mend the oxen's harness or sharpen knives. Or, if they both had work to do, one would tell about Ireland when they were young or really old Irish legends. We have stories at night, just like they did, don't we Mama?" Yes, Maureen will pass on the stories to her children, with a few of her own added, I'm sure. Her first baby won't be born for a few months yet, but I can already hear her saying "Why, when I was young, we didn't even have telephones!"

And poor James. He's a very intelligent man, my husband, but it still puzzles him, and maybe frightens him, too, that I just know when you need me. But Mary, he treats me with a respect above that which most men around here have for their womenfolk. Always, at supper, we talk, of books, of school, of town needs and farm problems; the children join in with their concerns. While one talks, the rest listen, most of the time anyway. That's the way James' family and mine did it, so we fit very well in that regard. Most of the families we visit with serve a lively meal, too. But our children have brought back tales of other supper tables, where the children may not speak unless spoken to. One German family sounds stifling: the wife feeds the children, puts them to bed, feeds her husband and his friends, then she gets to eat. I am blessed at our table and in our life by the respect we have for each other.

Whenever I think of deep respect for women, I am reminded of that evening, oh, it must have been thirty years ago, when James' father celebrated his seventieth birthday. The whole family was there, James and I, Margaret and her husband, Tom and Lizzie. John and Maggie related how they had come to Wisconsin and started their farm. John openly admitted taking Maggie's good advice on several occasions. (When our Ma got her way, she did it by getting Da to believe it was his idea in the first place.) I greatly admired John and Maggie, two people who shared a dream and worked together to reach it.

With his whole family present, John explained his will. To honor her share in their accomplishment, John gave the homestead to Maggie and he asked that she will it to Tom and Lizzie that they might be provided for, which she did. Tom and Lizzie are still there, managing the farm and taking care of the church and reading and socializing with their friends. Sometimes it seems a shame that neither of them ever married, but they seem contented enough in their quiet, good lives.

Anyway, though my James is not the great adventurer his father was, nor quite the fine farmer. If he only took after his father in one way, I would love him for the way he loves and respects me.

Our supper discussions follow the tradition of his family and ours, and so does education. James, his brother and sisters all went to Patch Grove Academy, which was started at the end of the Civil War to give children more than eight years of schooling.

Mary Anne, our eldest, finished at the academy in only a year, instead of two years, and went off to teach, staying with a family near the school. She told us she got paid considerably more than her Aunt Mary Anne got paid for teaching back in 1855, thirty years earlier. Her aunt only received eight dollars a month. James was not a man given to speaking of his pride in his children, but that pride lit up his face whenever Mary Anne's name was mentioned.

And now we have four daughters who are teachers, and one nurse. We'll see what becomes of Helen. Some things are beyond our knowing, but I still wonder that none of our sons, nor their father, seems to have the strong purpose that drove James' father, and ours, thousands of miles from Ireland, to settle in barely peaceful Wisconsin and establish very successful farms in their own lifetimes. Our daughters seem to have a great deal of spunk and ambition; our sons are good men and boys, but somehow less alive than their sisters. Well, Art seems adventuresome enough, but lacking in direction or how to make it all fit together, or something.

Oh my, I'm thinking strange thoughts about my family! But you understand, dear Mary, all my ramblings, and you never mind, even when I'm with you, my retelling the same things again and again. I'm coming, Mary. I'll listen to your frightful thoughts until you slow down; I'll comfort you, hold you, sing to you.

Oh, here's the bridge coming up ahead. I never really liked this covered bridge, crossing the Wisconsin River at Bridgeport. I don't dislike it as much as the old ferry. I was always afraid the ferry rope would break and the raft would go tumbling down to the Mississippi, and me with it, if I was

lucky enough to hang on. It did break a few times, passengers
got soaked and a few even drowned. The bridge seems safer,
although it gets battered pretty badly by ice every spring. I
just don't care to pay the toll. Seems to me, the farmers who
got together and put it up ten years ago get enough profit by
how much easier they can get their stock and crops to the
railroad station. They charge fifty cents for a team and wagon,
twenty-five cents for a horse and buggy, five cents for a walking person. Of course, you had to pay the ferry, too, but that
was different: the ferry man had to drop whatever he was doing and get you across. If the bridge was free, nobody would
have to waste time collecting the tolls and raising the gate.

It could have been an O'Neill, you know their way with
horses, but it wasn't. I can't remember who it was. Some
young man, they say, got out of his buggy, paid five cents,
walked across the bridge, and whistled for his horse to follow,
which it did, so he saved twenty cents. Until his father found
out about it and made him pay the twenty cents and fix the
gate. I always thought the story might have been invented by
someone like me, who didn't like paying the toll.

Well, the courting couples surely like this bridge; yes, even
some of my own sons and daughters have been known to dawdle
through the darkness, and I doubt if they were discussing the
stone supporting piers or the wooden structure.

Now what comes to mind, dear, is that our father had it
much easier than James' father; by the time Da brought us
here, twenty years after John had settled on his farm, life was
pretty tame. And Da had help from Uncle Patrick, his brother.
I guess you remember him better than I do — I was only five
when we left Ireland. But I thought he was the most handsome, charming man in the world! Years later, I accidentally
overheard Ma and Da arguing whether to accept Uncle Patrick's
latest beneficence. When Da saw me at the door, stunned by
their rare disagreement, he explained it all to me.

Uncle Patrick was a smuggler, as were many in his family.
Years ago, driven to recklessness by zealous customs officials,
Patrick and his men had lost their ship in a bad storm. They
had always spent as quickly as they "earned". So Da helped.
By providing some of the funds for a new ship, Da became a

partner and he was merely getting his share of the profits. But Ma was against accepting the money, after they had become established. Da told Ma that Patrick was merely keeping a little money in Ireland instead of giving it all to the English, which meant smuggling was considered a very honorable profession in Ireland. Besides, it made Patrick feel good that some of the money went to such honest folks; couldn't God more easily overlook their sin when it helped these worthy people? I guess Da won out, because now that he and Ma are gone, his share is split among you and I and our brother.

When my monies come, James and I sit down, after the children are in bed, and figure out where it would be best spent. If we strongly disagree, we sleep on it, then work it out the next night. We had been married some time before Da's share started coming to me. James was very uncomfortable about using "my" money for our farm at first, but at that time, we really needed some new cows and he accepted it. Naturally, a little always went for frivolities for the children, maybe something for James and me and a little set aside for something special that might come up. I am pleased to make this contribution, and very pleased that James accepts it and considers my views on it important. That is his way. Perhaps that is why, when he works on church committees or with groups of farmers or as one of the local politicians, he is so successful: he carefully listens to everyone, weighs the matter thoughtfully and then talks everyone into a common conclusion. I think because he treats everyone with respect, they are more likely to act together.

Dear Mary, I wish your problems were as simple as heating the church, because James could surely find a way to help you if they were. I hate to see you all twisted up, but riding to see you by myself does give my mind a rare chance to wander. And whether I'm talking to you in person or having an imaginary conversation, like now, I know you understand. And sometimes I think you hear me, even though it's only my mind talking to you, because you seem to know things you have no other way of knowing.

The Old Military Road. Seventy years ago, soldiers built this road, all the way to Green Bay, so they could better tame the Indian country; if the road wasn't any better then than it is now, it's a wonder the soldiers ever settled anything. Full of holes, curving, up and down hills, bumps built up across the road to keep the rain from running down and eroding big gullies all the way down. Luckily, it hasn't rained for a few days or the cart would get stuck so often I'd get to you faster by crawling.

Now the road winds between fields. Mary, I felt bad waving to farmer Johnson just now. That horse he's got pulling the wheat mower just doesn't look good. It seems like Mr. Johnson has gone downhill, since his wife died a year ago, leaving him with three babies. She died in the birthing, poor thing, so young and frail. Pretty she was, and happy; but three children in five years and the hard work of being a farm wife wore her out quickly. They say he's too grief-stricken to even look for another wife. Most of the many farmers around here who have lost a wife have another before six months have passed, she is that needed. It takes a strong heart and a strong body for a woman to survive here and I have been greatly blessed with both, though my health now isn't so good.

So you see, my Dear, I can understand the terrible frustration your husband felt when you sometimes couldn't manage your duties. I tried to talk to him, several times, but he was unable to listen, to realize that tenderness and calm were the best remedies for your problem. I could understand his early anger, but when, over time, his anger turned to cruel coldness, I came close to hating him, closer than I've ever been in all my life. Now, with you safe at the asylum, I've mostly forgiven him.

Dear Child, the first time I visited you there, it nearly broke my heart. So many empty eyes, no dignity, no joy, no one at home in those straggly bodies; one woman curled up in a corner, screaming to herself; another singing wordless, tuneless songs; all of them so disconnected from each other. But you helped me see that it was indeed a refuge for you; there, when your mind torments you, it doesn't hurt your children or husband. In time, I saw the joy a smile or a small treat brought to them. But, oh, how I wish life could be better for you! Why, Mary, does your mind run away from you? Why are you fine one day and not the next? Do you run away from harsh reality only to find a harsher unreality?

I must think of more pleasant things. Remember, Mary, our first winter here, we came home from school one Friday to find Ma and Da all excited. Sparkling eyes betrayed them, but all our childish begging couldn't force the details. We had an early supper, and after cleaning up, Da told us to put on our warmest clothes. When we opened the door, there was a new sleigh, with our horse dancing in front, eager to be off. We shrieked and squealed and climbed in under the rugs, found heated stones to keep our feet warm.

After a while, when we were calm enough to listen, Da told us that nobody went for a pleasure ride in Ireland for many years. The potato infection and bad weather ruined crops and then starvation invited disease until you could hardly leave your home without hearing that someone you knew was either dead or dying. The futile rebellion of 1848 against the English took more lives and rebels who were caught were shipped to the penal colonies. Some rebels escaped to America along with many who desperately sought a better life. Da said every family was cut in half, some lost even more. "So," he told us, "Look at how beautifully the full moon shines on the snowy fields. See, even in the dead of winter, the land is healthy. Know that this land is yours and will keep you well and never, never forget to thank God for bringing you here!"

What is wrong, child? Have my wanderings upset you? I'm coming, as fast as I can. Oh, my dear! Please don't fear death! Our mother waits for you in heaven. Although life has often been cruel to you, you were always kind. The Virgin Mary knows this, and how you have suffered. What a welcome you will receive!

There is a barred owl in that big dead tree just ahead. Who-who who-whooooo. Whoa, Paddy. Mary that owl shouldn't be out in the middle of the day! He's just sitting there, looking at me. Oh, Mary, he says you're flying away with him! Good-bye, owl. Good-bye, Mary. Fly to peace. There's no need to rush now. I'll just sit a spell and bid you farewell. I'll miss our talks. All those times I came to you when your mind went crazy and you were always so much better when our time was over; all I ever did really was love you. Why am I crying when I know you're finally at peace? I miss you already! I miss being able to help you. I miss your understanding, your kindness. Oh, Blessed Virgin Mary, take her gently to yourself and comfort me, for I have lost a much-loved and loving sister!

"Thank you, Annie."

Oh, was that you Mary? Yes, I believe it was. You're very welcome

3

(Grandma) Cece
On the Bridgeport Farm
May 1916

Five-year-old Marguerite's terrible screams woke me up. "There, there, it's just a bad dream."

I sat up in the hay and pulled her toward me, held her. Moonlight came in the open hay-mow door, so I could see the frightened faces of nine-year-old Elizabeth and baby Mary.

"Oh, Ma, it was Pa! He was talking to me. Then he turned into a monster!" Marguerite cried.

I thought, "Out of the mouths of babes comes wisdom." I said, "There, there, it's all right now." Didn't I just wish it would be all right, that it was nothing but a nightmare. I moved Marguerite to my side, keeping my arm around her, set Mary on my lap, and patted the blanket covering the hay, inviting Elizabeth to sit next to me, too. I couldn't let Art terrorize our children! I had to do *something,* but *what?* I couldn't think about that yet: I had to take care of the children first.

I started singing our nightmare chaser:

"There's an old bogey-man under my bed;
doo dah, doo dah.
He scares me when he blows his nose;
oh, dee doo dah day.
Gwine to chase him out,
Gwine to chase him out.

*I'll blow my nose right back at him;
oh, dee doo dah day."*

I felt Elizabeth relax under my arm. "Now let's all sing it." Elizabeth sang out; Marguerite just muttered along, until we came to "blow my nose." Whoever had the bad dream was supposed to make the nose-blowing noise. That night, she made a huge angry sputter and broke down in giggles.

Eventually, my lullabies put them back to sleep. I climbed down the ladder and went outside, into the bright moonlight. I walked furiously back and forth in front of the barn, staying close to my girls in case of more nightmares. I thought back over the day.

Before noon, Art had come dragging into the kitchen, covered with dust, bleeding from several cuts, angrily complaining about one of the horses he was trying to break before he sold them. He and his friend had captured twenty-six of the wild mustangs in North Dakota on their latest trip. I told him lunch would be ready soon, but he didn't stay.

The first time I was awakened that night was by Art's yelling and crashing around. I went to the kitchen. Apparently, Art had run into a chair and he had avenged himself on it by smashing it to bits.

"Art, go to bed," I said quietly.

He swore, grabbed a coffee cup off the table and threw it at me. I was too shocked to duck. It hit me on the shoulder, fell to the floor and shattered. Behind me, Marguerite yelled as one of the pieces cut her leg. I stared at Art, unbelieving. He gaped. Then I picked up Marguerite and saw that Elizabeth was there, too. "Come on, Elizabeth."

In the girls' bedroom, I told Elizabeth, "Get an old wash rag and towel and the pitcher of water." I threw two blankets over my shoulders like a shawl and picked up Mary, who was crying. We came out to the barn and lit the lantern that was there. I tended to Marguerite's cut, which was small; its ugliness came from its source. Then we bedded down in the hayloft.

Well, Art had been drunk many times before; he'd been mean, but never broke things or hurt us. Marguerite was so right: liquor made a monster out of Art. And who would believe it of gentle Art? No one, except his drinking cronies, and even they would never admit they believed it. But I didn't really care whether anyone believed me. I had to protect my children and nothing else mattered.

I must have walked for hours; my mind churned with disbelief and fear, with determination, with outrage and self-pity, with helplessness and righteous anger. Determination won out. I *would not* let Art hurt our girls! Finally my mind and my feet slowed down. Although I had no answers yet, I went back into the barn. I prayed for help and went to sleep.

Hungry Mary was the next one to wake me. As I fed her, I began to know what I had to do. And I felt the strength rise in me. Maybe the Virgin Mary was with me or maybe I had some of my father's feisty strength. Elizabeth and Marguerite woke up as I fastened my bodice. "Girls, I'm going to the house now. Please stay here with Mary." I would make sure the monster was gone before I let them in the house.

Art was sleeping heavily on the kitchen floor. He slept on as I fixed a huge picnic basket of food. I took it, and clean clothes, out to the barn. "Girls, get dressed. We're going for a picnic." My smile convinced them; they chattered as they dressed. After eating, we wandered around our farm, exploring the woods, the creek, and the fields.

Late that afternoon, I took the girls back to the barn. As I walked toward the house, I knew I might lose Art. Well, he was lost when he drank, but that was only once or twice a year. It would break my heart to take the girls and leave him, but even that if necessary.

Art was sitting at the kitchen table, eating bread and butter, drinking coffee. He looked terrible, but surprisingly sober; he was usually drunk for a week or two.

I poured myself a little coffee, filled the cup with water and sat down across from him.

"I hurt you last night," he muttered, looking at his bread.

"Yes, and Marguerite, too." He had cleaned up the glass and the broken chair.

"I'm sorry."

"I know you are." I said calmly. "But you've been sorry

before." I prayed silently: "Mary, help me." I told Art, "I can't stop you from drinking. I've tried. So from now on, when you get drunk, we'll go visit neighbors until you're sober. We'll get out of your way." I took a deep breath and spoke firmly. "I tell you this. If you ever hurt me or the children again, we will leave you for good. Furthermore, you are not to destroy our belongings. You bring in so little money, I have to scrimp and save to get what little we have. I'll not have you wreck any of it. If you can abide by this, we will stay with you. Otherwise, we will leave and not come back." Art stared at me, amazed, then convinced. Silently, I prayed: "Thank you, Mary."

"I'll call the girls in and fix supper." Art nodded.

A few nights later, after the girls were in bed, Art told me, "Cece, I've been thinking of selling the farm. Our neighbor Edward really wants to buy it. Then we could move into Prairie du Chien and I could work there."

I thought about it. "Yes, I think I'd like that."

It took just a year for hopelessness to take over my life in Prairie. Then I went to visit Annie. "Welcome, Cece," Annie said. "It's good to see you. James is gone, but you and I can have a good chat."

"Hello, Annie. I hate to trouble you on such a lovely day, but I'm at my wits' end." A week after the nightmare of Art's violence last year, Marguerite had stayed with Annie and James to prepare for her First Communion. Marguerite had her bad monster dream at Annie's and told her all about it. Annie also knew (the whole town knew) of our first six months in Prairie du Chien, when Art had tried to out-drink every drunk in town, while paying for their drinks. As if he couldn't get rid of the money from selling the farm fast enough by drinking, he took up poker with a vengeance, too. In six months, the money was gone and Art owed so much money for drinks and gambling that he quit going to the taverns. "It's Art ..." and I gave in to tears.

"There, there now, Cece, poor dear. What is it?" Warm, comforting Annie. I cried for a while, as Annie held me on the faded, lumpy old sofa, my mother-in-law's favorite listening place.

Finally, I told her: "Annie, I'm so shamed that my children have to come to you for a nickel to see a Jackie Coogan movie or to buy peppermints! Why can't Art be a provider for us? This whole last year has been a nightmare! First, his violence. Then coming here for a six-month drunk, followed by the last six months without money, except for what little he gave me from the farm money. Thank God, I made him pay for our house here in Prairie as soon as he got the money for the farm. A year ago, I thought I could handle anything except his violence. Now I find his improvident ways are driving me crazy. At least on the farm, I could sell a cow when I got desperate. I've got to feed and clothe my daughters, but how? Art is simply not capable of regularly earning money and I don't know what to do." So I cried some more.

When I quit crying again, I said: "You know, Annie, I haven't cried this much since my mother died. I was only ten, and I remember when they were going to bury her, I hid behind your mother's big monument, because Father said I shouldn't cry, but I couldn't help it. Everybody went to funerals at our church, so you were there, too. Soon after I found this hiding place, you came and put your hand on my shoulder, so gently. I looked up and you were crying, too. Then you held me while we both cried. I didn't want to let go of you; I felt so safe, but finally you stood back a little and said, 'My child, there is a time for crying and there is a time for taking care of others. Your little brothers and sisters will need your help; you must be their mother now. It will be very hard sometimes, but you are a very special girl. I will pray to the Blessed Virgin, Mother of Jesus, that you find the strength in yourself to do this.'

"Annie, I used to think of that moment whenever I was sad. I'd be standing on a chair, kneading the bread dough, one of my favorite tasks with Mother. Only when she wasn't there any more, it made me unhappy. Then I would punch and pull and push the air out of the dough and I'd be chanting to myself, 'Blessed Virgin Mary, help me be strong' over and over again. By the time I had a dozen loaves punched down and shaped and in the bread pans, I felt tired, but satisfied, because once more my tears and anger were gone, re-placed by good food for my family."

I smiled as another thought came to my mind. "I was so pleased to marry your son. The handsomest man around, he always said the sweetest things when we were courting. I was the envy of all the girls. And to have you for a mother-in-law! I wished you had stayed on the farm, though, instead of mov-ing here, because all too soon, life again turned hard. Eliza-beth was born a year after you left, followed by two who came too soon. The second one I lost was a boy. You always knew when I needed you, so I wasn't surprised when you came out. There I was, lying in bed the next day, thinking I'd failed Art because I couldn't give him a son. I couldn't get him to take care of the farm. I couldn't keep him from drinking. Worst of all, I wasn't sure I even wanted the boy because Art didn't seem to want any more mouths to feed and how could I pro-vide if he wouldn't? You saw the look on my face and said the right thing: 'Dear Cece, it is a sad, sad time when you lose a child. But you must never blame yourself. It's God's way of saying that you have enough to worry about right now.' Then you got a funny look on your face and said, 'But I have a feeling that your next child will live and I think she's going to be a real fine woman. You'll be proud of her.' I must have looked shocked, because you started apologizing for saying such things. But then my heart knew you were right, and I felt better." Everyone felt better after talking to Annie. She had a way of taking our sorrows to herself, which lightened them to where they were bearable. It wasn't the words she said. I don't know how she did it, only that she did.

"And Marguerite was born fifteen months later. Now she is seven years old and she already knows how to get what she wants. It was her idea to go begging to you for nickels. Now, I've had more miscarriages and a third daughter. Each time I've lost one, my heart breaks again, yet I'm grateful that I've only three to feed and clothe."

I sighed. "Annie, sometimes it seems like the only happy part of my life is living just down the street from you. Ever since my mother died, you've been a mother to me. I don't remember her very much, except her health was always poor.

But after she died, I always looked forward to going to church, for Sunday Mass or for a social, because you would be there and you always had a special smile for me and even if you said no more than 'hello,' it would brighten my day.

"Annie, I haven't let you get a word in edgewise, all this time, nothing but 'poor me, poor me.' How are you?"

Annie laughed. "About the same: ten bad days for every good one. Before you came, I had started some cookies. Why don't we finish them now and figure out what to do about our dear Art? I mixed up sugar cookies. Well, actually, I measured and James mixed, your recipe. The dough is on the back porch cooling. Why don't you roll it out and I'll get us a fresh cup of coffee? Do you think this fire is about right for the cookies? I've been baking in a wood-burning stove for all these years and I swear the hardest part is getting the right heat in the oven. Every kind of wood gives off a different amount of heat and you never have the same-sized chunks."

I checked the heat. "Hmm. I think it needs this one small chunk. Sugar cookies like a nice hot oven, in and out. Annie, I wish you'd teach Art how to make coffee. Yours is so good. In the morning, he puts grounds, water, and an egg to settle the grounds all together in the pot and boils it on the stove. At noon, he adds more grounds and water. At supper, he adds more grounds and water. After noon, I don't drink it unless I'm desperate, and then I boil up over half a cup of water and add a little of his black brew. By the time I throw the coffee out at night, the pot is half full of grounds!"

"I think Art is past learning from me." Annie laughed. "Besides, I'd rather watch you roll out the cookies, cut them with the upside-down glass and scoop them onto the cookie tin. You are an artist with dough."

I laughed, too. Seven minutes later, I peeked into the oven. "Look at that. A little golden brown creeping up around the edges. Perfect! Why don't you heat up our coffee and let's have some cookies!"

Annie reminisced. "These bring back memories. I suppose it was ten years ago we were at Maureen and Charley's farm for one of our family get-togethers, James and I, six or eight of our children and their spouses, a dozen or more grandchildren. I was looking out a kitchen window, out to the side yard, ignoring for a moment the hubbub of my daughters and daughters-in-law behind me getting the food ready. I admired the soft June sunshine, smiled at the children's laughter as they played in the front yard, noticed, near the barn, the half dozen wagons which had brought us together. None of those noisy horseless carriages then. Some of the food was already on the long tables, built to feed threshing crews and large family gatherings there in the shade of the huge old oak. It was all so busily peaceful and happy.

"Then Maureen's son, I suppose he was five or six at the time, swaggered over to the table and peeked under towels to see what delights he could look forward to. At about the fourth lifted towel, temptation hit. He paused to savor it. Behind me, Maureen said, over the noise, 'All right, Helen, you can ring the dinner bell. By the time they're all at the table, we'll have the hot foods and salads out there.' My grandson, startled, looked around quickly but saw no one watching him, so he grabbed a handful and darted to the back of the house. I was curious, so I went to a back window. Delight lit up his face as he crunched into one of your sugar cookies. At the second bite, his grin grew even bigger. A clatter behind me startled him and he looked into my window, embarrassed at being caught out, but thrilled to have an audience.

"'Grandma, they tickle my teeth!' You know, that boy is still getting away with great mischief."

"Annie, I love those gatherings, too, more now than ever, with your oldest granddaughters helping out. The earlier times, we women spent most of the time getting the food ready, serving it and cleaning up, which I certainly enjoyed, but the best part for me is when we all sit around and talk. The conversation is very stimulating, talking about the olden days, the parish and church problems, how we're going to get more education for our children, who should be the next president of the United States or the next town chairman. At first, I felt a little shy about venturing my opinion, even though I'd known your family as long as I can remember. But in spite of some teasing, the men do take our views seriously, usually. Except Art, when he's drunk. Then he makes me feel completely worthless." I grinned awry. "But I'm not good for nothing, am I Annie! He hasn't hurt me or the girls once since I gave him that ultimatum, even though we haven't been able to completely avoid him when he's drunk. I only wish I could prevent his nasty words — they hurt, too."

I shrugged. "Anyway, now that my girls are older, they enjoy the get-togethers more, too. Afterwards, they'll talk for days about horseshoes and croquet, pony rides, the swing in the big willow tree, the latest exploits of their twenty cousins. So, let's celebrate family by having another tooth-tickler!"

"You really enjoy baking, don't you, Cece?"

A wisp of sadness blew past me. "Yes, it was my favorite way to get a smile from my brothers and sisters after mother died." An idea came to me. "Annie, do you think I could sell my cookies and baked goods? Do you think people would buy them? I mean, if I could earn some money to take care of the girls, I wouldn't have to worry over whether Art is earning or not. Do you think Art would let me?"

"Cece, that's a wonderful idea! Let's see, who would buy them? Widower Jack, down the street, I'm sure he'd love to have cookies for his grandchildren when they visit. Prices' cook retired and they have a lot of dinner parties, so they'd buy bread and rolls maybe. Why yes, lots of people. As for Art, you just send him to me. I'll talk to him." Annie's determination would send Art's objections out the door, just like dust in front of a new broom.

I smiled at the thought, then frowned. "No, by God, I'll tell him myself. I can do that." I stopped, shocked at my use of God's name. "Listen to me! I sound like Art after he's been out West, catching wild horses with those hooligans. He'd usually be sober when he was breaking them, back on the farm, but his language was so foul, I'd take the little ones as far from the pen as I could get, until he was through for the day. Then I'd come back and fix supper."

"Cece, you didn't take the Lord's name in vain. You called on him to witness your right and good purpose. Actually, I think God is probably smiling right now, seeing you a little while ago, crying like a lost babe, and now finding a way out of your troubles.

"Please, dear, I want to help." With a tear in her eye, Annie said, "You know I'm shamed by him, too, maybe even more than you, because he's my son. I had hoped, when he married you, that he might get some direction in his life, but neither you nor I can make of him what he doesn't want to be. I don't want my grandchildren to suffer on his account. We both love Art, but we'll have to take care of your children without him. I want to give you some seed money. Consider it part of Art's inheritance that won't drown in his bottles."

I was overwhelmed. "Oh" was all that came out.

Annie continued, "Of course, Art should be providing nickels for the girls. But do you remember, just after your mother died, that I bought you a penny candy at the store? Do you remember how delighted you were?" I nodded. "Cece, your daughters need their treats, too. Life would be too harsh without them. Besides, I get my value out of those nickels when they come to see me. For them, my rule is that we talk only about happy things, so for a while, they can forget about the bad times. My nickels buy me some sunny smiles and buy them a treat and how better could I spend them?"

"All right. All right." I gave in with a laugh. "When you started talking about giving me money, I was ashamed of needing help. But that is a waste of energy, I think. Yes, I'd be pleased to have your help. By ... by all that's good and holy."

A surprising thought came to me. "You know, Annie, when I came here, I was so overwhelmed, I didn't know what to do. Life seemed totally impossible, even more than when Mother died, because I was too young then to realize how great a responsibility I had to carry. But now I can see a way and I know I can do it. Thank you." I rose from the table and Annie rose, too. I hugged her. "Maybe even if Mother had lived, she wouldn't have helped me as well as you have, over the years." Then I wondered, "By the way, why did you mix up the cookies when you haven't the strength to roll them out anymore?"

Annie just smiled.

As I walked home, I realized that there was no one else in whom I had ever — could ever — confide in as I had in Annie. I could tell her the deepest-down-in secrets of my heart, things I hadn't even realized myself until I said them to her. And, talking to her, I had found direction again. My determination would take care of the rest.

I needed to pump two buckets of water, one to clean the vegetables and one for the soup. My backyard was surely noisy. Automobiles chugged up and down Main Street, only two blocks to the south; children played next door at Anna Lucy's. A train was coming into the depot three blocks to the west, toward the river. But I had done well to insist that Art buy this house when he sold the farm six years ago. The Lord knows the rest of the money went for nothing. Our two-story brick house was fairly new, not falling apart like the old farmhouse. The bright warm sun played with the breeze which fluttered through the gold leaves in the huge maple at the edge of our lot. I thought, "It's early this year. I must tell Annie to come see it soon." Then my heart grieved. I had forgotten again. Annie was four years gone from this life.

An automobile stopped in front of the house. It was Art's sister, Maureen. I went to greet her, anticipating good conversation.

"Hello, Cece. What are you doing?"

"I'm getting ready to make a big kettle of vegetable soup. Today is Friday and you know how weekends are here. I suppose there's more traffic here than at the Burlington depot. It seems like half the passengers from the train stop here, plus my three girls are always bringing their friends home and our relatives like to drop in."

"And you love it, don't you?"

I laughed. "Yes, I do!" I paused. "You know, when we moved here, I had hopes that Art would change and take responsibility. Of course, he's still the same. But I really like living here. I like the constant company and I like earning money to keep us going."

"Can I help with the soup?"

"Of course. Come on out back and admire my maple tree

while I pump some water."

When I had enough water, I stood beside Maureen and looked again at the tree. It blazed forth its glorious gold against the bright blue sky . Suddenly I was smiling and crying: Annie was with us. Her presence magnified the joy I felt until I thought I could stand no more. Then it passed. I shook my head, looked at Maureen. She, too, was smiling through tears. I whispered "Annie was here."

She nodded.

Silently, savoring our wondrous experience, we carried the water in. I gave her a cup of coffee. Maureen put on an apron, found a knife, a bowl for peelings and a bowl for the vegetables while I started washing carrots, rutabagas, snap beans, potatoes, tomatoes, onions. Maureen sat at the kitchen table, peeling what I cleaned.

I thought back to other times when I had felt Annie's presence. I hadn't quite believed it before but sharing the experience with Maureen convinced me. And who better to share it with than Maureen, so like her mother. Maureen had Annie's great sensitivity and brought joy to all who knew her. But I didn't know how to say these things to Maureen.

When I finished cleaning the vegetables, I sat at the table to cut them up. "Good heavens, Maureen, do you realize we've been together for half an hour without saying a word?" We laughed at this very unusual behavior.

Maureen got a strange look on her face.

"What's wrong?" I asked her?

She hesitated. "After what happened outside, it all seems pretty insignificant."

"What does?"

Maureen began reluctantly, "Well, a few weeks ago, you cut Marguerite's hair, quite short.

"Yes, I did. When it was long, I would wash it and set it in rags. Every time I combed it out, she would cry. I don't know why her head is so sensitive. Elizabeth and Mary have no trouble. Maybe it's because of all her ear infections. Anyway, I decided it was ridiculous to cause her pain, now that women are cutting their hair short."

Maureen replied, "You had good reason. Did you hear

what Mary Anne's daughter, Marian, did?"

"No."

"Marian marched herself into town and had her hair cut. And then she took our Margaret in back of their barn and cut Margaret's hair. My husband had a fit! 'She cut off her crowning glory! No man will marry such an independent woman!' And on and on. I can't decide whether to laugh of cry about it."

I commiserated with her. "Oh, dear."

"Charlie was going to come over here and read you the riot act, but I thought it would be better if I came."

"Maureen, I am sorry that Charlie is upset, but he is being very foolish." I thought a moment. "You know, short hair is really much more practical. Just think how much easier it will be for Margaret when she plays on her high school basketball team." Silence. "Maureen, Margaret is a wonderful, high-spirited girl and Charlie dotes on her. He'll get over it. Besides, what does he want to do, shut the gate after the cows are out?"

Thoughtfully, she said, "It's more complicated than that. You know us six sisters. Our parents raised us to think for ourselves. Four teachers, one nurse and one to stay at home to take care of them. For years, I've been running the farm successfully, with our hired hand. I make all the decisions, pay the bills, even work in the fields and milk cows when I'm needed. Charlie is no farmer — he's a salesman, and a very good one. That's why he went to Chicago, to work with that big import company. Chicago was exciting, but we both missed farm life." She paused. "I think it was Dan Patch that brought us back."

"Do you mean the great pacing horse?" I asked.

"The very same. We saw Dan Patch race in Chicago. Another horse started with Dan Patch, so he would have a race, but the other horse was running full out, not pacing. Dan Patch was so much faster than any other pacer, no owner would put his pacer against Dan Patch. The first runner tried to keep up for a while. When he slowed down, a second runner started up. The magnificent pacer left them both in his dust. You know how Charlie loves horse racing. Myself, I enjoy a race, but it's not a soul-stirring event in my life, not even when young Charles rode in races. But watching that splendid horse was a moment of perfection." Maureen smiled, remembering that moment and I smiled, thinking of a very recent glorious moment, when Annie shared our joy in the beauty of a tree.

Maureen returned to her tale. "The owner of Dan Patch also owned International Stock Food Company of Minneapolis which provided animal feed all across the Midwest. He used Dan Patch to promote his feed and with such an awesome horse as a trademark, it's no wonder the feed company was so successful." Since a Dan Patch story, told by an Irish woman, was self-sustaining, I just listened as she went on, though I wondered what Dan Patch had to do with women's haircuts.

"Anyway, after seeing that race, Charlie started hankering to be back on the farm. Several years later, he quit hankering and decided to do it. He was smart enough to know he was much better as a salesman than as a farmer. So he went to the International Food Company and got himself a job as sales representative for this region. I was all for coming back, because I had been taking the children to the farm every summer during the Chicago years, so I could help run it. Life would be much simpler just staying there, and much better being close to my family all year round. So Charlie sells his feed and I run the farm and we both like what we do, but you see, I never flaunt my independence."

I thought of what she had said. "Then what you're saying is that you ran the farm, summers when you came from Chicago and you run the farm now that Dan Patch brought you back, but you let Charlie think he's the boss. Since Margaret's haircut is an obvious rebellion, you're worried that Charlie will realize that he's not in charge at all."

"Exactly."

"Maureen, a lot of men would be better off if they realized that." We both laughed. "But seriously, you know that he dotes on you, too, and for all that you may not belabor the point, I think Charlie knows perfectly well how capable you are. You are a partner to him, and I think he likes it that way."

"Hmmm. I suppose you are right. Mother always said you were very perceptive."

Although I didn't want to talk about feeling Annie's presence a while earlier, I loved talking about her. "I always felt special when Annie was around."

Maureen responded, "You were special to her. The amazing thing about her was that everybody felt the same way. She once told me that she was determined that no one could ever dislike her. She succeeded." Maureen paused. "You know, I used to think she could see deep down inside me and see the good in me and also the foolishness. She had a look that said 'It's all right to be a little foolish now and then, but don't take yourself too seriously when you're being foolish.'" She looked thoughtful. "You said Charlie and I are partners. I suppose we are, just as Mother and Father were partners, although Mother was very inconspicuous about it."

"How is your father?" I asked.

Maureen answered, "Poor Father. He was always so active in local politics, on school boards and town boards and very involved in church activities. He loved to tackle a problem and find a way to solve it for the benefit of the community. Farm life suits him better than town life, so it is good he moved in with us. He helps a little here and there and the children love to listen to his stories. But he misses the role of leadership and the respect it brought. Even more, he misses Mother. I think that may be why his mind wanders so badly at times."

"I remember at Annie's funeral," I said. "As everybody was leaving the cemetery, I turned around and there was your father with his white beard and his dark suit, standing under the big pine tree by her grave, sobbing. It seems like when she died, the heart went right out of him."

Maureen agreed. "He has been fading away, ever so slowly, since Mother died. You know, when Prohibition started, nobody around here paid much attention, just kept right on drinking. If it had been left to these people, everybody would still be drinking the same. But the regular liquor became hard to get, which resulted in everybody making their own moonshine or brew, which brought the federal agents here."

I interrupted. "I guess I know about that!" Art tried selling moonshine but when the feds caught him and put him in
jail, I was very angry. I didn't visit him once. When he came
home, he asked me why. I told him, "If, stone sober, you
haven't the good sense to obey the law, why should I mollycod-
dle you when you get punished for your foolishness." And
that was the end of his moonshining.

Maureen winced, remembering Art's disgrace. "Of course
you do. But anyhow, you know how Father loves his whiskey.
When he came to live on our farm, there was no liquor at all.
He was very crotchety. He managed to get some moonshine,
which made him very sick. Then he harangued Dr. Moody
until he wrote him a prescription to have a drink every night.
That works pretty well because it's not enough to get him
drunk, so he doesn't go wandering around looking for Mother,
but it does quiet him down.

"I send our hired man into Bridgeport to buy whiskey. I
won't go there myself. I have never seen such a tiny town
with so many seedy characters. The farmers use the depot,
but almost the only other businesses in town are the taverns.
But your father's tavern there is the only place I know where
they still sell decent whiskey."

"Well," I remarked, "your father is a dear old man, and I
guess when I'm that old, if I want illegal whiskey, I hope
someone will be kind enough to get it for me. All his grandchildren love him; he used to take them to movies and he
always had peppermints in his pockets for them."

"Cece, he dearly loves his grandchildren. Did you know
that in his will, he left everything to be divided among his
children except for one hundred dollars for each grandchild?
There are already twenty-nine of them. That's a lot of money!"

I said, "I'm sure my daughters will find good use for theirs,
but I hope he has many good years yet before they get it."
After a moment, my thought returned to an earlier topic. "You
said you didn't know whether to laugh or cry over Margaret's
hair. What's the funny side?"

Maureen answered: "The funny part is even more incredible. I think Margaret was right to cut her hair and I'm even

half-tempted to cut my own. Remember all the brouhaha in the 1920 presidential election campaign? Since women were finally allowed to vote, both Cox and Harding offered a bit of support for women's issues and a bit more, until October 1. Then Harding went all out, calling for equal pay for equal work, an eight-hour work day, the end of child labor, prevention of lynching, maternity and infancy protection, a minimum wage, national health care programs, the whole program set forth by the League of Women Voters."

"Yes, he had an excellent platform," I said. "I voted for him, but I haven't seen any changes yet."

Maureen went on: "Margaret is saying, 'I will not let men dictate to me how long my hair should be.' If this were a rebellion against morals, I would be very troubled. You read these days about the flappers. They have short hair, short skirts, and very red lipstick. Their lives consist of smoking, drinking and lusting. There is a great new freedom in the air for women, and flappers take the free-from-restraint road, while the League of Woman Voters are choosing the path of helping others improve their lives. Margaret is sound. She will never be a flapper."

"So, Maureen, you're saying that Margaret cut her hair to show her independence and that she'll use her independence well?"

"Exactly."

"Then why are you only half-tempted to cut your own hair?"

Maureen looked thoughtful. "I've always been independent and I guess I don't have to prove it to anyone. Of course, if necessary, I could always threaten Charlie that I'd cut mine if he didn't come down off his high horse." We both laughed.

"Well," I said, "now that we have haircuts in their proper perspective, I'll tell you about Marguerite's big adventure. She had quite a time visiting her Aunt Ruth in Milwaukee. She took the train, all by herself. After hearing your children bragging about their travels, she seemed very excited to go. I thought she could help Ruth out; her cancer is getting bad when she can't make it to family gatherings anymore. Ruth must have been a little better, though. Marguerite said Ruth took her shopping in the department stores. From all the clothes, hats, kitchen wares, and furniture Marguerite described, they must have walked for hours. Ruth had given her five dollars to spend, as thanks for helping. Marguerite bought a sweet little hat with it. When she got home, Marguerite told me, 'Aunt Ruth couldn't raise her arm to brush her hair any more, so every night I would brush it for her. She liked that very much.' And Marguerite found it very intriguing that they lived in back of the grocery store that Uncle Guy owned and operated."

I had a wicked, irresistible thought. "You mentioned the wickedness of smoking and drinking. What about Ruth and her smoking?"

"Cece, you don't miss a thing, do you?" She smiled. "Actually, I don't think any of those activities are wicked, of themselves; only when they become a way of life. But what a fuss when Ruth was discovered smoking in our outhouse at that family gathering, when, five years ago? She told us, with a perfectly straight face, that the doctor had prescribed smoking for her because it would relax her and take her mind off her pain. Poor dear; how she has suffered. It must be very hard for her husband. But I think that her doctor's prescription and Father's prescription for whiskey are much the same: they each wanted something and found a way to get it. I would do the same thing, if I were in their shoes. That attitude runs in the family, I think."

"It runs *rampant* in the family, I'd say. I'm that way, too. Maybe that's why I married your brother — I fit right in. My daughters are like that, too, especially Marguerite. When your brother John visited us a month ago, Marguerite woefully told him how badly she wanted a bicycle. John said his daughter wasn't using hers any more. When he returned to Wauzeka where he was station agent for the railroad, he put the bicycle on the next train coming here. She embarrassed me no end and yet I'm glad she finds a way to get what she wants."

Maureen looked thoughtful. "And what is it you want, Cece, that you use these dried-up vegetables?"

"You don't miss much either! I'm no good at begging for

myself, but I want my girls to go to college. I buy old vegetables from the grocer, who sells them to me for pennies. The money I save goes into their college fund. Oh my, I've never told that to anyone. Please don't tell Art. If he knew, he'd use the money on one of his drinking bouts."

Maureen replied: "What a wonderful idea! I won't tell anyone. You know I won't."

"Thank you."

"But what about the money you earn at the dress and millinery shop?"

"Most of that is for now," I answered. "I want all the girls to have four years at St. Mary's Academy first, then college. Catholic education is very important to me, in these turbulent times. I think you put it very well: our daughters have many choices before them, from flapper girl to social reformer. You and I both love our men, but we also recognize that men have made a mess out of things. You and I work hard to make our little corners of the world right. That is good and it suits us well. But who knows how great an influence our daughters will have?"

Maureen agreed. "I have spoken so strongly about college for our children, that Charlie says we'll educate them all off the farm. If that happens, so be it. Mary Anne already has a college graduate among her children. Maggie says she'll scrub floors if she has to, in order to get her children through college. Oh, her daughter Irene leaves for St. Teresa's College in Winona this Sunday. Yes, we all want our children to have as much education as possible. I guess that runs in the family, too.

"Grandpa John and Grandma Maggie built the first one-room schoolhouse in the area on their land. My Aunt Margaret and my sister Ro both taught there. It's amazing when you think about it. My Father had eight years of grade school and two years at Patch Grove Academy. My children, God willing, will have college. My Jennie and Charles have already started college and it brings tears to my eyes to think of it." She paused. "Do you think Grandpa John and Grandma Maggie can see from heaven that their great-grandchildren are getting so well educated?"

I said, "Yes, I think so, and if they are allowed a little pride in heaven, I'm sure they're busting their buttons, too."

"Of course, I miss my children when they're gone. Our Jennie is nearer, studying music in Chicago. Charles is farther, at Notre Dame. But they are so involved they don't get home too often. I miss them most on a cold winter evening, with a blizzard raging and the telephone wires singing in the fierce wind. That's our time for music. Charlie played the violin and Jennie played the clarinet; Bill on drums and Charles on coronet. Colleen and I like poetry. During a blizzard, I'd recite a dozen poems about snow and end with one about spring. Well, we still have our music and enjoy it very much. And Charlie still plays his fiddle for dances, though usually at the cheese factory now because there aren't many barn raisings."

I stood up to put the large bowl of vegetables into the soup kettle on top of the wood stove. I added salt and spices, and a little holy water from a small bottle, with a quick prayer that there would be enough to go around.

"Maureen, would you like more coffee or tea?"

"Tea, please. One cup of Art's coffee is plenty!"

When I sat back down at the table with our tea, I commented, "I see you're still driving the old Tin Lizzie."

"Of course! We got it in, let's see, 1910, I think. It's a cranky old automobile, but I like it. Charlie has his newer one, but once I found I could crank it up and start it myself, I claimed it for my own. You have to pull the choke first, then crank it a few times, then jump in the driver's seat and turn the ignition on, jump out and crank it quickly, with just the right touch."

"Charlie used to get so upset when it wouldn't start!" I said. "One time you came to see us at the farm and when it was time to go, he couldn't get it started. So he stalked back into the house and you got out and started it. You do have the touch! I wanted to laugh out loud, but poor Charlie! I was surprised he didn't walk home, he was that put out."

Maureen replied: "Oh, yes, I remember that. Then my brother-in-law Tom bought his Ford, so whenever he and Charlie got together, that's the first thing they discussed, the new doodads available for the Fords and any repairs they'd done. Tom took such pains with his Tin Lizzie. He wouldn't use it in the winter; he'd drive it into the second floor of his barn, which he had cleverly built into a hill. He let the air out of the tires, jacked it up, drained the radiator, covered it with canvas. Even today that Ford looks brand new. They only drive it for special occasions. I'm the opposite: any excuse, or no excuse, is good enough for me to go for a ride. Thank goodness, the war didn't last any longer! With the gasoline rationing and no driving on Sundays, I really felt put upon. Of course, I never complained about it, being very patriotic, and knowing that my hardship was small indeed compared with that of our soldiers, but ..." She smiled, that come-what-may smile of hers.

Then I spoke, "And our brother-in-law Will still hasn't bought an automobile. He thinks they are the devil's own invention. There is as much variety of opinions on automobiles as there is on haircuts. Tom is adamant about his daughters leaving their hair long, but he has a Ford. Here, we have short hair and no automobile. You, I suppose are the most venturesome in your family: you have both Fords and short hair."

Maureen continued with her thoughts. "Maybe what I like about driving is the challenge of it. Whenever I get a flat tire, I have to fix it right there. We've had to buy new inner-tubes several times, because the old ones had more patched places than unpatched. I have to get chains put on if I want to drive on muddy roads. I don't understand why the gas tank is under the seat so that I have to lift the seat out to put gas in from the gas can. And it happens fairly often, as much as I drive, that I run out of gas. Sometimes someone comes along and helps me and that is fine. I don't mind at all watching someone do the dirty work for me. Usually, though, I end up doing it myself. Then, by the time I get going, I'm quite pleased with myself for my little accomplishment, if I'm not disgusted with myself for being such an awkward wretch about it. In the winter, it's much easier to take a horse and sleigh, but even that isn't always easy."

I knew that well enough. If the snow came a little at a time, the horses pulled the sleighs and a lot of sleighs made a path. But when there was a big snowstorm, the men and boys had to get out and shovel, mile after mile after mile. It could take weeks. No mail, no school, no shopping, most likely the phone lines were down.

Maureen continued. "In Grandpa John's time, there were so few settlers, that roads were snowed in for most of the winter. Maybe the isolation brought on by a blizzard is what brings our grandparents to mind, because we always tell pioneer stories then.

"Speaking of snow," I asked, "wasn't that a job Mary Anne's sons took on last January for their sister's wedding?" They shoveled the eight-foot snowbanks off the sidewalks at the church so the guests could get in. No automobiles that day! Mary Anne was worried that nobody would make it, so soon after the blizzard, but almost everyone came.

"Ma, we're home!" called Marguerite as she and Mary came in the front door.

"Come see who's here!"

"Aunt Maureen!" Their faces lit up when they saw their favorite aunt.

"I made sugar cookies this morning. Would you like some?"

"Yes, please." They both responded quickly.

"Well, then, go change out of your school clothes. I've made tea and we'll chat for a bit and then you'll have to do your chores."

"Yes, Ma."

"May I ask Susan for supper tonight, please?"

I looked at Maureen. We smiled. "Certainly."

The next Sunday, Art's sister and her family stopped in. "Maggie and Matthew, Irene, Catherine, come in, come in! Maggie, did you take time off scrubbing floors to come see Irene off to college? Where is the rest of your family?"

Maggie laughed. "You know I haven't had to scrub floors to get Irene to college; my Matthew runs a good farm down by Lancaster, in case you haven't heard. Maurice is tending his sick calf and Mary is taking care of William."

"Cece," asked Matthew, "where should I put these preserves Maggie brought for you?"

The box he carried held a dozen quart jars of apples, pears, peaches and plums which she had put up from the trees in their orchard. I was delighted. "Put them on the kitchen table, please. Thanks, Maggie, these are wonderful. We'll surely enjoy them this winter."

My girls came rushing down the stairs and added to the welcoming hubbub, as Matthew came back. I told him, "Art went to Tom and Belle's after Mass. The girls and I were going to join him later, but as long as you're all here, why don't you walk over there and ask them to join us?" Art's brother Tom had enough years as station agent at the depot that he didn't have to work on Sundays anymore.

"That's a good idea."

"Elizabeth and Marguerite, get some cookies and milk for you girls and go upstairs to visit." They quickly disappeared.

When Maggie and I were settled at the kitchen table with tea and cookies, I said to her, "How happy you must be to have your first child leaving for college. How wonderful that she can go to Saint Teresa's, which has an excellent reputation for learning."

"Oh, Cece, I'm so pleased! Look at me, so pleased, I'm weepy." She remembered: "It was a lot different when I left home to finish my schooling, ninth and tenth grades at Patch Grove Academy. I went from our farm near Mount Hope all of eight miles to stay with dear Grandpa John and Grandma Maggie during the week. After I finished at the academy, I had all those wonderful years of teaching in the rural schools. How I loved pinching pennies so I could buy books and lovely things for our home, for Matthew and I had an understanding that when he got his farm built up, we would marry.

"I was very sorry I had to give up teaching when we got married, but our wedding was glorious. And what a sight we were, moving my things to his farm, where everything would become ours: my books and bookcases, silverware, Haviland china and Irish linen, carefully packed on a wagon. For if Matthew wanted the security of a good farm for bringing up our children, I wanted them to know beautiful things."

I remembered my young niece, Helene, after a visit to

Maggie's, telling me that Aunt Maggie was the most beautiful woman she had ever seen. Aunt Maggie had served toast
with butter and jam at the dining room table, using her china,
silver and linen; served with such beauty, Helene thought it
was a feast. I thought, "She walks in beauty." Where had I
heard that? Probably from Maureen, who was always putting
poetry into conversations. That was Maggie: she brought
beauty to everything she did. Then I recalled something I
had heard. "Didn't you used to teach the teachers after you
got married?"

She smiled. "Yes, I did. Young women had only eight or
ten years of schooling before they started teaching and some
of them were very poorly prepared. I missed teaching so much,
it was a godsend for me to be able to continue in that small
way. Eventually, teachers went to school longer and my dear
husband and children kept me so busy that I didn't have time
to miss teaching any more. And now, Irene is following in my
footsteps, planning to become a teacher. I couldn't ask for
more!"

"Yes, it is good," I agreed. "And how is Matthew taking
this, his daughter going to college?"

"Matthew is satisfied that his children will do better than
he did. I think the hardest part of my marriage is seeing his
frustration. He hates farming, but he feels trapped there by
his lack of education. He is a good farmer and a good man,
but he can't see anything but what he isn't. So he gets really
stubborn about things. Mother cautioned me about marrying an uneducated man. It didn't matter to me then and it
wouldn't matter now, except that it bothers him a great deal,
and it does come back on me. Anyway, our children will be
free to choose what they want."

"Now they are getting old enough to make choices," I
commented. "It seems like just yesterday that I heard how
Irene, then a toddler, saw her favorite uncle in the back pew at
church and crawled under the pews to get to him."

Maggie laughed. "Yes, even as a child, she went after what
she wanted! And wasn't it your daughter Marguerite who
came into town from the farm to stay with Mother and Father
while she prepared to make her First Communion?"

"Yes." I knew what was coming.

"She had a loose tooth, so she went into town and had it pulled. Much to everyone's dismay, she received her First Communion with a front tooth missing."

I added: "When she came home, she raved about the delicious bread her Grandma made and complained about her Grandpa's poor hearing, 'Every time I wanted to talk to him, I had to pull his sleeve to get his attention and then I had to shout very loud so he could understand.'"

"I like Charlie's ghost story," Maggie said. "He told his children, and they believed him for many years, about Joe, the fellow who used to cut wood for him. Joe and Charlie agreed on how much wood he should cut and Charlie paid him in advance, as usual. But when Joe left to go home, he was struck by an automobile and killed. After that, whenever the trees cracked and snapped in the cold, Charlie would say, 'I guess that's old Joe, cutting wood. He got paid for the work and he's determined to get it done.'"

"My favorite story about our children is about Maureen's son, Charles. When they lived in Chicago, just after the turn of the century, Maureen would drive to Carson-Pirie-Scott for shopping. One time, six-year-old Charles hid in the back of the buggy and fell asleep there, only to fall out on Michigan Boulevard. Maureen heard him cry out, turned around and picked him up."

"And then there was Mary Anne's son, Arthur," responded Maggie. "When he was learning to drive, he would complain about the 'thank-you-Mom' bumps in the roads. The hills had bumps across them to prevent the rain from running downhill and creating big gullies. If Arthur went too fast over these bumps, he'd hit his head on the roof of the automobile, which prompted a wry 'thank you, Mom' for the reminder to slow down."

I smiled. "We have so many wonderful stories of our children, we could go on all day with them. But how is your little William?" William's birth four years ago was very difficult for his fifty-year-old mother and, a few weeks later, the influenza epidemic hit. Three of her children, including William, were very sick but she nursed them through it and then got sick herself. It's a wonder they all lived through it. That was the epidemic that killed hundreds of thousands of Americans. Both Maggie and William have kept their health but poorly since then.

"William is such a serious little fellow," Maggie answered. "He is stronger now, but I doubt if he will ever enjoy the robust health of his brothers and sisters. For myself, I have never regained my strength. My older children are wonderful helpers, but it grieves me not to be able to do my work as I used to. Matthew is good to me. He doesn't understand me — he never did — but when I quietly insist on something, he will agree."

Maggie laughed her pleasant laugh. "When we married, I asked him if I could have something on our farm which I could take care of to earn a little money to buy nice things. He thought he should just give me a certain amount of money each week for household expenses. He couldn't understand that I liked earning money or that household expense money simply could not be spent on frivolities. We went around and around about it. I was always calm and pleasant. He was insulted, angry, and puzzled, but my persistence wore him down. The chickens and their eggs became my source of pin money and Matthew learned that when I want something important, none of his arguments made any difference. College for our children was one idea that we agreed on from the start. He wanted better for his children than what he had."

"Cece, I haven't talked this much in a long time. You are a good listener. You remind me of my mother in that way."

"Yes, I cried on her shoulder more than once," I replied. "Annie was a woman of great understanding and sympathy. To this day, I find myself thinking, 'I must tell Annie the maple is golden' or 'Annie will be sorry to hear her grandchild is sick.'"

"Mother's last few months, when she was so poorly, all my brothers and sisters took turns staying there, helping out. I came too, but that was right after William's birth. I was so weak that I was more bother than help. And then we were so sick with the influenza that we couldn't even come for her funeral. I felt really terrible then. I know I did what I had to do, but even now, four years later, it hurts me that I had to miss her funeral."

I reached over and took her hand. "Your mother knows, Maggie, she knows." That had been a very hard time for Maggie. Then I thought about her sister, Helen, whose recent months had been very difficult. "When your sister, Maureen, was here Friday, I forgot to ask about Helen. How is she doing?" Helen's husband had gone to town for supplies and she found the house was on fire. She was due to deliver her baby in only a few weeks, but she tried to drag all the furniture out of the house before it burned up. Two days later, the twins were born, only one of them alive.

"Poor Helen," said Maggie. "It's a good thing she had twins so at least she has one baby. In her letter last week, Helen wrote of their rebuilding and refurnishing. Their new home sounds even nicer than their old one. Her little girl is fine, but I fear Helen blames herself for losing the boy. Yet she continues to be the fine mother, wife and sister we all love." Maggie's eyes were wet, as were mine.

I sympathized. "It was bad enough when Ro's and Maureen's homes burned; no deaths, but some priceless possessions lost, like Maureen's family letters from way back and all the family history she had gathered. Well, she has put much of it back together, but how does Helen replace her child? Of course, family and friends help out with food and clothes, which is fine and good, but sometimes I wonder why life has to be so cruel. And yet, we do go on, don't we?"

Art called out as he came in the front door, "Cece, look who's here!"

"Hello, Tom and Belle. Ro and Will, what a surprise! Hello, children. Well, Matthew, you brought back more than you bargained for."

The men squeezed kitchen chairs between the sofa and the arm chairs that circled the potbellied stove in our living room. We had no fire that lovely day. We women passed around cookies, tea and coffee. When we were all happily crowded in, I asked, "And how is our famous Mount Hope farmer today?"

With a crooked grin, Will answered, "You mean our progressive brother-in-law Mike, the first man to put in a silo, the first to plant hybrid corn, the first to use commercial fertilizer, the first to practice soil conservation, the man who loves his land and his animals, the father of the winners of the junior livestock show, the father of the first college graduate in the family, the man ..."

"No, no," I laughed. We all did. "I mean how are you?"

"Then you should have asked, 'How is our infamous Mount Hope singing farmer?' I'm looking at good crops, fair prices for them and for the beef cows I'll sell. We're not getting rich, but we're not getting poor, either. The county agent who brought in all those newfangled ideas to increase production during the war did have a few good notions that I've tried. Seeing how successful Mike has been, I had to break down and change a little."

"Ro, what's new with you?"

"We got a letter from our son. He told us all about his work in the Chicago hospital. I miss him, but I'm pleased that, after college, he chose a job helping the sick."

Loud giggles came from upstairs. I said: "Elizabeth and your girls are probably talking about boys. Elizabeth is terribly preoccupied with them these days. It's a good thing she's going to St. Mary's school, for girls only. If she were in public school, I think she'd be too busy about the boys to listen to her teachers."

"As much as I hate to leave," Maggie said, "I think we'd better get Irene to the train." We all followed them outside.

"Good-bye!"

"Good luck!"

"Good to see you!"

When Matthew started up his Ford, Will's horse snorted, but he had been around enough automobiles that he didn't run away. Will didn't like much that was modern, but he did have a water pump in the kitchen, so Ro wouldn't have to haul water in from outside.

After everyone left, I made deviled eggs with some of the eggs Ro had brought for us, heated the last of the soup and mixed up some biscuits.

At supper, Marguerite asked, "Mother, may I go to St.

Teresa's when I get older?"

Her question startled me, but I answered, "I hope so. It will be many years yet and a lot could happen, but I'm planning and working for just that." Art looked surprised, but didn't argue.

I looked around at my family. It had been such a pleasant day. Some days, I'd just as soon trade Art for a bag of rutabagas, if I could. But only if I could keep our fine daughters and the rest of his family. Then I wondered, when our daughters were grown up, would they remember good days like today, or the bad ones, when Art was drunk?

Eight years later, we saw Marguerite off to St. Teresa's. She looked very grown-up in her new Pendleton plaid suit. Then Mary started crying and Marguerite joined in and she looked far too young to be leaving home. Afterward, the closest Mary came to admitting she missed Marguerite was complaining that she had taken all the clothes with her.

Elizabeth was working in Chicago as a medical technician then and all too soon she wrote to ask my advice, which made me feel my age.

June 15, 1933

Mama darling,

Sebastian and I went to storage houses after church on Sunday, all afternoon. Our big ideas have come down to $5 beds and $35 dining room sets! We have been wanting to get married instead of waiting and while we were discussing it, Seb suggested that I ask you what you thought of it — without any money hardly — just a lot of enthusiasm. He is so blue and lonely all the time and discouraged. It seems I have a little black magic because I can make him forget his troubles. I am not afraid and I know he wants to go ahead but I guess he's afraid I'll be unhappy if we are poor. The thing I had hoped to do was to have a very small wedding in Chicago and have you family come. Could you afford it as a wedding present? I expect to ask Con to be bridesmaid; maybe some of her family might drive you. At least you and Pop could come. This depression seems to be lasting and we both hate to wait any longer. I, too, am a little lonely, or had you noticed?

Well, Cece, what think you? Are we crazy or are we crazy?

Best love and kisses

Eliz

4

(Mom) Marguerite
Prairie du Chien
1936

I breathed a sigh of relief as I left the sheriff's office. I had had to type really fast to finish all the reports so I could leave. Sheriff O'Hara, my boss, was a crazy bounder. I liked working for him, but I wished he wouldn't regale me with his wild stories when I wanted to finish my work and go, especially on a Saturday. I had to talk to Dot, then rush home and get ready for my date. Tim, the undersheriff, was nice; he said we could borrow his car Sunday afternoon.

I rushed up the stone stairway in the courthouse and around the corner to the Register of Deeds office, where Dot worked for her aunt. "Hi, Dot. We can use Tim's car tomorrow. Let's go for a picnic on the bluffs. I'm hungry for a hamburger cooked over a fire. It's cold yet, but at least the snow is gone after that preposterous April Fool's snow storm. We'll get Jane and Betty and Rosemary, too." I had just spent two weeks at home getting over my appendicitis operation. I loved having the company, Uncle Dave and Aunt Helen, Uncle Mike and Aunt Mary Anne, Uncle Charles and Aunt Maureen and all the others who came to wish me a speedy recovery, but I was ready to move again. I wanted to do! I wanted to go!

Dot caught my excitement, "Sounds good to me! What are you doing tonight?"

"Joe is taking me to see *Follow the Fleet* with Fred Astaire and Ginger Rogers."

"Marg, I don't know what you see in him. He's just a big bumbling bumpkin."

I grinned. "Maybe that's why I like him. Besides, if I had to pay for all the dances and movies I want to go to, I wouldn't have a quarter to buy hamburger for the picnic tomorrow. Five dollars a week doesn't last forever, you know. And I give half of that to Ma for room and board. She worked hard to get me a year at St. Teresa's and a year at secretarial school. I owe her." I doubted if my two dollars and fifty cents even paid for the food I ate. I didn't know how Ma could do so well with so little money, especially with all the company we had. But she refused to take more. She wanted me to have fun with my money.

"I'll bring some ground coffee and my metal pail to make coffee in," Dot offered. "Betty and Jane can buy gas for the car. Three gallons, at fifteen cents a gallon, will get us there and back with a little extra for 'thanks, Tim.' Rosemary can bring the other food from her Dad's grocery store."

"I'll pick you up at one, then. Oh, can you call Rosemary and I'll talk to Jane and Betty?" My cousins lived next door to me. I looked at the clock. "Got to go now. I don't want to be late for Fred and Ginger. 'Bye."

Sunday afternoon, five chattering, giggling young women in the old Ford chugged up the hill to the park that the CCC men had started last fall. At the entrance, Jane got out of the car and moved the sawhorses with the "Road Closed" sign, so we could drive through. "Do you think they'll catch us sneaking in?"

"Who would bother looking for picnickers in April? Besides, Marg works for the sheriff. He won't arrest *her*."

"Look, the CCC men have been working; they've cleared out a lot of trees. This is going to be really nice."

"They've started building a shelter over there."

"The sun is shining and the wind is blowing and it's good to be outside."

"Let's get the fire going. I'm starved!"

When I finally bit into my hamburger, I proclaimed, "Aaahhh, this is the best hamburger I ever ate!"

"Marg, you say that every time we have a picnic."

"It's true every time."

When the food was gone, Dot took the pail of boiling coffee off the fire and poured some into our tin cups. We all lit cigarettes, and quietly watched the last ice chunks float down the Mississippi. I always liked watching the river shove winter out of our way. The almost warm sunshine brought a smile to my face.

After a bit, Betty said: "Boiling coffee in a pail over a fire without even an egg to settle the grounds sounds awful, but it always tastes good. I guess everything tastes good on a picnic."

"Marg," Dot asked, "I've been wondering, how can you put up with all the teasing you get in the sheriff's office?"

I grinned. "It wasn't easy at first. Some of the men were pretty mean. So I blew my nose right back at them."

"What?"

"When I was little, Ma taught us a 'nightmare-chasing' song. It was silly, so when we sang it, we forgot about being afraid. But it was smart, too. In the song, the bogey-man scared us by blowing his nose, so we scared him right back by blowing our noses. Well, Grant was the worst tease, so I decided to give him back what he was always handing out. The next time he started in on me, I looked him straight in the eye and asked him 'Do you get paid extra for being mean or is the meanness just part of your personality?' Grant was shocked speechless. He stalked out of the office. He never apologized, but he quit teasing me. Now they tease me and I tease them right back and we all have fun."

Betty asked, "Say, Marg, how were Fred and Ginger last night?"

"They were so good I made poor Joe sit through the movie twice. In one number, Fred lost all his money gambling and he came out of the casino ready to commit suicide, and then Ginger came out and was going to drown herself and he started singing *Let's Face the Music and Dance* and, when they danced, I wanted it to last forever. I love their marvelous dancing! By the time the second show was over, Joe had to take me right home because he had to get up early this morning to do his farm chores. He couldn't even take me to Kaber's for a nickel hamburger. How was the dance, Dot?"

"Great! Say, I saw your cousins, Colleen and James, talking to two very tall, very good-looking men. I wanted to go up and introduce myself, but I didn't quite dare."

Jane spoke up, I'll tell you who I think is handsome, Rudolf Valentino."

"How about Cary Grant?"

"Clark Gable! I loved him in *China Seas* with Jean Harlow. He sure does handle his women. And I can't wait to see *Wife vs. Secretary;* Gable and Harlow and Myrna Loy. It's coming to the Met in two weeks."

Rosemary asked, "Did you read in the paper that Shirley Temple was the biggest money-maker in Hollywood last year?"

"She's awfully cute and I like the way she goes after what she wants."

"How about Jeanette MacDonald and Nelson Eddy? Wouldn't you love to have him sing to you 'I am calling you-ou-ou-ou-ou-ou?'"

"Yes!" We all shouted.

"Or would you like to marry a man who would give up being king to marry you, like King Edward in England?"

"Yes!"

"It's so romantic!"

"Lucky Wallis Simpson!"

I grinned my disagreement. "I'd rather marry a man who could keep on being king when he marries me."

"I wish I could attract men like Mae West did in *I'm No Angel.* She's incredible. She never really said anything bad but oh, the innuendos, and the looks she gave the men!"

"That movie was so wicked, so deliciously wicked!"

"*I'm No Angel* was funny, but nothing tops *Night at the Opera* with the Marx brothers. I saw that a year ago, and still laugh thinking of how they messed up the opera."

I commented, "I loved *Follow the Fleet* and *Rosemarie,* but the most memorable film I ever saw was *20,000 Leagues Under the Sea.* I was just a kid. It scared me and thrilled me and made me think there was a great big world out there."

"Are you going to see the world, Marg?"

"Yes, I think I will."

"Did you see that *Connecticut Yankee* with Will Rogers is coming back to the Met?"

"I cried last year when I heard he died in a plane crash in Alaska. I still miss his column in the newspaper. One time he wrote about crime and how we can't seem to stop it, so why not make it legal and tax it, tax it so high that a thief couldn't afford to rob anyone. As long as taxes are putting other industries out of business, why not try it on robbery?"

"Speaking of the illegal, Marg, do you have any slugs?"

"No, I'm all out. The sheriff will probably raid the slot machines in a week or two. Then I can get some more and we can play the slots."

Jane asked, "Marg, have you stolen any dates lately?"

"No, I can hardly keep up with my own." Exaggeration wasn't lying. "But Betty and I sure had fun that night, locking you and Elizabeth in our bathroom, where you were busy trying to get beautiful." Then we told their dates that they weren't feeling too well and wanted us to go instead. We went to a dumb cowboy show, where Betty and I giggled so much, the boys insisted we tell them what the joke was. They couldn't decide whether to laugh at the joke we played on them, or be mad at us for separating them from their dates or be afraid of what Elizabeth and Jane would do.

Betty said: "Your sister, Elizabeth, always had boys mooning over her because she's beautiful, so I couldn't help laughing when the joke was on her."

"Elizabeth told me once that the worst time she ever had was at senior prom," Jane said. "One of the O'Brien twins asked her to go and the other twin asked that Bohemian girl with the bad accent and worse reputation. Elizabeth didn't know about her until the two boys and the girl came to pick up Elizabeth. Worst of all, the other girl had on exactly the same dress as Elizabeth was wearing."

Elizabeth had her two years of college, worked in the x-ray department in a Chicago hospital and married her Seb in '33. I said: "With her gone, there's less competition. I swear she used to come in one door with one date and go out another door with another date."

Rosemary had a question. "What was the story about your sister Mary going to Hollywood?"

I laughed. "Well, Mary and our cousin Irene felt destined for Hollywood. They sent their photographs to MGM Studios. They ran to their mailboxes every day for months before they finally gave up."

"It's starting to get pretty cool. Maybe we'd better get back," Jane said reluctantly.

"Why don't you all come over to my house and we'll listen to Wayne King, the Waltz King," suggested Rosemary. WLS from Chicago broadcasted his show from the Aragon Ballroom on Sunday nights at seven. Dot was the only one who couldn't. The rest of us jumped at the chance.

On the way back, we had a flat tire. We got out the jack, pump and patch kit. Rosemary was plenty strong from working in her father's store, but in spite of our advice, muscling the tire off required a few bad words. Jane scratched the scraper around the puncture, put glue on the patch and put the patch on the inner tube without any trouble. Getting it all together again was a lot of trouble. We took turns pumping air in.

In town, we stopped for gas at the Red Crown station. Bob pumped three gallons up into the glass container, then let it drain into the car's gas tank. Jane paid him.

Rosemary's mother just happened to have some food in her icebox, so we feasted again on chicken, cheese, bread and jam, canned peaches and chocolate cake. As we ate, Rosemary asked, "Should we have a truth party?" That meant each of us would have to say something true about the person on her right.

"I used to like those, but then they weren't so funny when somebody got hurt," I said, meaning somebody like me. "I'll pass on that."

"Well, how about a rubber of bridge? Then, when Wayne King comes on, we'll listen as we play."

We all agreed to that. My partner, Dot, and I got the good cards and played well. Even though we trounced Jane and Betty, I didn't gloat too much. The game ended before the music was over, so we sat around. In my best languid, sophisticated manner, I told Jane, "Give me a drag off your fag." She handed me her cigarette and I inhaled deeply. Afterwards, we went home to get a little sleep before we went back to jobs which we worked ten hours a day, six days a week.

Cousin Colleen came to see us Monday evening. "Marg,

how would you like a date for the Will Osborn dance band playing in Gutenburg next Saturday?"

"Are you kidding? I'd love to go!" Will Osborn played a lot of swing and I loved the new dance craze. "But only if my date is tall, dark, handsome and rich."

"He is, except for the rich part." We laughed. "How did you know?"

"Dot saw you and your brother talking to them at the dance Saturday night."

"They just stood there for the longest time, so I asked James to go talk to them and after a bit, I sauntered over to be introduced. Aren't I the proper one? I liked Dave and he asked me to go and could I find a date for Ben. They're the two engineers who designed the new park. They're in charge of the CCC men who are doing the work. Want to go?"

"Sure." CCC workers usually had money even when nobody else did and these men were good-looking besides. "Can he dance?"

Colleen laughed. "If you wanted to keep on winning dance contests, you should have stuck with Ed. Ben's not a great dancer, but he's easygoing and easy to get along with."

I grinned, "What time?"

"Eight o'clock?"

"Great!"

Saturday night, it was six thirty before I got home from work. After my bath, I put the tea kettle on the stove and when the water started boiling, I stuck my head into the steam and pushed waves into my hair. Every time I did that, I remembered Ma cutting my hair, freeing me from the rag curlers and painful combing. Short, my hair didn't snarl and I didn't have to set it in rags. Getting ready for a date, I missed my sisters. Mary's blue sweater would look really nice with my dress. Well, at least I'd been working long enough to be able to buy some ready-made dresses. Ma did make pretty dresses out of patterned flour sacks, but I felt so much more worldly in the store-bought ones. I tried to put aside fifty cents a week for clothes so when I saw a five- or ten-dollar dress I liked, I had the money for it.

The radio downstairs was tuned to WLS National Barn

Dance, four and a half hours of music. I, the very sophisticated Marg, didn't admit it out loud, but they did play music
that made it hard to sit still. Of course I liked Wayne King,
Guy Lombardo and Benny Goodman much better.

I heard Colleen at the door. They were early. "Hi, Aunt
Cece. I'd like you to meet Ben and Dave." I could hear them
walk between the stairs and Ma and Pa's bedroom toward the
living room, which was right under my bedroom; Ma called
upstairs, "Marguerite, your date is here."

"I'll be right down."

As I put on lipstick and a little rouge, I heard Uncle Tom
and Aunt Belle come in for their Saturday night card game.
The mirror assured me that I was as gorgeous as I was going to
get and my purse held all the essentials: comb, lipstick, rouge,
mirror, handkerchief, a little money, just in case.

I heard Ma start a story. "Ben and Dave, I'm sure you
know what hard times we're all having. My brother, Ed, sent
some pigs by train to Chicago. He received a telegram saying
that the sale price was two dollars less than the transportation
costs, so would he send the money. Ed's telegram replied
that he had no money, but he could send more pigs. They
didn't bother him again."

I timed my entrance perfectly. At the end of the laughter,
I stood in the doorway to the living room. All eyes were on
me. "Hello, everybody." Colleen introduced me to Ben and
Dave. Ben towered in front of me. He must have been a foot
taller than my five-foot-two. And he was just as handsome as
he was tall. Besides that, he was, well, I didn't know what,
but I surely wanted to find out.

We all sat down and Pa asked, "Ben, how do you come to
be in Prairie du Chien?"

"Well sir, I studied engineering at the university in Madison. My grades weren't too good, but back in Watertown, my
brothers had put me on the ballot for city engineer. They
must have done some good campaigning, because I was elected.
I guess the university figured if I already had a job as engineer,
they'd better give me a diploma. When I came up for re-
election, the fellow who ran against me was a veteran of World
War I. Watertown always elected veterans, so I got a job su-

pervising CCC work and they sent me here."

I watched Ben. I watched Ma and Pa watching Ben. Comfortable. Good.

After chatting a while, I stood up. "We're keeping you from your card game. We'd better get going."

"Have a good time."

"See you later."

Iowa had voted to stay dry when Prohibition ended, so we went to Kaber's for a few beers. We didn't stay long because the jukebox was too loud for talking and we wanted to dance to live music.

At the large hall in Gutenburg, the exciting music kept hundreds of dancers moving. I never saw so few wallflowers. We danced to *The Way You Look Tonight, Isn't It Romantic, My Blue Heaven, Stompin' at the Savoy, Wrap Up Your Troubles in Dreams, I'm Getting Sentimental Over You, I've Got You Under My Skin.* Jukeboxes were fine, but the Will Osborn band, there in the flesh, really put the music "under my skin."

I forgot about Pa and his drinking. I forgot about being poor and seeing people every day who were even poorer. I forgot about "Make it do, do it over or do without," the ugly Depression slogan. I pretended Ben and I were Fred and Ginger and everything would be fine. Well, Ben's dancing was far short of Fred's, but I found his unassuming way quite charming. So we danced the night away and had a lovely time. Then we went back to Kaber's for hamburgers and more beer.

When I finally got up the next morning, Ma asked if I'd had a good time.

"Dreamy." But I didn't want to admit to her or to myself, just how dreamy. "And he asked me out for next Saturday night, too."

"That's good. I liked him too."

"Did you win at 500 last night?"

"Sometimes. We switched partners after each game. Mostly, whoever was Belle's partner lost. I enjoy her company but she's not much of a card player. She's afraid to bid and never keeps track of the cards."

Ma's laugh caught my curiosity. "What's so funny?"

"Your poor pa. As clever as he is about playing cards, even there, he gets his comeuppance. Last night, when Belle was my partner, I passed, Tom bid seven diamonds and Belle muttered about the 'worthless whippersnappers' she held. After Belle passed, your pa, counting on help from the blind and figuring his partner had at least one bower, bid eight hearts. Art had four trump, the joker, ace, king, and queen, plus two aces and their kings. He'd figured rightly: Tom had the right bower. But Belle's 'whippersnappers' included the left bower and five little trumps. Being set by Belle was a hard pill for your pa to swallow! It nearly ended the game." She looked at me. "Now tell me about Ben."

I couldn't help smiling as I thought of him. "He's German, the youngest of four brothers. His father died when Ben was only six years old. He likes tennis and ice skating and he plays the trombone a little. He sounds like he's very honest and conscientious about his work. He's not a bad dancer, but I'll have to teach him more steps if we're going to do much dancing."

"You'd better get ready for church now. We don't want to be late."

The next Saturday, we went dancing again. Sometimes Joe or Tom or one of the other fellows I knew asked Ben if he could dance with me and Ben was nice about letting me, as if he could stop me if I wanted to dance with them. But after the third time, Ben said, "I guess I'm not much of a dancer compared to those guys." Perfect opportunity. I offered to teach him but he wasn't very keen about that. So mostly we did a box step, slower to the waltzes and fox trots, faster to the others. Sometimes he would twirl me around for a little change. But I enjoyed being with him a lot.

During intermission, Ben told me, "I was senior class president in high school, so I had to go to the prom. My sister-in-law, Caroline, taught me how to dance, but I only danced once."

He must have been very shy, I thought. I found his diffidence a pleasant change from the braggadocio that infected most of the fellows I knew. After I told him some of my farm memories, he said, "When I was little, we spent the summers at my mother's family farm. I wanted to play with the baby pigs one time. I must have been about five then. I talked my cousin Evelyn, who was a little bigger than I was, into standing guard between the mother pig and me. Well, the pig knocked Evelyn flat in the mud, so I quickly jumped out of the pen, leaving poor Evelyn to take care of herself."

"When I was a kid," I said, "I missed so much school on account of ear infections that I was kept back a year. I hated it, because only dummies failed and I wasn't a dummy."

Ben talked about his work, overseeing the CCC boys as they cleared trails leading to scenic and historic points, built rustic benches, graveled roads, built check dams in gullies to prevent erosion, cleaned out debris from the woods.

I told him about writing and typing reports on drunken drivers, thieves and bounty abusers. "A man turned in dead rattlesnakes in Grant County and collected the bounty. He found out where the snakes were buried, dug them up and turned them in again in Crawford County, to collect their bounty, too. But he got caught."

We argued politics. He was all for Roosevelt but I thought FDR was getting us into worse problems than ever. "He is playing God in the White House and one God is enough for me."

Ben teased me. "If it wasn't for Roosevelt setting up the CCC camps, I would never have met you, so he must be doing something right."

"Well, it's an ill wind that blows *no* good."

We traded silly jokes, "The Lord helps those who help themselves and Uncle Sam helps the rest."

"There are two sides to every question, but, like flypaper, one side may be sticky."

"Sometimes marriage is a partnership and sometimes it's a battleship."

When we came back to my house, we loitered on the front steps for a bit, but he didn't try to kiss me good night. In bed, I couldn't sleep. I kept thinking about my two dates with Ben, how easy it was to be with him and how easy to talk with him. He didn't seem to mind when I disagreed with him and he didn't try to change my mind, even though I tried to change his. How flattering that he was so considerate about opening the car door for me. Of course, most fellows did that, but Ben seemed to like doing for me. He seemed to like spending his money on whatever I wanted. Not that I blamed the other guys or thought they were stingy; I knew how hard it was to earn those nickels and dimes. And Ben was so handsome! I could hardly wait until next Saturday night.

After a month of Saturday night dates for dancing or movies, Ben started asking me out more often. And he would come over for a Sunday afternoon visit at my house, where he met lots of my many cousins, mostly from Pa's side of the family, and was surprised at how much everybody seemed to enjoy each other. He liked his cousins from his mother's side but didn't see much of them since they grew up; he hardly ever saw his father's relatives, who were nice enough, but distant. He was amazed at the constant coming and going at my house. He, too, felt my mother's warm welcome and he always seemed comfortable, whether we were alone or with a crowd.

So when I made my announcement regarding Memorial Day weekend, I felt fairly confident. "Ben, unless you want to help out at the Centennial Celebration of St. Gabriel's Church, I'm afraid you won't see much of me Memorial weekend. Ma is in charge of the dining room service and I'm the number one assistant." Ben read the papers and he knew it was going to be big. Saturday and Sunday would be filled with doings, Memorial Day services, processions, special Masses, eighth grade graduation exercises, blessing of the new grade school (already paid for), pageants and rallies, with every Catholic in Prairie du Chien's two parishes and many from out of town participating. "Ma is in charge of the luncheon for clergy and notables to be served after the Pontifical High Mass Sunday morning. I doubt if we'll get to see the processions or other excitements, what with planning and preparing and feeding the two hundred and fifty or so who are expected. Father Blank wants a really nice meal served."

I watched Ben's face as I enthused. He showed surprise and amusement, then I could see he was taking me seriously.

"Ben, this is all very exciting for me. My family has always been active in the church and there will be this wonderful celebration and I get to be part of it. And Father Mazzuchelli — maybe you read about him in the paper — he started St. Gabriel's a hundred years ago. He's the same priest who used to come to my great-grandfather's home to say Mass in the pioneer days, before there were any churches. He traveled all over this area, saying Mass, marrying people, and baptizing children and wherever there were enough people, he helped them to build a church. He baptized my Grandpa James and his brothers and sisters."

Ben didn't go to church, but he never teased me about my religion. Would he be willing to help? "Well, I knew your Ma was good at feeding people, but that sounds incredible. How will she do it?"

I laughed. "Two hundred fifty people — that's a piece of cake. In the May 5th *Courier*, everybody was invited to the luncheon. Ma talked to Father Blank after that. They guessed that with the local Catholics, out-of-towners, and some local non-Catholics, there might be fourteen hundred guests, and Father Blank wanted something better than pot luck with all its casseroles. Ma went home and figured. She calculated she'd need at least four church kitchens to prepare all the food. Even if the lowly Bohemian Catholic Church and the Lutheran and Episcopalian churches agreed to let us use theirs, that was only the first of the complications. So she went back to Father Blank and told him she could do it, but very likely it would be a mess. She could manage a pot luck for that many people with only slightly less chance of disaster. If he wanted a really nice banquet, it could only be for two hundred or so. So the May 12th paper stated the luncheon would be for clergy and notables.

"Then Ma went over to the school auditorium, where they'll have the luncheon, with a bunch of her friends, and walked through the serving so she could figure out how many women and girls she'd need. The women will dish up the plates and the girls will serve them. She'll practice with them, so they know exactly what to do. Of course, they've all helped out with wedding and funeral meals, but they're usually pot luck and served family style or buffet style."

Ben asked, "What will she serve?"

"Ham, potato salad, green beans, dinner rolls, cole slaw, and apple pie with ice cream. And relish plates and things. Her best helpers will make the potato salad, cole slaw and bake the rolls at the school kitchen Saturday, while others set up the tables and chairs. Her best bakers will be at home baking the pies. Other women will bake the hams at home Sunday morning and bring them, already sliced, in plenty of time for lunch. They'll fix the beans and relishes Sunday."

"Where will all the food come from?"

"Well, the manager at Kroger's is Catholic, so Ma talked to him and he'll donate some and sell the rest at cost. Father Blank will convince some of our rich parishioners to donate money to pay the bill. Ma talked Luick's into donating ice cream and it's going to be butter pecan. Won't that be a treat on apple pie! Luick is even going to open up his store for us to pick up the ice cream Sunday."

I was awed by this side of my mother. What a terrific job she was doing on the planning! Ben looked intrigued. I asked him, "What will it be? Do you want to help or do you want to do without me?"

Ben smiled. "I think I'd better help. Otherwise I'll never know how your Ma could manage such a feat." I smiled. Working together on these things was a lot of fun and wouldn't I look good with such a handsome fellow to show off?

Because of Memorial Day, neither Ben nor I had to work Saturday, so we spent the day running errands. "Get extra dishes, silverware, pitchers, tablecloths."

"We need more coffee."

"We'll have to have more dish towels."

"Find us six more large garbage cans."

I liked running errands with Ben.

Sunday morning, Ma and I went to five o'clock Mass, then ate some breakfast out of our bags, along with coffee at the auditorium, together with a dozen women who were there to work. We put on the tablecloths and silverware, salt and pepper shakers; we fixed the relish plates and got the beans ready to cook. Ma had a list of what to do when — she was a marvelous organizer. The "flower brigade" appeared with vases of bridal wreath, irises, lilies of the valley and wildflowers. We put cole slaw at each place, put on butter, baskets of rolls and relish plates and poured water. Ma and I had gone over every detail. Everything was ready and there were ten minutes before the guests arrived. So we grabbed a bite to eat from our bags and told jokes so we wouldn't seem nervous. This was a really big deal. Why, even President Roosevelt had sent us a congratulatory letter.

Our lookout spotted them. "To your places everyone." Even Ma sounded excited.

The bishops entered, chatting quietly with each other, followed by all the priests, nuns and a few laymen. This august assembly of holiness couldn't possibly want something as lowly as food. When everyone was seated, Ma signaled. Close to the kitchen, women at two tables served the food (several women kept them supplied from the kitchen) and ten girls carried the plates from there to the guests. They were beautifully efficient. Other girls followed the food servers with pitchers of milk and coffee. Ma and I were expediters. She watched over half the tables and I watched the other half. If anyone wanted more food or coffee or the butter dish was empty, we signaled a helper. As the guests finished eating, I signaled for a girl to clear the plates. Now there was no rush, so we waited until all the plates were cleared up before we served the pie and ice cream.

As the guests left, there were many, many compliments on the food and the service. I was very proud of my mother and all of us. When they were finally gone, I found that Ben was in the kitchen helping to scrape and stack the dirty dishes. Then all of us workers grabbed plates and heaped them to overflowing (Ma had planned for this, too) with the delicious food. We savored the meal and the sitting down time before we all went back to work cleaning up, sorting and returning the borrowed things. We were all delighted with ourselves over a job well done and I was especially pleased to have Ben helping beside me. Finally, Ben and I loaded his Buick with clean dishes and other borrowed things to return them.

Back at home, Ma had already gone to bed, even though

it was only seven o'clock. Pa was still up, reading a Zane Grey cowboy story. "Ben," I said, "I'm beat. If you and Pa want to talk, go ahead. I'm going to bed." And I did. As I went to sleep, I realized I had missed all of the celebration except the luncheon. But I had seen my mother magnificently master-mind the gracious, efficient serving of a lovely meal for two hundred fifty people. I was very impressed with the whole thing and pleased to have been a part of it.

I was all agog after the phone call. "Ma, Ben and Dave are going to a landscape architects' meeting July 16th and 17th in Black River Falls and they're inviting Colleen and I to go along."

"That sounds exciting. Can you get off work?"

"I'm sure Sheriff O'Hara will let me — I'll try to find somebody to take my place while I'm gone; I haven't missed work for two years, except when I had my appendix out. So it will be all right." Well, that was easy — I had expected at least a little fuss about us going, unchaperoned, to another town for a few days. I thought I had enough money put by for the luscious little pale green dress I'd been eyeing. I won-dered if Betty would let me borrow her new dark green neck-lace and earrings. I hoped Colleen's folks would let her go. She was only nineteen, but she was very sensible; her folks and mine thought the world of Ben and Dave.

The past two months with Ben had been so much fun! Dancing two or three nights a week at a dozen dance halls, wherever the best bands were playing. We even danced to Al Kavelon's WGN band in Dubuque. When we went to Ga-lena, Illinois, to dance to Ted Weems, Pa muttered, "Pretty soon, you'll be going to London for lunch."

We'd gone on picnics, visited relatives, gone to the free band concerts in Artesian Park, celebrated the Fourth of July. And movies, in Prairie or anywhere we could drive to. Ben liked cowboy movies, war movies and the Marx brothers. I liked musicals and romantic dramas, like *Magnificent Obses-sion,* with Irene Dunne. We both loved *Showboat* with Irene Dunne, so we saw it twice. I hummed its songs for weeks afterward. *The Trail of the Lonesome Pine* was pretty good for a western, but there was too much feuding to suit me. It was the first all-technicolor film I had seen.

Sometimes just Ben and I went; other times, Dave and Colleen came with us. Or, if there were cousins or friends around, we'd all pile in Ben's car and go.

Wednesday evening, before the meeting, Ben and Dave and Colleen picked me up after work. I had brought my bag with me that day, so I was all ready to go.

For the trip, I persuaded Ben we should take Dave's car so we could sit in the rumble seat. The wind felt wonderful; it had been another scorching day. The heat and drought were causing dire predictions about fall harvests. I tried not to notice the scrawny, yellow, foot-high corn in the fields. It made me thirsty to look at those dried-up plants, thirsty in my mouth and in my heart. But sitting close to Ben made it easy to forget the harsh side of life.

We stopped for supper along the way. By the time we got to the Lodge in Black River Falls, it was late, so Colleen and I went to our room; Ben and Dave went to theirs. Through our open window, the waterfall's murmur sang us to sleep.

The next day, while Ben and Dave went to their meeting, Colleen and I walked around the small town and in the afternoon we walked along the river where it was mostly shaded. When the men came back, we decided to go for a swim in the river, just below the waterfall. It felt wonderful after the heat of the day — probably over a hundred again. We swam and splashed and giggled and acted like little kids having a very good time. Then we went out to eat; we talked and laughed at the table after we finished eating and then Dave started playing the jukebox and we danced. A very pleasant day.

Colleen and I were lazy the next day. We found a nice spot by the river, got a little sun, a little swim, a little talk, a little nap. It was so beautiful, so peaceful, so far away from the Depression and drought.

That night there was a good band in town, so we danced until the wee hours, went to the lodge and left the next morning. On the way home, I tried to thank Ben for the lovely vacation, funning with people I liked, traveling to a new town. I didn't know if he understood me, because I stammered around, but he must have, because the next few months, we went to visit his mother in Watertown, his friends in Galesville, my sister in Chicago, and everyone else we could think of.

Ben had warned me that sometimes his mother was a bit standoffish, so for that visit, I put on my most studied nonchalance, pleasant but not too serious. His mother was distantly gracious. His sister-in-law Caroline was a dear. His brother Leon was a likable rogue, just as outgoing as Ben was shy. We didn't meet his other two brothers; Ed lived in Michigan, Carl lived in Seattle.

On the way home, Ben told me that after he lost his re-election back in 1933 as Watertown engineer, he went to Seattle to stay with his brother Carl for a while. "I snuck on top of a coal car to ride it to Minneapolis. When I jumped off, a railroad detective caught me. He told me I should have jumped off the train two miles sooner, at an intersection where the train for Seattle slowed down so I could jump on. So I walked back. A railroad man was walking around and he opened a box car so I could jump in. Oh, the detective also told me that I should get off when the train slowed down, get food and hop on again after it started up, about every eight hours. The last leg of the trip, I was on an open-slatted cattle car and the temperature got down to twenty below zero. I had on long underwear, boots and a leather jacket, so I didn't get as cold as the others in the cattle car."

I interrupted, "What difference can a few clothes make when it's that cold?"

Ben kept right on. "In Seattle, I tried being a Fuller Brush salesman. I went door to door, giving away potato brushes or soap caddies, trying to sell the bottle brushes, fingernail brushes, back brushes, tooth brushes — a dozen for only $1.99 — and scrub brushes. But in 1933, nobody was buying. I earned seven dollars the first month and not much more the next two months, so I went back to Watertown and made ten dollars a week at my brother Ed's filling station."

I didn't envy him that miserable trip, yet I wished I could as easily hop on a train and try a new life somewhere else. And what was it about Ben that the railroad detective, whose job it was to catch and jail men who tried to bum rides on the trains, helped him instead?

We got back from Watertown just in time: *San Francisco* with Jeanette MacDonald and Clark Gable was on in Lancaster. Ben and I saw that movie twice. I loved the romance, the excitement and Jeanette's marvelous singing. Later on, when it showed in Prairie, the film exploded and burned, right during the earthquake scene. The fire stayed in the projection booth, but Jane and Betty told me that everybody was screaming about the earthquake on the screen, when suddenly the screen went dark and the audience smelled smoke. Then they really screamed and everybody rushed to get out. Fortunately, nobody was badly hurt.

Ben's stories indicated a self-deprecating sense of humor. He could poke fun at himself, but he wouldn't make fun of others. Yet he enjoyed my stories when I ridiculed some of the unsavory characters that showed up at the sheriff's office. Where a story in the paper about government waste or dishonesty would distress him, it would encourage me to mock the culprits. In bed at night, I always fell asleep thinking about him, usually with a smile. What was it about Ben that, in a group, everybody listened to me — I loved being the center of attention — but they always talked to Ben? He was always glad to see me, but he never seemed to notice if I was in rags or if I was all dolled up for him. When he wasn't around, everybody told me what a great fellow he was. But who told me how great I was? Yet I loved dancing close to him; I felt so secure in his arms. It seemed like all my hopes were safe with him. And other times, I got all strange inside when we danced. He was a good, honest man and exciting, too. And what was it about him that I kept thinking about him, not just the fun we had together, but wondering, "What was it about Ben?"

I snuck quietly into Ma's bedroom, careful not to wake Pa. It was well after midnight on a Saturday, and I had just come home from dancing with Ben. There was enough light from the street lamps to see my way to touch Ma's shoulder; when she woke up, I beckoned for her to come with me. She put on her robe and followed me to the kitchen table.

"Ma," I whispered excitedly, "he finally proposed!"

"Oh, Marguerite, how wonderful! Tell me about it. Was it as romantic as you always wanted?"

I laughed. "Ben is a good, thoughtful man, but you know as well as I do that he's no more romantic than a bushel of potatoes. He said his job here will soon be finished and he didn't want to leave without me, so maybe we should get married. He was so nonchalant about it, I almost laughed, but I've been waiting so long for him to propose that I didn't dare laugh for fear he might change his mind."

"What did you say?"

"I asked if he loved me."

"And he said?"

"He said 'Of course. Don't you know that?' So I said 'I love you, too!' And he asked, 'Does that mean you'll marry me?' Then I said 'Yes.'"

"Marguerite, I'm so happy for you!"

"Ben wondered if he should ask Pa for my hand in marriage. What do you think?"

"I think Ben is a gentleman and it would be a gentlemanly thing to do, even though we all know you would do what you have a mind to do, regardless of what your pa says. But your pa likes Ben as well as I do. What about religion?"

"He's willing that our children be brought up Catholic, but he says he won't become Catholic."

"I wish he were Catholic, but he is a very good man. I'm glad you're marrying him. When do you want the wedding?"

"As soon as we can get it all arranged — how about the middle of October? I guess it will have to be a pretty small wedding. Neither Ben nor I have much money and I don't suppose you do either."

Ma laughed out loud. "You should know me better than that by now! Remember when your pa went out to Montana last spring and brought back all those wild horses? He didn't break them, the way he used to when we lived on the farm, but he still got good prices for them, considering the times. As always, he gave me half of the money, for the house. As always, I put most of it away, saving it for something important. Now I know what that something is — your wedding."

We talked and planned for hours. Then we realized it was

getting light out so we went to bed for a few hours of sleep before we had to get up again for Mass.

I told Jane and Betty my good news before I left for church. I knew they would put it in the paper. They reported the social news for the *Courier* and they were paid by the line, so every time anyone had company or went somewhere, it made the paper. What with our relatives coming and going all the time, we helped Jane and Betty's incomes a lot. I was a little embarrassed when they put in about our trip to Black River Falls, but nobody fussed at me.

Ben wanted us to go to Watertown to tell his mother the next weekend, so we went. When she heard, she was no longer distant, she was angry. I wanted to tell his mother off, but I managed to hold my tongue. Maybe, in time, we could get along. Dear Caroline, his sister-in-law, said it was because of religion. Two of her sons had already married Catholics and this was too much.

On the way back, I suppose to lighten my glum mood, Ben told me about his first car. "I went to the Ford salesman in Watertown, paid $585 for it and, after a few instructions, I drove off in it. About a year later, I was driving at night along a country road. My lights were on; another car came from the opposite direction and turned left to go into his driveway. Only my car was in his way. It was a total wreck and I had a badly cut scalp. So the farmer took me into his house where his wife bandaged my head. They insisted that I sleep there for the night and drove me to Watertown the next day. I wanted another car, but I couldn't afford another new one, so I bought the old Buick I'm driving."

Then Ben started talking about the tree planting project that some of the CCC boys were working on; this was to provide windbreaks to help prevent erosion.

I asked Ben, "Did you see that poor South Dakota farmer who was wandering around Prairie, looking for his farm?"

He grinned. "We'll probably finish the Prairie swimming pool this fall."

I answered with another joke from the paper, "They say the standard of living in the U.S. isn't fixed, it's just a few steps ahead of our standard of earning."

The next Sunday after Mass, Father Weiss, who had re-placed Father Blank a month ago, said he wanted to talk to me when everyone had gone. I was puzzled, but I waited.

"I see by the paper that you are planning to get married. Your boy isn't Catholic, is he?"

"No, Father."

"You have to have a dispensation from the bishop for that, and he really doesn't like to give them out."

I thought fast. If I couldn't get a dispensation, we'd get married by a judge. I didn't say it though. It would sound very disrespectful and Father Weiss was very old.

"Wait a minute. How old are you Marguerite?"

What does that have to do with marrying Ben? "Twenty-five."

"Oh, then you'll get one all right. You'll probably never get another chance."

When I realized what he was saying, I was so angry, I almost cried. I turned around and left. I found out, many years later, that after Ma had heard what he'd said, she'd given him one good tongue-lashing. Ma, who would lay down and die before she ever protested a priest doing her wrong, would not stand for cruelty to her daughter. At any rate, when Ben and I went to him for instruction, he was nice enough.

We would get married in the parish house, since Ben wasn't Catholic, with his best man, Martin, and my sister, Mary, as attendant; his mother, brother Leon and Caroline, my ma, pa, Eliz and Seb would be there with us.

I found some beautiful dark red velvet material for my wedding gown. Most brides wore white, but I felt adventur-ous and Ma liked it, too. Mary's gown would be made of midnight blue velvet. We'd both have matching caps. Ma's cousin was making them for us and they would be gorgeous.

Aunt Maureen gave a shower for me; there must have been thirty-five or forty women there. I received towels, and doi-lies, sheets and a frying pan, a small throw rug and even a very glamorous nightgown. We snacked and then some of the women left and the rest of us played cards. I was so touched by it all, I didn't even make any smart-aleck remarks.

The wedding day itself was one very happy blur in my memory. We got married at five o'clock in the evening in the rectory. Then thanks to my mother's thrifty ways, all the family that came, about forty of them, had a splendid dinner at the hotel. After the dinner, Ma and Pa hosted a reception for family and friends at our house. They had set up borrowed tables and chairs in the back yard, with kerosene lanterns for light. It was a good thing it didn't rain, because if we had all been inside, we would have been standing on top of each other. There were refreshments and drinks (because of Pa there was no liquor) and more presents; everybody had a good time and I kept thinking, "All this for me and Ben, too?"

About ten o'clock, the young crowd left for Kaber's and beer. When Ben and I left there, he was in a hurry to get to our hotel in Minneapolis for our one-day honeymoon. Too much of a hurry. Just outside of Winona, Minnesota, a sheriff pulled us over. He ordered us to follow him in to the justice of the peace. Ben apologized to me, again and again. The fine was five dollars for speeding. Poor Ben. He looked so miserable. He took out his wallet and told the justice of the peace, "You see, I can pay the fine so I won't have to go to jail, but then we can't have our honeymoon."

"Well, young man, I tell you what. You look like an honest fellow. If you promise to send me the money as soon as you earn it, I'll let you go — but no more speeding!"

"Yes, sir, I mean no, sir. Thank you, sir."

"Have a good honeymoon."

"Thank you, sir, thank you."

We obeyed the justice. Ben didn't speed and we had a wonderful honeymoon.

In a few weeks, Ben mailed in the fine. It came back several days later, with a note: "You are a very honest young man. Keep the money for a wedding present."

What was it about this husband of mine? Was he just so darned nice that he brought out the niceness in everyone else?

5

Cece
December 1942

The train to Chicago grumbled and growled past
snow-covered fields and farm buildings and stopped in
every town, where soldiers and civilians hustled on and off the
train at every stop. I saw all this vaguely as my mind wandered through the past, thinking of the great changes in this
land. About a hundred years ago, when my grandparents and
Art's grandparents had come here, this was great wilderness of
forests and prairies. A few whites lorded it over the remain-
ing, conquered Indians. Then, if one of those airplanes could
have flown over this area, there would have been just occasional signs of man. But in the last hundred years, men and
women have transformed the land with farms and towns, so
now someone up in an airplane would hardly see anything
untouched by man. More recently, this farmland had seemed
ready to die, well, not the land itself, but the farms. The
Depression was so bad that buildings were run down, unpainted. Old machines and cars rusted away like peoples hopes
and many farmers went bankrupt. But the war brought prosperity back so that, even in winter, the farms seemed more
alive than they had during the Depression.

Trains certainly had made it easier to travel. Grandpa
Daniel and Grandma Sarah had driven a buckboard with a
team of oxen from Philadelphia to western Wisconsin. They
had planned to go farther, but the last oxen died near what
later became Patch Grove and Grandma Sarah had her first
child, Robert, who was delivered by a medicine-man from a
nearby Indian camp. They had eight children but black diphtheria killed five of them one winter. In 1851, Grandma and
Grandpa were crossing the river when the ice broke and she
fell in. Daniel got her out, but she caught pneumonia. She
and her unborn child died soon after that. Grandpa Daniel
wrote back to Scotland asking his distant cousin to come be
his housekeeper, which she did. She raised the three chil-

dren, Peter, Matilda and Margaret. Grandpa built the first frame house in the area and built a one-room schoolhouse at the end of the yard. Papa told us these stories on dark winter evenings as we munched on popcorn or apples, just as his Papa had told him.

Papa Peter married Elizabeth and we were born: Daniel, me, Jack, Christine, Betty.

My earliest memories were happier than later ones.

The teachers would board with us. If we misbehaved in school and got punished, we were punished again at home. That gave us plenty of incentive to behave, which we usually did. I liked school, especially arithmetic and reading.

Christmas Eve was joyful. We went to Midnight Mass at the old church on the hill, St. John's, started by Art's grandfather. We went in a bobsled with sleigh bells on the horses and buffalo robes and hot stones on the bottom of the sled to keep our feet warm. All the neighbors would wait for us to go by and yell "Merry Christmas!" Santa would have been there when we came home and then we had a big breakfast.

I remembered each fall we'd get up and leave in the dark. We'd take the big wagon to the grist mill where they ground our wheat and corn, enough to last the winter.

I remembered the covered bridge at Bridgeport with the horses doing the Highland fling waiting for the toll collector.

Then came the bad times. Mama died from appendicitis and her sister's husband died. Aunt Aggie had two children and no money and no place to live. So Grandma and the Priest said Papa and Aunt Aggie should marry, which was the worst thing to do. Only one of Peter and Aggie's three children lived. Aunt Aggie never did take care of us and after her babies died, she couldn't. So I still had to take care of my brothers and sisters and the house. As I grew older, she took to overusing the bottle.

Of all my brothers and sisters, my sister Betty has had the most exciting life. Back in 1914, our sister Christine had gone to Chicago but became sick. Betty left our farm where she had been helping me, to go help Christine. When Betty arrived, Christine was in the hospital and they wouldn't let her go until she paid the bill. So Betty called our brother

Dan and he sent the $350. Christine and Betty stayed with
Aunt Lena, who was in show business, until she moved away.
Then Christine married.

Betty was down to her last nickel, out of work and the
rent was due. She was walking along the slushy, sloppy sidewalk on a grey winter day, there in Chicago, when she saw a
pay phone. She decided to call our cousin. But Betty dropped
the nickel and though she dug around in the snow for a long
time, she couldn't find it. She looked up. Across the street
was a luxury apartment building. She went in and asked the
manager if there was anyone living there who might hire a
cook. He looked skeptical, but sent her up to a top floor
suite. Betty told me she just stared at the very handsome
young man who answered the doorbell; then she pulled herself together and offered to cook him the most delicious dinner he ever ate if he would buy the groceries. And if he liked
it, he could hire her as a cook. She got the job.

Later, married but childless in Los Angeles, Betty started
a catering business and catered for the movie stars, including
Spencer Tracy. Dear Betty. She is a great storyteller like our
father. If she starts up a story in a crowded room, everybody
stops talking to listen to her. Well, Betty had her exciting life,
which suited her well, but my life suited me, too. Except for
watching so many dear ones die.

Papa died as he lived, in a fight. Back in the twenties, in
spite of Prohibition, Pa became constable while he ran a tavern in Bridgeport. I guess that shows what kind of town Bridgeport was. A road crew came in to drink and Papa was giving
them a hard time. Later, one of them hit him from behind, in
the head, with brass knuckles. He fell and broke his skull and
died instantly. I found out about it the next morning at
church. That was terrible!

Papa loved causing commotion. He used to give his granddaughter a nickel whenever she beat up one of her school-
mates who teased her about her red hair. And yet, when my
brother was so ill with diphtheria, Papa was the one who did
all the chores while Dan was laid up. A much-loved man, if
the number of people at his funeral was any indication. He
was always good for mischief and for stretching the truth, but

he was always there when you needed him.

My brothers Jack and Dan died of strokes and Art's sister Ruth died of cancer in the twenties and just last May, his sister Ro died of cancer, too. All of Ro's sisters took turns helping out during her last months, just as they had helped their mother, Annie. How hard for Ro's children: her husband had died six years earlier, then one son died in a car accident. When Maureen's husband, Charlie, died last year; she was devastated. A well-matched couple like that should last forever — I guess that's what heaven is for. And Amelia Earhart. Her death was hard for me, stranger though she was. I suppose millions of women the world over mourned the loss of our great aviatrix. Her courage showed us that women, too, could be heroic adventurers. Sometimes, I got so lonesome for all those who had died that I wished I was up there with them. I missed Papa and Annie the most, even though they'd both been dead for many years.

Maybe I wouldn't have to wait much longer to join them. Last August, I had a slight stroke. I was frightened when I woke up in the hospital, not knowing how I'd gotten there or why. But Art nearly went out of his mind. So when he called our girls, they thought I was dying. They each dropped everything and caught the next train to Prairie du Chien, Elizabeth from Chicago, Marguerite from Kansas, Mary from Washington, D.C. Marguerite came charging into my hospital room. After one look at me, sitting up in bed talking cheerfully to Elizabeth, she passed out. When she came to, she asked Elizabeth to get her three children, ages four, three and one, out of the cab and take care of them while she recovered. It turned out the children had measles and there was no one to take care of them, so she brought them along. On the train, it was very hot and crowded, because of all the servicemen. Marguerite had them all wrapped up in blankets because she was afraid they'd be kicked off the train if anyone knew they were sick. The poor babies were sick and hot and miserable and bawling the whole way. And what should have been an eight or nine hour trip took fifteen hours because of all the soldiers getting on and off. What a horrible experience for her. I was deeply touched that she went through all that for me, but I didn't know how to tell her.

My mind returned to the present as the train pulled into Muscoda, about fifty miles from Prairie. There was a young soldier, saying good-bye to his mother, father, little sister and his wife. They were all dressed up in their farmers' best.

Life was such a mess sometimes. The soldier had four people crying as he left. I had had no one, because I had walked off behind Art's back. When he left for the tavern that morning, still not sober from the night before, I walked over to Thompson's store and asked my brother-in-law to buy my stove. He drove the delivery truck over, picked it up, paid me the ten dollars I wanted for it, same as the other times, eight dollars for the train ticket to Chicago and two dollars just in case I needed something.

Then I called the high school and left word for Janet to go to Lucy's instead of to my house. When Janet came from her farm home to board with us so she could go to high school, we had talked of this possibility, so she knew what to do. Janet helped around the house and paid a little for room and board. I liked her company, so it worked out well. It was like having another daughter. Like my own girls, Jane had three dresses, one for church, one for school one week, one for the next week at school. She liked hand-me-downs about as well as my girls did, too, which wasn't much, but none of them had any choice.

Then I called my friend Joanna and asked her to take my place at the 500 games until I got back. I enjoyed playing cards and I liked the women who played. Then I packed and left. And, same as the other times, when Art wanted me back, he'd have to get together enough money to buy back the stove and buy my return ticket. I loved him dearly, but...

Life with Art was filled with ups and downs. Just a week before I left, Art and I had walked to the theater to see Sonja Henie in *Sun Valley Serenade*. She was such a delightfully charming young woman! The ice skating and the skiing were marvelous. On the way home, Art held my hand. I don't know what people thought of two old fogies walking home from the movies holding hands, but I enjoyed it.

Then Art went off on another bender. When the girls still

lived at home, I used to take them next door to Art's cousin's house when he drank because I didn't want them around for his drunken rages. He might go six months or a year between binges, which lasted a week or two. After our daughters moved out, I would go to my daughter's in Chicago when he got drunk. I always left him a note, telling him where I was going and that I would return when he had money to get me back.

Art's latest attempt at earning money was to run a poker game at Zach's tavern. He collected a nickel from each player for each game; that was money for the house; he was paid out of that money. Ironic, that he should get paid for losing his money.

A man's voice pulled me back to the present, "Excuse me, ma'am, is this seat taken?" I had the whole seat to myself for a while, which I always liked, having time to think my thoughts, but with so many servicemen on the train, there were very few empty seats.

"No, you're welcome to sit here." It was the young soldier whom I had seen saying good-bye.

"Thank you." He put his duffel bag on the overhead rack and sat down. "I'm Jack." He smiled a sweet, shy smile.

"I'm Cece. Where are you going?"

"I'm going back to Camp McCoy. I finished my training, so when I get back, I'll get my orders for overseas." The poor boy was terrified and tried hard not to show it. The newsreel before *Sun Valley Serenade* had shown England being bombed, fighting in Africa, the Japanese taking over the Pacific. When I saw the news, I knew we had to fight back, but when I saw this innocent boy, loved by his wife and family — he might never come back or he might be crippled — I hated war and wanted to end it, regardless of what happened. If Jack had watched that newsreel, no wonder he was afraid. I decided it was up to me to distract him for a while.

"I believe I saw you at the station, saying good-bye to your family and your wife. Have you been married long?"

He blushed. "Two days, ma'am. I kind of thought we should wait until the war is over, but she would have none of that. We had a big argument over it, and when she started crying, what else could I do?"

"Have you known her long?"

Jack smiled. "We went all through school together and attended the same church; her father's farm is only five miles from our farm."

"I'm surprised you weren't deferred — you must be needed on the farm." I commented.

"I enlisted. You see, my older sister lives in town and she has two boys in high school who will help Dad on the farm. As long as the farm can get along, I really had to do my duty and join the army. We've got to stop the Nazis and the Japs!"

I asked, "Weren't there some Japanese-Americans training at Camp McCoy?"

"Yes, ma'am. At first we were all pretty suspicious of them, but they were very polite and respectful and worked hard at their training. They were all Americans, most of them second- or third-generation Americans. They were just as angry about Pearl Harbor as we were. And now out on the West Coast, especially in San Francisco, they're rounding up all the Japanese-Americans and putting them in detention camps for the duration of the war, so they can't help the enemy. Their property has even been confiscated."

"How awful for them! Sometimes war is an excuse for great cruelty. And if it is so necessary, why not detain the German-Americans, too? I suppose that wouldn't do, because there are too many of them."

Jack looked upset. "My grandparents all came from Germany. Why, I'll bet half the people in Wisconsin have German blood. And most of them are Lutherans." Then he commented on the irony. "The two synods of Lutherans are always fighting. In peacetime, Lutherans fight Lutherans; in war, Germans fight Germans. It's rotten!"

"I'm Catholic," I answered. "We fight along ethnic lines: in Prairie du Chien, we have two parishes, the Irish and the Bohemian, the old-timers and the new immigrants. It's considered almost worse for an Irish Catholic to marry a Bohemian than for an Irishman to marry a Protestant. Wouldn't you think that all the cooperation in the war effort would get rid of some of our prejudices? My daughter Elizabeth writes about scrap metal collections and paper drives at her children's school.

Marguerite's little children even collected milkweed pods, to be used to make life preservers. The Red Cross collects blood; movie stars hold war bond rallies to get money for the war. Food and gas are rationed. New cars, even new tires, are impossible to get. Women are working in factories. Everything is changed during this war." I sighed. "Wouldn't you think we could overlook the differences between Irish and Bohemian or between one synod of Lutherans and another at least long enough to see that those horrible Nazis and Japanese don't take over the world?"

"My buddy is from Kenosha," Jack told me. "He says that all the industries there are turning out war goods: from combat vehicles and aircraft parts to engines and heavy munitions; from boots and underwear to raincoats and blankets for our soldiers. He says swarms of workers have moved into the industrial towns. There is plenty of work and the pay is good, but they're having a terrible time housing them all. His mother takes in several boarders, which helps her, but families can't find a place to stay."

"Prairie du Chien has no industry to speak of," I said. "It has been a very sleepy town ever since the railroads replaced the Mississippi riverboats for transporting people and goods, sixty years ago. The main war effort around there is providing food: meat, dairy products, and vegetables."

Jack spoke proudly. "Our farm has nearly doubled production in the last two years, thanks to better hybrid seeds and better fertilizers. We have four hundred acres and Dad and his dad have carefully used all the newest ideas in farming. Why, we even got a tractor five years ago!"

I laughed and explained why. "My nephew insisted that they get a tractor, way back in 1929. Bill used it less than a year when it tipped over as he was going down a hill. He wasn't hurt, thank God, but he put the tractor in the barn and it hasn't been used since. Do you have electricity on your farm?"

Jack grinned proudly. "Yes, we do, in the barns, for lights, milking machines, and refrigeration for the milk. Not in the house, of course."

"The cows are more important than the women?" I retorted. "Jack, your mother deserves better than that. I want you to get electricity in her house the first chance you get." I could see that Jack was startled with my strange thought. "I'm sorry, Jack. Your father's way of 'cows first, then the wife' is common around here, but it isn't right. And it isn't right for me, a stranger to you, to order you around. But please consider the idea."

I never thought of it before," he said slowly, "but I think you're absolutely right. I'll do it."

"Good for you!"

Jack had to change trains at Madison. Before he got up to go, he leaned over and kissed me on the cheek, blushing furiously. He stammered, "Ma'am, I surely do appreciate your talking to me, so nice and all." He jumped up, grabbed his duffel bag and ran, before I could even say, "You're welcome." How good it was to be so warmly appreciated.

Such a nice boy. My eyes watered, as I thought of the loss to his family if he should get killed over there. There should be a law that only bullies and criminals and the worst sinners could fight in wars. Better yet, in every country, the only ones who could start wars would be mothers, and then only if their favorite sons would be fighting.

"Is this seat taken?"

"No, do sit down."

When the young woman sat down, she immediately opened a book to read. I didn't think I wanted to talk more, anyway. You got to liking a person a little and then you said good-bye, forever. Usually that wasn't so bad, but Jack might never return to say "hello" again to his loved ones.

I asked the Blessed Virgin to see him safely home. And I thanked her for not giving me sons. I would have had to let them go, but I couldn't have let them go! My brother had a son in England and Art's sister had a daughter who was an army nurse. I couldn't do that, work every day with brutally wounded men and know that their families suffered with them. Mary's Andy is in the Navy, and I know she is on edge, wondering when he will have to ship out.

Across the aisle, a young woman whined to her husband about food rationing. I almost laughed out loud. I've always had to ration; two and a half pounds of meat per person per week was a rich week for us. I glanced over at her and saw a face that looked like it was weaned on a pickle.

It would be good staying with Elizabeth for a while. Her Sebastian had become quite the important lawyer, but Elizabeth was not too happy at the long hours he put in at the office. At least he was too old to be drafted. They were both afraid of marrying during the Depression, but they went ahead, and did well enough for themselves. I enjoyed playing Old Maid with their three children and reading to them and giving them baths. It still amazed me to turn a faucet and have hot and cold water come out. It was a lot easier than hauling water in from the back yard and heating it on the stove.

Marguerite's three children made me six times a grandmother. Poor Marguerite, losing her newborn son last February. I cried with her. She learned how hard it is to lose a child — one of life's harsh lessons that I surely wish she could have been spared. Then they moved to Kansas City where Ben worked with the Civil Aeronautics Administration. What a brouhaha over his name. His parents had put the old German spelling on his birth certificate, but Ben had always gone by the anglicized name, so his mother had to go to court with him and swear that both names belonged to her one son.

Marguerite's last letter sounded pretty glum. Ben's job was taking him all over Kansas and Missouri, engineering airports. Housing was a problem with three little children. In her letter, she said they had found a basement that had been finished off; the war prevented the first floor from being built. She said she had found a few dead bugs in the kitchen, but hadn't thought much about it. But one of the many nights Ben was gone, she had to go to the bathroom. She walked barefoot in the dark to the kitchen, hoping not to wake the babies. She heard a funny rustling noise. So before she stepped down into the kitchen, she reached around and switched on the light. The floor was covered with cockroaches. How gruesome! But she said his salary was good, even if most of what she wanted to buy was either rationed or unavailable.

My dear little Mary; I tried to tell her in a letter, but it didn't do any good.

Dear Mary, it was nice Andy could spend a few days with you. What does he go to Washington for? It seems very dumb. I have hoped and prayed so hard that you could be married at home. This awful war it seems you are getting so little for your money. You go away and live among strangers at the most important time of your life. You will remember every little detail of your wedding and if you don't see one dear familiar face there, you miss something that you can't do over again. I was so disappointed when I got your letter, I was nearly sick for a few days. I do wish you would change your mind and come home to get married. It's nice having Eliz here and the children are good. Aunt Helen and Aunt Carrie were here for supper tonight. It's nice and cool here. Love and kisses and I'll be looking for your next letter.

Mother

But she married her Andy in Washington, D.C. I was very unhappy that the wedding couldn't be at home with her family and friends, but at least Art, for a change, had enough money that he and I could go. All three of my girls married good men, good providers. But they all moved so far away. Almost all of their cousins moved away, too. I had nieces or nephews from Puerto Rico to Alaska, to Hawaii; from Texas to California; from Madison and Milwaukee to Chicago. The younger generation seems to have inherited my grandparents' and Art's grandparents' yen for faraway places. Our ancestors found their right places. I hope the young ones have found theirs.

Back in the twenties and thirties, I never knew how many I would have for a meal, even breakfast. Nieces and nephews would come in from college, any time of day or night. If they were late, they would just sleep on a sofa in the living room. I think it was Irene who informed me that I had a living room, not a parlor or sitting room. Their house had a parlor and a living room both, so she knew the difference: a parlor was for occasional use, more formal; a living room was a place where everybody congregated.

Maureen and Maggie's children especially spent many

nights at our home. Irene, after college, taught in Wauzeka, twenty-five miles from Prairie. She took the train on a Saturday so she could go to Mass on Sunday, because there was no priest in Wauzeka. With all the company, we might have run out of food, except on their way back from the farms, they always brought vegetables or eggs or whatever was on hand, or they left money in my household jar.

By the forties, most of my nieces and nephews had settled down to start their own families, far away, so Art and I didn't have as much company any more. Sadly, family gatherings had become less frequent and much smaller. Other changes were better, like indoor toilets, my gas stove, my agitator washing machine. Some things never changed, like loving Art, hating his drinking, working hard or enjoying a visit with family or friends.

Twenty years earlier, Maureen and I had talked about the unlimited possibilities opening up for our children, especially the girls. Had they accomplished great things? Of James and Annie's thirty-five grandchildren, there were fifteen teachers, three of them in universities, a few farmers, a few businessmen, a few secretaries, a few women married without working outside the home. We had not raised an Amelia Earhart, an Eleanor Roosevelt, a John D. Rockefeller nor a Yehudi Menuhin. But our children earned their money honestly and had small adventures making a good life for their families and for those they worked with. Though there were no great musicians, many of our children had music in their souls. I was proud to be part of the recipe that made them and I was glad I had a few moments to appreciate the recipe.

I had certainly been thinking of a lot of hard times on that trip: the war, deaths of loved ones, Art's drinking, everything changing. But seeing my daughters and their cousins become such fine people — yes, it had been worth it!

The Milwaukee depot was chaotic. There was a huge frantic crowd, getting off, getting on; tearful farewells to servicemen, porters yelling. I was glad I didn't have to change trains there.

"Is this seat taken, ma'am?"

The book reader had gotten off. I looked up at a smiling elderly gentleman, who spoke with a faint Irish lilt to his voice. "No, please sit down."

A trip was like a game of cards, or like life. You never knew what cards you would get. There were good hands and bad ones. But leaving home always helped me get a better perspective on my bad hands, because I found that other people's problems were often much worse than mine. It seemed to me that if you played the poor cards and the good ones well, you ended up a winner. And that was the best way to face life, too. So I set myself to savor some moments with this charming gentleman so I'd have yet another fond memory to help me through the next rough time.

6

Maureen
Shawnee, Kansas 1946

On the way to school, a public school kid teased me about my uniform. I got mad and he kept teasing. I told him he was going to Hell because he wasn't Catholic. He was surprised; then he started crying and ran away. I was sorry I made him cry but I was glad he quit picking on me. I was gladder than I was sad.

I liked first and second grades at St Agnes School. But Mom always yelled at Dad because our house was too small. She didn't like having the baby in their bedroom. Dad said there weren't any houses because all the soldiers came back from the war. Mom just yelled more. If he didn't find a big house, she would. Mom won. We moved. Mom found other things to yell about. She was always mad at us kids or at Dad.

I started at St. Joseph's school in third grade. All the kids there knew how to write. At the old school, kids printed until third grade, so I was behind. But I was good at reading and arithmetic. At the new school, all the kids knew each other; I was a stranger. They didn't like me, so I didn't like them either. I hated St. Joseph's. It was all Mom's fault; she shouldn't have made us move.

Joe and I had some matches in back of the empty chicken house. I lit a match to some weeds. Then we stomped out the fire. Joe lit a match to start another fire. We stomped again. We let each fire get a little bigger. Suddenly a fire got too big and I was scared.

When the fire reached the chicken coop, I ran into the house and yelled for Mom. She was in the basement. I ran downstairs and I begged Mom not to kill me. She wanted to know what was wrong. I bawled. I wanted to tell her but I was afraid. Finally I pointed. She ran up the basement stairs, out the back door and saw the smoke. She called the fire department. Pretty soon, I heard the fire engine and the screaming truck drove in our driveway. The whole world heard it. I was ashamed.

After supper, Dad took Joe and me behind the chicken house. He asked us what happened. I looked at it. The back wall was burned nearly through. The neighbor's garage was burned some, too. We told Dad what we did. He told us fire was very dangerous. We should never play with matches again. He didn't yell at us. But we never played with matches again.

Frank, Joe and I got to stay up way after dark one summer night. Millions of lightning bugs lit up the alfalfa field behind our house. We chased them. When we caught one, we put it in a canning jar and popped the lid back on. When we each had a dozen or two, we went back to our yard. We sat on lawn chairs and admired the delightful bugs. The next morning they were all dead! We had killed the magic! After that, we let them go the same night we caught them.

7

Marguerite
Saint Joseph's Hospital
Kansas City, 1948

I could hardly believe it: there I was in a hospital, with nothing to do but wait a week or so until my seventh child was born. Ben had taken me to the doctor the day before, after I fell trying to get out of bed.

It was no wonder I had collapsed for the day before that had been very trying. After Sunday Mass and lunch, I started fixing supper. But Mrs. Miller came storming over with her son to accuse Frank of shooting out a window in their garage with his BB gun. She demanded that Frank pay for it. It was about 97 degrees already and I felt miserable. I looked at Frank. He said he didn't do it. I believed him, but Mrs. Miller kept right on shrieking. I gave her two dollars, just to get rid of her. Frank was very upset. But how could I explain to an eleven-year-old that a woman who is nine months pregnant, when it had been 100 degrees or more almost every day for the past two weeks, gets rid of trouble any way she can? Besides, it would be better for him to learn to take care of himself, like I had to. But I wished it hadn't happened. Frank was my best helper around the house and he seemed to understand better than Ben or anyone when I got crabby. He was always on my side.

After the Millers left, I told Frank to stay away from the Miller kids and I went back to making potato salad. I worked long hours in the hot kitchen. Maureen had disappeared, as usual, and Frank had too, so I had no help. But I wanted a nice supper because Bleak was coming. His wife was visiting her parents so Ben had invited his coworker over. Bleak was an awful nickname for a usually enjoyable man.

Finishing supper, Ben and Bleak were at one end of the kitchen table, I was at the other end and five kids sat along the sides. The platter was heaped with chicken bones, the bowl of potato salad was bare, a few seeds decorated the tomato plate, the corn cobs were piled high on two more plates. The kitchen was stifling; I was tired and uncomfortable when Bleak started, "Well, Marg, this child will be your sixth." He didn't know about the one we had lost. "Then there will be number seven, and number eight, then number nine and number ten ..." He stopped abruptly because the corn cob I threw had just hit him right in the middle of the forehead! Then I left the table and went outside, where the shade and a little breeze felt very good. My anger kept everyone away, so after a while, I calmed down. That was Sunday. Monday morning, I collapsed.

It seemed ridiculous for me to be glad I was in the hospital, but I was.

My doctor back in Wisconsin had told me after the first three kids that I shouldn't have any more because of the varicose veins in my legs. So Ben and I tried rhythm and Ben was impossible to live with, but we still had David. That was terrible. Even though it was a small town hospital, the doctor knew quickly that there was something wrong. I never had anything wrench me apart so awfully as when the doctor asked me if he could operate on my three-day-old child. A picture flashed through my mind of my poor tiny baby, cut open for surgery, bloody, dead. I screamed, "Nooo!"

The doctor was a kind man. He took my hand and muttered soothing things until I calmed down. "You know, Marguerite, he will die if we can't find out what is wrong and fix it," he told me gently. Desperately though I wanted him to live, I fiercely wanted to protect him from the awful surgery. "Marguerite, surgery is his only chance." I didn't know how to tell him David would die anyway. How could I explain to a doctor what my heart knew?

The doctor found that David's intestines were hooked up wrong, so they fixed that, but he died anyway. Years later, Dr. Wiseman told me that they probably didn't know about blood types yet at that hospital and gave him the wrong type of blood for the transfusion.

After David died, I was alone for a few hours and I yelled and screamed at God for putting David and me through all that. I wasn't making any noise — I didn't want everyone in the whole hospital to hear me, but when Mrs. Richards moved into the next bed, they gave me a sedative, so I wouldn't upset her, I guess.

When I woke up, I remembered dreaming about my mother. In my dream, Ma sat beside my bed, holding my hand. We didn't talk, but I knew she was suffering with me. I remembered all the miscarriages she'd had. I understood her suffering then and knew that she had never become bitter. If she got through it, so would I. I felt calmer about David's death, but the pain was deep and lingered for years.

Maureen's birth, my second-born, now that was something else. When the contractions got going good, Ben took Frank, fifteen months old, to our friends there in the duplex and we went to the hospital. Jerry and Joan said that Frank screamed the whole time I was in labor and quit as soon as Maureen was born. That was ten years ago, and I'd always been able to tell when something was wrong with Frank, whether he was in the room with me or miles away. I think he felt my troubles, too, but I doubt if he realized what was going on. I've never told anyone about it, though. I can just imagine what Father Lutz or Peggy or Vivian would say if I ever tried to tell them about it. I knew it was as real as the pain of childbirth and I wasn't about to invite anyone to tell me I was nuts.

I didn't know if anesthesia during childbirth was unknown in the small-town hospitals where I had my first four kids or whether it was still considered unsafe. I only knew that it was a hell of a lot of pain, especially the first time. I didn't like the feeling of helplessness I had when they've put me under for the last two births, but it was a damn sight better than all that pain. I apologized to the Blessed Virgin for thinking bad words, when I should have been praying to her to get me and my baby safely through all this, but somehow, I thought, since she was a Mother, that she would understand. I asked her to please convince her son Jesus to forgive me and help me out. "Hail Mary, full of grace, blessed art thou among women ..." Yeah, I guess she was blessed — she only had to have one child. Uh oh, sorry Mary, that just slipped through.

"Hello, I'm Sister Anne Marie. How are you doing?"

"Good afternoon, Sister. The temperature in this room must be about twenty degrees cooler than outside; how hot is it out there by now, 105 degrees? And the thought of no supper to fix for five squabbling kids and one indifferent husband is absolutely the greatest joy I've had in months, maybe years. I'm feeling better already. But don't tell Dr. Wiseman. I don't want him to send me home just yet."

"Dr. Wiseman insisted on an air-conditioned room for you. Isn't it great? I can see that it's helping. Enjoy it — it's 107 degrees outside. And you're due in about a week, right?"

"Yes, Sister."

"Let me take your temperature and blood pressure."

"Yes, Sister." I already liked Sister Anne Marie. She was older, grandmotherly. There's nothing worse than having a dried-up witchy nun around, pretending to great holiness, when she has no idea what it's like living with the day-after-day exasperations of a husband and kids. When I was having Ellen, before I went into the delivery room and had anesthesia, there was skinny old shrew of a nun with me and when I had a contraction, she'd say, "offer it up" and I would have sworn she was smirking inside and thinking, "See where all that wickedness gets you?" I remember thinking I was not at all pleased about where *it* got me. I used to like *it* all right, until I'd suffered through childbirth all those times. But she was nasty to gloat!

Back to the present: "Sister, how did a Jewish doctor ever come to be working in a Catholic hospital? I've often wondered, but my other deliveries here were so rushed, I never thought to ask."

Pain shadowed her face as Sister Anne Marie answered. "I'm sure you know he's one of the best. He practiced in Germany, traveling a great deal to learn the newest and best methods. He spent several years, in the early thirties, in the United States. When Hitler came to power, he was one of the lucky few with his eyes open; he came back to the United States. He had known our administrator when he was here before, knew Dr. Johnson didn't consider healing to be monopolized by Catholics, so he came here. Perhaps he is so compassionate because of all he and his people have gone through."

Sister Anne Marie was like my Grandma Annie, I thought; when others suffered, she felt their pain. I liked and respected Dr. Wiseman, but suddenly, it seemed that the cost of my receiving his good care was the death of millions of his fellow Jews. I had seen a newsreel of some of the Jews released after the war. I ran out of the theater and threw up. I still didn't go into the movies until after the news was over. I guess that cut my sniveling down to size.

"It looks like everything is fine here. Is there anything

you'd like before I go?"

"Yes. A Scotch and water." We both laughed. "Or, if I can't have that, how about some more ice water?"

"Of course."

"Thank you, Sister."

Between the medication, having my feet up and the coolness, my legs felt much better; I even felt good all over, in spite of my bloated, clumsy, grief-ridden body. And somebody else was changing Martin's diaper and doing the laundry. What was it the receptionist had said? Yes, when I told her this was my seventh pregnancy, her eyes went soft for an instant and she said, "Oh, the seventh child always brings great joy." I knew she was right.

But the laundry. With my legs so bad, I'd have to do something about that. I had to go upstairs, get the kids' dirty clothes and sheets, carry them down, collect Ben's and mine, and gather diapers and towels. In the basement, I'd sort them, put a load in the agitator, (cleanest first, so I could reuse the water), cut some chips off the soap bar. Then I'd go upstairs while they washed, then downstairs again to feed the clothes through the wringer into rinse water (with bluing for the white clothes), feed them through the wringer into the second rinse water, then through the wringer into the clothes basket, carry them outside and hang them on the clothesline. I'd bring them in when they were dry, dampen the clothes that needed ironing, fold the rest and put them away. I got tired just thinking about it

Last month, we had bridge at Peggy's house and she showed us her new washing machine and dryer. The washer not only agitated the clothes clean, it automatically drained the wash water, automatically added rinse water, drained that and rinsed again and then spun out most of the water. Then she would throw the whole load into the dryer, which was right next to the washer.

I wondered how Grandma Annie got through it all. She didn't even have an agitator, just a washboard, so she had to scrub each piece, do all the wringing out by hand. I vaguely remember her stirring a huge kettle on the stove, boiling the white clothes to get them bright. Grandpa had to lift the clothes out with the big wooden paddle though, because she was so frail. It seemed like she'd always do everything she could, then she'd ask Grandpa or one of my aunts to help her. It seemed like everyone was always glad to help her. And Ma, too. The way she had everyone working at that church centennial dinner! That was over ten years ago, but the memory was vivid. She drew the best from all the helpers and the banquet was flawless. Why couldn't I get my kids to help without their making a big stink about it?

I remembered when my mother got her agitator. She managed to get it before the war stopped production on such civilized niceties and grabbed all labor and materials for itself.

I was glad Ben wasn't drafted. He was almost too old and had a wife and three kids, but I supposed it was mostly his work as airport engineer that kept him out of service. Someone had to keep our home airports going to transport people and materials to where they were needed.

I had to tell Ben, when he came to visit, about getting a washer and dryer. I wouldn't be disagreeable about it. I just wouldn't do the laundry until I got them.

But how was I going to convince him that I couldn't, *absolutely couldn't*, have any more kids? The Catholic Church would not allow us to use birth control. It was either abstain or have kids, or use rhythm and have kids. When we tried rhythm, I missed *it* and Ben was unbearably grumpy and we had David anyway. *It* was definitely more fun before I had all those kids — knowing what I was getting into cast a definite shadow.

It made me mad to think that when the Holy Catholic Church dictated about having kids, the decision came from a bunch of men who had never carried a child in their bodies for nine months. Oh, dear, I got carried away again.

I'm sorry, Mary, that's blasphemous or heretical or something, I suppose. I'll put these thoughts out of my head. If being pregnant weren't so terribly hard for me, I would never be thinking such wickedness. Forgive me, Lord.

"Hello, Dear. How are you feeling?"

How nice. Ben was here. "Hello, Ben. I'm a lot better, but still not good." He looked sad, preoccupied. I guessed

I'd better tell him anyway. "Ben, you'll have to get me one of those new washing machines and a new clothes dryer. I'll never be able to do the laundry with the old agitator any more." There, I got it out without sounding crabby, just the facts.

He looked surprised. "Oh, okay, sure. Uh, Dear, I saw Dr. Wiseman before I came in."

Afraid, I asked, "Is something wrong with the baby or me?"

"No, no, nothing like that. It's uh... it's just ... well, he said ... "

"What? What did he say?"

"He said, 'No more kids.'" Ben blurted out. Then, relieved to have it out, he seemed puzzled. "He practically threatened to put a bullet through my head if he ever saw you pregnant again."

"Ben, I'm sorry, but he's right." My quiet tears were as much relief as they were sorrow for what we would miss.

So I changed the subject. "How are the kids?"

"Oh, they're all fine. I left them in the tank, fighting as usual." Ben had bought a tank that had been used to water cattle, about two feet high, round, about ten feet across. The kids loved playing in the water.

"Uh, dear, I think I'd better get somebody in to fix meals for them."

I was surprised. "Why, what happened?"

"When I got home yesterday, I decided to fix them scrambled eggs for supper. Do you remember a few months ago when we had scrambled eggs with limburger cheese at Davis' party? I really liked it, so I thought I'd try to make it. But it got so stinky when I fixed it, the whole house smelled and the kids wouldn't even come in the house, much less eat it."

Poor Ben. He looked so sheepish, but I couldn't help laughing. Life was so cruel to him just then, I shouldn't have, but ... Then he laughed, too.

Finally I told him that the cheese is supposed to go on top of the eggs after they're cooked, not cooked with the eggs. "Why don't you see if Rosemary can come in for a few hours each afternoon to check on the kids and fix supper? If you buy a couple of pounds of lunch meat and make sure there's plenty of peanut butter and grape jelly and bread, Maureen can see to it that they get sandwiches for lunch."

"Okay. Say, did you hear that Truman got the Democratic nomination for the presidency?"

"That haberdasher!" When Roosevelt died, vice-president Truman had taken over. "He ended the war by ordering that horrible atomic bomb dropped, not once, but twice, on Japan. And what has he done since? Housing is still impossible, prices are preposterous, labor unions have been pushing for strike after strike, Russia is taking over Eastern Europe and China. Why, Russia may even know how to make atomic bombs! And has Truman gotten Russia to stop blockading Berlin or are we still flying in hundreds of tons of food and fuel a day?"

"Marg, it's not Truman's fault that Russia is so greedy. He's taking a stand against further Russian expansion, but he's also trying to avoid another war. As for the problems at home, he announced he's going to call a special session of congress to deal with them."

"Congress is Republican. It won't do anything for Truman."

"But Truman said the Republican platform for Dewey is pushing for all the things Truman wants done, so if they do nothing, it's the Republicans who are to blame, not Truman. But, if you believe the papers, Truman doesn't have a chance against Dewey, so you'll soon have Republicans in power again."

"Well, it's a mess. And Russia with its Iron Curtain and its atheism — it's a frightening world to be bringing a baby into." I didn't want to think of all that garbage any more. "What did you bring in the bag?"

"Oh, I almost forgot. Your *Ladies Home Journal* came yesterday and there's a letter from your mother and I picked up a few books from the library for you, Edna Ferber's *Showboat* — didn't we see that movie back before we got married?"

"Yes, it was a wonderful movie. What else?"

"The librarian gave me Daphne du Maurier's *Frenchman's*

Creek and for variety, an Agatha Christie and a Zane Grey."
He was reading titles and authors as he pulled them out of
the grocery bag and handing them to me.

How sweet of him! "Thank you, Ben. That should keep
me out of mischief for a while." I kept my voice light, not
wanting him to see how touched I was by his thoughtfulness.

Ben said, "Oh, Bleak says he's sorry about teasing you the
other night."

"He'd better be!" I said, "Tell Bleak, he'd better learn to
be more careful with his teasing!" I paused. "I guess I'm not
mad at him anymore. I accept his apology." I wasn't mad, at
least partly because of the immense satisfaction I got from
seeing the look of pure shock on his face when that corn cob
hit him! I laughed out loud at the memory. Actually, I wasn't
so angry at him even at the time; I was mostly upset over
feeling so lousy and so hot for weeks on end.

After Ben left, I thought about his limburger cheese ex-
periment and started laughing again. Ben was very good at
being ignorant when he wanted to get out of something. When
we first met, I tried to teach him new dance steps. He would-
n't try new steps in public and he found other excuses not to
try in private.

After we married, we'd have friends over to dinner and I'd
want to play bridge. But Ben didn't want to learn how.   So
one time, I just asked our company if they wanted to play.
They did, so we played and Ben has been playing ever since.

My scheme didn't work as well with chicken-carving. I
wanted him to carve the chickens I cooked. He didn't know
how. So one evening, when we had company, I just handed
him the knife and asked him to carve. The chicken landed in
his lap and he never carved again.

I decided it was good to be in the hospital, for more than
one reason, because I realized again that even though Ben can
be terribly exasperating sometimes, I really do love him. It
was awfully hard to feel very nice toward him, though, when
I was at home, buried under the endless work and constant
frets of five kids, soon to be six.

Pa used to write the most pathetic letters whenever Ma

went to stay with Eliz, but this time, I almost felt sorry for him.

Nov. 27 1949

Dear Marguerite, I can't afford to call you, so I will drop you a few lines. Eliz called to say Cece is back from the hospital after her stroke. Mary was there, so I talked to her, too. Cece can't walk and it's hard for her to talk. She won't get better this time. Eliz says Cece can stay with her. I got the rest of my bottom teeth out. My mouth is awful sore. Then my ear had to start aching. It hasn't quit yet. They want me to come to Chicago for Christmas, but I don't know whether I will be able to go or not. Call if you find time or write me. I am always glad to hear that you are all right.

Pa

8

Maureen
Shawnee
1949

I screamed at Mom, "I don't want to go to the beauty shop and get my hair cut! I want my hair long!" Mom had just come back three days ago from Chicago, where Grandma was sick.

"I let you have it long and you don't take care of it. You never set it and half the time, you don't even comb it. You're going and that's all there is to it!"

As the woman cut away, she said to me, "You have such beautiful, thick hair." Maybe she was trying to make me feel better; I was crying.

The woman in the next chair was getting a permanent and it smelled terrible. She said, "I wish my hair was that thick!"

When it was cut, Mom told her to thin it. That really made me mad! Why? Everybody there admired the thickness and Mom said get rid of it!

Back home, I wished it was summer so I could climb up

in the neighbor's huge maple tree. I liked climbing way up to the top and letting the wind blow me around. I would look down at our big house or at the neighbor's big vineyard and orchard and let my troubles fly away. As I changed clothes, I noticed my camera on my dresser. There were only a few pictures left, but I didn't feel like finishing the roll of film. I liked my camera. I had gotten it with twenty-five cents and a Wheaties box top. The hard part was waiting for the pictures to be developed.

I was restless, so I went walking in the orchard. There was a little bit of snow on the ground and more falling. It was pretty, but I felt ugly. In the summer, I could lie down under an apple tree and daydream for hours. It was too cold for that. I should have worn my pea coat and my plaid wool scarf. I had worn a little jacket and nothing on my head. I was cold.

Sometimes, I baby-sat the Lyons' kids across the street. I earned twenty-five cents an hour. I liked having that money to spend on whatever I wanted.

I decided to go to the library the next day. I could get another *Black Stallion* book and a dog book. I loved to read. At Christmas, I always opened the books first. My second favorite present was maple sugar candy. Dad's Uncle Ben sent some every year that he made himself.

I thought I'd get some candy on the way home from the library. A Butterfinger wasn't as good as maple sugar candy, but it was better than wishful thinking. These important decisions sweetened my mood as I headed for home.

Mom told Frank, Joseph and me that she had new blankets for us. She gave each of us a pencil and a piece of paper. She said she would bring them out to the living room. We weren't supposed to say one word. We should just write down our names on the paper and what color we wanted. They were very pretty. One was gold, one was pink and one was light orange. The gold one was the prettiest. I was afraid my brothers would want it, too. It would be just like Frank to take the one I wanted. I didn't much like Frank. He was bigger than I was and he always got his way. He was Mom's pet. Frank chose the orange one; Joseph chose the pink one. I got the gold blanket!

By sixth grade, my grades were getting better. I had caught up with my classmates. I even got three A's that spring. I was very good in arithmetic. When we finished our other work, we could get an SRA card from the box, read it and take the test on what we read. I was way ahead of everybody on those. I hadn't fought with the kids at school for a long time.

Our teacher, Sister Humbeline, taught church music to our class of thirty kids. We learned the *Kyrie Eleison*, the *Gloria*, and other Latin songs that were in every Mass. Then we sang at Masses before school. Some of us learned the Requiem Mass, for Saturday funerals. They were very gloomy.

We were pretty good singers, especially Margie, Judy and I. Sister Humbeline taught ten of us girls the songs for Holy Week and Easter services. That was a lot of singing! We had practice after school for weeks. I really liked it, being part of that very solemn and joyful celebration. I felt like I belonged.

I didn't fit too well in the kitchen. Mom had a phone call, so she asked me to watch the bean soup that was in the pressure cooker. When the steam started, I shut the valve on top. Then I watched a squirrel playing in the back yard and forgot to turn the heat down when the pressure built up. So the pressure got higher and higher and blew the rubber stopper out. Bean soup shot out of the hole. I ran to the far side of the kitchen and screamed. Mom ran out and looked at me. She looked at the bean soup volcano and quickly stepped over to turn the burner off. What a mess! Bean soup dripped down the walls and off the ceiling, bringing plaster with it. It smothered the stove and splattered all over the floor. Mom went to the sink and rinsed the beans off her hand with lots of cold water. The soup must have burned her. I was in bad trouble. But she didn't even yell at me. She just said I could go outside and play.

Mom and our neighbor, Nikki, were sitting at the kitchen table. "Mom, I want to show you something." I was worried. "Can't you see we're talking? Show me later."

"Mooom..." I guess she saw that I was upset. She followed me to the bathroom. "Last night I found a few drops of blood in my underpants and now this." I showed her my pants. There was a big, bright red patch of blood.

"Oh, is that all? You're all right. That just means you're growing up into a woman. All women bleed, about once a month. It's called 'the Curse.'" She went to her bedroom and brought out a sanitary belt. She took a pad from the box in the bathroom cupboard. She showed me how to use them.

That evening, I was setting the table when Dad came home from work. Mom turned away from the stove, so Dad could give her the usual quick kiss. He seemed happy.

"Well, Dear," he announced, "today I applied for a job in Africa."

Mom just stared at him. Then she turned back to stirring the gravy. I thought he was joking. Like when he told us how he got the scar on his head. He said it was from Indians trying to scalp him. Years later, he admitted it was from a car accident.

After supper, Dad took me outside. He tried to explain to me about the birds and the bees. I didn't know what he was talking about. I didn't think he knew either. It didn't matter. I didn't want to be a woman anyway.

Mom told us she was going to listen to the *Telephone Hour* on the radio. She didn't want to hear one peep out of us during the program. Jascha Heifitz was going to play the violin. We could go to bed. We could go outside until it was over. We could not bother her during her program. It was wet outside, but the rain was over. We went outside. Dad, too. I heard a little of the music. It made me feel sad and lonely. It was pretty, even if Mom did like it.

The next weekend, Dad made me a bedroom. I wouldn't have to sleep with all my brothers and sister in the big bedroom upstairs. He put up a plywood partition from the backside of the furnace room wall to the outside wall. Mom found a wardrobe for me to hang my clothes in. They bought an old skinny bed; it could open out into a double bed. Dad nailed a piece of plywood over four upright orange crates to make me a desk. He put two shelves on the wall for my books. I watched, unbelieving. Frank had gotten the old coal bin for his hobby room years ago. Ever since then, I had been begging for a room of my own. I didn't know why I suddenly got one, but I was thrilled with the privacy. And what riches! All those things for my very own.

A few days later, I followed Frank to his hobby room. He had model airplanes hanging from the ceiling, a framed butterfly collection, a bug collection, classic comic books, and stuff all over. I asked him if I could borrow his *Tarzan* books. He could read my *Black Stallion* books. He wasn't even nice about saying no.

Back in my room, I looked at the size of my books. Yes, it would work. The next time he went to a Boy Scout meeting, I went to his room. I put *The Black Stallion* inside the jacket of *Tarzan the Ape Man.* I took *Tarzan* to my room, put it in *The Black Stallion's* jacket and read it. It was much more exciting that way. I read a lot of his books.

Frank was the oldest, then me, then Joe. After five years, came Ellen, then Martin, then Peter. We were the three big kids, they were the three little kids. I liked the little kids better when I didn't have to be around them all the time. I even let one of them sleep with me every now and then.

9

Marguerite
Shawnee
1951

Eleven-year-old Joseph lay in the hospital bed, flushed with fever. As Ben and I approached him in that stark, six-bed ward, several children were moaning. They all looked very sick. A nurse wrapped steaming hot towels around the legs of a boy who watched her fearfully. Joseph tried to turn his head toward us, but he couldn't.

"Hi, Mom and Dad," he muttered calmly, weakly. Earlier, I had seen his fear when he saw the monstrous needle they stuck in his spine to test for polio. The test showed polio but Dr. Johnson said it was a light case. He could tell better in a day or two, when the fever went down.

How could God strike innocent children like this? I thought. Blessed Virgin, here I go again! I'm blaming God for letting this happen to my son and begging you to get him to forgive me. I guess you know the anguish of watching your Son suffer! Please, Mary, don't let him be crippled! Please don't let him die!

I couldn't show him my fear." Hi, Joseph. How are you doing?"

"Mom, I feel awful. Do I have to stay here?"

Mary, help me, I prayed. "Joseph, I hate to leave you here, but these people can help you more than I can. When you're better, you'll come home." I hoped I sounded convincing. As Ben started talking, I turned away to hide my anxiety. I looked out the window, but that didn't help. From the fifth-floor window of that hospital on a hill, I had a perfect view of the horrendously flooded Kansas River. What should have been a river meandering through the industrial districts was one huge lake dotted with tree tops and roof tops. Some pigs from the stockyards were stranded on top of railroad cars. The water raced forward, carrying trees, buildings and oil storage tanks. Some of the tanks had exploded and the fire had spread over several blocks. Dozens of firemen stood in waist-deep water with their hoses, trying to put out the fire. Farther downriver, many men were sandbagging to prevent further flooding. It was too terrible to look at. I turned back toward Joseph.

"Joseph, we have to leave now. They will take good care of you. If you need help, just ask the nurses." I knew I sounded abrupt, but I had to get out of there before I fell completely apart.

When we were in the car, I told Ben, "I've got to have a drink. Let's go someplace where no one knows us."

"All right."

A few blocks later, I screamed at Ben, "I've read about the flooding all over eastern Kansas and the fires. But when I looked out of the hospital window, it seemed like *everything* was ganging up on Joseph! If *polio* doesn't get him, the *fires* and *floods* will. They said Argentine and Armourdale were protected by levees — they would be safe — but yesterday, the dikes broke and they flooded. They said the Turkey Creek pumping station was safe. It flooded this morning and now we have no water. Damn it, Ben, how can I believe *anything* anymore? Is Dr. Johnson right about Joseph's polio being a light case? Will the flooding get worse and hit the hospital? How can the hospital take care of Joseph and the other patients without water?" I could hear myself shrieking, but I couldn't stop it. "I want to go home to my mother and cry on her shoulder, but I can't, because she's *dead!*" I was terrified for Joseph, for our family, for myself. How could I get through all this?

Ben stopped for a red light. He looked over at me. He didn't say anything, but his fear brutally wiped out mine. I thought: *My God,* he's even more frightened than I am! If I fall apart, he won't be able to pick up the pieces. I stopped screeching and started crying. Ben pulled over to the side of the street and held me for a while, as I cried my fears and my inadequacy. Ben was crying with me, the only time I ever knew him to cry. And the rain cried with us, too. It seemed like it had been raining almost every day for months, only the past week, it had been two and three inches a day. I hated the rain and all the misery it brought.

That night, I couldn't sleep. I kept seeing Joseph's face — pained, abandoned, surrounded by floods and fire. I wanted to go out to the kitchen, get down the bottle of Scotch and drink myself senseless. I could barely keep myself in bed. Ben couldn't stop me — nobody could. So why not? An ugly picture flashed into my mind. My sister Mary was about five. She had fallen, her head was bleeding badly and she was screaming bloody murder. What did Pa do? He yelled out the back door for Ma, then left for the tavern. His drinking ruined every good time we ever had and made the bad times worse. Maybe I was just like Pa — I sure felt like drowning myself in the bottle. I hated him — I wouldn't be like him! I wouldn't do to my kids what he had done to us. I'd be strong like Ma. My thoughts churned. I tossed and turned. Ben slept on. Finally, I knelt by our bed and said a memorare. *Never* had I begged harder for Mary's help. After that, I went to sleep.

The next day was another rain-dulled Saturday. The flood news was worse. We had to go to the park to get drinking water and we'd have to boil it. The fire truck came and filled the kids' swimming tank with water for flushing the toilet. No sirens, unlike when they came to put out the fire that Maureen and Joseph started — it seemed more like an admission of defeat than heroes to the rescue. Fairfax was underwater. Turkey Creek flooded Merriam only eight miles from our house. Our friends, Tom and Vivian, in Rainbow Village, were flooded out of their house again, three times in three weeks. The damage estimates were up to eighty-five million dollars.

I was tired of all the rain and flooding. I hated worrying about Joseph and whether the other kids would get polio. I didn't even have enough energy to yell at the kids. When the Manor Man came around with his truck of bakery goods, Maureen wanted a pecan coffee cake. I just said okay.

It was awfully quiet around the house, with Joseph in the hospital and Frank at summer camp. His counselor called to say that Frank was sick yesterday. They had put him to bed, thinking it might be polio but I thought it was heat exhaustion — why did they take the boys on a five mile hike when it was 95 degrees out? Anyway, he was fine Saturday when the counselor called.

Poor Maureen. She didn't have Frank to fight with or Joseph to play with and she was old enough to be frightened by the polio and the flooding. At least Joseph's fever was down a little and he was still able to go to the bathroom by himself. I could almost begin to hope that he'd be all right. The three little kids didn't seem to realize what was going on, but even they were being pretty quiet.

Sunday was another wet day with more dismal news. The Kansas City council declared a state of emergency. They closed down everything except health services and grocery stores, radio and newspapers. There were no buses or trains. We'd have to borrow a car and get a pass to go to the hospital, because sightseers were getting in the way of the firemen. Life was drowning me.

Sunday afternoon, it wasn't raining for a change, so I chased everyone outside. I went into our bedroom and knelt beside our bed. Looking at the statue of Mary on the dresser, I said a rosary. Then I stayed there and just begged for help. After a while, I seemed to hear a voice inside myself, "You are strong enough. You can do it." Was it Mary or my mother? I tried to believe it.

Tuesday, Joseph was a little better, but Ellen came down with polio. Her case appeared to be very light, so the doctor said to watch her temperature very carefully at home. "She will probably be just fine in twenty-four hours. With the flooding and all, it will be better for her at home, unless she gets worse." I didn't think I could go on, but after supper, I took the kids into my bedroom and we said the rosary to-gether.

Wednesday, Ellen was much better and so was Joseph. Two of the six municipal water pumps were working. We were at the edge of the water district, so that didn't help us yet. The floods began to recede. The end was in sight.

Friday, Joseph came home from the hospital and Satur-day, Frank came home from camp — we were all healthy! So, I gathered all the kids in my bedroom to say thanks for our being together and well. When we finished the rosary, I told Ben to get us two tickets for *Roberta* which would start at the Starlight Theatre in two weeks.

The flood waters left a horrible mess behind: as much as eighteen feet of water had covered over two million acres in Kansas; the damage estimates were around a billion dollars. Floods, fire and polio had ravaged Kansas City, but they couldn't destroy the city, nor could they destroy me.

10

Maureen
Shawnee
1951

I was scared. Really scared. Six-year-old Ellen was in the big crib in the living room. She had polio. Joseph was in the hospital with polio. The newspapers told about iron lungs. They were used to help polio victims breathe. Would Joseph and Ellen have to spend the rest of their lives inside iron lungs? Would they die? Would we all get polio?

The quarantine sign on the front of the house announced our contamination to everyone. We couldn't go anywhere, not swimming or to the movies or even down the street to play baseball with the other kids. We were trapped by polio germs. Our neighbors brought us groceries and left them on the porch. They brought us drinking water, too. Everybody had to get water at the city park, because of the floods. Mom put pills in the water and boiled it. It tasted terrible. It made even lemonade taste awful. I drank milk.

Mom wasn't even yelling at us. When she saw us looking worried, she told us to pray to the Blessed Virgin. Every evening, after we did the supper dishes, Mom would take us into her bedroom. We knelt around their big bed and said the rosary and a memorare. There was a statue of Mary on the dresser. Mom kept fresh flowers there.

Ellen got better pretty fast. When they brought Joseph home from the hospital, we all went into Mom's bedroom again and said the rosary to thank Mary. While we were praying, Mom's voice got funny. She was crying! Frank was kneeling next to her. He put his hand on her arm. I cried, too, but I didn't want anyone to know, so I didn't make any noise. Ellen and Joseph were both fine. The rest of us never got sick. When they finally turned the water back on, we all stood around the kitchen sink as Mom turned the faucet on. The dirty water sputtered out of the faucet. We laughed.

Grandpa Art came to visit us. Mom said he was lonely since Grandma died, but she wasn't very nice to him. I wondered why. He was very old and sad.

Grandma Cece came to visit once when I was little. She baked sugar cookies for us and read stories to us. I liked her and Mom liked her, too.

We had to get a new septic tank. When it was in, there was a three-foot circle of bare ground on the north side of the house. That became my flower garden. I planted moss roses and waited eagerly for them to grow. I kept it weeded. Sometimes I even weeded around the roses and gladiolus and all the other flowers. Gardening was good work.

Our driveway ran alongside our house, back to the garage. Between our driveway and the neighbor's driveway, Dad had planted a dozen rosebushes and a dozen other flower beds. It was hard to mow the lawn with the push mower, because you had to go around all the flowers. Halfway back from the road, Dad had raspberry bushes, then the vegetable garden. This was only about twenty feet wide and thirty feet long. Dad planted the big vegetable garden in our neighbor's empty lot.

When we first moved to Shawnee, there was an old upright piano in the basement. Mom decided that Frank, Joseph and I should take piano lessons. My brothers quit after a year. I kept on, but after eighth grade, I decided I had had enough. I wanted to quit the year before, but Mom said if I continued piano lessons, I could also take voice lessons. She said, "You like to sing. You're always singing around the house and at Church." For a change, I liked her idea. So, in eighth grade, I took piano and voice lessons. I didn't like my teacher and I still hated practicing when my brothers and sister were playing. I told Mom I wouldn't take lessons in high school. I was determined and she knew it. I won.

Summers were good with swimming lessons, summer camp, hide and seek, no shoes except for church on Sundays, staying up late playing cards on a rainy night. And bicycling, except that my bike was a used one with skinny tires and kids teased me about that.

Ours was the first class to start in the new high school. Fifteen kids came from other parishes, which enlarged our class to forty-five. We had very good teachers.

When I came home from school one Friday, Mom said, "Maureen, I've got some clothes for you. Try them on." There were four skirts and blouses. I only had a few before then. The skirts were pretty pleated plaids and the blouses matched them. We wore uniforms to school, but not to dances and ball games. I was excited.

I walked into the kitchen to show Mom the first pair I tried on, an orange and green plaid skirt and orange blouse. "They fit. Good. Joan's mother brought them over," Mom said.

Joan was my classmate. I couldn't wear her clothes! I hung them in my closet, but I never wore them.

Saturday, I baked pecan rolls from scratch. Freshman Home Ec had taught me that I liked to bake. I didn't want to know how to cook, though. That was too useful, too necessary. I liked seeing my brothers and sister devour the rolls or cookies or whatever I baked.

December 28, 1953

Dear Aunt Elizabeth and Uncle Sebastian,

Thank you very much for the sweater you sent me for Christmas. It is the prettiest sweater I have. I'd like to wear it to school with my navy blue uniform. But Mom says I have to save it for good. I'll wear it to school dances and stuff like that. Lots of the girls have dates, but I go by myself. I don't dance much, except sometimes with other girls, but the music is fun.

My report cards are very good now. I get all A's. Mom and Dad never say much about them.

I walked home from school with Margie last week and all she could talk about was how handsome our new assistant pastor is and what a beautiful voice he has for singing at Mass. It's true enough, but it seems to me that it's a pretty dumb way to talk about a priest.

I'll tell you who I think is handsome. Dave Wedgewood. He came to visit us last October. Mom said he used to work with Dad in Prairie du Chien when she first met Dad. I guess that makes him kind of old. After we went to bed, I could hear them, because my bedroom is right under the kitchen. They were drinking beer and laughing a lot. Mom doesn't usually laugh much.

It has been very cold here, so cold that the pond over by Judy's house froze up. Dad found a pair of ice skates, ugly black ones, for me, so I got to go skating twice. I didn't even fall down once, but all the other girls had white shoe skates, which kind of spoiled my fun.

How are you? Did you get nice Christmas presents? And how are your kids? We are all fine except Peter lost another baby tooth and Ellen and Joseph have colds.

Thanks again for the sweater.

Love
Maureen

I hated shorthand. It was so stupid! Why had I let Mom talk me into it? Even the teacher was no good. I goofed around and Sister Martha just tried to ignore me.

Typing last year wasn't so bad, but when I told Mom I wanted to quit shorthand, she told me I had to take it because if I knew typing and shorthand, I could always get a job if I needed it. That settled it! I was not going to be a lowly secretary, ever. So, in shorthand class, I made a nuisance out of myself, until I was sent to the principal's office. Instead of yelling at me, Sister Elizabeth Ann looked at me and asked why I was misbehaving. I had never been a troublemaker before and suddenly I was ashamed of myself. I started crying, one eye tearing from shame, the other from self-pity.

"I don't want to take shorthand. I want to take physics," I mumbled. "But Mom won't let me quit shorthand."

"All right. I want you to go back to class and behave yourself. I'll see what I can do."

I got out of shorthand, but it was too late too get into physics, so I went to study hall.

I liked my other classes, especially Trig. When we worked

at the blackboard, I could zip out answers almost as fast as Sister de Montfort gave out problems. I had no idea that girls weren't supposed to beat boys in math. In English IV, Sister Pierre loaded us with work, memorizing poetry, reading books, writing compositions. I loved the challenge.

Last summer, after years of swimming lessons, I passed Senior Life Saving class. I was proud of that, because Frank had been one of the victims for the test and he had made it very hard for me to bring him in both times I had to rescue him. But he had passed a year earlier, and if he could do it, so could I! So when he thrashed around as I pulled him in, I got mad but used both arms, across his chest and back and held my hands tightly together. I wanted to squeeze him hard enough to hurt him, but I wasn't strong enough.

They had finished the bowling alley in the high school basement when I was a junior and we had a high school girls league and one for boys. I was good at bowling, not as good as Dad, but I had the highest average in our league. I was secretary of our league, so I kept the statistics. I would write them up for our school paper: who got the highest single game and highest three-game total, who picked up splits, and team standings.

I even had a boyfriend my senior year, from another school. He wasn't Catholic, which sometimes bothered me. But Mom never fussed. How could she, when Dad wasn't Catholic? I had friends at school, Mog, Clara, Louise and a few others, but I still felt like an outsider. I liked bowling a good game, writing a good test, laughing with my boyfriend, but... But what? I had no idea.

Mom wanted me to go to college where she went, St. Teresa's, in Winona, Minnesota. I agreed, but only because it meant getting away from her. After graduation, I found summer jobs: I worked in the concession stand at the drive-in theater; I was an assistant supervisor at the summer playground for kids; weekends, I was locker-room attendant at a new country club. For a while, I worked seventy hours a week. I put all the money in a savings account for college.

One night at the drive-in, as I made popcorn in the huge

kettle, the concession stand manager complained to another worker, "They're going to let niggers swim with whites at the Swope Park pools!"

I decided to poke fun at his complaint. "That's good!" I grinned as if I hadn't heard the disgust in his voice.

He looked at me, "Do you want to swim with them?" His raw, ugly hatred battered me. I wondered how Negroes could stand it.

At the end of the summer, Mom took me to the Shawnee Bank to get my money. I got to hold it, all $423.22 of it, all the way into Kansas City, where she put it into their bank. Besides what I earned, I had received a scholarship, a loan and a work grant that would cover three hundred dollars of the costs. I was proud that I could take care of most of the nine-hundred-dollar fees for room and board, books and tuition.

Mom took me shopping; after buying a lot of boring necessities, Mom told me, "My folks didn't have much money when I started college, but they bought me a Pendleton suit, and you can have one, too."

I was wondering what kind of ugly thing she was going to try to foist off on me, when I saw the most gorgeous suit I could ever have imagined. I stopped. "I want that one." I barely whispered, pointing to a mannequin. I didn't dare hope for the bright red, straight skirt and the jacket with bold, three-inch squares of red, black and gray. Much to my surprise, Mom bought it for me, even though it cost almost fifty dollars. Usually, I didn't pay much attention to clothes, but that suit made me feel grown-up and important.

College meant starting all over again — hundreds of new classmates, new teachers, dorm life. The newness swamped me for a while. After about a month, Sister Thomas a Kempis kept me after calculus class. She wanted to know why I wasn't doing better. I fumbled around with excuses, "This logarithm stuff doesn't make any sense."

She was very gentle, "You had logarithms in Algebra II, didn't you?"

"I never took Algebra II. Mom made me take typing." So she explained some and I caught on. Then she said, "You scored very high on your college entrance exams, especially in math. You wouldn't be in calculus class otherwise. I know you can do the work, Rena." Her kindness and confidence in me were amazing. So I put my brain to work and earned A's in her classes from then on. My other grades suffered for a while longer as I adjusted to college life.

There were dances at the nearby Catholic boys' college and at St. Teresa's. At first, I danced some, but never more than one dance with the same guy. At a November mixer, I was dancing with a fellow and he asked, "What's your major?"

"Math," I told him. He stopped dancing and looked at me. "Oh." He finished the dance and disappeared.

After the dance, I talked to Mary Ellen. She was good with boys. "It seems like as soon as I tell a guy I'm majoring in math, he's gone. Why?"

"Boys don't want girls to be smarter than them. Don't tell them math."

"I don't want to lie."

"Just say you're going for an M.R.S. degree." She thought it was funny.

I thought about that, even tried it, but it just didn't suit me. Mary Ellen was only about five foot two. I had seen her looking up to a fellow but I couldn't do that because both my body and my spirit were too tall, especially if he was so stupid that my brains scared him.

I bowled in the mixed league, formed between the two colleges. We were a very good team. John had a 160 average, mine was 150. Gary and Jean weren't as good but they were a lot of fun, so we enjoyed ourselves as we stayed in first place. Hiking the bluffs along the Mississippi river was neat. So was the pool in the dorm. My lifesaving certificate was still good, so I signed up for lifeguard duty. I took up smoking and bridge.

From seven to nine in the evening was study time, nine to ten was recreation time week nights, eleven was lights out. Smoking was allowed, but only in the four smoking rooms, never on the street. Drinking was forbidden. We had to wear hats and gloves when we went to town. We could wear slacks to go bluff climbing, but we had to leave by the back door when we wore them.

The nuns were pretty fussy about our behavior, but they were also excellent teachers. The three nuns who taught me calculus, physics and English all had doctorate degrees, earned during the Depression, and they were as good at explaining as they had been at learning.

I worked in the dish room, to pay part of my fees. One evening, I left the dish room to wipe off tables. There was a large bakery cart with empty trays and one tray with apple pies. I looked around. No one in sight. It was irresistible! I took a pie and hid it in a drawer, where I could pick it up later. Several other girls came out to do tables.

As we washed tables, I told Jeanette about the pie. She grinned. "Let's meet in my room at nine." Even divided into slivers, the pie was much better than what we had for supper. Two days later, Jeanette told me Sister Gertrude was calling in the dish room girls, one by one, to cross-examine them about the stolen pie. I figured most of them knew I'd done it, but Jeanette said nobody had told on me. When I was called in, Sister Gertrude asked me if I had taken the pie. I replied, "Yes, Sister."

She was so surprised at my honesty, she didn't know what to say for a minute. She gave me a lecture and I respectfully yes-Sistered her at all the appropriate places and No-Sistered her at all the others. I wasn't the least bit repentant and she knew it. I wasn't going to do it again and she knew that, too, so she let me go.

The college production of *Oklahoma* was great fun, but when the ballet came (required attendance), I sat way up in the balcony so I could sleep in peace. The first dancers flitted out and I was hooked as pure white souls flew in graceful patterns across the stage.

So, I studied and worked and socialized and after the culture shock wore off, I did just fine.

Dad was promoted and sent to Los Angeles, where Frank, Joe and I had a ball the following summer. All three of us worked at a beach club, went to ballrooms for dancing, played bridge with other college kids and bowled in a summer league.

I didn't even have time to miss fighting with Frank.

Back at St. Teresa's, I was restless. It took me a month to realize why. I stayed after class to talk to Sister Thomas a Kempis. "Uh, Sister, can I talk to you?"

"Yes, of course."

I stammered around, then blurted out, "I want to become a nun." We talked a while and she told me to make my request for admission to the Mother Superior. She made it all easy.

That night, I called Mom. When I tried to tell her, I got all weepy with the magnitude of my decision so I had to repeat myself twice before she understood me. It was a good choice for me at the time. I could devote myself to God and teach math. I was, or trying to be, very noble and self-sacrificing.

All of us postulants stayed at the college to get in a year of study, along with religious training, so I continued my classes. Our religious training seemed overinvolved with externals. We were to severely detach ourselves from all persons and things and that part was all right. We were supposed to meditate for half an hour every morning, but I couldn't stay awake for that no matter how hard I tried.

I became Sister Mary Anne, one of fifty new novices. For our two years as novices, we stayed at the Motherhouse. We kept the huge stone building clean with its hundreds of tiny bedrooms, the old nun's infirmary, guest parlors, chapels, dining rooms, recreation rooms and administration wing. We did the cooking and laundry. We had classes in Church History, Franciscan History and our order's rule book. For prayer, we had meditation, Office and Mass in the morning, Office at noon and afternoon, Office and night prayers at night, plus our private rosaries and other prayers.

That was how we spent our time. As I saw things then, these were the surface occupations we were to use on a relentless search for perfection. I decided that perfection was doing my job perfectly (washing pots and pans, collecting garbage or whatever) and promptly; don't think for myself; just do what I was told, do it the way I was told to do it, whether it was folding sheets or praying. Poverty wasn't so bad, even if it meant patching the patches on my underwear, but I didn't understand why, if patches were honorable symbols of our poverty, we had to wear new underwear to see the doctor. I patched dutifully. Chastity in thought and deed was no problem. All emotions were suspect at best; we weren't supposed to like anybody or anything, but we were supposed to love God and love our neighbor; I never did get that to work. I was far too preoccupied with trying to be perfect for anyone to like me, which was the way I thought we were supposed to be. The devotion to God, supposedly expressed in our prayers was a problem. Sometimes, I felt the beauty of the liturgy, awe at the solemnity of the Mass, but mostly the prayers seemed not to reach all the way to God or all the way to my deepest self. I still slept through meditation.

Those were the two most frustrating years of my life! No matter how hard I tried, the novice mistress was always annoyed with me: I broke too many dishes in the dish room, I chewed my fingernails, I broke needles in the sewing room, I got mad at others if they held me up so I couldn't get my job done in time. The harder I tried, the more she found wrong with me and the more I found wrong with myself. She always gave me the dirty jobs, which I felt, deep down, were meant to degrade me. One time, she bawled me out because my laugh sounded nervous, another time because I thought I was smart, as if I could change that. I'm sure she thought she was doing the right thing, but cruelty in God's name was very cruel, indeed.

When we started as novices, Sister Marcelline, the choir teacher, asked each of us who had taken piano lessons to continue with piano and organ lessons. I didn't understand why, but I politely said no; I didn't like myself for it and she didn't like my refusal, either, but she didn't push it.

The best singers among the senior novices (second year) were in the Schola; they led the singing at Mass. The novices who were a year ahead of us had some very good voices — they were good at everything. In my class, we felt vastly inferior. When we became senior novices, I was in Schola. Sister Marcelline berated us about our singing; she said no one could hear us in the big chapel. I tried singing louder, but then I'd get off-key. The harder I tried, the worse it got. Then, at Schola practice one day, Sister Marcelline started in on *somebody* who was singing off-key. She called me to the front of the room and made me sing by myself. At first I was all right, but she was looking to find me wrong, so she found wrong. I was demoted, from the back row to the front row and told to sing very quietly. If she had asked me, I would have told her I was the guilty one, but that wasn't her way. Being humiliated in front of the others was bad, but being cut down for trying unsuccessfully to please was excruciating. I crawled further into myself and tried to be inconspicuous.

After we took our three vows of poverty, chastity and obedience, ten of us were sent back to the college to get our degrees. What a relief it was to be studying again I knew I was good at that. And with no energy wasted on the "mating game," I put my brain seriously to work on math, still my major, philosophy (fascinating), history (there were two sides to the arguments that led to the Revolutionary War?). My brain was as agile as a ballet dancer's body and I loved it!

We were meditating in the chapel at five-thirty one winter morning when the telephone shattered the silence. It was Mom, calling from Washington, where she was going to have surgery to see if she had cancer. She wanted me to be with her. It was awful and sweet that she needed me. I asked our Juniorate Mistress; the rules of our order wouldn't allow me to go, she said, but I could write to her every day and I could ask all the nuns to pray for her.

11

Marguerite
Liberia, Africa,
1960

As always, when Ben received a promotion, he moved to the new city and left me with the job of moving our kids and our belongings. Only this time we went overseas to Liberia. So I sorted, packed, stored and shipped.

It was exciting and scary.

Then I drove all over with Ellen, Martin and Peter to say our good-byes. They were a little better-behaved by this time, so I didn't have to resort to comic books. When I drove the kids from Shawnee to Los Angeles, I gave them comics to read in the car, which made them carsick. They quit fighting.

We went to see Sister Mary Anne at the Motherhouse in Rochester, where she was a novice. At least there was one in the family who was settled. Frank was in graduate school and Joe was in the army. We visited Eliz in Chicago and Mary in Washington D. C. In New York, we saw friends and went to Radio City Music Hall and the Empire State Building.

Joe got leave from his army unit in Germany and met us in Paris. We saw Notre Dame Cathedral. It was huge and beautiful and needed a good cleaning. Peter and Martin climbed to the top of the Eiffel Tower; Joe and I did the night-club tour. I enjoyed the sight-seeing and visiting — it beat doing laundry any day.

We landed at Robertsfield, near Monrovia, Liberia on August 8 in a miserable rainstorm. Ellen and Peter were sick after we landed and threw up all over the place. What a beginning.

Two experienced overseas wives met our plane. They took us to a nurse to check the kids. She said it was probably just the excitement. Then we checked in at the dilapidated old City Hotel. We had three rooms and a bath. At least the food and service were good. We were very tired and numb from all our traveling.

We stayed four days at the hotel, three weeks in a house and finally settled in a second house.

The agency that sent Ben to Liberia, USOM, knew how slow shipping was. They furnished a hospitality kit, which included everything from dishes to bedding. Our goods sat on a ship in port for ten days before they finally unloaded it on October 17.

While we waited for our things, two of the ladies took me to call on the ambassador's wife, the wife of the director of USOM, and the wife of the assistant director. I had no calling cards. That was a bad breach of etiquette. And I thought calling cards went out of style ages ago.

Pauline, who was as knowledgeable as she was fun, found a house boy for me. Johnny cleaned and did laundry; he was a good worker. She also took me shopping. The shops were interesting but horribly filthy and very expensive. You could find most anything if you looked long enough.

I found schools for the kids. Martin quit two schools and Peter quit one. I got a home study course for Peter and, after much frantic arranging, I put Ellen and Martin on a plane. They would go to boarding schools in Atchison, Kansas. The same Benedictines who taught in Shawnee ran these schools. Ellen would be a freshman, and Martin only in eighth grade. They were very scared-looking kids. I could have cried buckets, but I didn't. I hoped it was the right thing to do.

Before we even settled in, we had to join the social whirl. We went to cocktail parties, dinner parties and silver teas. I didn't like being around people you had to be on guard with, but it was exciting to be with the bigwigs. We met the ex-president of Liberia and the bishop. Bridge was very important among the wives but sometimes I won so often I was embarrassed. I slowly learned to play mah-jongg. For relaxing, Ben and I went to the lagoon to swim in the warm ocean or we went to a movie. I wished my mother were alive so I could tell her all this.

For our wedding anniversary, Peter made us a banana cake and then went up-country with several of Ben's coworkers. Ben took me out for dinner and gave me a very pretty string of local beads; it was a nice anniversary.

The next day, I took five very nice sailors sight-seeing and had them for dinner. One of them came back in a cab with nine cartons of cigarettes for me.

In November, we finally had an air conditioner installed in the kitchen and they made a terrible mess, but it surely helped — cooking in tropical heat was no fun!

My mouth was sore again, so I went to a native Liberian dentist, Dr. Jupiter. It kept getting worse, every time I went to him, but finally cleared up. At the same time, Ben was throwing up sick for two days.

Our Christmas presents started coming in January, with a

tape recording from Ellen and Martin. We rushed right over to Danny's so we could use his recorder to listen. I enjoyed hearing Ellen and Martin so much I cried.

After that, Pauline and I had coffee at her house and then we went downtown shopping. A nail punctured a tire on the way in, but a nice young fellow stopped and put the spare on. I went to the hairdresser and asked for a shampoo and a color rinse. It turned out pink!

Before we got to Monrovia, Ben had taken up tennis again. He played two or three times a week when he could. Often, he invited his tennis boys to our house for a beer afterward. As if that wasn't enough, he started playing tournaments. In January, he played in the Air France Tennis Tournament. He and his partner won their first and second rounds, but lost the third. Ben was exhausted each time and very proud of his wins. I played with him just once, for only fifteen minutes, and it wore me out completely. I thought they were crazy to play so hard in this heat. Sometimes I got so fed up with tennis I wanted to wrap the racket around his neck.

The professor from India was the only one of Ben's tennis buddies that I liked. His daughter had died in an airplane crash in September. In January, a printed announcement invited us to her cremation. Everybody went to their house at eleven that morning, but there was a delay because they had to get permission from the Public Health Department to take the wooden casket out of the steel one.

The mourners, headed by a local band, left the house to walk two miles in the boiling heat to a lovely beach area. They put the coffin on a bier, stacked firewood underneath and started the fire. It was very sad and gruesome.

I sold tickets for the Louis Armstrong concert. There was no mad rush to buy them, even though they were only two-fifty and five dollars each. I bought tickets for Ben, Peter and I as well as Dr. Jupiter and the Barajos. We had a wild rush to get there on time because Ben was late getting home from tennis. The concert was wonderful. We all enjoyed the music and Satchmo's antics, even though the audience was small.

The next night, we went to Wexel's for a buffet supper. George was nice but his wife wasn't. Ma would have said,

"She's like a crow, beautiful and graceful, but as soon as she opens her mouth, you can't stand her." Marcel was there and he gave me another big pitch about letting Ben play more tennis. He is starting to annoy me.

The supper was a delightful high calorie meal. I knew that if I didn't cut back, I wouldn't be able to get into a lot of my clothes, especially several of the lovely cocktail dresses I had to buy before I came here, and Maureen's Pendleton suit. Maureen couldn't wear it any more, but I had already let it out as far as I could, so if I wasn't careful, I couldn't wear it either.

The city ran out of gas for stoves for a week, which was a nuisance, but the water shortage was ridiculous. Once in a while, we had cold water, but never any hot water. So the boys carried water from down the road. We'd go to the beach with Pauline and Ed, then have a shower and hamburger at their house.

I didn't get to Mass on Ash Wednesday. It wasn't a holy day of obligation or anything, but I felt bad. Liberia is considered a "mission country," so I didn't have to fast or abstain during Lent. That was a good thing, because Ben and I were expected to attend all kinds of cocktail parties and dinner parties and I couldn't possibly follow the fasting and abstinence rules without offending everyone.

In February, I had dysentery and the curse both, with terrible stomach and leg cramps and Ben felt miserable, too. That was the day they had to take the stove out to fix it, again. It amazed me how calm I was about all these nuisances. If they had happened in Shawnee, I would have been raising hell. I guess I wasn't cut out for the endless work and frustration of raising six kids. I really liked living in Liberia, with only a little work and a lot of fun.

Fortunately, I was better the next day, because it was an important day at the embassy. They celebrated the Fourth of July on February 22, because July was in the rainy season. Six or seven hundred Americans came and I cooked delicious hot dogs while and Ben served beer. They had a program, dancing, singing and a speech by the ambassador. Afterwards, we went to Stewart's for a few drinks. It was fun and we were exhausted.

We met the chief of a tribe of natives at a cocktail party. He was a charmer, with many fascinating stories to tell. He invited Ben and me to be his guests for a month in Nigeria. Ben couldn't leave his work for that long, but it sounded intriguing. We met him again a few days later at another party. He told us more stories and repeated his invitation. I invited him to our house for dinner for a good talk with him. After he left, Ben said, "You're really living it up, aren't you kid?"

When I was little, I missed a lot of school because of ear infections. Pa's drinking set us apart, too. I usually felt left out. But there I was, at the center of the social whirl, with plenty of money and hardly any work.

After Thanksgiving, a year and a half later, I discovered a lump on my left breast. I went to see Dr. Johnson who examined me and cheerfully sent me to Dr. Cooper. I had to wait two hours for him. He seemed quite sure that it was cancer but no outgrowth so far. He said the lump must come out right away. I'd have to go to Washington.

We had company for dinner, which was a mess, but it kept me quiet and I drank too much. I got the curse, too. Two long days later, Ben went to the embassy and Mr. Ross sent a cable to Washington requesting evacuation for me. I hoped I could get out in a few days.

The nuns at the convent had a tea for the people who helped with the bazaar. They had a lot of really good food, but it didn't appeal to me. Sister Edmund kept everyone laughing. It was good because I was so jittery I couldn't stand myself. She distracted me for a little while. I'm telling everyone that I'm going home and asking them not to tell anyone. It's funny. It's scary. That night, Ben had chills and fever. He was never sick before we came here. The next day, I had my hair done, just in case.

But it took three days for Washington to answer our cable and then they said I was to go to the Firestone company doctor for consultation. He examined me and concurred with the others. Ben sent another cable. We played bridge that night. I lost miserably, but it sort of kept my mind off myself.

Barbara, Betty, Alice and Mildred came to see me, which was nice of them. But I didn't like to be needing their encouraging words. The seamstress brought over the skirt and blouse she made for me, so I modeled them for my company. They looked real cute.

Again it took them three days to answer our cable, but this time they said I should go to Washington for the surgery. At least they didn't want to send me to Casablanca. I was to leave Sunday morning and arrive in New York that evening.

Ben won in the first round of the Liberian National Tennis Tournament but it really beat him. My plane broke a window so it would be late getting to Liberia.

We went downtown for Sunday Mass and then to Robertsfield. Joe was out of the army and living with us again. He and his girlfriend went with us. The plane left at 5:30 p.m. Idlewild was fogged in so we went to Bermuda for several hours. It would have been so nice if Ben had been with me.

I finally arrived at Idlewild at 2:30 a.m. I went through customs then to the International Hotel. I took a long warm bath but that didn't help. I called Ellen at school in Switzerland. She didn't recognize my voice. I told her why I was going to Washington and that I would stop and see them on the way back to Liberia. The phone call cost twenty-two dollars. I called Maureen. I asked her if she could come be with me. She said she'd try to get permission.

I went to Mary's in D.C. I was glad I could be with my sister. She went to Bethesda with me, where they examined me. They gave the same verdict, but couldn't operate for two or three days. Then we went shopping for a lot of things that Ben, Joe and I needed.

The next day, Andy took me downtown where I took a train to Baltimore. I had blood tests, a physical, a vaginal cancer test and a chest x-ray. In between, I tried to bury myself in a book. In my hospital bed after supper, I wrote to Ben, Frank, Eliz and Maureen.

The next day was horrible! They wouldn't let me eat anything, in case they had time to operate. I tried to read, to pray, to walk, to take a nap. I couldn't do anything to make the clock move faster. Finally, at 3 p.m., they started getting me ready for surgery.

I woke up in the recovery room and found out they had taken out two large cysts and six small ones, all benign. I had my first good night's sleep in weeks.

The next morning, the doctor dismissed me. Mary and Andy came to see me and I went home with them.

After a week of visiting, shopping, and resting, I flew to Switzerland to see the kids. Ellen, Martin and Peter met me in their friend's Alfa Romeo. We ate lunch and they showed me their school. We ate a good dinner at a small hotel in Chunby where I stayed. I nearly froze, but it was good to see the kids and know they were happy.

They came to get me for Midnight Mass at Les Avants. It was a pretty little church with a stove in back. The kids brought Christmas presents, a musical cigarette lighter and a letter opener for me, a musical toilet paper roller for Ben. The kids had lunch and dinner with me, went sleigh riding Christmas afternoon and to a party that night. I was lonesome; it was my first Christmas without Ben.

My plane landed at Robertsfield the next morning, but Ben and Joe didn't get there until noon. It was so good to be home and warm; I had really missed Ben.

The next day, I fired Johnny. There were more than a dozen fifths of liquor and several silver dollars missing, among other things. He was very hurt but I was sure he was guilty. He had been leaving the house open and going away. Besides, the house was just plain dirty. I had my hair done and shopped for groceries.

On New Year's Eve, we went over to Burwells' house after dinner and played bridge, then went to a New Year's Eve party where we danced and drank.

It had been a large year and a very large December.

12

Maureen (Sister Mary Anne)
Rochester, Minnesota,
1961

I finished my degree in a year and a half and was sent out to teach high school. Of the twenty nuns there, one was definitely weird, one was a kindly old saint, one turned out later to be an alcoholic, another had had a nervous breakdown and most were very good teachers. We had an average assortment of problems and an above average dedication to teaching. We were absolutely separate from each other, held apart by our holiness, or lack thereof.

Sometimes I had a cold and lost my voice. Then I would coach a boy or girl from each class and he or she would explain the algebra lesson for the day and then they would all work on their assignment. The kids liked that. One time, Davy got up to teach; he was the shortest boy in the freshman class and also the cutest. He stood up, looked around at all the kids and said "Steve, put your gum in the wastebasket and put your dime in the pig." At this perfect imitation of me, the class burst into laughter. Steve threw away his gum and put a dime into the piggy bank. It was a bleach bottle with a hole for coins, cloth ears and a painted-on face. Steve paid a lot of gum fines, which was one of the reasons that my home room often won the weekly contests of collecting money for the missions.

The kids were mostly good kids, who were there to learn. Gum-chewing and talking without being called on were usually the only misbehaviors the teachers had to deal with.

On a bright day, my love of learning was contagious: half of each algebra class worked factoring problems at the blackboard. Their busy chalk beat out a staccato rhythm which kept all their brains dancing. Or the general science class competed in a "basketball game" review for a test; the kids chose sides and a pair of them went to the blackboard; the first one with the right answer earned two points for his or her side; occasional free throws penalized rambunctious behavior. But if I was tired or grumpy or unprepared for a class, it reflected right back to me from the kids. I'd get sloppy for a while, then pull myself together again and work hard.

I didn't like the science book, so I invented units; the kids especially liked the atom and periodic chart, with all the patterns, and the car engine. When we studied engines, I told the girls, "I've always heard that boys are smart about engines. But I bet you girls can do as well as they can." Tests showed them about even, all with excellent scores.

One day, Jim came in after school to get help on a physics problem. His question answered, he asked, "What do you nuns do when you aren't teaching?"

I answered, "Well, we get up at five-thirty, start prayers at six, eat breakfast, do a little housework, and come to school."

"What do you do between five-thirty and six?"

Before I could come up with a way to say that nuns had to dress and go to the bathroom, too, he realized what we did. He blushed furiously and got out of there very quickly.

I didn't get a chance to tell him that we took turns helping our cook prepare meals and do laundry. Or that during our recreation hour between seven and eight at night, we played cards, built picture puzzles and talked. I wouldn't have embarrassed him or me by saying that some of us walked over to the hospital on Friday nights and went swimming. Friday was nun's night at the pool there. Some nuns played a good game of bridge; sometimes, I played, but their sour seriousness spoiled the fun. Silence was not as strict as it had been: in the novitiate, we could barely greet each other during the day; after night prayers, silence was absolute. Now, talking during the day wasn't so fiercely frowned upon; night silence was still strict.

After I'd been there for several months, I took my place with other nuns and laypersons in the most incredible line I'd ever seen. In calm triumph, we slowly advanced the three blocks into the public school gym, where we received the new oral vaccine against polio. Tomorrow's kids would not have to be quarantined. They wouldn't have to worry that their brothers might have to live the rest of their lives in iron lungs. I wanted to ... but no, nuns were not allowed to feel excited or thrilled, much less to express these feelings.

So, the days passed, a lot of gray days, because when I wasn't all involved in teaching, I realized that my prayers weren't getting me any closer to God. I said my prayers, except when I slept through meditation, but it was like talking into a dead telephone. There were black moments, too, when isolation threatened to smother me, moments escaped by plunging into fancier lesson plans or frenzied house cleaning.

I walked past the teachers' lunchroom. The door was open but instead of the usual chatter, the only voice was from the TV. "We repeat, President Kennedy has been shot." I couldn't stand it. I went on upstairs to my general science class.

One of the kids asked me what was wrong. I couldn't even answer, only shook my head. A few minutes later, our principal's voice came over the P.A., "We have just heard that President Kennedy was shot and killed in Dallas, Texas. This is a terrible tragedy. Will each teacher please lead the class in saying the rosary for Kennedy."

I opened my mouth, but nothing came out. Then Ron, who was sometimes a nuisance but not a bad kid, started praying and the others followed his lead. I nodded my thanks to Ron.

It was too terrible to be true! I had voted enthusiastically, for the first time, for Kennedy. He was such a charismatic figure, the promise of a bright future. How could he have been assassinated?

I muddled through my next two classes. At the end of the day, our principal announced there would be no school Monday out of respect for Kennedy.

Though we nuns seldom watched TV in those days, most of our group spent the next few days doing nothing else. It was too sad and ugly for me. I sat in my room, trying to blot it all out by doing schoolwork.

In the summer of 1965, I went to Brookings, South Dakota for a summer of studying PSSC Physics, the newly modernized course for high school. Mrs. Anderson showed me the college dormitory where I would be staying. We looked down a long corridor, with twenty rooms on each side.

"This end of the hall is for married couples. Single men are downstairs. Nuns and single women will stay at the far end of the hall," she said as we walked along the corridor. "Here is the bathroom for this floor," as we reached the half-way point. At the end of the hall, "And here is your room." I muttered, "Thank you." I was appalled!

I had carefully checked the National Science Foundation brochures for a course on teaching the new physics because I had muddled through teaching the course for a year and figured I could use some help. The government, after the Russians had put Sputnik into space, was paying science and math teachers to go to summer school so they could go back to the classrooms with better courses. Our order of nuns was strong on education and encouraged us to seek these summer grants.

I was glad to be accepted at Brookings, because they offered "separate quarters for nuns." But these separate quarters were just down the hall from the married couples. And the men would be sharing our bathroom. There was one big shower room with eight showers, not even a curtain separating the showers from the toilet area. I disliked the idea of a woman seeing me naked, but a man walking in on me was too terrible to even think of. It wasn't just ordinary modesty; I was a nun. I couldn't be seen naked!

I met, but didn't see much of, the other three nuns and the two single women sharing the end of the corridor. One evening, I saw Sister Theresa walking toward the bathroom with her towel and soap. I blurted out, "What if one of the men comes into the bathroom while you're in the shower?"

"Oh, didn't you know? They use the bathroom downstairs." What a relief! I had been going to the bathroom fully dressed, brushing my teeth there and soaping up a wash-rag to use in my room. I thought about it for a while, put on my nightgown and robe and head wrap (like an oversized hanky, pinned at the back of the head). I didn't want anyone to see me undressed, as I was walking down the hall, or naked in the shower, but I made it unobserved, and as the days went by, I began to relax. Then one evening, I was brushing my teeth at a sink in the bathroom, and the door opened. It was Olivia, Alice's friend. She looked at me in the mirror and I looked back. She was even more shocked at seeing me than I was at being seen. She backed up and the door swung shut again.

When I returned to my room, it started, a laugh from deep inside myself, not loud enough to hear yet, about how foolish I was. The sun and moon wouldn't stop in their tracks just because I had been seen with a little half-inch-long hair showing up front (I'd cut it very short so as not to bother about a haircut during the summer.)

A few days later, Alice, a Mexican-American teacher from El Paso, studying chemistry that summer, appeared at my door. For the first week, I had kept it closed, for privacy; it had become too hot for that and besides, I was beginning to feel like opening doors.

"Good afternoon, Sister."

Alice was polite, but the slight Mexican accent and the proper words couldn't quite hide the impishness in her eye. I liked her. "Hello, Alice."

"Olivia and I were wondering if you and the other sisters would like to fix supper with us at the Newman Center Sunday evening, since the cafeteria is closed."

I had been buying a few things at the grocery store for Sunday meals. "Yes, that sounds good. What will we have?"

"How about weiners and beans and potato chips? I could get the groceries, if you'd like to pay for part of them. There are plates and silverware and all that at the center."

"Sure, that would be fine. Let me know how much money you want." The NSF not only paid our room and board, tuition, books and transportation, it gave teachers six hundred dollars in spending money to lure them away from summer jobs. I really liked having money in my pocket again, after all those years, but at the same time, I felt duty-bound to use it sparingly and turn most of it in at the end of the summer.

Alice was a good organizer. She had gotten a fire going outside in the fire pit. Sister Theresa had put the canned beans in the fire. I was inside, gathering plates and things, when seventy-year-old Sister Louisa came in shrieking, "My ham exploded! My ham exploded!" She couldn't eat wieners, so she had been heating her ham on a stick. There was something all over her black wool habit, but it wasn't ham. Sister Theresa had put the beans into the fire without punching a hole in the lid, so when they got hot, the can exploded. A science teacher, who thought her ham exploded. It was maybe more pathetic than funny. Poor Sister Louisa spent hours washing the beans out of her habit and more hours ironing it dry because she only had one habit with her.

The next Sunday, Alice and Olivia fixed a Mexican dinner and invited about twenty people. She was not a conservative cook, so she and Olivia and Sister Theresa and I ate Mexican leftovers for three nights. The food was spicy and I drank a lot of water with it. The locals said their water had a lot of magnesium in it. Whether it was the water or the food, I had a few days of staying close to the bathroom.

One of those evenings, Alice mentioned swimming. I had my tank suit with me, but I hadn't expected to be able to use it. "I wish there was some private place where I could swim. It's hot and I love swimming."

Alice looked at me and said she'd see if she could find a place. Sister Theresa said she'd like to go, too.

A few days later, Alice told me "I found a place for you to swim! It's a private beach on a lake about ten miles from here and nobody is ever there during the week and it's fine with the owners. Shall we go out Wednesday after the lecture?"

The shadow of modesty flitted across my mind, pushed out by the pleasurable thought of a nice cool swim. "Yes!"

Every Wednesday afternoon, there was a guest lecturer. As we went in, we got a ticket which entitled us to a free ice cream cone at the dairy bar. We were slow getting out of the lecture hall, so there were about fifty teachers from the math, chemistry and physics classes ahead of us to get their cones. Alice had a big mouth. She yelled, "Hey, you guys! Let us go ahead, please. We want to go swimming!" Fifty teachers, mostly men, turned around and looked and gawked when they realized "we" were Alice and two nuns. Silence. A path appeared, like the parting of the Red Sea before Moses. My red face made up for a lifetime of non-blushing. I wanted to disappear, but Alice moved blithely forward, yelling happily, "Thanks guys." I followed. Well, ice cream on a hot day was a necessity.

Of course, Alice had to drive us to the lake and she had to bring Olivia along and they had to swim with us. I tried to be embarrassed, but the water felt *so* good, the prude in me gave up and I enjoyed the swim and the other women.

I studied hard and really understood the course. One day, our teacher asked what problems we had trouble with, as usual, and asked for volunteers to put the solutions on the board. I wrote out a tough one. There were several questions and then someone blurted out, "Yeah, but she's got an answer book!"

I had told Alice I had it and she must have blabbed. I had looked at the answer book on that problem. I thought the solution was long-winded and ridiculous and, besides, I didn't understand it. So I had worked out a totally different one. I had worked hard and I was proud of myself. I looked at the class. "Yes, I do have an answer book. I taught the course last year. But if you were to look at their solution, you'd see that mine is completely different." I was dignified in my reply, but there was dissatisfaction in the room

Our teacher said, "She's right. The solution is her own." He paused, feeling the resentment. "But as long as she has one, I'll pass out all the answer books after class instead of waiting until the end of the course."

I had only taught the first three units, so when we got to the fourth and last unit, it was tough. I learned a lot, but didn't have the complete understanding that I had had for the first parts. We had more picnics at the Newman Center, ate at a few restaurants and went swimming once a week. Sometimes one of the married couples came for picnics, and Olivia's and Alice's boyfriends, sometimes just Alice, Olivia and I. It was a great summer, lots of fun and some serious studying. It was the beginning of a new me, a me that could enjoy what I did and who I did it with. I had started to belong in this world, to belong to myself.

By 1967, the Vatican Council, instigated by Pope John

XXIII, had finally produced an awakening in our order of nuns. Slowly, fearfully, our powers-that-be had decided that all who wanted to could wear short habits, mostly brown suits with a short veil. So I began teaching at my new assignment, Pacelli High School at Austin, Minnesota, in human clothes.

The next two years would be the best years of teaching I ever had. I taught the familiar, modern PSSC physics course and, to juniors and seniors, I taught the modern math courses that stressed thinking and processes over memory work to juniors and seniors and senior physics. The math courses were new to me, so I had to work hard to keep ahead of the kids. What amazed me was how hard the kids worked.

A month after school started, Sue, getting a little help after school, admitted she usually worked three to four hours a night on her math homework. She was embarrassed about asking so many questions in class, but I encouraged her, "Keep asking. Your questions are good ones and there are probably others wondering the same thing, but they don't want to ask." She liked my response.

They all did so well on tests and quizzes that I didn't want to slow down. We challenged each other to stretch our brains to the utmost and it was marvelous. After a while, I realized that I could relax and enjoy these unusual teenagers. They were excellent students, good kids, fun people.

And our principal, Father Tighe, was the best. He was a man of integrity, who expected the kids to behave. When a teacher put students on detention for being tardy or fooling around in class, Father Tighe kept them after school for an hour. They respected him for his firm discipline and they liked him, too.

As the fall progressed, a great adventure loomed before me: a visit with my folks, who were in Thailand. I hadn't been for a home visit for many years, because after Mom and Dad were in Liberia for several years, they went to Afghanistan, then Thailand, where Dad was once again in charge of updating airports. He worked for US AID, which helped underdeveloped countries. They decided that if my sister Ellen could get one of her stewardess-discount tickets from Pan Am, they could afford to pay for my trip to visit them in Bangkok.

After much fuss and bother I went, during an extended Christmas vacation. As soon as I got to their apartment, Mom insisted I open one Christmas present. A camera and film. How thoughtful of her! I took pictures of their servant, of brilliant red bougainvillea and huge poinsettia bushes, of golden curlicues dancing up from temple roof edges, of elephants carrying monstrous logs with their trunks, of mosquito netting draped over a bed, of tame monkeys, of Christmas decorations on palm shrubs, of three-wheeled taxis, of small trees trimmed to the shapes of elephants and tigers, of bicycle-powered rickshas, of exotically dressed Thai dancers, of the canal where small boats peddled vegetables and where the people bathed, brushed their teeth and relieved themselves. I saw several Thais taking a bath. They wore capes into the water, so that even if the water hadn't been opaquely muddy, I wouldn't have seen any flesh below their necks.

What a welcome change from snow-buried Minnesota! And how nice to have Mom fussing over me, "Would you like to...?" And "What would you like for dinner?" She was a marvelous hostess, and I loved being her guest. Evenings we played cards a lot and they talked about their experiences overseas. We even went for an overnight stay at an ocean-side resort, where I swam in the Pacific Ocean before breakfast on December 27.

I hated to leave. Surprisingly, it seemed like Mom was sorry to see me go. Fortunately, I really liked Pacelli. Teaching was great and the rules had been relaxed at the convent, so we could start being adults with responsibilities, instead of silly children. The feeling was spreading in the Church that religion was a guide through life's joys and sorrows rather than shackles to prevent us from being human. When I returned, the cold was a terrible shock after two weeks in the tropics, but it was good to see the kids and some of the nuns again.

I liked the kids, but I was still pleasantly surprised when Chelle and Dan stopped in after school one April afternoon to ask me to go with a group of them to Minneapolis to see the movie *Camelot*. They liked my company.

Chelle, Dan, Bob, Mike, Dave, Mary, Sister Avis and I went. I found that all these kids loved music. Besides taking their third year of chorus at school, they also sang at the new guitar Mass on Sunday. They talked about summer jobs and going to college. They teased in fun. They laughed a lot. On the way home they marveled at the music they'd heard and the huge screen that drew them into the movie. I had a good time and admired their friendship for each other. Later, Chelle admitted that they figured they had a better chance of getting their parents' permission if they asked a nun or two to go along.

So when I decided to go to the Twin Cities looking for cheap science equipment, I took these friends along and we had another good time. Much to my surprise, all those years of nunnish withdrawal hadn't killed all the humanness in me. I had started to open up. I had friends. Well, I'd had friends at summer school, but that was easier, because I would probably never see them again.

In May, the junior girls were gone from class one day to take a standardized test. Next day, the boys were gone. When the boys came back, Bob wanted to know what we had done while they were gone.

I told him, "Not much. We just talked."

Dan said, "Oh, come on, what did you do?"

They didn't believe the truth, so I said, "We played tiddly-winks with manhole covers." Bob's eyes grew big as he tried to imagine flipping manhole covers instead of quarter-sized pieces of plastic.

"You're kidding! You couldn't do that," Dan objected.

Bob said, "Us guys didn't get to play. Can we do it to-day?"

I answered, "We took all the manhole covers back. Now let's work," and I started writing math on the blackboard. When I turned around, Bob had his hand up.

"Bob?"

"Sister Mary Anne, if we bring manhole covers to class tomorrow, will you show us how to do it?"

Was he serious? I had a vision of the boys stealing manhole covers, leaving behind big holes in the road; I pictured them being picked up by the police, brought before Father Tighe, telling everybody, "Sister Mary Anne is going to show us how to play tiddly-winks with manhole covers."

Me and my big mouth! "Bob, I was just joking!" Bob grinned. What did I expect? If I teased them, why shouldn't they tease me?

The next fall, Saint Edward's parish started a series of awareness weekends, where over one hundred people gathered to talk in groups of ten or so. There would be a theme for the weekend, a few rules, like disagreeing is okay, but not disagreeableness. The idea was to open up intellectually and emotionally to the people in the group. My students were there, too, making music and joining the discussions. I found that I could share with these people and when I listened to them, I discovered that a lot of people, not just nuns, felt emotionally stifled and we reached out and touched each other.

While I was reaching out, so was my brother Martin. He was a Marine, fighting in Vietnam and he wanted mail: letters, books, sweets. I mentioned this in class one day, and Chelle and two other girls came in after school to get his address. I told them of his recent letter, in which he described sitting under a tree, reading. He got up to go to the bathroom, leaving the book behind. When he returned, the tree and the book were gone, blown up by artillery fire. I was sure Martin had seen a lot of ugly things, but he never wrote about them. He wrote good letters and I answered them quickly and sent him paperback books and coffee cans full of cookies. It took a month before he got the cookies, but he always thanked me enthusiastically for the crumbs. He liked getting letters and books from the girls.

Before Christmas, I went up to the Twin Cities to see *2001: a Space Odyssey.* It was incredible! Late that night, back at the convent, I sat in the parlor smoking. I had taken up smoking, probably because it felt naughty without being nasty. Visitors smoked in the parlor, so I figured an occasional cigarette of mine wouldn't be noticeable. The light from street lamps was all I needed.

After finishing my cigarette, I sat there, not exactly thinking, just letting thoughts come. Suddenly, I felt the awesome presence, implied in the movie. It was way beyond our words for God or about God, beyond understanding, beyond imagining. Incredible! I had finally begun to know people and I had finally met God, even though I still slept through meditation.

I wanted to share this experience with my friends, so we borrowed Chelle's Dad's station wagon and my visiting friend from summer school, Alice, drove her car and twelve of us took off for Minneapolis on New Year's Eve. Before we got to the theater, though, the station wagon died. I coaxed it to a filling station. The mechanic put a can of Heet into the gas tank and said to let it sit for a while. Alice took a car full on to the movie, so we wouldn't all be late. When I started the station wagon, it seemed all right and we weren't too late for the movie.

The kids weren't much impressed with the movie, some were downright bored; it certainly didn't shake their souls as it had mine. But that wasn't the worst. Driving out of the Twin Cities in the already bitter cold of early evening, I found that the station wagon would go all right at forty miles an hour, but coughed and spit and threatened to die at higher speeds. Another can of Heet. It didn't help. As we neared Owatonna, I pulled over and Alice followed.

"Alice, this car isn't going to get us home at any decent hour. It's New Year's Eve and I don't want to be on the road late tonight. I think you'd better take home your car full of kids and I'll find a motel for the rest of us and crawl back tomorrow."

"Okay."

"Who wants to go and who wants to stay?" Some wanted to get home for a party, others thought it would be a good adventure to stay behind.

I called the convent and told my buddy, Sister Gilbert, our plans and she said we should stay with her brother in Owatonna. The kids called home, so their folks wouldn't worry. One of the girls said her dad absolutely refused to let her impose on strangers so she should stay in a motel. Okay, I hadn't called Sister Gilbert's brother yet, so we would all just go to a motel.

In the motel room, Chelle and I were getting ready to sleep in one double bed, the other two girls in the other.

Mary whined, "I can't go to bed without brushing my teeth."

I was tired, the responsibility for these kids and the worry about the erratic car felt heavy and I was coming down with a cold. I tried to be patient. "Wipe your teeth with a wash cloth; that will get the worst off."

She came out of the bathroom again. "All the wash cloths are dirty."

I had no patience left and I'm sure everybody in the room knew it. I glowered, "Then use a towel."

In the morning, I called Sister Gilbert to let her know we'd make a late start because of the 45-below-zero temperature and take the long way on better traveled roads to be on the safe side.

"Where have you been? We worried all night because I called my brother to see if you got there safely and he hadn't heard from you."

I groaned. I had tried so hard to make sure we were safe and to make sure everybody knew it. The whole trip was a miserable flop.

When I finally got home, I collapsed in bed for a day with a monstrous cold. Alice also had it. She said Sister Gilbert and Sister Dominique had been really sweet, bringing her food in bed. Before she left, I abjectly apologized and she just laughed it off. I was relieved that she didn't seem to mind.

After we'd been back in school for a few days, Chelle came in to tell me that the problem with the station wagon was dirt in the fuel line; the gas couldn't get through very well. She also said that Bob had told about our misadventures for a speech class assignment and the kids loved it! I was embarrassed, no, mortified. Then I started laughing. At least the speech class got some fun out of it.

A month later, I wrote a derivation on the blackboard for my senior math class. Each of the four lines was quite long, but the patterns made it relatively simple. "That will be your quiz for tomorrow." They sputtered. Then I pointed out the patterns.

Mike commented, "The only paper wide enough for that is toilet paper." Dan agreed.

I thought. "Yes, you could use toilet paper. But you know

what happens to toilet paper."

"You wouldn't, would you?"

"What do you think?" I was having fun with him, but I made myself sound pleasantly serious.

The next day, Dan and Mike showed up with toilet paper. I asked, "Are you sure you want to do that?" Dan chickened out, but Mike used the toilet paper.

After school, I corrected the quizzes, entered the scores, mostly perfect, in my grade book and flushed the toilet paper down the toilet. That evening, I was with the kids and Mike asked about his quiz.

"I flushed it."

"You didn't!" Mike was really upset. He was very grade-conscious, getting A's in all his classes. Dan grinned, glad that he'd played it safe.

I told him, "It's all right, Mike. It's only one quiz."

"But ..."

"Besides, I gave you your score before I flushed it."

His relief was immense. When he realized that I had been giving him a hard time, just as he'd been giving me, he looked at me and grinned weakly. "Okay, I asked for it."

Another time, Tom asked in physics class how come a Trix top worked the way it did.

"What is a Trix top and what does it do?"

"It comes in a box of Trix cereal. It's like half a ping pong ball and where the other half should be, there's a stem that you use to start it spinning. When it spins, it turns upside down until it slows, then it goes right side up again."

"Well, offhand, I don't know. I'll give you an answer tomorrow."

"Okay."

That evening, the kids gave one of their great choral concerts and I was late getting to my school work. Then I remembered the Trix top. Tom wasn't in the "in group," so his question was as much a demand for attention as a demand for an answer. I looked in several books. The only things I could find that might be relevant were fluid friction and gyroscopic principle.

Sister Dominique passed my doorway, towel and soap in

hand. "Hey, Dominique, what am I going to do about this? Tom asked me a question and the best I can find may or may not be right, but I've got to give him an answer."

"Why don't you write out the solution in shorthand, make copies on the ditto machine and hand them out?" That was the kind of answer that was no answer at all, so I did it.

I gave each student a copy of my solution. My shorthand skipped most vowels and many consonants, leaving just enough for me to recall the words, so I expected their reactions, "What is this?" "I can't read this!" After the protests died out, I read it as quickly as possible, "Fluid friction of the air inside the top causes it to turn upside down; gyroscopic principle keeps it in the same position until it slows down and reduces the friction and it falls down."

Mike looked at me. "You made that up."

He was right, but I just shrugged and replied, "You don't have to believe it, but that's my answer."

Before school, a week later, I got the gyroscope out of its box and looked at the yellowed paper with it. After the usual gyroscope explanation, there was a picture of the Trix top and the words: "Scientists aren't sure how it works, but they think it is a combination of internal fluid friction and gyroscopic principle." When Mike came in for physics class, I beckoned him into the lab, took down the gyroscope box and handed him the paper. He read it. His eyes got big and his mouth gaped open. He looked at me, read it again. I knew exactly what he was thinking: he knew I had made up the answer, so how could I be right? But the obviously old paper showed I was right. Impossible! But true. I took the paper and gave it to the kids to pass around so they could all read it.

Father Tighe had a small mission parish. Sister Dominique, Chelle and I went with him on Saturday mornings to teach religion to the children. He didn't go with us one bright February morning, so I took my camera along. Now I knew he wouldn't have minded stopping for me to take a few ordinary pictures, but I wasn't looking for an ordinary picture. The snow-plowings were piled up over ten feet high along some roads and I wanted a picture that showed it all.

After our classes, we drove along, stopped at a likely place.

I looked through the camera. It showed snow. Big deal. "Chelle, would you climb up on top?"

"Sure."

She clambered up and crouched on her hands and knees. I looked through the camera. No. "Sister Dominique, would you stand just below her?" Her head was far below Chelle and a telephone pole stuck out of the snow, only a foot of it showing, next to Chelle. Perfect. "Smile." Click.

Before Easter, I asked Chelle to stop by after school. "Chelle, when I have my Easter Saturday religion class, I'd like to make it a celebration instead of a lecture. Do you want to join me with your group?"

"Sure."

"I'm thinking of singing and dancing. These kids are small, so it won't be anything fancy. But they could stand side by side, hands on each others' shoulders and do a few easy steps, a simplified Zorba dance."

Chelle caught my enthusiasm. "I could get Tony to come along to play his guitar for the dancing."

"Great. And they could learn that triple *Alleluia* we sing at Mass. It's short and easy."

Chelle asked, "Will you explain to them why we're singing and dancing?"

"Yes. Let's see. A short explanation, practice the singing and dancing, then do it. Sounds good."

The first to fourth graders were very solemn about it, awkward with the dancing, off-key with their singing. Poor Tony. His solo guitar-playing was sadly lacking and he knew it. I was glad Sister Dominique and Father Tighe had declined to join us with their groups because the kids were reflecting my awkwardness very well and the fewer witnesses, the better. I wanted to make a celebration of Easter; I wondered if even one of them understood what I was trying to do. Years later, I realized I couldn't lead those kids in a celebration of song and dance because my heart didn't know how to sing and dance.

The following summer, I finished up a master's degree in math, thanks again to NSF funds. The next school year, my graduated friends were replaced in the classroom by a mostly uninterested, uninteresting group of kids. I was much the same. There were a few bright spots during the year. One was that I met Leona, who quietly found a lifelong place in my heart. And I continued friendships with some of the couples I had met at the St. Edward's weekends. Mary Ellen and Don and especially Gen and Mike were good friends who helped me through a rough time. I had reluctantly come to the conclusion that I would leave the convent. With the help of my friends, I had grown enough to see that I had a lot of growing left to do, and that I could not do it as a nun.

13

Maureen
Minneapolis, 1970

I left the convent and found a job. Two months later, I went to a Volkswagen dealership. Big, friendly Bill sent me off on a test drive, which didn't take long, because I knew exactly what I wanted, and the brand new, bright red, inexpensive "Bug" was it.

Then he asked, "How will you finance the car?"

"I don't know." I had thought I'd just make payments to the dealership.

"Do you have any references for getting a loan?"

"Not really. I never had any money until the last two months." That didn't sound creditworthy. "You see, I was a nun until June." He was surprised. "But I have a contract to teach here in Minneapolis." I took it out of my purse and gave it to him.

He looked it over. "You were a Catholic nun?"

"Yes."

He looked thoughtful. "I have eight kids in Catholic schools. The nuns do a terrific job with them."

Uh oh, I thought, he probably thinks I'm terrible for leaving.

Bill looked at me. "I'll bet you were great with them, too. All right, here's what you do. First, we'll fill out the papers." Then he told me how to get a loan, using his name for reference, and where to get insurance.

Two weeks later, after a big grinning "Thanks" for Bill, I drove out of the dealership in my own new car.   A small waterfall spurted out of my eyes. I had no idea where I wanted to go, but I could get there on my own power and at my own speed.

December 9, 1970

Dear Alice,

Merry Christmas and all that good stuff! Have to get my Christmas letters out early because I'm heading to Puerto Rico; that's where Mom and Dad are now and all of us kids are all going there for Christmas. Should be fun.

It's absolutely delicious to plan a trip like that without asking permission from Mother Superior. You wouldn't believe all the botheration I went through to go to Bangkok, when Mom and Dad were there. It was a fantastic trip, though, and it definitely whet my appetite for more traveling.

Why did I leave the convent? Because I was spiritually, physically, socially and sexually constipated, repressed, suppressed, freeze-dried, dried-up and disconnected. When I entered, I expected nice neat little boxes, where everything was right and good and simple, so I would go to heaven when I died. But after some years, I knew my life as a nun was not a nice neat little box and the box didn't fit anyway. Then Pope John came along and said life wasn't supposed to be a box and finally I realized that I needed to leave so I could grow out of my box and find out who I should be.

So I got a job as a live-in housekeeper for the summer. My master's degree in math is nice, but I needed to feed myself until fall. In August, I bought a new red Volkswagen for less than two thousand dollars and already I have it nearly paid for.

Teaching in Minneapolis has been hard, but I'm getting into it now. The kids here are not over eager to learn, so I have to keep it lively or I've got trouble. I really don't like the discipline part of teaching.

As soon as I got my first paycheck, I went out and bought clothes. What fun! My favorite outfit is a green, red-orange and yellow plaid pair of slacks, matching vest and red-orange sweater. I wore it to school. After school, we had a faculty meeting, so all forty teachers and the principal saw my new clothes. The next day, Mrs. Johnson asked me if anyone said anything about my outfit. I told her I'd had several compliments, even one from the assistant principal. Then she explained that women teachers weren't allowed to wear slacks to school. I was the first to wear slacks there. I had undermined the dress code without even realizing it and having the fun of rebellion! Since then, quite a few women have started to wear slacks.

I share an apartment with another ex-nun. We aren't getting along too well probably because I have a boyfriend and she doesn't.

I've been to Milwaukee to see my brother, Peter, over several weekends and at Thanksgiving.

The U. of Minn. has an excellent series of dance programs, ballet, folk dance, etc. I've joined a singles club for alumni of Catholic colleges; good enough people, but not overly exciting; I enjoy their twice a month volleyball games. I also bowl in a teachers' league; I average 152, not bad for being out of practice for all those years.

I suppose you think I should tell you about my boyfriend. He's okay, but nothing to write home about. If we go bowling and I get 200, that's an exciting date.

When school is out next summer, I think I'll pack up my VW and go see everybody, friends, relatives, in-laws, outlaws. I'll drive south to New Mexico, east to Georgia, north to New York and back to Minneapolis, stopping here and there for a few days to visit all the people I haven't seen in a while.

I would love to visit you. I have enjoyed our letters, but I want to meet your hubby (I remember one of your first letters, bemoaning your "old-maid" status) and your adorable little girl; there is so much to talk about, old times, now times and everything in between. I could get to El Paso to see you about the middle of June. Will that work? Later, I'll settle my itinerary and let you know more exactly.

Well, I hope you, your hubby, and your daughter are all fine and that you have a wonderful Christmas and New Year.

See you soon, I hope,
Rena

A salesman showed me around the undeveloped recreational development; "There will be a golf course and ... and half-acre lots for sale, but half the land will remain as it is." Which was Wisconsin woods.

"Show me a cheap lot." When we arrived, I said, "Please disappear for fifteen minutes." I'm sure he thought I was weird, but he left.

I walked through crunchy leaves to a small clearing fifty feet from the road and sat down. *Aaahhh.* When I heard his car, I walked to the road. Grinning, I said, "I'll take it." I looked at the boundary markers. "On second thought, I'll take two lots." So my neighbors wouldn't crowd me.

After teaching physical science for two and a half years, the school board decided I wasn't qualified for the job. I went on a year's leave of absence. I set up a trailer tent on my acre of Wisconsin woods and commuted to school that summer and fall to get certified. After classes ended, I packed my Bug and headed to Florida to stay with Mom and Dad during the worst of the winter.

Christmas was uncomfortable — whenever my brothers and sister and I got together, sparks would fly. I thought that we all wanted attention too badly to get along with each other. After they left, I decided to drive to a nearby state park. Mom, Dad and I went to Epcot Center; Dad and I went to Busch Gardens. Which was all very nice and passed the time pleasantly, but most interestingly, Mom and I didn't fight. Maybe I knew if I wanted to stay there a while, I'd better keep my prickliness well under cover.

Sometimes Mom and I stayed up way late, playing cards or just talking. One night, she told me about my birth and how Frank screamed the whole time she was in labor. She said, "He didn't stop crying until you were born. And you started fighting me the day you were born."

"But, Mom, part of the reason I became a nun was to please you. Yet you never said you were happy about it or proud of me or anything."

"Well, my mother never complimented me either. It just wasn't her way and it isn't my way. Besides, I never thought you'd last very long." Mom looked sad. We talked a little longer and then went to bed.

Another night, Mom and I looked through old pictures of hers. She talked about picnics on the bluffs, her drunken father, how hard her mother worked. She told me she grew up always feeling like an outsider, like someone from the wrong side of the tracks. When she talked about her friends and family, except for her father, it sounded like she was well-loved and well-liked, but she seemed to cling to the negative, so the love couldn't really touch her.

I returned eagerly to my woods in mid-February, away from the screaming city. I shoveled snow up around the sides of my trailer-tent, threw a couple of packing blankets over the top, covered the floor with some carpet scraps and settled in to *be*. With my penny-pinching ways, money was no problem. I had no one to answer to, no one I owed money to. I walked in the woods, admired the deer, befriended a skunk. I always threw my garbage out the door of my trailer tent, so little creatures wouldn't be coming in after it. The garbage attracted a grouse and her chicks, chipmunks and a skunk. Skunk showed his appreciation by never spraying me, not even when I came rushing out of my trailer tent and almost stepped on him.

I wrote poems, like:

At the edge of the woods
Graceful fragile ferns form a carpet
For the eye to walk on
And the wind whispers, "Follow me in."

I listened. I listened to the sounds of the trees, the wind, the birds. In the spring, the frogs' croaking sounded glorious! I had made it through the winter, which included a 30-degrees-below-zero weekend in March. Those two nights I had kept my electric blanket on inside my sleeping bag all night and visited people in real houses all day. I did a little baby-sitting, a little tutoring, but mostly, I just listened. I listened to my innermost self. Self said: "Here is where you belong." I decided to quit waiting for Mr. Right to come along and make a life for me. I would make my own life, here in the woods. First, I needed a job, then a home. I heard a song on the breeze:

Oh, give me a home
Where the deer and bear roam,
Where the skunks and the butterflies play,
Where the wind in the trees,
Sets my spirit at ease
And my heart is not cloudy all day.

I applied for teaching jobs in the area, and when I found one, I visited friends' homes and measured, figured, drew up a floor plan, took it to builder-man, who gave me an estimate, which I took to the bank and applied for a loan.

Gus, my builder-man, built my log cabin, with a cement basement. In order to have a drive-in basement garage, the basement had to stick way out of the ground, so from the outside, it looked a little weird, but inside, my log cabin was me, sparsely furnished, unfinished, becoming.

The small bedroom and walk-in closet sat in the southeast corner; on the west side was my living room and kitchen, separated only by a set of cupboards and the sink; the laundry, coat closet and basement stairs took up the northeast corner; the bathroom was in the middle, so that I could take a bath without cold winds rattling through a window.

I sprayed clear sealer on the interior walls, stained kitchen cupboards dark brown, bought a new, brown, red-orange and white plaid hide-a-bed sofa and a used refrigerator and stove. I had a card table and a TV from my folks.

During the summer, I had worked in a factory and, with permission, had saved a lot of throwaway wood, pieces with knots or wrongly cut. The foreman set up a machine on a Saturday, so I could feed them in and get them tongue-and-grooved. A neighbor nailed them down to make my living-room floor. I took other wood scraps and made a breakfast nook and coffee table, butcher block style. I used clear sealer on the floor, breakfast nook and coffee table.

I thought I was doing all this because of money. My teacher's salary was half what it would have been if I had stayed in Minneapolis and my mortgage payments seemed huge. I was scared of being so deeply in debt and didn't want other bills, too. But there was also a do-it-yourself handy-woman aspect of myself that wanted out. I did a lot of work, saw every flaw, and did all those projects anyway. I even started changing the oil in my car. I amazed myself.

During a summer break from these projects, I took another look at my woods and wrote:

LIFE'S FLIES
Noisy and germy, small houseflies annoy
Big ugly horseflies are no fun, no joy.
Butterfly's wing is a beautiful sight;
Dragonflies dart on their rainbow-gay flight.
Menacing deerflies load spite in their bites;
Fireflies make magic on summery nights.
Life will not fail to give beauty and pain;
Which will I cherish, from which will I gain?

I finally decided to tackle the kitchen floor. I bought six-inch-square tongue-and-grooved wood tiles to glue down. My neighbor Mike put down underlayment for me. Gus' wife and kids, Nancy, Doug and Annie, helped me glue some of the tiles. Then Mike told his friend Roy he'd better help me. And that's how I met my husband, after I had decided to give up on Mr. Right and make my own life.

Roy was over six feet tall, his face was aged beyond his forty-five years. He was an alcoholic, sober for three years, the oldest of ten children, born of an alcoholic father and a nagging mother, who currently ruled the roost by virtue of her poor health. Roy had been accepted in a program to get six months of training to become a counselor for alcoholics. The program started the next summer.

When he told me about his drinking himself out of three marriages, about his long struggle to sober up, about Skid

Row, I heard a child talking about his refusal to grow up and I heard a man starting to take charge of his life. I accepted the man and fought the child. I guess he accepted the woman in me and fought the child, too — I hadn't had much practice in the give and take necessary in a close relationship.

This big, gentle man slipped quietly into my life, fitting in like water in a sink full of dishes. I loved him and that was great; he loved me and I found that incredible. An ex-nun and an ex-bum: what a combination! We were two lonely people who looked at each other and saw more of ourselves, our better selves.

Roy's proposal came only three weeks after we met. We were cuddled up together in bed, in the dark, and he nonchalantly said, "I suppose we should get married."

I thought for a minute and calmly asked, "Do you want to get married?"

"Well, yeah, I guess so."

"Do you want to marry *me?*"

Finally his voice admitted some feeling, "Yes, I really do. I love you very much."

My answer was shaky, too, "I love you, Roy. Let's get married. We talked all night, then made love again, reaching out to the Other in each other, the Other beyond ourselves.

Roy wasn't very busy with his TV antenna business, so he spaded up a ten-by-fifteen-foot garden. We planted gladiolus along the back, potatoes, peas, onions and beans in the middle, low-growing moss roses in front. Except for the bugs, I liked working in the garden, so I didn't mind that once he started the garden, Roy abandoned it.

He had two dogs, Boots and Kachit. When Kachit was killed by a car, Roy buried the dog, then sat on a downed tree. I went out and found him crying there. I put my hand on his shoulder; he looked up, just for a second, and I saw his pain. I stayed for a few minutes, then left him to finish his grieving.

Boots was terribly lonesome, so one day, Roy brought home a springer spaniel puppy. I named her Tinker and Boots quickly house-trained her. Then Roy left for counselor training and

Tinker became mine. I had a dog when I was a kid, but I neglected it so badly, Dad gave it away. I took good care of my darling little Tinker and every bit of love I gave her, she gave me back doubled.

A few months into their program, each counselor-in-training asked an "important other" to join him or her for a few days at the treatment center, so she or he could better understand their training. Good idea.

Roy was working under John, a big lovable counselor. The first time I went down, I mostly listened to the eight men and women, old and young, in John's and Roy's group sessions, and in conversations at meals and in between times. The atmosphere at the treatment center was tense with patients' attempts to work on their problems, which the center defined as ten percent alcohol abuse and ninety percent emotional immaturity; the ninety percent led directly to the ten percent.

With Roy talking every weekend about drug and alcohol abuse, I had come to realize that Mom was an alcoholic. And Peter? I called him. "Peter, I'm worried about you using marijuana and cocaine." I had seen him use both.

"Well, I'm just fine." He sounded very cold. "But if you really want to worry, here's something to chew on. I tried smack last week." He waited for my reaction.

I didn't know what to say. "What's smack?"

"You know, the big H, heroin. It was pretty good stuff."

Afterward, I wasn't sure whether he really meant it or if he was just pushing my buttons, or, most likely, both.

At the treatment center, Roy was too busy to talk. At the first group session, John said, "Rena, you look like something is bothering you."

I didn't want to parade my woes in front of patients, but John's voice was kind. I blurted out, "I talked to my brother last night and he's not just doing marijuana and cocaine anymore; he tried heroin. I want to help him, but there's nothing I can do and Roy's too busy to talk to me. I know this group isn't here to solve my problems, but I feel all alone with this. And I'm jealous because all of these people are getting help and my brother isn't." Then I cried a little.

Don, one of the patients, said, "You could try a confrontation. Get together all the family and friends who know about his drug abuse and tell him how badly he's behaving. That's what brought me here."

"That sounds like a good idea, except that our family is spread out all over the U. S. and none of them knows about it except me. His only friends are users, too." They couldn't solve my problems, but it seemed like they cared, so I felt a little better.

John said, "After lunch, Rena, why don't you and Roy come to my office and we'll talk more?"

There, John gave me some brochures about how to handle an alcohol or drug abuser, and suggested Roy and I stay there and talk after he left.

So I told Roy how close Peter and I had been and how all the things I had learned at the treatment center made me very frightened for Peter and I hated losing him to drugs. "And I feel so awkward here. I didn't mean to blab about me in the group session. And then I dropped my tray in the cafeteria. I don't want to mess things up for you. I'm proud of you for getting this training so you can help others." I looked at him for a while. "Thanks for listening, counselor. I don't feel so alone now." I smiled weakly.

Then Roy laughed. "You think you feel awkward? The first week I was here, I broke a tray of dishes, too. And I made a pot of coffee for our group, ahead of time, because we all drink a lot while we're talking. Only I forgot to put in the grounds." I laughed, too. "And the next time, I put in grounds, but I forgot to plug it in." Then he became serious. "Look, I don't know if this confrontation thing would work, but you could at least tell your family what is going on."

"Hah! I know just how well my alcoholic mom would receive the news of her favorite son's drug abuse, coming from her least favorite daughter."

"I just know that if my kids were using, I'd want to know about it."

That evening, we went for a ride. I told Roy, "Your comments in the afternoon session were really right to the point.

You're going to be a good counselor!"

He muttered, "When I'm right with you, I'm right with myself and then it's easy." He found a secluded parking place and proceeded to show me how right we were together.

Back home, I called Mom. Frigid denial. I called Ellen. She understood but didn't see that we could do anything. Joe agreed with Ellen.

That weekend, when Roy came home, I told him about the calls I had made. I said I thought I had alienated my whole family. He was sympathetic.

"When my Dad came home drunk, Ma always gave him tomato soup. She wouldn't fix him anything else. He hated tomato soup. She even had him sent to get dried out, thirty days worth, a couple of times. But Dad still goes on his binges, although not as often as he used to. Alcohol and drug abuse tears families apart no matter what they do about it. At least now your family knows about it, so they're not as likely to enable him, make his abuse easier."

I thought about this and then I wanted to get away from it. "Let's go for a walk."

"Okay."

The sprinkler was watering our little garden; the evening sun kissed the water into a rainbow. We stopped to admire it and then we spotted a hummingbird showering in the rainbow. We stood silently, letting the beauty refresh our souls.

As for Peter, he cut himself off from the family for years, because I had "betrayed" him. Later, when he did come to family gatherings, he was aloof. He wasn't obviously using drugs, but who knew for sure?

When Roy moved into my house, it evolved slowly into our home. I was reluctant to change anything, but knew it had to be. After a few months here, Roy complained that he wanted to shower, not take a bath.

"Well, you can put a shower in the basement. The pipes and everything are there." He stomped downstairs (that wasn't the response he wanted) and looked at the pipes. He kept complaining, expecting me to take care of it, and I kept repeating my answer. After a while, he and our neighbor put in a shower.

Roy had brought his recliner, floor lamp and several end tables. He looked so comfortable in his recliner that I bought one for myself, rusty red-orange. He thought the house looked like a barn without curtains, so I found beige curtains, which wouldn't distract from the log walls, and a few rusty red-orange throw rugs. I put up some pictures and knickknacks and he hung a tapestry he'd bought at a county fair. It looked homey.

But the biggest change was the heat. I always kept the electric heat as low as I could stand it, because it was so expensive. He thought we should burn wood. "Fine, but where does the wood come from?"

"I'll cut it. I can get a permit to take wood from county land."

I loved Roy and I knew he loved me, but I still wasn't secure about our future. "Will you be around long enough to make it worthwhile?"

He was surprised by my question. When he finally answered, he was calm and sure. "Yes."

So we went out to the county land where he cut and I loaded the wood into a borrowed pickup. All the bending and lifting bothered my back, so I took it slow and then he'd start nagging me. After a few days of this, I refused to go with him anymore. "I pay the mortgage and other bills; you can provide the heat. Besides, after teaching all week, I like to sleep late on weekends." He wasn't very happy about that, but I was firm; he did it by himself.

At Thanksgiving, his daughter Dorothy, her husband Jim, and their daughter Jennifer came to visit for a few days. I got along fine with his family, in spite of Roy's introduction: he had called Dorothy from my house, "Is it all right if I bring Rena with me when I come for Christmas?"

Dorothy must have asked, "Who's Rena?"

"Oh, she teaches go-go dancing at the prune factory." He liked teasing me about eating prunes (or anything else) but that was his wildest line yet.

"Roooy!" I protested.

"No, she's a school teacher; she lives near me."

His family helped us bring the wood into the basement. With all of us carrying, we brought a lot of wood in quickly. Jennifer was amazing: she scuttled back and forth faster and longer than any of us and she was only ten. I really appreciated their help — if they hadn't pitched in, I probably would have ended up doing it all by myself.

Several times Roy had asked other counselors-in-training here for the weekend, which was supposed to be, I thought, our time just for each other. So my appreciation for their help warred with my frustration over his inattention. And there was another problem. Jim had gone deer-hunting and killed a buck. Roy asked if I would park my car outside so Jim could keep the deer in the garage, where it would be safe from animals. I agreed, but kept forgetting; every time I opened the door to the garage, there was the carcass. To me, it seemed ugly to murder one of those beautiful creatures. It wasn't that they needed the meat; he just liked hunting.

With these things fretting me, I got peevish and snapped at Roy and his family often the last two days they were here. But before they left, I explained to Dorothy and apologized. After they were gone, I told Roy what was bothering me.

Several days later, I realized an amazing change had taken place while his family was here. He had told me that he always teased Jennifer, sometimes until she cried. I had told him that was awful and he'd better not do it around me. He didn't tease her! A picture came into my mind: Roy and Jennifer sitting next to each other on the couch. Jennifer's face glowed as she talked to her *listening* Grandpa. "We got a little puppy. We call him Sammy. He's a beagle and he's only this big." She held her hands about a foot apart. Roy's eyes studied her, saw her, smiled at what he saw. He had heard me and done what was right. I was humbled and proud, but I didn't think I wanted that much power over him.

It was hard to stick to the speed limit, I was so eager to be with Roy. It was a two hundred and fifty mile drive. It would be at least nine o'clock before I got there, even though I left right after school. I distracted myself by thinking up a love poem for Roy.

I didn't like him working so far away from home — it was bad enough when he was a hundred miles away getting his counselor training. But he got the job offer: counselor at a halfway house for alcoholics. When he told me about it, I could see he really wanted the job. If I had said, "No, I'll be miserable with you so far away," he probably would have refused the job. Then he'd be unhappy and I'd feel lousy anyway. Better one of us should be miserable than both of us.

We had planned to leave the halfway house right away, drive a hundred miles to his brother's house where we would stay overnight, then drive fifty miles more to be with his folks for Christmas. But when I arrived at the halfway house, he showed me around and introduced me to everyone. Then he took me to his room to exchange Christmas presents.

"Roy, go away for five minutes, please."

He looked puzzled. "Please." I wrote down my poem; it nicely complimented the practical present of a shirt — his TV antenna fixing coveralls didn't quite suit his counseling job. I put the poem on top of his present.

"Okay, Roy, you can come in now." We were both grinning. "You first," I said. He read the poem. He read it again. He didn't say anything, but he held out his arms and gave me a good warm hug. He liked the shirt, too.

I read his card. All excited, I ripped open the box. A fake fur jacket. It was pretty. It was the last thing in the world I wanted. Oh, well. I pretended to like it.

We finally headed out. I followed his car in mine. After an hour, I signaled for him to pull over. "Roy, I'm terribly tired. We'd better stop in the next town so I can get a cup of coffee. And my legs are killing me. Whoever owned this VW before me must have weighed three hundred pounds. The center of the seat is caved in so the rim is cutting into my legs."

We left the freeway at the next town, but it was after midnight and everything was closed. "Do you think you can make it? It's only about fifty more miles."

"I guess so."

Back on the freeway, I lost him or he lost me, but I thought I knew where to go. I took an exit and realized I was on the wrong road, so I pulled over to try to figure it out. I just sat there; my mind was blank. A police car pulled up behind me. "Is anything wrong?"

He sounded so nice, I started crying. At last I calmed down enough to blubber, "I was following my husband and I lost him and I know where to go, but I don't where I am and I'm so tired I can't see straight so if I don't get some coffee, I'll never make it."

He explained how to get to an all-night restaurant, a mile away. I must have looked pretty blank, because he offered to lead me.

"Thank you, sir."

After a cup of coffee, I called Roy's brother and told him what happened. Roy had missed me and called him, too, frantic with worry. I told Jerry I would leave in another fifteen minutes and wrote down his directions.

I found Jerry's place, only to find out we couldn't stay there because all they had was one couch extra. So I got in Roy's car with him. He started in on me, "What the hell happened to you?"

"Roy, I got up at six thirty this morning, taught all day, drove two hundred fifty miles to see you. Then you gave me that stupid coat. I don't want a fur coat. Even if I did, where did you get the money for it when you can't even pay your bills? Just yesterday, I got another call from somebody who wants the money you owe him. And that damned car! I wanted a new car, but you insisted I get a used one and the seat digs into my legs so they hurt something awful. And how am I supposed to be nice to your family when I'm so mad at you? I don't want to be around you or your family!"

He pulled over. "What do you want to do?"

"Take me back to Jerry's. I'll sleep on their couch and go home tomorrow."

He was mad and he was hurt, but I was madder and a whole lot more tired. Sometimes we really oiled each other's vinegar!

He stopped the car at Jerry's and as soon as I got my bag out and slammed the door, he took off. I felt really dumb, knocking on their door at three in the morning. Jerry and

Jeanette both came to the door.

"Rena, what's wrong?"

So I blabbed out my woes. Jerry sympathized with Roy. "I went with him to shop for that jacket. He spent hours and went into a dozen stores before he found the right one. He was really happy he found you such a nice present."

"It's not just the money thing. That fur coat isn't me. It's who he wants me to be." Still, I was impressed that he had gone to so much trouble for me.

Late the next morning, Roy called. He sounded so miserable, I couldn't stay mad. I went to be with him and his folks and we had a nice Christmas. After that, I always told him what I wanted for presents.

December 18, 1978

Dear Aunt Caroline,

Merry Christmas and Happy New Year to you and yours.

Here's your copy of the family stories. I have a study hall this year, due to the obnoxious principal, instead of teaching physics, the one course I enjoyed teaching here. But I've been using the time to organize the stories you have told me. As I reread my notes, I enjoyed again our times together. I wish you lived next door to me so I could collect volumes of these tales instead of pages. Now that I'm married, I probably won't be coming to see you as often. I am curious about Dad's father's relatives. They seem to have disappeared.

My sometimes very dear husband, Roy, was working on a grant program of placing alcoholics into foster homes to see if that might help them stay sober. Now he's starting up a group home for alcoholics, funded by his employers, the county agency that deals with alcoholics, mentally ill and so forth. He should be getting residents after the first of the year.

I'm still not used to being married. It seemed like almost as soon as we got married, Roy became preoccupied. When I first met him, two years ago, he was very attentive. Six months later, he went into training to become a counselor. For six months, he was home only for weekends. Then he got a job as a counselor, two hundred and fifty miles from here, and again he was only home for weekends. When he found a job here, I thought, "Aha! Now we'll have time together!" Ha!

It has been very hard for me to get used to sharing so much with another person and yet feeling so separate sometimes. I finally tried talking to him about how alone I felt; we ended up having a terrible fight.

I went to visit a friend of mine and I talked and I cried; she had been married many years, so she knew exactly how I felt. When I calmed down, I asked her to tell me how to make scalloped potatoes, because Roy likes them.

When I got home, I made scalloped potatoes. And a few days later, I noticed how hard Roy was trying to please me. I have decided that love must be very strong indeed, for two people to put up with so much and still keep trying.

More pleasant thoughts. Yesterday in my general science classes, I had contests; the kids, in groups of four or five, wrote down every gadget they could think of that runs on electricity. Every one of the hundred or so that they listed came to use during your lifetime! Which set me to thinking. Men invented cars and airplanes, landed on the moon and wiped out smallpox during your life. You have lived through the administrations of seventeen presidents. The changes you have seen — it boggles my mind! Is it true that "The more things change, the more they stay the same?"

Have a nice Christmas.

                                                    Love
                                                    Maureen

Roy always gave me nice cards for Christmas and birthdays, but this one came with a perfect present, without any suggestions from me; he gave me a gift certificate for four rose bushes. When he wanted to, Roy could please me perfectly, but perfect presents came so seldom in my life that I'd get all flustered and I'd hardly be able to say thanks.

FOR MY WIFE WITH ALL MY LOVE
My every dream begins and ends
With loving thoughts of you.
And you're the most important part
Of everything I do.

You're on my mind, you're in my heart
Each moment of the day.
And no one else in all the world
Could make me feel this way.
HAPPY ANNIVERSARY.
Love
Roy

I growled to myself. I hated housecleaning. Especially when I was cleaning up after Roy. I didn't figure there was that much more dirt with two of us, but he was so *messy*! He just threw his stuff anywhere. Before he hung up his trousers, he emptied the pockets onto the dresser. So there was an ever-growing pile of pennies, books of matches, pens and dirty handkerchiefs. He always threw his coat on a chair. There were dirty socks on the floor, a dirty shirt on his chair. Before Roy moved in, I would clean house in an hour. Getting his things in order so the house looked neat as well as clean added at least two hours to the job and added a *lot* of aggravation. I hated cleaning up after him! Not that I cleaned house that often. But when it got so bad I couldn't ignore it any longer, and when I ran out of excuses, I'd wash dishes, do laundry, dust and mop and put everything away and feel very satisfied, for half an hour or so, when the house would start looking rumpled again.

Roy was usually here Saturdays, but one of the guys at his group home got sick and Roy had to go see to him. He had quite a bunch there, mostly elderly alcoholic men. Roy said that they all had considerable brain damage from alcohol, so if you added up all their IQs, you might get up to a hundred.

I finished cleaning about five o'clock and I didn't feel like fixing supper. So I sat down to read a book. Roy came home at six. I was still mad at him because I had had to clean up after him.

"Hi. Looks like you've been busy," he commented.

"You know, Roy, I hate picking up after you. There's no reason in the world you can't put your own dirty clothes in a the hamper or hang up your own coat or put your pennies in a drawer instead of all over the dresser."

"Look, I'm in no mood to argue tonight. Edgar had a stroke and I had to get him to the hospital and when I got back, Richard was drunk." He looked around the kitchen and saw no evidence of supper. "I'm going to the restaurant and eat and then I'm going to AA. There's a new group starting at the community center. They're going to have an Al-Anon group, too, for spouses of alcoholics. Do you want to go with me or not?" He was mad and so was I.

"No!"

After he went, I fixed myself some supper and thought. I decided to go to the Al-Anon meeting.

There were six women at the meeting. I listened to Susan describe trying to please her drunken husband. Angie told of bills her out-of-work husband couldn't pay. Mary said her husband was always angry when he was drunk. She looked afraid, I thought and wondered if he was violent, too. Judy just joked around as if she couldn't even begin to admit her problems.

Alice spoke up, "According to Al-Anon principles, we don't have to let our husbands make us miserable."

"That's it!" I exclaimed. "Susan, don't you see that your husband is impossible to please? You don't have to take the blame. When he complains, it hurts. But if you hold on to that, it's you hurting Susan, not him. Mary, you are so afraid of your husband. You do have a choice: you could leave him. Angie, the bills aren't getting paid. Fretting about it just makes you unhappy; what can you *do* about the bills?" I looked around at five surprised faces. I saw resentment about my oversimplified solutions to their problems. Then I laughed. "I hope you realize, it's not really you that I'm trying to convince. It's Rena I'm talking to. My husband has been sober for years, but pushing buttons is still his favorite pastime. So what I'm really doing tonight is lecturing myself. Just because he throws his coat on the sofa doesn't mean I have to get mad. I have choices: I can hang it up or leave it or throw it in the garbage. I can get mad at his sloppiness and then forget it; or I can use it for an excuse to get mad and stay mad for a month. But if I choose to stay mad for a month, my choice is about as smart as chewing on eggshells instead of spitting them out." Then we all laughed at ourselves.

At home that night, I calmly told Roy, "It was really dumb for me to get mad at you today. From now on, you can clean up after yourself or leave it; that's up to you. I won't pick up your socks or clean up the mess on the dresser or clean out the bathtub after you, unless I want a bath. If I clean out the tub before I use it, I'll leave it dirty when I finish." He was surprised. "But what is really bothering me is school. I'm tired of teaching. I talked about quitting after we got married, but you were uncertain about your job future. Then you were working two hundred fifty miles away. You wanted a job around here. You got that and now you've started your group home. Now it's my turn. I want a job I can enjoy and I'm going to get one!"

Silence. He looked thoughtful. "You like old people, like your Aunt Caroline. Why don't you start a group home for the elderly? I know how to do it so I could help you."

My turn to be surprised. It sounded like a great idea! And we could work together on it. Could I do it? Did I dare try? Could we work together and make a go of it?

Driving to volleyball, I told Myrna I was thinking about starting a group home for the elderly.

"I know just the place. It used to be a nursing home. I worked there when I was in high school, but no one is using it now. It belongs to Marion. Why don't you call her and see if she'd sell?"

I was excited, "Sounds good to me!"

Buoyed up by the real possibility that I could get out of teaching, I played very well, maybe not by the standards of kids those days, who were taught skills of setting up and serving, but in that group, we all played as best we could, skilled or not. I had been playing here and there for quite a few years and when I was good, I could hit the ball hard and right where I wanted to.

That Wednesday, there were only four on each team. The other team was serving. I was straight ahead of the server, front line. He hit it very high and it was coming down to me. "Look out!" I yelled as I leaped up, higher than high. I reached way back and then swung my arm forward, smashing into the ball with the palm of my hand, aiming it at the center of the court. As I came down, I watched the ball hitting hard, right where I had aimed it, and the four players were scattered respectfully off at the edges of the court. That felt *good!*

When I got home, I told Roy about my great spike. Then we talked quite a while about the group home. Roy was very interested and planning together increased my hopes and fed my excitement. I decided to call Marion the next day, as soon as I got home from school.

It took a while, but at last I was at Marion's old nursing home, now vacant. I unlocked the door, walked into a wide forty-foot-long hallway, painted green, with three bedrooms on each side, also painted green, mostly empty except for a few beds and dressers. Halfway down the hall, I stopped. I felt a good warmth here. The place looked ordinary enough, but it felt like a big grin spreading across my face and around to the back of my head. I wanted a place for older people to come to when it became too hard for them at home; a place, unlike a nursing home, where they could belong, not just vegetate out the rest of their lives. This was *the place*. The hall ended at the living room, also green except for one wall of stained plywood; there were a proud, sagging sofa and a few end tables. Through an open doorway, I reached the kitchen, all sterile white, except for a lot of water stains on the ceiling and some walls. Yet it felt like homemade bread. Upstairs were two small rooms, cozy pine board ceilings and walls.

A week later, I went back to meet Marion there. She would show me around and talk price. As Marion got out of her car and came toward me, her smile lit up my heart. She was very short, white-haired, plump, bent over. I felt like I was meeting someone that I'd been lonesome for all my life. She had run the nursing home here back when there weren't so many stifling regulations. Her residents made end tables, baked cookies, and generally made themselves at home. *She* was why I felt so good as soon as I walked into this home.

We set up the loans and other paperwork so we could sign the papers at the end of May. But the bank found several judgments filed against Roy, for money he owed. I was so mad at his irresponsibility, I yelled at him *but good*. He took care of the debts and *finally*, on July 2, we signed the papers. The bank insisted that Roy co-sign the loan. I was too excited to make a big stink about that.

Roy brought residents from his group home to help tear out the kitchen for remodeling. His dad came up and the two of them tore out the kitchen windows and put in new ones. They put up new ceiling tiles, patchwork patterned paneling and new linoleum. Roy hired an electrician to update the wiring and a plumber to plumb the plumbing. He knew all the state specifications that had to be met to start a group home and he helped me get the place ready for inspection.

Some days I worked by myself, painting bedrooms. My dog Tinker would lay down in the doorway and watch me. Except for chewing on a bone, there was nothing Tinker liked better than to be with me, especially if it meant riding in my car. Then she'd lie on the floor behind the driver's seat so I could reach back and pet her as I drove.

I picked out all the materials myself, because I didn't like Roy's decorating sense. At his group home, there were red velvet drapes, left over from funeral parlor days. To go with those drapes, he chose country style wooden chairs and sofa with brown and beige plaid cushions. He painted all the metal cupboards an awful shade of purple.

After Labor Day, we had an open house at the Haven, inviting social workers and doctors, friends and neighbors, and anyone who might know of possible residents. It was all very exciting to work closely and well with Roy as I started a new chapter in my life. I was amazed that he helped so much, but when I tried to tell him how I felt, he got all embarrassed and changed the subject.

One day, Roy brought me a ledger and showed me how to record the income and expenses of my group home, for tax purposes. I liked doing my own bookkeeping because then I knew where I was financially so I could budget accordingly.

Then Roy decided there should be a new furnace and new steps and sidewalk for the kitchen entrance. He was right, they needed replacing, *but* ... The borrowed money was nearly spent and there were no residents yet. I was very edgy about money. I would continue teaching, but my salary had to pay on the loans and the bills at home. I felt that Roy would keep on spending money indefinitely, as long as it wasn't his.

I blew up. "You're just spending money like crazy and you have never been responsible about paying debts, so paying them is up to me and I won't let you get me into a hole I can't get out of!" We argued. I ended my say with, "I hate you for getting me into this!"

After that argument, I was angry for days. When I calmed down, I looked carefully at the money situation. Roy had said the used, wood and fuel-oil furnace he'd found would cost eight hundred dollars, the sidewalk one hundred dollars.

"Roy, you can go ahead on the furnace and the sidewalk. That leaves very little money for unexpected needs and I'm very uncomfortable about that. But if you want to spend more than that, you'll have to use your own money." He looked relieved that I had given in. "And I'm sorry I blamed you for getting me into this. It was your idea, but I chose to go ahead with it. You have no sense about money." I smiled to soften my bluntness. "But other than that, you have been a great help, and I do appreciate all you've done." Then we hugged.

In November, a hospital social worker called, looking for a place for Bob, who was forty-two and had muscular dystrophy. Bob lived alone and wasn't taking care of himself so he was frequently in the hospital. He was thin, homely-cute, seemed like a not-much-of-anything.

Sometimes Bob would go with Roy to his group home, where he'd sit in a corner, not speaking to anyone all day. Sometimes he'd stay at the Haven and sleep all day. Other days, he'd surprise me when I got there after a day of teaching, by telling me he'd washed all the windows or dusted all the furniture and paneling.

Before long, Bob was talking freely to me about his deceased parents, his dogs, farm life, the nurses at the hospital, brothers and sisters. But he never had much to say to Roy.

On one of Bob's monthly visits to the doctor, I decided

we had time to stop at the hospital next door so he could say hello to his nurse friends. I ignored his lack of enthusiasm. At the nurses' desk, I said, "Look who's here to say 'Hi!'" Bob stared mutely at the floor. I had very stupidly exposed his secret: not only was his admiration for these women unspoken, he couldn't even greet them, he was so shy!

I knew he had a huge crush on me, so I started calling him my favorite adopted brother. He liked that.

By summer, I had seven residents, thanks to Roy, and I decided to get them to do the cooking. Four sets of manager-cooks had come and gone and I really didn't want to bother with any more. Although not all the men were over sixty-five, we had arranged for them to eat lunch at the senior citizens' center. Jim fixed breakfast, so all we needed was a supper cook or cooks. Three men volunteered to try, with me assisting, to cook a meal of their choice. Bob cooked liver and onions and it was a great success. One comment was, "It's much better than the liver and onions we had for lunch!" That they could take seconds and thirds when they'd had liver for lunch amazed me.

Bob loved all the praise and he loved to work with me. He evolved into being the supper cook. He made a few mistakes, like using curry powder instead of chili powder in the chili. Since no one else wanted to cook, they cheered the good results and kept unpleasant comments mostly to themselves.

The following winter, Roy came in after a frustrating day at work and asked Bob, "What's for supper?"

Painfully shy, yet proud of his work, Bob replied, "Chicken zucchini."

"Chicken zucchini!" my sometimes terribly tactless husband bellowed, "I hate the goddamned stuff!"

Before I could rescue him, Bob swallowed his hurt and replied with great dignity, "Then don't eat the goddamned stuff."

Roy stared, astonished at this new human being, then sat down and ate two helpings.

Bob liked cooking, but he loved baking, especially when company asked him for his molasses cookie recipe or his secret for such good pie crust. I told him he baked good things because he put so much love into them. As the other residents and I came to depend on him to satisfy our sweet teeth, he acquired considerable status.

In the first years Bob was there, he only fell occasionally, as he helped with nearly everything. Joe and Tom were stronger, so they would spread manure on the garden, but Bob would help with planting and weeding.

On our first day of planting, I always had a special ritual: I took off my shoes and wiggled my toes in the good dirt, grinning as I made my connection with Mother Earth. The guys probably thought I was nuts, but that was all right. They were cutting up potatoes while my feet called forth a blessing for our garden. When they had quite a few cut, Bob continued cutting as he sat on a stump. Tom and Joe spaded aside the dirt; John and I dropped potatoes in the holes. When the potatoes were in, we planted onion sets, lettuce and peas. Working on his hands and knees, Bob planted the peas, while I handled the tiny lettuce seeds and the others pushed onion sets into the soft ground, following the lines of string across the garden.

The first years, Art did most of the weeding, but sometimes our whole gang went down and worked the garden over. Bob and I weeded on our hands and knees, up close to the rows, while Joe, Tom and John hoed the rest. What a sight we were, four men and I, men who were alcoholics or mentally ill or retarded, hoeing and pulling weeds in a one-hundred-foot-long row of young onions or lettuce or radishes. Thanks to the manure, lime and ashes we added to the soil, we always had a splendid crop of vegetables and weeds, and how we loved eating the fruits, no, the vegetables of our labor, especially corn on the cob and tomatoes.

I was terrified! In the fall of 1981, Roy had a small growth in his lung, probably cancerous. The doctor said they would have to take his whole lung out because it was such a mess on account of his smoking. When he breathed, half the air went into the rotten lung and never went out into his body. With only the "good" lung left, all the air he breathed would be circulated, at least as much as that lung could work it.

Roy wanted to get things in order before the surgery. I wanted him to get it over with, right now! It was his body. He waited.

His daughter and I saw Roy off to surgery. In the waiting room, I stared at page one in my book. I paced. I tried to talk to Dorothy. If the clock hands had gone any slower, they would have been going backwards! Four hours and six minutes later, the doctor came out and told us, "We got it all; he'll be fine. He's in post-op now, where we'll watch him closely for a few hours; then you can see him."

I was crying my relief. After I calmed down, Dorothy asked if I wanted to get something to eat. So we went.

The doctor's optimism hadn't prepared me for what I saw. Roy was very pale, his breathing labored, oxygen tube up his nose, IV hooked into his hand. He looked just about dead. What had they done to my Roy? I could have cried, but then he looked at me. I pulled myself together. "Hi, Roy," I said quietly. "How are you doing?" I went over to the bed and took his free hand. "I'm going to stay here until they kick me out. If you want anything, just let me know."

"Okay." His voice was so weak, I could hardly hear him.

"Do you want something now? A drink of water? Are your pillows okay?"

"Okay." Roy closed his eyes, so I sat down to stare at page one in my book some more. Then Dorothy came in; she had been phoning her husband. When she saw her dad, she looked like I felt. "Dad, you look like hell!" He gave a twitch of a smile. "I have to go now so I can get to work tomorrow. The doctor said you'd be all right. But if you need me, just call and I'll come right back."

I went out to the hall with her. "I'm glad you were here so I didn't have to be alone." We hugged and she left.

The next two days, I sat by his bed, giving him water, helping him eat. The nurse said he needed to cough up as much as possible, to prevent fluid from settling in his lung and setting him up for pneumonia. To make it easier for him, I was to hold a pillow to his chest and another to his back while he coughed. At first, I had to help him sit whenever he needed to cough. His puny coughing hurt him terribly, even though he was getting morphine for the pain. I had never known that somebody's pain and weakness could hurt me so much! His pain slashed and shredded me until my heart wailed like a banshee. I waited on him and that was fine, but what I really wanted to do was wave a magic wand and make him all better. I felt so helpless against his suffering.

They started him walking on Sunday, so I figured he'd be okay. I went home, tried to unload on Carol and Bruce, but the burden was too huge for relief.

When I brought Roy home, he was still in a lot of pain. He announced he was going to quit smoking, so for a month, I went to the basement to smoke when he was home. Then I found an ashtray in the bathroom with a cigarette butt in it. When I confronted him about it, he grinned. "I just can't quit."

"All this time, I've been going out of my way not to smoke around you and you've been sneaking them!"

"Well, at least when I was smoking on the sly, I was smoking less." He was still grinning, trying to convince himself that this was just another game. He was caught with his hand in the cookie jar.

I flinched — I knew better. But before I could say anything, his face darkened. He knew. I wanted to cry. "I really wish you wouldn't smoke, but I know I can't make you quit."

He had less pain over the next months, except when it was humid or he overdid it. Slowly he regained some strength.

The summer of 1982 was a good one at the Haven. Thanks to Roy, there were twelve residents. Leonard was fixing breakfasts. They still had lunch at the senior center, and Bob and I fixed suppers. Dan did the laundry. Tom, Dan and John cleaned, somewhat haphazardly. If we were expecting company, or if it was looking too dirty, I would organize a good cleaning. The ones without other jobs did dishes. There were flower gardens all around the house and some at the far edges of the lawn. Summer evenings, after a day of some gardening and fishing or house cleaning and horseshoes, the men liked to sit outside on the lawn chairs, smoking and watching for deer, and I would weed the flower beds until the mosquitos drove me into the house.

And I could enjoy it, every blissful moment of work and play. In February, the principal at school had pieced together a false accusation against me. Rather than fight it, I quit. I didn't like quitting that way, but even if I proved them wrong, there had to be a lot of bad feeling to create the accusation. I had two classes with the rottenest bunch of kids I'd ever seen. I didn't want to stay there any more than they wanted me. More importantly, I did want to be full time at my group home, the Haven.

With my salary and the income from the residents, I had already paid off the two smaller loans taken out to start the Haven, and I had a small chunk out of the biggest one.

Roy was on salary, running his group home. He wanted to buy a place out of town, away from six bars on every block, and run it on his own. I began to understand that maybe he had been so helpful with the Haven because it was a trial run, to see if he could do it on his own. That was all right — I had gotten what I wanted: a job that I *liked.*

Roy showed me the places he was interested in. One was larger, more expensive, and very dark and gloomy inside. That was the one he wanted, but the price tag was bigger. I told him, "I like the smaller one because it's much more cheerful and with the addition you're talking about putting on, it will house eighteen men; if you're uncomfortable about the cost on the bigger place, you'd probably do better with the cheaper place; and finally, the smaller one has a great banister along the stairway. But it's your money and your group home, so do what you like."

It turned out that he could get the cheaper one on a land contract. He wouldn't have to try getting a loan from the bank. He bought it.

When Dorothy, Jim and Jennifer came for their annual summer week of fishing, they stayed at his new place; I liked that. The summer before, Roy and I had had one of our big fights over families. I wanted him to go with me to Florida to visit Mom and Dad. Because my family was so spread out, we had never visited any of them, except Peter, once. We went to see his family a lot, which was fine, but if he couldn't go to see my family once every few years, I wouldn't be going to his either.

He went, but he cut the visit short; he said it was because all we did was talk and play cards.

"And with your family, all you do is fish and play cards. When they come up, I'm supposed to clean and cook and play hostess. And you ignore me the whole time they're here. I like your family, but I hate the way you treat me when they're here."

"Well, it's their vacation. I can't ask them to help."

"It's my vacation, too! It's *your* company — why don't *you* do the cooking and cleaning?" That was a year earlier.

With Roy busy running one group home and starting another, Dorothy, Jim and Jennifer did a lot of fishing without him. We went out to eat together several times, played cards, and had a picnic at the lake; while they fished, I dangled my feet in the water, enjoying the warm sun and quiet lake.

Then his folks came and one of his brothers with his family, so there were kids for Jennifer to play with. I took the kids blueberry picking and made blueberry pancakes for the whole mob. Dorothy and Jean fixed the eggs and bacon. I had enough to do with the pancakes. It was fun and the pancakes were delicious.

The best part of this visit was that Roy treated me as a person of importance in all the nice little ways, in front of his family and when we were alone. He'd ask, "Would you like to eat out tonight?" instead of telling me about plans already made. He'd put an affectionate hand on my shoulder at the picnic. He'd talk with me at the end of the day.

Roy was easy to be with — no, he was *good* to be with. He used to bad-mouth Native Americans until he became good friends with an Native American couple. He used to belittle blacks, until he got help starting his first group home from a black. He used to ridicule people with college degrees until he got one himself. He found out that he'd get a better salary if he had a degree, so he collected all his transcripts for credits earned at a lot of colleges when he was in the Army; one of the colleges added them all up and gave him a degree.

Roy had collected some ugly prejudices and a nasty vocabu-
lary during his many years in the army, but that summer, he
was busy setting up a third group home — his own. His confidence was so high, he didn't need to use foul language or
look down on others any more.

I helped a little with his group home, but he seemed to
want to do it himself. I shopped garage sales for kitchen gad-
gets. I suggested he put the coffee pot in the dining room,
out of the small kitchen. I drove the Haven van and he drove
the pickup to Minneapolis for remodeling materials. He listened to my suggestions on paneling.

He started moving men to the new place that fall and
planned to have them all there by the end of the year. That
fall, his residents came from the new place, four miles away,
to the Haven for weekend suppers. Bob and I would fix a
roast with potatoes and vegetables, or a huge kettle of homemade soup. The nice part of making those meals was that my
residents would peel the vegetables and potatoes, so we had
twice the fun out of it: fixing it and eating it.

At Roy's January cancer checkup, they found cancer in
one of his kidneys, so they operated again. It was a much
easier operation, but the doctor said there would be more
cancer but no more operations.

Dorothy was there the first day. When she left, I called
Mom and Dad to tell them the news. I was so devastated, I
couldn't even talk, I could only cry. They caught the next
plane up. I was surprised Mom and Dad would do that for
me, and *very* grateful. They stayed for two days, while I pulled
myself together. It seemed like all that held me together was
bubble gum and baling twine.

The cancer killed "us" before it killed him. We did great
things together, but we gave up, not with a big fight, just a
sigh. What I needed from him was not there; what he needed,
I didn't know. But it was fall: there was wood to haul against
the winter cold, manure for the garden for a rich harvest next
year. I cleaned my house, graveled the driveway, planted the
tulips, dug up gladiolus. Busy, busy, busy. So I didn't have to
think or feel.

Winter came and he was still gone. It was peaceful, home alone, a relief, no thwarted expectations. And lonely. Should I have given more, hoping he'd come to terms with his cancer? Did I leave him when he needed me most? The divorce settlement was peaceful; we agreed easily on what was his and what was mine. Strange, for two who'd fought so well. The snow fell softly and kept falling, for many hours. The bitter cold that followed froze my very soul. Or did I freeze it when I sent him away? We warmed each other but I didn't warm myself too well. I felt hard and cold at work and play.

Spring at last: we planted the garden; joyful daffodils bloomed and happy tulips. And still no man. We were married in the spring, "A time of new promises and great beginnings." But I was still frozen inside. I knew his thoughts, even when he was away. He didn't want to come back; I'd know it if he did. I always knew before. And yet sometimes I wanted him back *so* bad. I knew it wouldn't work because he couldn't take responsibility, not even responsibility for my few needs.

I called Roy on business one day in June. He was very grumpy. Later I remembered that damp weather aggravated his pain. So he had an excuse to be rotten to everybody. But what was my excuse for feeling so uptight at the same time? I always sensed how he felt, up or down, insecure or loving whether we were hugging or far from each other. It was time for me to let go, to quit being affected by his feelings. It was time to turn off the E.S.P. I should hang tight to the good he found in me and let the rest go. I'd tell myself to let him go and promptly forget my resolve.

I felt like screaming and hollering and throwing things! Why did life seem like such a waste between men? Oh, the twisting, writhing hornies! I said good-bye and waited to get over him so I could start again. I knew it would be like that. Marlene Dietrich could leave one man and walk into the arms of the next. But I wasn't made like that. Maybe it was just in the movies. My body yelled, "Get a man!" but a man meant so many concessions. Oh, sure, if you cared about someone, living with him, you wanted to consider him, plan around him, let him decide some things, wait on his whim or fancy sometimes. But it was *damned* hard! Was my need for control greater than anything else in me? If I had stayed in the convent, I could have avoided this mess. But I guess I wouldn't want to have missed the whole fourteen years.

I'm amazed at how giving I was. When I first met him, he had sobered up; he seemed so gentle and fragile. When he went into training to become a counselor, I got to know him, deep down, as I took part in the training with him. I was his strength. I believed in him and he kept going. As he started his new career, I encouraged him, every step. I also badgered him, demanding that he be his best self. And he tried. It was awesome how hard he tried; inch by inch he pulled himself forward. I told him how I appreciated that. He helped me start the Haven so I could quit teaching. I would never, could never have started it without Roy. I would always be grateful for his help.

We had a painful mix of giving and fighting. He'd back away, be in his own world for a month or two. Then I'd blow up, yelling at him about all the dumb shit and the big things, like sex and money and responsibility, mostly trying to say, "I'm here! Pay attention to me!" I learned to let the little things go. But the big ones kept billowing up like thunderclouds, released only in verbal violence. I tried not to hurt him when I yelled. No name-calling, just told him how I felt.

But it didn't matter. He'd hurt and then he'd try. We'd be okay for months until he'd wander again and I'd feel sorry for myself again and we'd fight. He used to need me so badly that he'd keep trying. It's funny: he needed me but he didn't really like me, at least not in the beginning. He didn't like my clothes, my housekeeping, my cooking. He said my house was a monument to me, not a home. He didn't like me being aggressive but he didn't want me to depend on him for *anything*. He didn't like my ideas, but he hated making decisions. Amazing that we stuck together through all that garbage! But we did and we both grew up.

After I quit teaching, we had ten gloriously happy months. We were good friends and good lovers. All our troubles faded away. As he started his own group home, our love was miles and years away from our first love. How could we let that go?? It *hurt* to think about the good times!

We had beautiful moments of *us;* we had bleak moments of loneliness when our hearts seemed bitterly opposed to each other. Did I hang on to the bad times, let them build up in my heart to smother the good times?

We were good for a while, then cancer struck again and we fell apart. Maybe we had stretched so out of shape growing up that we just had to snap back again.

It was time to let go.

14

Maureen
Northwestern Wisconsin, 1984

"Beep, beep, beep. We interrupt this program to update you on the severe weather." Four angry red and yellow storms showed on the radar map and one of them was headed right at us. "Okay, guys, it's headed our way, so let's get ready for it. Joe and Tom, will you bring in the lawn chairs and set them up in the basement?"

John said, "I'll take my radio down."

"Thanks John. Dan, will you shut all the bedroom windows and the two doors."

Ed picked up three ashtrays. "I'll take these down."

"Good, Ed."

"Should we shut the windows in here?"

"No, it's pretty hot; we'll shut the TV room and kitchen windows later." I went outside and moved the van, the pickup and my car as far from trees as possible.

"Does everyone have plenty of cigarettes?"

When the TV broadcast the warning for our county, I sent the men downstairs. Bob's legs didn't take kindly to stairs, so he and I went into the office, in the center of the house.

The wind and rain battered and screamed. I made weak jokes to hide my fear. The radio's voice was buried in static, so I turned it off. After many hours, or maybe half an hour, I went out for a look-see. The heavy rain blocked the view from west and south windows, so I went to the east door and looked out from the porch. The wind drove the rain almost horizontally and was so heavy, I could only see a hundred feet. I went back to the office.

Much later, it quieted down. I went to the basement to tell the men they could come up. The electricity was out. It was several hours before sunset, but heavy clouds still darkened the sky as we gathered in the TV room. Looking out the windows to the west, we saw the driveway was covered with trees, reaching almost to the house. As I saw the downed trees, I cried quietly, for their destruction, for our safety, for letting go of our fear. John reached over and put his hand on mine, comforting. I couldn't talk, I just nodded.

After I stopped wobbling, I asked, "Joe and Tom, do you want to come outside with me and check damage?" A dozen oaks and pines littered the driveway, crying silently as their lives ended. The top leaves of two of them had been all that hit the house. One downed oak had been three feet across. The wind had shoved it down and dragged its fifteen feet of roots right out of the ground; it must have been born about the time the first settlers came to this area. The garden was flattened. The van, truck and car were untouched, as were the house and garage.

The fierce destructiveness of the storm was overwhelming, yet we were safe. Safe, but feeling very vulnerable.

Then I wondered if Roy's group home was all right. The phone was out, so Tom, Joe and I drove over to find out. They were only four miles away, but they had no damage. They offered to help us clean up the next day. Roy was gone on vacation, so I couldn't lean on him. Back at the Haven, I made sure they all had flashlights ready in case they had to get up in the night and the electricity was still off. Then I went home. No damage there.

The next day, I called our noon cook to come early, because we still had dirty supper dishes and no electricity for the water pump or anything else. We did have gas stoves (on purpose because the electricity went off fairly often). I dragged myself over to the Haven by nine o'clock.

Herman and Bill, both in their seventies, started up their chain saws. "Tom, Joe, Alvin and John, you clear up after Herman. Any wood that's big enough to burn, stack it right here, away from the driveway a ways. Take the brush down there, away from the house and pile it up. Kim, Einar, Dan and Alvin, you do the same for Bill."

Then I went in the house and started Bob on a batch of cookies for us to snack on during our breaks. I found three five-gallon buckets and took them over to the little store to get water. When I got back, it seemed the men had hardly started, so I crabbed at them a little. I wasn't mad at them, I just wanted all the destruction out of sight, *right now!* Maybe I could too easily picture my life snuffed out had I been in the way of a falling tree. I felt totally helpless in the face of such power and I didn't like the feeling one bit!

I went for more water, for making stove-top coffee, washing dishes, flushing toilets. Then I emptied the freezer and took that food over to Roy's group home. Fortunately, there wasn't much, because I usually stocked up in the fall, when prices were lower. When I got back, the older men looked like they needed a break.

Seated at the long kitchen table, a dozen men solemnly drank coffee, smoked cigarettes and ate fresh cookies. Maybe they were pondering their own mortality or the huge job before us. Our puny strength sweated against what nature puffed down.

"You're doing great, you guys. Are you ready to get back at it?" Revived by their break, the men settled into a rhythm: the two veteran chain saw men unconsciously tried to outdo each other and the haulers had to move faster to keep up. Some were forgetting the forgetfulness caused by years of alcohol abuse. Others were facing a painful reality in spite of years spent ignoring reality in mental illness. The retarded ones understood that there was a mess at their home and of course they would clean it up. The fellows from Roy's home, with the same kinds of problems, found themselves able to help somebody and worked harder than they knew how. The eighty-year-olds walked more slowly than the forty-year-olds, but with no less will. Those who weren't strong enough to work outside helped our cook doing dishes and getting lunch.

After lunch, I saw that the men were doing fine without me. "Hey, you guys are really moving now!" I went for more water and started Bob on another batch of cookies.

They worked for two hours; then I called for a break. This time, the work was nearly done. The 85-degree heat wilted their bodies, but their spirits were flying: we can do it! We laughed wildly at the same silly jokes we had been telling for years. Joe told us, "You know, when I was flying back from Alaska, the weather got so bad, even the automatic pilot bailed out."

"Do you know what a smart ass is?"

"It's someone who can sit on an ice cream cone and tell you what flavor it is."

By four thirty, the driveway was cleared, so I took the men back to Roy's place, thanking them again and again and I asked if some of them wanted to come back and help pick up the small branches that were scattered all over the huge lawn. So Wednesday we twigged. Thursday, we relaxed and the electricity came back on. Friday we cut up the downed trees by the road, finishing in the early afternoon.

When Kim carried off the last branch, I yelled "Hooray for us! We did it! Can you all get cleaned up by five o'clock?" It was 93 degrees and humid. They just looked at me, like, what's the rush? "Because if you're all dressed up by then, that's when I'll take you all out for fish fry at the restaurant."

"We'll be ready!" Their grins were tired but satisfied.

At the restaurant, as we waited for our food, I tried to tell them how proud I was of them, but I choked up and couldn't get the words out. My eyes went blurry on me, but I could see that these men were sitting tall, proud of themselves, and they knew what I meant.

At home, after the cleanup, I decided "*off with the hair!*" I had let it grow long when I left the convent, fourteen years ago, sometimes below my waist. It was the sixth month anni-

versary of my divorce and the date when I could legally re-
marry (fat chance of that — marriage was just *too hard*) so I
decided to celebrate and cut off all my hair. I rigged up a
second mirror in the bathroom, so I could see the back of my
head. I had my hair down to a "boy cut" and I wanted more
light to trim it neatly. As I plugged in another lamp, it sparked.
I unplugged the lamp and flipped the circuit breaker to re-
store the circuit. Nothing. I flipped it harder. Nothing. So
I moved to another light and finished my hair. Then I washed
it. I unplugged everything on the dead circuit and flipped
the circuit breaker again. Nothing. Uh oh, no water either.
An hour later, I tried the dead circuit again. It worked! But
still no water. Weird!

Next day, I called everybody I could think of that might
know how to get the water back on, but nobody was home.
Finally, I reached the well man. He came and put the water
pump on a different circuit. Then the lights went out again.
An electrician said the circuit breaker was giving out. So I
flipped it again. It worked. I bought a new circuit breaker
and found out how to put it in, just in case. (I never did have
to use it.) So, cutting my own hair cost me forty-five dollars.

The garden, flattened by the storm, rose up again. Ah,
the garden! Nothing could stop it, not deer, potato bugs, or
storms. We gathered potato bugs and eggs by the millions
and kept potatoes thriving. We put tin can lids up as wind
chimes to keep the deer off. The hail only damaged a few
plants and the rest straightened up after the wind. We ma-
nured it well last fall, threw ashes from the furnace on it all
winter, added lime in the spring, weeded it well in June, so
we were already eating potatoes, spinach and 'bagas; soon we'd
have tomatoes, corn, and turnips. We already had nine quarts
of cukes pickled, seven loaves of zucchini bread frozen, eight
quarts of beans canned; we had eaten lots, given away some,
and it was still only July.

We also had a record blueberry pick: thirty-five quarts!
The picking wasn't that great, but we were having fun so we
just kept picking. We had to go one last time for the two
quarts that would break our record. Just when it was time to
quit, heading back to the van, I found the best patch of all.

There were millions of blueberries. So we picked there for fifteen minutes and wished all the picking had been so good. Of course, we had to celebrate our new record with a fishing picnic. Knowing the catch would be small, in spite of their great fun, I took hamburgers to grill, buns, beans and all.

We had a good time, yet that night, my mouth was full of acid and I had the runs. Was it because Roy seemed to be in a decent mood and I wanted him back again? Or because Herman wanted to move out and that would leave me with only nine residents? I handled the storm, the garden, the inspection. I had even bought a pickup so I wouldn't have to borrow Roy's. But he had always gotten me residents. Was I afraid I couldn't do that? Maybe I just didn't want to manage *everything* by myself.

We managed the inspection just fine without him. As Mick, the man from the state, and I toured, I commented, "Notice how neat Art's closet is.

"Joe did the edging when we painted bedrooms. Didn't he do a great job! Everybody took turns painting the walls.

"Not much wood left in the basement now. In the fall, this room is full with fourteen cords, which the men cut, split and bring in.

"In the fall, these shelves are full of canned tomatoes, beans and pickles from our garden. Tom is my chief assistant, but they all help cut up the vegetables. Underneath the shelves, we store boxes of squash, onions, and huge bags of potatoes.

"Dan does the laundry; when his sister came to visit him last month, she said he'd never done anything so useful in his whole life.

"Bob does all the baking. You'll be able to sample his ginger bread at lunch."

I finally ran out of ways to brag up my men. Mick looked at me. "You know," he said, "I wish all group homes were this well-run. The Haven should have a special award, but there isn't one."

His praise felt *good*! Hmm. "Well, why don't you tell the men how great they are and give us a perfect inspection. That would be the best award you could give us." My grin told him that this was a request, not a demand.

He complimented the men, not once, but many times. And he cited *no deficiencies*! Inspectors love to cite deficiencies, find things wrong and demand that they be fixed. I framed the no-deficiency report and called Roy, trying to sound very woebegone. I said I had something to show him; would he stop by? When he read it, he was incredulous. "You son of a bitch!" he yelled, but his grin was almost as big as mine. So for weeks, everybody had to listen to me brag, "Inspector-man said we're perfect!" We were mighty proud of that.

With much botheration, I had taken care of fixing up after my hair cut. I ran out of gas for my stove at home and the gas tubing was bent. I took care of that. An electrician had put in a heavy duty outlet for the air conditioner at the Haven, but the cord stuck out so that every time anyone walked past it, they would rub the cord. It wasn't safe so I made him fix it. I did all that, but sometimes I got tired of being in charge all the time. I wanted someone to take care of me, make some decisions, call the repair man.

A few nights later, I was looking for an old address book and found my old poems. I read through them and suddenly they fit together in a new way.

> *As I stand at the edge of the woods,*
> *Graceful, fragile ferns*
> *Form a carpet for the eye to walk on*
> *And the wind whispers, "Follow me in."*
>
> *He enters my life.*
> *We dance with the wind*
> *As it whirs through the firs*
> *And rustles through the birch.*
> *We soar and swoop*
> *Play with clouds and grass.*
> *Blow us, wind, with you we go*
>
> *Child of wind, the lightning comes;*
> *We fly the storm together.*

Lightning, lightning, lightning
Darting through the sky
Darkening what was light
Lightening what was dark
Splitting what was one
Joining what was split.
Come
Lighten
Darken
Split
JOIN!

The storm is gone and so is he.
Blow me, wind where I must go.
Restless wind, violent storm
Is there no home for you
Or me?

Right before Memorial Day weekend, I had found another dog for the Haven to replace the one that had been run over. She was a black and white Springer, eighteen months old. She was hyper, but free, so I decided to try her. She hadn't had her shots. Thirty dollars. Not quite free. The men named her Chrissy. She was shy, scared of the men at the Haven, but made up to them. She snarled at Rusty, the springer at the Haven, but then made friends with him. She didn't like Tinker, who always came with me, but she learned to tolerate her.

Unfortunately, Chrissy was snarly with company and might hurt someone, so I decided to give her back. I'd wait until after Memorial weekend, when their company would be gone.

Memorial Day, my phone rang. It was Bob. "Rusty and Chrissy are stuck together somehow." He sounded worried.

"You know how cows mate?" I asked the farmer's son.

"Well, yeah."

"Were they mating and that's how they got stuck?"

"Yeah, I guess so."

"How long have they been stuck?"

"About half an hour."

"Okay, it happens sometimes. Just leave them alone and they'll be all right."

It had happened to Tinker, but I called the vet. "How long can they be hung up together before there's a problem?"

"Don't worry, they'll be okay."

They were stuck together for two hours. When I got there, they were apart, but Rusty's penis was still swollen and hanging out. He looked so pathetic. This was his first time mating and look where it got him.

Because he was still swollen the next day, I took him to the vet. The vet greased him and tried to push it back. It wouldn't stay. The skin around the tip was so tight, it would stay swollen until it was back in. The vet gave him anesthesia, pushed it in and it stayed. Rusty was patient through all this distress. I kept him in the basement at the Haven and brought him home at night, afraid if he were near Chrissy, he'd get a hard-on and start the whole thing all over again.

Rusty didn't eat, he was still swollen, and his nose was warm. Back to the vet. Rusty seemed bewildered and in pain, but he knew I was taking care of him. Poor Bob was just as bothered. "Will he ever get better?" Well, it took two weeks, but he did get back to normal.

I was so busy taking care of Rusty, I forgot about giving Chrissy back. She had settled down, so I decided to keep her until the pups were born and if she stayed calm, we would keep her.

Two months later I greeted our company, "Hi, Fred and Joan. Come on in. Hi Dorothy. Hi Ellery. Hey guys, we've got company!"

Several years ago, a group from the nearby Lutheran Church had adopted the Haven. Once a month, two couples brought prizes over, like small bags of chips and candy bars and we played bingo. They also helped us celebrate birthdays and Christmas and other fun times. Only a few of the men went to their church, but they didn't fuss at those who didn't go. They were good friends, and the men really appreciated them.

"Hi, Tom." "How are you doing, Joe?" "Well, Bob, what did you bake for us today?"

Bob smiled proudly, "Blueberry pie, best crust in town!"

"Hi, Dan."

"Art, are you going to win all the games, today?"

"Hi, John."

"Who wants coffee and who wants lemonade?" As we started to settle down, I told Fred, "Chrissy seems restless. She's about due to have her puppies, so if I need to stop playing, just go ahead with the game."

"Oh, okay."

"I 16 ... B 3 ... G 48 ... N 33 ... B 12 ... O 67 ..."

Ed interrupted, "Hey Fred, where'd you get such a good-looking wife?"

"I met her at church."

"Do you think if I keep going to church, I'll find one, too?"

Fred laughed. "You never know, you might. I 24 ... G 56 ... O 72 ... I 22 ... N 43 ... B 7 ... O 68 ..."

"Bingo!"

"Good for you, Tom. Call your numbers."

"B 3, I 16, free, G 56 0 68."

"You've got a bingo. Pass him the prize basket." Tom chose a candy bar.

"Hey Ellery, did you hear about the Norwegian who threw himself on the ground ... and missed?" Laughter and groans answered Joe's joke.

Fred asked, "Regular bingo again?"

"Yeah." "Sure."

"B 15 ... G 59 ..."

After a while, Chrissy started whining, so I sat on the floor and cuddled her a bit and she calmed down. Her water broke as John called "Bingo!" for the final game of blackout.

"Joan and Dorothy, would you please dish up the pie and ice cream? Tom, please clean this up. It's time to take Chrissy to the basement."

Tom cleaned up, Joe brought out the ice cream and I took Chrissy to her nest, two old blankets folded up and covered with an old sheet, and clean sheets to use as needed. Poor Chrissy, whimpering, squealing, squirming for over an hour after her water broke, but no puppies. I called the vet. "Bring her in."

I put Chrissy up on the examination table and she growled at the vet. I held her head and talked to her while he examined her and gave her a shot to strengthen the contractions. The vet said it should be a while, so Joe and I went to buy a quick supper.

When we returned, she had had a puppy but it was dead. Then she easily pushed out another messy black baby. Yes, she was fine now. The vet thought he should probably keep her there until she was finished, but he wasn't very enthusiastic about it, because of her snarling. I agreed with the vet that she would be more comfortable at home, but I didn't know her like I had known Tinker when she'd had her three litters. "How can I tell if I need to bring her back in?" His answer was vague.

We went back to the Haven, Joe sitting in back with her, talking to her, petting her, just as he had on the way in.

We no sooner walked in the kitchen door, when out popped another puppy. As soon as Chrissy cleaned it up, I took her and the puppies downstairs. Over the next two hours, Chrissy fretted out four more hand-sized little squealers. Then she tucked them under her and calmly looked at me, tired but pleased with herself, grateful for my soothing presence during the birthing, but would I please leave them alone now. I knew she was fine, so I went upstairs.

I did like midwifing, though my only contributions were comforting and going for help. It was a very special experience to watch the beginnings of new life and see the first squirm, "Ah, it's alive!" and hear the first little yips and yelps, watch the mother clean the pups, and push them to where they could start nursing.

Most of the men had stayed up late to hear the news, "She had three black and three brown puppies, two males."

"Can we go see them?"

"Better wait 'til morning. Chrissy is pretty tired now. And when you approach, go easy because she may be very protective of her little ones. If she growls, back off slowly," The men were pleased to have these new residents, safe and well with their mother.

Mostly the men stayed away the first week, a little over-awed maybe. Then I talked Chrissy into letting me take two puppies upstairs. She was nervous about it, as Bob and Tom tenderly held her babies. At first, we only stayed upstairs a few minutes, then longer.

When Chrissy's former owners came over with their five-year-old grandson to see the puppies, I left Chrissy outside. But someone let her in. I heard her running down the steps. I told young Robert to back up and stand very still. Chrissy ran in, sniffed the puppies, then jumped at Robert. She didn't bite him, just scratched his cheek. But that settled it. She'd have to go, as soon as the puppies were weaned. It was too bad. The men loved her. When she cuddled up, she was really sweet. But I didn't want anyone hurt.

The brown male was an amiable fellow, just like his father. We'd keep him. When the puppies were a month old, we put together a pen, out of pieces of plywood and cement blocks, too high for the little ones to get out, but low enough for Chrissy to get in and out. It was in back of the garage, where they would have some sun and some shade.

How the little ones yipped when their mother came near! We'd let them out and sit on the ground to play with them. They'd crawl all over us, investigating everywhere, even up Tom's pants leg. They rough-and-tumbled with each other. If Chrissy came around, they tore after her and she'd lead them a merry chase, as their stumbling developed into running.

Every resident I had found the dogs irresistible. As soon as a new fellow sat down, one dog or both would come up, sniff him and look up with big eyes that begged, "Pet me." For many residents, the dogs were their first friends in a long time. But the puppies were young and full of life and their delightful antics brought grins to every face.

Then the little darlings learned how to dig their way out of the pen. We filled the holes and blocked them with cement blocks and they'd dig somewhere else. One day, John said, "Rena, the puppies are out again." I blocked the hole and put them back. One was missing so I listened and I heard a puppy crying. I followed the sound out into the cornfield. The poor baby was really scared. "Here puppy; here puppy." There she was, shaking and whimpering. "Well, you know if you hadn't been naughty, you wouldn't have gotten lost!" She looked sorry for her misdeed, so I picked her up and she cuddled close, safe again. I put her back in the pen and she snuffled up to the others, telling them about her scary adventure.

I advertised springer spaniel puppies for sale. Wouldn't you know! The first couple that came fell in love with the brown male that I wanted. No other dog would do. Okay.

Now which one would I keep? Chrissy told me, "The black female with the lopsided white marking on her nose. She's the one for you." I accepted her choice and named her Sunshine, so we could have sunshine, even when it rained. She cuddled up to my heart and has stayed there ever since.

Again I had acid in my mouth, with the runs and a four-aspirin headache besides! I never had headaches, well, maybe one every ten or twenty years. It took me until that night to realize that what was bugging me was Roy's cancer checkup. They would be checking everything and he was terrified. Was it his terror that was eating at me or my own terror? I kept thinking he should cope better with his cancer. But if I was sick before his checkup, how well was I coping? Judging by my stomach, I figured he would go the next day. I *hoped* so! I wanted it over with. Why did I let the E.S.P. go on? I supposed my indecision brought on the headache. I should work at pulling him together telepathically or let him go. I told myself, "Let him go, Rena. Drop the E.S.P. But be patient; it takes time to undo seven years of loving, caring, fighting, frustration, building, working together, arguing, hurting each other. Be patient, but *let him go.*

I dreamt that night. I was still a nun, reporting to teach at the high school. "Go teach at the grade school." Upset, because that was not my domain, I went anyway. "You aren't supposed to be here." I was elated, free to do what I was good at. But still I wandered through each empty classroom, duty nagging at me. Then I left.

When I woke up, I knew the dream was about my divorce: Roy knew how his pain hurt me, and that hurt him. He had wanted the divorce to spare me and to spare himself, because he needed all his failing energy for protecting the inheritance for his daughter and son, whom he had failed repeatedly when he was drinking. He had wanted my support in putting together this legacy, but he had to pass it on to them by himself. He needed to give it to them as badly as they needed to receive it. He'd give them his group home, which he had responsibly built up to care for and care about the residents. This dream-insight was a great relief: he had dismissed me, I hadn't run out on him.

The fluorescent light in my bathroom at home was out, my wood stove was belching smoke and the critter was back in the crawl space above my ceiling. But the way things had been going, I didn't know if I should try to fix them myself or not. Last month, my bathroom faucet leaked. I turned the water off, tried to take it apart, ran out of time and left.

I came home, turned the water on and took Tinker for a walk. But I had left the bathroom faucets on and the drain was poky so a monstrous flood poured out, drowning the control box for the electric garage door opener, below the bathroom. The garage door came up and kept going, jamming into the control box. My good neighbor Mike spent three hours fixing it. I finally put new washers and springs in the faucets, but then one went clockwise and the other went counterclockwise. That bugged me! I took them apart again to figure it out. I couldn't understand it, so I put them back together. They still turned opposite, but they leaked again.

The fluorescent light had been out since August; I had tried all possible combinations of three bulbs and two starters, then gave up on it. It was simple, once I got to it. I pulled out two nails, cut two wires (with the electricity off), took the whole thing to town and bought another one just like it. I wired the white wire to white, black to black, pounded the two nails in and it worked!

I stepped on the bottom rung of my Haven-made ladder to climb up and clean out my chimney. "*Eeooww!*" The rot-

ten wood fell apart and I was back on the ground! Good
thing it was the bottom rung! I called my neighbor to borrow
a ladder.

While waiting, I decided to clean the stove pipe leading
to the chimney. I took it down and outside, banged it against
the basement wall to knock the creosote loose. It was pretty
flimsy. I went to town and bought new pipe. I put it in, but
smoke still backed up. Gus brought an extension ladder and
he spotted a gray squirrel peeking out of a hole next to the
chimney. My critter. I took the light, wadded-up chain onto
the roof, which was covered with six inches of wet slippery
snow. I dropped the chain down the chimney and it hit with
a strange clunk, like it was hitting a piece of broken off chimney liner, instead of soot collected at the bottom. Getting on
the ladder without sliding off the roof was scary, but I had to
go down and get the tow chain; it was heavier and might
break up whatever was blocking the chimney. While I was
down, I lighted a piece of paper in the stove and the smoke
came back at me. I took the heavy chain up, dropped it several times; it didn't help. Then I took the new stove pipe
apart and looked into the chimney from the basement. There
was the problem! I had pushed the new pipe all the way into
the chimney and smashed the end of it when I dropped the
chain on it. Back to town for an unsmashed piece of pipe.
The stove worked again.

Next day, I moved the ladder to the side of the house with
the vent up near the peak. I had to lengthen the ladder.
When I raised it up, it kept collapsing. I finally got it up, but
it was at 45 degrees instead of nearly straight up and down. I
went up four rungs; it shook so badly, I couldn't stand it. If I
fell and broke a leg or something, I'd have to drag myself
around the house and up the stairs to phone for help. I stood
on the fourth rung, terrified to go up, too proud to give in to
the fear. Of course Joe and Tom would be glad to help me,
but I would feel awfully silly telling them why I couldn't do it
myself. I let my mind wander. Up another rung. I looked
up. Ten feet to go. I wondered if my guys heard my knees
knocking, fifteen miles away. Another rung. I waited. It took
me about twenty minutes to climb up fifteen feet. I pulled

the bottom nails out, bent the vent up, shoved in the moth-balls and some rat poison, bent the vent back, all in five min-utes, and climbed down. It took two weeks before the smelly moth balls drove the squirrel outside, where it could squeak and chew all it wanted.

To celebrate getting all that stuff done, I went over to the Haven and asked Bob to make my favorite cookies, peanut butter with chocolate chips.

October 24, 1984

Dear Mom and Dad,

We have six inches of snow already. Don't you wish you were here? Fortunately, it came after my trip to the cities.

At the paperback book exchange I traded my grocery bag full of books for another bag full of Agatha Christie, Charlotte MacLeod, Margaret Truman, Isaac Asimov, Arthur C. Clarke, Louis L'Amour, Zane Grey, Anne McCaffrey, Michener, Danielle Steele and more. I'll have lots of good reading to enjoy now that the flumdusterating, botheratious fixings are done. Mom, I love to stay up all night reading, just like you do. Then I go to the Haven about noon.

After shopping, I had dinner with Marion and her daugh-ter Elayne. I moaned and groaned about my inept repair jobs, but pretty soon they had me laughing at myself. Then we went to a great Canadian Brass concert.

Yesterday, when it was snowing, Bob baked molasses cook-ies and while we sat at the table sampling the hot cookies, Joe said, "We ought to go on a picnic." Then Dan remembered a picnic we had last August. Cookie and Merle and Fred and Joan were there, celebrating Joe's birthday. Some of the guys went fishing and I started the grill and discovered I had for-gotten the hamburger. It seemed like my guys were glad, that the picnic would just have to last longer. Well, it was a warm, sunny afternoon, excellent company, and delicious ham-burgers (eventually). Life's good moments are too short!

I'll be seeing you soon.

Love
Rena

I was edgy about visiting Mom and Dad. A month earlier, Mom hadn't even come to the phone when I called to wish them happy anniversary. What was she mad about? A week after that, we met at Aunt Caroline's funeral. Mom was nice enough. Was it because I had cut my hair? I hadn't told her about it because I did it for myself, not her. Anyway, when I got to Florida, I was wary. I had decided not to start a fight, but if she was obnoxious, I'd stand right up to her. She came with Dad to the airport. I was surprised. As we sat up talking the first night, she asked me if I wanted to go with her to Munich for a Christmas shopping weekend. I was very surprised! I wanted for us to be friends and that could be a big step. And I was scared, scared that if we were friends, she could hurt me worse than she always had. And no doubt, I would hurt her more, too. "Uh, yes, I'd like that." I watched for signs of her alcoholic bitchiness.

I chatted with her as we fixed meals, played tennis with Dad twice, taped some of their music, got passport photos and application.

Then we went to her cousin's for dinner and cards. The year before, we had gone there and Mom got into her "Maureen-go-help-Irene," "Do-this-do-that" routine. So when she started it again, I told her calmly, "Mom, I wish you'd let me act like an adult and see for myself when to help." She meekly replied, "All right."

I waited until Mom and I were alone that night to tell her how I'd been feeling about coming to Florida and she got upset and I got mad. She called off the Munich trip. I calmed down and said I hadn't intended to yell at her. I just wanted her to know how I felt. I told her I understood how Dad had provoked her into an argument on the way to her cousin's. I didn't beg for the trip, but if the offer of friendship was real, I didn't want to reject that. I was relieved about the trip. It seemed too much for two old enemies to handle, especially with her bottle between us.

On the way to tennis the next morning, I told Dad we'd had words and the trip was off. I knew it would be nice for him to be away from her for a while, but, "I'm sorry, Dad, but I would be very uncomfortable taking the trip with her." The passport was wasted, but that was no big deal.

I won the first game of tennis and the next. That had always been my limit. Then it was 2-1, 3-1, 3-2, 4-2, 4-3, 4-4, 5-4, 6-4. I won the set! I let out a humongous whoop. Of course, he could easily have won, just by hitting the ball where I wasn't, but I still had to get it back to him. I only played a few times a year, while he played in tournaments and was nationally ranked in the top half of his age group of players. We played three more games and I hardly got a point. He wanted to be sure I understood. I did. But that didn't spoil my elation over winning a set.

As I thought about it all on the way home, I realized that in all my watching, recognizing the "poor me," the "wait on me," the alcoholic that was my mother, I wasn't really angry any more. Other visits, I had been so mad when I left, I would swear I'd never go again. I recognized a lot of her in me, but it wasn't eating away at me anymore, which was certainly marvelous. And Dad had picked a fight by his driving rather than tell Mom he didn't want to go to her cousin's. I would never have spotted his aggravating behavior before my marriage. Even that was okay because somehow, I didn't need for them to be perfect anymore.

Poor Pastor Arvid called yesterday. Some of the church people had complained about Ed, putting the pastor in the middle, and which side was more in the wrong? Ed talked during services; as Pastor Arvid got ready to give his sermon, Ed spoke out, "Those sure are nice flowers you have there!" Pastor thought Ed's comment was good in a way: his loud outburst woke people up. But after services, Ed went up to a woman and asked her if she was married, told her he was looking for a wife. Ed was about five feet tall, nearly bald. He was sweet, but between alcohol abuse and mental illness, he didn't have much brains left.

I thought it was pretty funny; anybody who would get mad at Ed deserved to be aggravated. But it wasn't funny to Pastor: his parishioners expected him to change Ed. "I've seen Ed do that; while he waited to see a doctor, he asked a woman if she was married. She was surprised but she answered with a smile. Ed talked with her for a few minutes and then he sat down, quite satisfied." Behind Ed's back, I had smiled my appreciation for her kindness. I explained to Pastor Arvid, "I think he's just trying to reach out to people and he's very awkward about it." A lot of the Church people liked Ed and were big enough not to be upset at his unorthodox ways.

"Pastor Arvid, I understand that some of your parishioners are unhappy with Ed's behavior, but I can't change him any more than you can make them be more tolerant. I'm sorry they put you in the middle. If your people insist that he be kept out of church and you and Pastor Kim agree, I'll keep him home, but I hope it doesn't come to that, because Ed needs God, too, even though he isn't as proper as some would like."

After talking to Pastor Arvid, I remembered when Ed first came to the Haven. Ed had resisted helping; he would do dishes, but that was it. Then we painted bedrooms. I didn't ask him to help paint, I told him it was his turn. I got him started and left him working. Half an hour later, I went to see how he was doing. Surprise! He had painted a big part of one wall. "Ed, you're doing a great job!" He was bewildered by my compliment and looked over what he had done.

"Uh oh, there's a holiday."

"What's a holiday?"

"That's where I wasn't working and missed a spot. That's what we called them when we painted ships when I was in the navy."

"Well, keep it up, Ed. You're painting this afternoon, so you don't have to do dishes tonight."

He grinned. "Okay!"

When we went to see Fourth of July fireworks, Ed jumped every time there was a loud one. They really scared him. I asked him if he was okay.

"That noise reminds me of when we invaded Italy." Poor fellow! That was over forty years ago!

"Do you want to go home?"

"No, I'm all right.

Pastor Arvid didn't complain to me again about Ed. I hoped the parishioners weren't bothering him any more.

Marion, our favorite adopted Grandma, knit an Afghan for one of the Haven sofas. We all admired it and Bob said he used to knit. Realizing the there would be less and less he could do as his muscular dystrophy got worse, I encouraged him to start again. I bought him needles and a skein of yarn. He'd knit a few dozen, ten-inch wide rows with a lot of hits and misses and a wide variety in the number of stitches in a row. Then he'd pull it apart and start over, again and again. So Marion came to help him.

He wanted to knit an Afghan for the other couch. I bought yarn, dark blue merging into light blue merging into white. He figured he would knit ten-inch wide strips, then sew them together. Marion came over to help sometimes. Pretty soon, the other residents were rolling the yarn into balls for him. It took five months for him to finish it. I thought his patience would be all used up, but he immediately started on one for his bed. He chose sixteen different yarns, most of them having three colors. He knit six-inch squares, then sewed the different colored patches together. This was the same fellow who used to wear only dark brown or navy blue clothes! The Afghan was so colorfully, preposterously fun, it was impossible to find his frequent mistakes.

Every week, we went to town, twelve miles away. The residents did their shopping and moseying around and waited at a cafe until I finished with grocery shopping and errands. I knew that Bob had started talking to friendly waitresses and nurses and even took cookies or zucchini bread to them. But then he started knitting scarves for his new friends. He wrapped a scarf in a brown bag and wrote, "To Debbie, my sweetheart," or, "To Jan, my dark-haired angel, from Bob."

When one clerk opened hers, she reached right over the counter and hugged Bob. A friend of our cook thanked Bob with a bouquet. Since we cheered for the Minnesota Twins, another friend gave him a Twins T-shirt. In the drugstore, I saw Jean. "I hear Bob calls you Smiley."

Jean smiled. "One day he came in and told me I was much prettier when I smiled. I've been going through some rough times lately, but now every time I see him, I smile and it makes me feel better."

Bob was as happy as a dog with two tails! The not-so-much-of-anything who came into my life had changed. He had developed his baking and knitting talents to make others happy. He was the most loving and loved man I knew.

I worked myself into a mild case of jitters, getting ready for the state inspector that May, which was silly because he had written us up as perfect a year ago. We had fixed the TV room ceiling, where rain had leaked in, darkening the tiles, and painted the whole thing. Then we had to paint the kitchen and living room ceilings, too, because it was obvious how bad they looked. We cleaned closets, bedding, windows (inside and out) and curtains; we cleaned under the refrigerator, on top of door frames, even the walls.

Mick, the inspector, was great. He wrote us a perfect inspection again. He told me Roy was getting chemotherapy. I shrugged, trying to pretend it was none of my business.

A few days later, a friend of Roy's and mine called to tell me Roy was in the hospital, very sick. And that the housekeeper at his group home, who had told her, said Roy was adamant that I should not know about it.

I went to see his housekeeper. "Wilma, what's going on with Roy?" I was calm and quiet, but I wanted answers and she knew it.

She was very agitated. "He won't let us tell you."

"Two people Roy and I know have told me he's in the hospital. I'll never tell him you told me anything." I reassured her.

She looked relieved, as though she'd much rather tell than not. "All right. Roy was on chemotherapy for two weeks, but the pain and reactions were so bad they took him to the hospital. He was delirious all the time."

"Is anyone with him?"

"His girlfriend." At my look, Wilma said, "You didn't know about her? They've been living together since October." So that was why he hadn't been bothering me telepathically! She looked worried, probably wondering how I'd react to this news, but it was a relief. If she hadn't been with him,

I'd have felt obliged to be there.

At home, that night, I turned all my energies inward and told Roy to fight the cancer. I felt an immense power going from me to him. A few nights later, I woke up in the middle of the night. I felt something dreadful going on with Roy. It was very strong and wouldn't go away. So I called the hospital. The night nurse said he was much better, even lucid when she talked to him a few minutes earlier. Maybe with his return to rationality, he was again trying to push me out of his life.

The next day, when I started thinking of Roy, I wanted to stop, but then I realized this message was different. Before, he'd been afraid or in pain, but it was all just whimpers and whining. Now there was desperate need and he took my strength, knowing it for what it was. He let me see into his soul, welcomed me there, acknowledged all I had done for him. He loved me. He needed me. Of course I would help.

During the following week, I talked a lot to Roy. Sometimes I yelled at him for hurting those he loved. Sometimes I cuddled him mentally. Then my sister called to say she was coming for a visit. Since my house was totally filthy, I had five nights of massive dirt removal.

When Ellen and I weren't at the Haven, working and playing with the men there, we were talking; mostly I was talking. She had divorced her alcoholic husband and she was also interested in psychic phenomena. Most of all, she was a good listener. It was a tremendous relief for me to be able to talk freely about the last few weeks, knowing she'd understand and accept.

I met cousin Ann in Canada, where we stayed with Leona, my friend from Austin. Leona's husband had died of cancer four years ago, so she was glad to have company from the States. We went to several plays, did some sight-seeing, and again I blathered. The problem was, I had no idea how long Roy would live. I wanted to help him die, but I didn't want to spend the rest of my life doing it. Ellen had listened, but Ann wanted to solve my problems with advice. We went to a showing of Native American art. There were several dozen pictures by Norman Knott, positive, powerful depictions of animals, with a short explanation of the symbolism in each. I looked into each picture then went back to absorb them, especially the deer, bear, geese and loons. His bear symbolized inner strength. The male deer had a female shadow to show that each human had male and female aspects, as inseparable as a deer from its shadow.

I wanted to talk to Roy, the normal way. I saw and followed his car until he stopped, and asked him what he'd found out about insurance for our group homes, but he had no news. Then I said I'd like to talk to him about some stuff.

After running a few errands, he came over to the Haven. I asked about his cancer. He said "I have some small lumps in my lung and some on my rib. The chemotherapy reacted with the calcium released into my system from the rib and that made me delirious and caused some memory loss, which is still bothering me. But as soon as the calcium is gone, they're going to do more chemo." He talked quietly and I listened quietly, but I cried inside.

Then I tried to tell him about the messages I'd been getting from him lately. "Roy, you know I've always known how you're doing, even when you're far away. What I've been hearing from you lately is 'Help.'"

Naturally, he denied the telepathy, but I wasn't sure he believed his denial. As he sat there smoking, he was obviously in a lot of pain. I told him, "Roy, it's really lousy to have people on the street tell me how sick you are and not be able to find out anything." He said he'd tell Bill to let me know in case of emergency, after making flimsy excuses about his secrecy. It seemed like he wanted to be decent to me, but he wasn't quite sure he could manage it.

A month later, Roy went back to the hospital. It was only supposed to be for putting in an implant for painkillers, but he'd been there for two weeks when I went back to Rochester.

I drove up to the Motherhouse, all jumbled up. My classmates in the convent had invited us "exes" to the celebration of their Silver Jubilee. I had been such a cold inhuman being in my search for perfection. Would my inhumanity plug right back in as soon as I walked into that cold stone building? What had become of my classmates? It would be good to see them again. As I neared a parking space, two women walked by. One was Lucy. So I jumped out of the car, and we hugged and hollered. And it was Aggie with her. And there was Sister Rosemary! Rosy looked absolutely beautiful.

Well, there was no doubt after that: huge grins and "Good to see you!" were the perfect greetings. More happy meetings happened on the way to my assigned room, in great contrast to the sacred silence that used to reign in those halls twenty-five years ago.

Wine was served at the reception (how wicked!) and several of us smoked (more wickedness!) I knew some of the older nuns there, a dried-up old prune, a pathetic nothing, and Sister Timothy, a happy, gentle woman, even after sixty years in the convent. Our "Mom" classmate had brought films she'd taken when we were postulants; we looked so young. The movies were too dark to see well, but plenty good enough to laugh at.

Then we classmates retired to the council room to chat. That was where the moguls used to sit as they decided our fates. And there we sat, drinking beer, smoking, and telling our life stories. There was pain, growing, achievements, mistakes, growing. Some of us stayed until three thirty in the morning (no bells ordering us to go to night prayers or to bed). We were up for eight o'clock breakfast and more talk.

When the kiss of peace came during the afternoon Mass celebrating the Jubilee, I found myself getting out of my pew to greet each of the jubilarians. After I hugged Sister Rosy, I said, "You are absolutely beautiful, all lighted up from inside with the rightness of yourself."

"Sister Anita, I don't know why I should say this, but the answers to the questions that are bothering you, these answers are within you."

I told Sister Marcie, "You really have your right and good place in life, haven't you?" She looked surprised, then she smiled. "Yes, I do."

I decided to receive Communion, even though I hadn't

been to church in years, because it was right to be in union on that day of jubilation. Our classmate nuns gave out Communion, even to the visiting priests. I loved that! And Sister Bernadine and her parents had taken the offerings up earlier. Great! In the "good old days," relatives were suspect. No loves, friendships, concerns were blessed then, because they might threaten our attachment to God.

On our walk to the grotto, I told more classmates good things about themselves. I seemed very sensitive to their innermost selves and found neat things to say. I told one nun it was time to forgive herself, though I had no idea why I should be saying that. But she seemed to know, so it must have been the right thing to say.

After I thought over what had happened, I realized how profoundly we had changed. We had a moment of closeness to see each others' paths as different from our own, yet each path led a woman to become more alive, more loving, more able to give her special gifts to her part of the world. Some talents were as small as a happy laugh, others as big as a vision of women working together as women.

We had all entered the wilderness of ourselves, found and fought some dragons, found and loved some beauty. *Mea culpa* was turning into "I'll do it better next time." Fear of the worldly was changing into loving and using it with respect. Not content with just surviving, we demanded of life. Not content with just receiving, we passed it on to others. We saw how strong and beautiful we all were, each of us. And together, we were awesome.

Roy was dying, the doctor had told Wilma, who told me. So when I got home, I talked to him in my mind: "Go in peace. It's all right to die, now. Your son Mike will run your group home." Then I snoozed and I dreamed he was looking for a safe place. When I awoke, I thought maybe he had died. After a while, I knew he was still alive. So I asked him, "Do you want to die now?" Before I even finished asking him, I heard, *"No!"* I asked again and heard the same answer. I thought about that, and wondered if it was just me, wishing he'd consciously make his peace with me. That wasn't it. I knew he wanted to do something before he died. So I turned all my energy inward and told him, "Tell them what you want!"

Later, when I went to bed, I asked him, "Are you ready to die?" Then he answered, "Yes." I told him, "Go to peace." I had just gone to sleep when Wilma called to say he had died.

I called my sister the next night and told her about Roy's death. "I'm not sure if it was Roy talking or just me."

Ellen replied, "Maureen, I got goose bumps when you told me about it. I'm sure it was Roy."

Then I told her about the nuns' Jubilee Celebration. "Ellen, after Roy's second cancer surgery, I babbled to my friend Carol. I was afraid that if Roy died, I'd go back to being a cold nobody and all the love at the Haven would dry up, too. Carol said, 'Ninety per cent of the things we fear never happen and the other ten per cent we make happen.' I didn't turn into an ice cube at the Motherhouse. So the love that is in me won't dry up and the Haven will be fine."

"Maureen, those thoughts will keep you going through the mourning. So, happy mourning."

I heard "Happy morning," too, for the new day coming. A while later, I realized, "I'm free!" Watching and helping Roy die had been excruciating. I had helped him and now he was safe; a huge weight lifted off my heart.

At Roy's funeral, I found out that his son Mike had been on his way to the hospital when Roy wasn't ready to die. That was what he'd been waiting for.

On the way home from the funeral, I stopped to admire the sunset. Ember-red clouds outlined black ones. I saw a magnificent black stallion, rearing on its hind legs, surrounded by fire. That was Roy. He had tamed me as I had tamed him. Our fiery love had been good.

As I drove out of the last town before home, I sped up, before the speed limit allowed, and suddenly there was a flashing red light. I wept a little about coming home from my husband's funeral. The officer lectured me gently but didn't give me a ticket.

Looking back over the last years, I saw how much Roy had given me. I'd seen it before, the Haven, my loving dog and mostly, he found me lovable, at least for a while. I still got angry that he had to cop out, but mostly I realized that what he gave me was enough. I was okay. I would be okay. He hung on to me the last two years, but I let him and discovered that I was fey. Like my Celtic ancestors, I could see into the heart of things or people and find good and give strength. I did my duty, until death did us part, and I was free, free to use the gifts he helped me find.

I found a man willing to teach first aid right at the Haven. He was good and the fellows enjoyed him. They weren't so stunned at passing as they had been the year before, when we had all taken it for the first time, as part of our strategy to prove to the inspector-man that they didn't need constant supervision as required by a new law. Our plan worked; we got an exemption. This time, they were proud to show the teacher what they knew. Their confidence was a joy to see. The teacher liked us so well, he sent us four cans of salmon that he had caught and canned himself.

I kept thinking of Norman Knott's art, so I ordered a bear (for inner strength), deer (for androgyny), geese (for friends — my symbol, because my friend in Canada found the exhibit for us), loons (whose lonely call is for family). I took the prints to a frame-it-yourself shop, framed them and hung them in my living room.

We hauled twelve pickup loads of manure for the garden. The smell upset my stomach, but the men liked doing it. It was a simple job, load it up, dump it off. And there was a feeling of feeding the garden so that is would feed us.

Without Roy to watch over the Haven, I made my Christmas visit to Mom and Dad in November. Mom and I started off wary of each other. I beat them both badly at cards the first night. I played tennis with three seventy-year-olds the first two mornings. They wore me out. And one of them went on to her exercise class.

The fourth evening, we went to Mom's cousin's house for dinner, where fights with Mom had started the last two years. Much to my surprise, she didn't order me to go help in the kitchen; she let me go on my own. And she passed up an after-dinner drink, saying she wanted a clear head so she could beat us at cards. Usually, she blamed the cards or her partner, rather than liquor, for her losses. She did win. It had made me sad the last few years to see her lose at cards, because she was quite shrewd when she played well.

Dad and I played tennis against two of the seventy-year-old women. He wasn't doing too well, and I suddenly knew that, right then, he couldn't be a good partner for me. I didn't know why, but that was where he was at.

We went to a show and Mom invited friends over for a drink afterwards. When we had settled in the living room, Dad picked up Rudolf from the coffee table. (Rudolf was a foot-high, red, stuffed reindeer, with a red nose.) Dad squeezed one of Rudolf's hooves and Rudolf played "Jingle Bells," his nose lighting up in time to the music. He said, "When Julie told us about Rudolf, I went right out and bought one."

"When I was a kid," Julie said, "my dad used to buy us the most fantastic toys. I remember a drummer boy that beat on his drum and a wooden dog with a moving head and legs." She grinned. "I'm still a sucker for a great toy."

"I love him!" I exclaimed. "I'll bet my guys would love him, too."

Julie asked, "Who are your guys?"

Always ready to brag, I answered, "I run a group home, for men who can't quite make it on their own, because of old age or alcoholism or whatever. In a group home, these men do things like gardening and cooking instead of rotting away in an institution."

Mom said, "Maureen's best accomplishment in her group home is teaching a retarded fellow how to cook and bake." Mom was bragging me up in front of her friends! That had never happened before, not in my whole life.

Before we went to bed, I said, "Mom, you know, when you bragged to Julie about me tonight, I felt so good, I ..." She just shrugged, but our hug was very warm.

Next day, Dad and I were alone in the living room. He started talking about things precious to him. Joe had one of them. And he wanted me to have the other. It was an ivory carving of a woman's head. It was lovely, not something I'd have picked out for myself, but if it was precious to him, it was precious to me. He also had me pick out some of their "treasures" to take with me. I chose an ebony carving of a woman and a Thai painting. Dad never thought he could verbalize very well, so his words were probably a greater gift than the ivory.

In the morning, Dad and I played tennis. Since that was my sixth day playing, I was vaguely respectable. We were halfway through the first set, grinning at each other. I knew deep down that we were both enjoying each other and liking each other a lot. He won, 7-5, but I made him work for it, at least a little bit.

On the flight home, I was upset. I suddenly realized that Mom had been putting on a good show and I knew why. Her two aunts had both been senile before they died. They were pathetic. Mom had been to see her sister in August and she too was senile. Mom saw how wretchedly her sister lived, at home alone while her husband was gone twelve to fifteen hours a day. With senility running in her family, and her alcohol abuse to help it along, Mom knew she was next and she was terrified. It was so sad. We had wasted so much time fighting. Well, maybe the fighting wasn't a complete waste; part of it was our challenge to each other, our way of saying, "I care about you, so be your best." Mom and Dad had always disagreed with each other. Maybe that was what they were trying to say, sometimes anyway. Mom always seemed frustrated and unhappy. Having six kids wasn't really her choice, it was her duty. She did her best, but even after we were all grown and away, she generally found more to fret about than to take pleasure in. And that was the biggest waste of all.

Dad sent us a Rudolf for a Christmas present.

I had told Mom, over the phone, that I planned to get tickets for several concerts, including one with Yehudi Menuhin, the violinist. She had said, so wistfully, "I always wanted to hear him in person." I told her, "Well, I'll get two tickets then. You can fly up from Florida. I'll meet your plane, we'll go out to eat, then to the concert; you can fly back the next day." I hadn't expected her to come, but I had hoped she would. And she did!

As we ate, I asked her, "How is Dad doing in his tennis tournaments?"

"I don't know why he has to spend so much time playing that stupid game!" Mom looked disgusted. I shouldn't have asked.

"Well, at least you see more of him than Aunt Elizabeth sees of her husband. He's been working twelve hours a day for over fifty years now."

"I would never have let Ben get away with that," Mom said calmly. Her certainty surprised me but her attitude sounded like mine.

"I really like staying up late to watch the old movies on TV. There have been some good ones lately, like Jeanette MacDonald and Nelson Eddy in *Maytime*. I love their singing."

Mom smiled. "Yes, they were quite the rage when your father and I met. My favorite couple was Fred Astaire and Ginger Rogers. He was such a charming rogue, and his dancing ..." By the look on her face, I guessed that her mind's eye was watching him again, losing herself in his grace and elegance.

"I've seen some of the great comedies, too, like *Bringing up Baby* with Katharine Hepburn and *My Favorite Wife* with Irene Dunne."

Mom laughed, "Hepburn and Dunne were two women who surely knew how to get what they wanted! My mother was like that. She was determined that Elizabeth, Mary and I would get at least a little college. We did, but to this day, I don't know how she managed to scrape together the money for it." She paused, then continued softly, "So many times, I have wished she was alive, so I could tell her that my children went to college or that I got to travel and live all over the world."

"Did you get what you wanted out of life?" I asked her.

Mom answered, "Well, I'm going to hear Yehudi Menuhin and I always wanted to. And I'm not poor! I certainly wanted that."

When she stopped, I asked, "What about Dad? If you had it to do all over again, would you still marry him?"

"Of course." Her voice was definite but a wisp of "What if... " flitted across her face. I wondered if it was "What if I hadn't had kids?" But I didn't dare ask.

As we sat listening to Menuhin's magnificent playing, I felt Mom's great pleasure and I was very pleased to be sharing that moment with her. Afterward, we went backstage to meet him. There he was! I stepped forward, shook his hand and said, "Thank you." Then I stepped aside so Mom could get closer, but she shyly mumbled something and Menuhin moved on.

After we got ready for bed, we sat up and talked a while. Mom told me, "When I was a little girl, I listened to violin music on the radio and wanted to learn to play, too. But there was no money for lessons."

"Those piano lessons you made me take when I was a kid haven't gone completely to waste: I like going to concerts, even though I don't play music myself," I told her. "You know, Mom, I'm really glad you came. It has been wonderful to share this evening with you." After a good hug, we went to bed.

On the first day of spring, it had been 10 below zero and there were eighteen inches of snow on the ground. Several weeks later, on Easter Sunday, it got up to 64 degrees. There was some bare ground, some still snow-covered.

Grandma Marion came over to join us in eating out. Tom offered her a cup of coffee and John offered candy. When she admired our stuffed animals, Dan took down a teddy bear, squeezed its paw, handed it to Marion and told her to say something.

"What should I say? Hello, everybody?" The teddy bear repeated what she said and we all laughed.

"Rena's dad sent it to her for her birthday."

Bob took a brightly decorated egg from the basket of Easter eggs and candy on the table. "We knew you were coming so I made this egg just for you. I even put your name on it."

"Thank you, Bob. How are you doing with your knitting?"

"I'm knitting neck scarves now. I give them to people and then they are my adopted sisters and brothers. When Pastor Kim came over for bingo, I gave her one and she even wore it for church services." He named other adoptees. I've given away seventeen so far. Would you like one?"

"I'd love one! Thank you, Bob."

I complimented Marion, "That's a beautiful pink pantsuit you have on. And we're all gussied up, too. Should we go to the restaurant and show them how gorgeous we are?"

We heaped our plates full of ham, beef, potatoes, rolls, a bit of vegetables at the buffet and after a while, Dan asked Marion, "What do you call a cow after she's had a calf?"

"I don't know."

"Decaffeinated." We all laughed.

Marion asked Joe, "Have you been cutting wood lately?"

"Not now. There's been too much snow." Joe grinned. "But Rena bought twenty-five pounds of macaroni the other day and I've been busy drilling holes in it. She got the curved kind, so it's really a tricky job." More laughs.

Back at the Haven, we changed into everyday clothes and everyday manners. We relieved ourselves rambunctiously by having a very wet snowball fight in our shirt-sleeves. Then we noticed our horseshoe stakes were snow-free. "Let's play four on a side: then we can all play." I was good at making up weird rules. "And remember, everybody stands as close as they need to so that they can get some points."

Marion stood about halfway between the stakes, Art and I stood about two-thirds of the way back. The other men refused the help. Since none of us were much good, we only played to fifteen, so the game wouldn't take forever.

I took pictures of us all dressed up, of our snowball fight and our horseshoe game. I would add them to the five albums of photos we already had at the Haven; they showed my men in all their glory, doing everything from gardening to housecleaning, from cutting wood to painting bedrooms, from cooking to eating, from playing badminton to playing cards. Many times our company found their way into our albums, along with pretty flowers and ten-foot-high corn. Every time

I brought developed pictures in the door, the men clustered around to admire themselves.

Ireland had called me. So in the spring of 1986, I went to the land of Mom's ancestors, land of the fey and the fairy, where maybe I could get away from the grief and guilt of my divorce and my husband's death, where maybe I could find ... I didn't know what I was looking for, a new direction, a new strength, something. At any rate, traveling alone in a foreign country would be a good test to see if I could get where I wanted to go.

After eighteen hours of travel, I arrived at Shannon airport at eight in the morning. I found my luggage and the currency exchange, where I handed over the pale blue traveler's checks and received a fistful of bright colorful patterns. The Irish money was fun to look at!

The fellow at the car rental booth offered, with a huge grin, to upgrade my car. "No, thanks, it's okay."

"If I don't upgrade, that yellow one over there is yours. Why don't you look it over?" he suggested.

I got into the tiny yellow car. The dash was starkly bare and the driver's seat wouldn't adjust to suit me. But I didn't want to pay more for a car. I wanted to splurge on "unnecessities." "It will do."

Cheerfully, the car-man coaxed, "But I thought all Americans liked big cars."

"Not me. I drove a Volkswagen for eight years. I'll take the yellow one." No cute, plump, grinning blond was going to con me out of my money.

Leaning forward, he said with a conspiratorial wink, "I'll upgrade it anyway, no extra charge." What a pleasant surprise! But even my impatience to be off adventuring barely kept me awake through the endless paperwork.

"Now, how do I get to Galway?"

"It's easy," declared the Cheshire cat. "Follow the road out, take a left ..." My mind collapsed under the barrage of information; all I could see or hear was his grin.

"Slow down, please," I pleaded, and he repeated the directions until I had them straight.

When he even put my bags in the luggage compartment for me, I felt ashamed of my mistrust. As if in response to his bright smile, the sun popped out and glistened off a rainbow of a hundred shiny, rain-spattered rental cars. A good omen for my trip.

Half an hour later, I passed a restaurant sign, so I turned at the next street to go back. There were no cars coming, so I started to make a quick U-turn. There wasn't enough room to make it in one swing, so I tried to get into reverse. He had said, "Lift the gear shift lever and pull it back and toward you." It didn't work. "Concentrate," I ordered myself. "Your reward is food." The eighth try worked. By then there were six cars waiting for me to get out of the way. "Sorry, folks," I thought, "and thanks for your patience." Not one horn had honked.

The restaurant sign was at an American-looking motel. I would have preferred a quaint little Irish place, but I was hungry. There I heard my first music in Ireland, a Spanish song sung by Julio Iglesias. At the next table, an American pompously lectured a young Irishman on the correct way to make pancakes. He boasted of the efficiency of fast food restaurants and the superiority of American machines. So why didn't he stay home, if everything was so much better there? About the only Irish touch there was the lack of makeup on the rosy-cheeked faces of the lovely Irish waitresses.

Back on the two-lane highway, refreshed by breakfast and almost awake, I puttered along. As always when I drove, I felt in charge of my destiny, yet at the same time, I was alert to whatever fate might offer. I enjoyed the golden gorse blooming in the rain, the three-foot high stone fences latticing the landscape, cows grazing in one pasture, sheep in another. The sun brightened the daffodils that bloomed in front of neat cottages painted white, yellow or pink. There were many old stone buildings, some only ruins, others in good repair. People walked, hitchhiked, rode bicycles, drove cars or trucks. Unlike big cities everywhere, the pace was easy.

When I was near Galway, I stopped at a gas station to get directions to the airport. I would fly to Inishmore Island in

Galway Bay, where I had a Bed and Breakfast expecting me for the night. "Go back to the stop light, turn left and go about two miles."

I found the little airport quite easily, considering I was driving a strange car on the wrong side of the road in an unfamiliar country with peculiar road signs (what was a lay-by?), some distances in kilometers, others in miles. Somehow, I had immediately caught on to the local custom of driving on the shoulder when anyone came up behind me, wanting to pass.

Because of fog on the islands, I sat at the airport for an hour and a half. When we finally left, I knew it was going to be a very long one-hour flight. It was like riding on the back of a grasshopper, lurch up, plunge down, jerk to the side. Was the plane making any forward progress at all? I was seated next to the pilot in the ten-seater. I concentrated on a gray spot just above the pitching gauges in front of me. I kept telling myself, "You took your airsick pills so you'll be all right." Myself answered, "Bleagh!"

Finally, I saw the island. I could make it. The only sign of a landing strip was a line of half-buried car tires in the grass. There was a tiny shack for a terminal. I could make it. No, I couldn't. What a mess and what a relief!

A decrepit van met the plane. This was the local taxi-delivery service. The big burly driver delivered several people to the plane, picked up two of us who had just come in and some packages. He drove to meet the boat, which didn't come in because of bad weather. I was feeling shaky, but better, so when he stopped at a grocery store for a delivery, I got a can of 7-Up and some crackers, to soothe my stormy stomach. The driver chatted in Gaelic with the other passengers and I realized he was an important link in the information and rumor network on the island.

After the others got out, I asked how many people lived on the island. He replied, "There are about nine hundred and fifty islanders, some fishermen, mostly farmers."

"How can they farm when it's so rocky?"

"They use seaweed for fertilizer; they gather it every winter." His Gaelic accent was so strong, I had to ask him to repeat sometimes.   Gaelic was the first language on the three Aran Islands and small parts of western Ireland and English was taught as a second language in primary and secondary schools. For the rest of Ireland, the reverse was true.

The stone fences here enclosed some areas smaller than my house. I was appalled to think a family would depend on that tiny piece of land for a living. But the driver said, "A family owns many of those pieces." They seemed to be mostly pasture, but it was early spring; gardens and crops were yet to come. At last, eight miles and two hours from the landing field, we arrived at my Bed and Breakfast.

After tea, scones and cheese, I loaded up my camera case, and set out for the ancient fort, Dun Aengus, two miles away. It had been built four thousand years ago, repaired a hundred years ago.

I set out, warm in my layers, even though the wind was nasty. At the end of the road, the village, with its half a dozen two-story houses, looked cold and forbidding, as gloomy as the overcast sky, perhaps because the homes were an unpainted gray. Past the homes, the signs started. I looked up a long rocky hill, dotted with a few green plants, crisscrossed with the ubiquitous stone fences. Off to my left was a waterfall, ten feet wide and one foot high, part of it enclosed in an old two-foot-by-two-foot, man-made, roofless stone enclosure, about seven feet high. There were stones in the pool at the bottom of the waterfall that I could walk on, so I stepped into the open side of the walls. I listened. If rocks could talk, what would be their mysterious tales? I heard nothing.

I climbed the hill, opposed by the fierce wind. At the outer wall of the fort, a sign explained that four thousand years ago, when there were raiders, everyone moved inside, cattle and all, and warriors set up their first defense at that wall. The second semicircular wall enclosed a few acres of rocks. The walls of the fort ended at the cliffs, several hundred feet above the Atlantic.

I had wanted to be at an ancient site on summer's eve, because the times and places of change were magic to the ancients. Here I was, at the border between winter and summer, at the border between land and sea, at the border in my life between past and future. Had fate led me here for some great vision? But the stones were silent, so I left.

Back in the cold-looking village, I saw two fifty-year-olds, weathered faces reflecting hard lives, their dark clothes reflecting a somber outlook on life. He was rebuilding the stone fence around his small yard, which doubled as pasture for two cows. He'd chipped the stones to size, placed them and was mortaring. She admired his work. I agreed. He worked carefully and it would take years to finish.

The woman said, "Wasn't that terrible about the nuclear power plant that exploded at Chernobyl? And now another one has exploded in Japan! What is the world coming to?"

I looked back at the fort. She said, "That church to the left is twelve hundred years old. The large stone barn on your right is about two hundred years old." He was building a new fence. Before me was the near and distant past, the present and the future, because these stones would endure.

As I walked through the rest of the village, it seemed less forbidding because now it was the home of two people who worked hard and well and counted their struggle as worthwhile.

Dinner was a feast! A lobster cocktail, lamb chops, salad, vegetables, a bit of wine left over from the proprietors' dinner party, even a fresh rhubarb dessert. In between bringing food, my hostess sat nearby and we chatted. She said her husband was a lobster fisherman, he raised sheep, he had built their house himself and she had decorated it. She was quietly proud of him and of their home. The picture window gave a splendid view of Galway Bay.

Afterwards, as I sat by the TV she came in and said her husband was off on his evening walk to the pub. "Can I help you clean up?" I asked, hoping to talk more with her.

"Oh, no, it's all done." She seemed embarrassed by my offer. I wanted to turn off the TV, but I was afraid if I moved, she'd leave. She said, "I guess you can tell, I'm a little tipsy. I never drink, but we had wine at dinner."

I complimented her for being such a charming hostess and a wonderful cook. "I went to London to cooking school before I got married," she said, as if apologizing for her talent.

"And you have a lovely home!"

"One guest liked it so well, he wrote a magazine article about it. He sent us the magazine, but we can't read it because it's written in Norwegian." Then we talked about religion in Ireland now, about ancient beliefs. We exchanged glimpses of our childhood and all the other things you talk about when you're alone with a stranger after a bit to drink.

I was sad. It seemed that she had a decent life, but couldn't really enjoy it. Because of guilt or fear that it would be taken away? Was that a Celtic trait? Or was it the mentality of any people who, generation after generation, have been ruled by others?

Back on the mainland, I stopped at a souvenir shop to buy little presents for my guys back home. A shillelagh, shamrock seeds, worry stone, or leprechauns would show I'd thought of them. I chose a beautiful, thick Aran-knit wool sweater for myself. I bought a tweed cap because it looked so cute on me, even though I knew I'd never wear it.

I took off on the back roads, headed east, then south, on a roundabout trip back to Shannon for a medieval banquet. The sun came and went, the rain came and went, but the wind blew me away every time I got out of the car to take a picture. (Did the wind give the Irish their rosy cheeks?) I took pictures of the unique: the gorse, stone church ruins, stone buildings with thatched roofs used for livestock, medieval monasteries in ruins. I snapped shots of universals: dandelions, TV antennas, and a plow horse welcoming spring by gamboling ponderously across his muddy pasture. Looking for the picturesque kept me constantly aware of the beauty around me.

I felt relieved to be away from all the harsh, hostile stone on the island. After I was back home, I realized the desolate island was a place where nature constantly challenged human survival. The rocks seemed to say, "This is how strong you have to be to survive here." But even they would be destroyed eventually by wind, waves and frost. I felt puny and powerless thinking about it.

About one o'clock I thought, "Hmm, I think I'm lost." A bit farther on, I spotted a grocery store, the only building in sight along the narrow road; the few trees gave a view of green fields with a few cows. The store was closed, I supposed for lunch, but there was a handsome, young, black-haired Irishman in a car. Map in hand, I asked, "Can you tell me where I am, please?"

He showed me; surprisingly, I was still on the right road. He thought I should go over to the main road and head south. I laughed. "I've already been on that road." I had to repeat that several times, before he gave up. He probably thought I was crazy, but he didn't seem to mind.

At the medieval castle, we went up the steep, narrow spiral stone stairway. A pretty young woman, dressed in a long emerald green velvety gown offered us a bite of bread to dip in salt, as a sign of hospitality, then we went up some more.

In the top room, we had a delicious glass of mead (honey wine). We looked at the sparse wood furniture, blackened by age, and at tapestries and carvings. I felt a twinge of loneliness; I seemed to be the only one by myself. Our host told us that the room we were in had been the women's quarters; maybe they had brightened it up. I hoped their whole existence wasn't as dark as this room made it seem. Ten lovely women in a rainbow of velvety gowns sang several Irish tunes, accompanied by a lute and a violin.

Downstairs at the banquet, over a hundred of us sat at long tables set close to each other. We ate salad and chicken with our fingers, breaking off chunks of bread with our hands. After plenty of good food and some tomfoolery, the women, our waitresses, sang again, some sad, some rollicking, all very good. But when they sang "Danny Boy," its exquisite beauty froze the rowdy crowd into silence and forced its way gently into the nameless sensitivities of the heart. As we left the castle, there was a young man bagpiping away. The whole day had been great fun.

Afterwards, I found a B and B. The rooms were tiny and the breakfasts were huge, which suited me perfectly: orange juice, corn flakes, choices of breads and toast, eggs, Irish bacon, sausage, coffee or tea. The bacon was saltier and meatier than in the States. When I had coffee, it was richer than back home and likely to be lukewarm but the tea was always piping hot. I would have enjoyed eating with the families, but there were always separate dining rooms for guests.

On my way to Cork, where I planned to see an international folk dance festival, I took a quick side trip to Blarney Castle. On the grounds were intriguing rock formations, some man-made, some natural, some both. In the castle, I climbed the spiral stone stairs, peeked into tiny rooms along the stairs (where servants had slept?). The floors between stories were gone, except around the edges. At the top, I laid on my back, lowered my head into the large hole and kissed the Blarney Stone. I had felt hemmed in by the stone on Inishmore Island, but here I was kissing a stone. I even bought a certificate stating that "... having kissed the Blarney Stone, (I am) now sent forth with the gift of eloquence which this stone bestows." Most curious behavior!

The folk dancers were excellent, lively and fun. Driving to Dublin was pleasant; the rocky west had given way to richer countryside. None of the cars went much over the fifty-five-mile-an-hour speed limit, even without policemen. Maybe the three dollars a gallon for gas was policeman enough.

In Dublin, I saw ancient artifacts at the National Museum, congested traffic, the art museum, and a delightful shopping center: a three story, square-block-sized building housed arts and crafts and food shops with their backs opening on to a skylighted, open area where a guitarist and a flute player entertained the cafe-goers. The flute's melody followed me to a leather shop, a booth full of paintings, and a jewelry shop. The crystal was exquisite, its many faces transforming ordinary light into tiny bursts of red, yellow and blue.

At fifteenth-century Trinity College, one building of the library held a large collection of old, old books. I paused just inside the door; it was about a hundred and fifty feet long, thirty feet wide and two stories high, with bookcases reaching almost to the ceiling on each side of the wide center aisle. As I stood there, I felt the wisdom of the ages as an awesome presence and my soul genuflected.

The bookshelves were roped off from visitors. I hoped the books were available to scholars. What a waste to have saved all that learning if no one could use it. In the center aisle, glass cases displayed old books and maps and the Book of

Kells, a twelve-hundred-year-old Bible, handwritten and illustrated by Irish monks. Two volumes, copies of the original, were open in glass cases. The books were fantastically
illustrated; the beginning letter of a chapter was huge, filled
with intricate interweaving. Illustrations were surrounded by
complex designs of geometric patterns, plants, animals, faces.
Ancient pagan art forms lived on in that very Christian art.

Back on the street, mobs of people scurried through the
rain at their big-city pace, expertly dodging each others' umbrellas. More women here used makeup than in the smaller
towns and more wore slacks. Here and there, in the midst of
centuries-old stone buildings, were some modern ones, like a
bank building or a MacDonalds, but no skyscrapers. Dublin,
with its 700,000 population, had received influences from
many cultures and many invasions. It had mellowed these
influences over the centuries and molded them into a robust
heartbeat.

It took me two frustrating, exhausting hours to find a Bed
and Breakfast. I asked directions a dozen times and they all
insisted, "You can't miss it." Hah! Finally I realized there
were no B and B signs in Dublin; I had to find the address.

I had an outrageously expensive meal at the Lobster Pot:
shrimp, potatoes, carrots, wine ... the kind of meal to eat alone,
undistracted by friends, savoring every bite for at least ten
minutes. The waiter treated me like royalty, even though my
jeans and sneakers lacked the glamour of the other diners'
evening dress. A highly pleasurable "unnecessity."

I called Michael, a Dubliner who was a friend of Mom's
cousin, and he offered to show me around the next day. He
came, wearing a gray suit and tie, in contrast to my usual
jeans. His round cheerful face topped a slightly plump, short
body. He looked like the perfect gentleman, sixtyish, perhaps
shy, but ever the charming host.

He drove us to a park, one of his "favorite places." My
cold feet dampened my appreciation of its rainy foggy beauty.

At a medieval monastery he said, "These three-hundred-
year-old tombstones always remind me how long I'll be dead."
The sheep wandered about, "mowing the grass."

We stopped at the peat bogs, where he had come as a boy.

"World War II made other fuels too expensive and hard to get, so I'd ride and push my bicycle up the thousand-foot hill, collect some dried peat and ride back with my load. And woe betide anyone who stole peat from my family's peat land!"

As we ate lunch, Michael asked about my work and talked about his clerical job with the bus company, his wonderful travel benefits and his work with the Vincent de Paul Society as a social worker in Africa. I told him my plan, "I'll drive west to Galway, then south to the Shannon airport." He wanted me to take the direct route to Shannon. "I've already been on that road" made no sense to him.

On the road to Galway, I stopped for two young women hitchhikers, who said they were studying late and missed the last bus. They wanted to bicycle through Europe, but were afraid of the terrorists. I said, "Oh, do have an adventure before you settle down! It will open your eyes so that when life presents opportunities, you'll be able to see them."

On the plane coming home, when I wasn't sleeping, I tried to understand the trip. Playing tourist was fun, but why had Ireland called me? I kept hearing myself say, "I've already been on that road." and "Have yourself an adventure."

For the first week back home, I was exhausted. I decided it was a great adventure but a lousy vacation. I did the same things in Ireland as I did at home: made decisions, drove, ate, slept, and I wore myself out besides. Maybe I was just too old for adventure. No, I had enjoyed my trip. But why had Ireland drawn me? I kept hearing, "I've already been on that road." Then I recalled a conversation with my sister before the trip. I had tried to explain to her my feeling that *fate* was drawing me there. "Maybe ancient voices will speak to me or maybe I'll meet a wise woman."

Ellen had replied, "Maybe you'll be your own wise woman."

I realized that my wise self was telling me to try new roads. I liked the road to my group home just fine, but I should explore new pathways.

15

Maureen
Marshfield, Wisconsin
December 1986

"It's cancerous." I hated the nasty doctor, so I shut out his face and crawled back under the anesthesia.

When I woke again, my hand hurt, from where they'd had trouble getting the I.V. needle in, and my breast hurt. A nurse stood over me. "It hurts."

"They were very sparing with the painkiller. I'll give you some in the I.V." She was a big, comforting woman. "It will make you sleepy."

I was in and out for a few hours and then it was time to get on with it. My parents would be there soon.

"I'm thirsty."

"Would you like Coke, 7-Up, or water?"

Her kindness relieved the starkness of the recovery room, where two other patients were lying on the hard skinny beds on skates, I.V. bags testifying to our helplessness. I sipped slowly and asked for more. By the time I asked for the fourth refill, I was feeling pretty sheepish. "Oh, that's all right; they dry you up before the surgery so you need the liquid."

Nurse Comfort helped me to the bathroom, and helped me pull my shirt over my head because I couldn't raise my arm. I liked to think of myself as a GDI (I stands for independent). I wasn't used to asking for help, but her gracious assistance was easy to accept.

Then I sat in the lounge, waiting for Mom and Dad, wishing I could forget what had happened and what was yet to come.

A month ago, I'd noticed a quarter-sized shadow on my breast. I had ignored it for a few weeks, while we finished up the fall work at the Haven. Then the doctor said the lump was probably not cancerous, but I should have a mammogram, just to make sure. The mammogram expert said it should come out. So I came here to the specialists at the big clinic.

Was it just yesterday that the hated doctor had said, "You need a radical mastectomy"? He said "You may want reconstruction. If so, we can do it right away. I'll do a needle biopsy. You can come back in an hour for the results." I wanted to ask sensible questions, but my mind was buried by the weight of the news.

After calming myself over a cigarette, I went to the insurance counselor, who would help me find out if my policy covered reconstruction. We were calmly discussing costs, as if it were about car repairs, when I started sobbing. It was *my breast* he wanted to cut off!

"You have every right to cry." Bless her heart. And it was even all right to smoke in her tiny office. She found out reconstruction was covered.

Relieved a little by my outburst and the insurance news, I went back to find out about the biopsy. It showed no cancer, but Doctor Hateful wanted the lump out to be sure. He would do it as outpatient surgery, but I should have someone with me for twenty-four hours after surgery, just to make sure I was all right. I knew it wasn't cancerous, because I'd just had a mammogram four months ago; I was ridiculously healthy, eating right (sort of) and physically fit (more or less). I hadn't been in a hospital since I had my tonsils out in 1943!

"Why not just do a lumpectomy if it's cancerous?"

"Your lump is much too large; a lumpectomy is for very small lumps. But even if we took only the lump and the half inch or so around it, over half your breast would be gone."

"Can you take the lump out for the biopsy tomorrow?"

"I'll see if I can arrange it."

As his nurse showed me where to go for the pre-operative physical, she asked, "Who will be with you tomorrow?"

"Oh, my folks will come up," I said, never intending to call them or anybody else. I could take a taxi to the motel and drive home the next day.

"Do your folks live near?"

"Sure, in Florida."

I guess she didn't think Florida was too close to Wisconsin, because pretty soon I was summoned back to Doctor Hateful, where he and I had a brief, fierce fight. He had already demanded no eating, drinking or smoking after midnight, and he also demanded that someone be there at nine in the morning, when surgery was scheduled, or he wouldn't do the biopsy. At the surface level, he was professional, but I was raw and I sensed his deep-down vindictiveness. He not only wanted to chop off my breast and hack at my armpit, but I would give it to him on his terms or I could go to hell, for all he cared.

I went back for the physical. The nurse rushed me off to get blood tests and x-rays, before they closed for the day. When I got back, I told the nurse what Doctor Hateful had said. I told her that nobody I could ask could get there by nine. My folks could arrive in the afternoon, (how I hated to ask them!) about the time they'd want to discharge me, but what good would that do? And I had to have it done tomorrow. If I waited, I didn't know if I could do it.

She was really sweet, dealing with an exhausted, bewildered version of the usually very-much-in-control Rena. Nurse Helpful soon had me talking to Mom and Dad. "Call us back in ten minutes. We'll see if we can get a flight." Ten minutes later, "We'll be at Minneapolis at eleven tomorrow morning."

"Nurse Helpful, they can be here by about three. Do you think Doctor Hateful would accept that?" She paged him and asked. Yes, he would do it.

Just that morning, I was waiting in the lounge before they prepared me for the biopsy, chatting with a nurse. The pitch of my voice got higher and higher. "It seems like Dr. Hateful wants to cut me all up, even take my head off, just in case it has some cancer, too!" I knew I sounded slightly hysterical, but that was how I felt.

I lay on a gurney while they prepared me for surgery; one woman washed and shaved me and another tried to get an I.V. needle in my hand for the anesthetic. Tears started, as I thought, "This is what my Roy went through and he died of cancer." The nurse paused in her shaving to wipe my face. I kept crying, even as I thought, Millions of people are worse off than I am. and They're only taking the lump. I kept crying until I lost consciousness. When I woke up: "It's cancerous."

Finally, I heard Dad, around the corner from the lounge, asking for me. I rushed out. We half-hugged, to avoid my cut-up side. "Mom, did they tell you?"

"No, we just got here."

"It's cancer." Then, to forestall my coming tears, I said, "Let's get out of here."

After a fine steak dinner, we returned to the motel, where the motel-keeper had turned up the heat in their room, as I had asked him, so the switch from Florida's 70 degrees to Wisconsin's 20 degrees would be less traumatic. We called a few people, talked a few nothings, then retreated into a card game. As our tiredness caught up with us, we got sillier and sillier, until we were laughing more than we were playing.

We watched the weather forecast and made our plans. "Maureen, you'd better not drive back here. You might not be able to drive home afterwards. Oh, I'm not trying to boss you around."

"It's okay; I'm just glad you're here. That's a good idea. What time do you want to get up tomorrow?" As we hugged good night, I thanked them again for coming. Mom and I had spent so many years fighting. Yet she had come up to this miserable cold, which she hated, on a last-minute call for help, to be with me when I needed her.

Friday night at home, I was too tired and numb to do anything, but Saturday I pushed the panic button. I called a nurse friend, who might know a doctor I could talk to.

"Lucy, I've been told I need a radical mastectomy. I think the doctor is a very good surgeon, but an egomaniac. If I go get an official second opinion, he'll know about it and he'll be all pissed off at me. Do you know of a doctor who believes in taking the least amount possible? I need to ask some questions." At the time, I thought I sounded fairly calm, even though talking about it made it more real.

Lucy called back in a few minutes. "Dr. Kindly said you could call him now. Here's his phone number."

"Dr. Kindly, how small must a lump be before you'd do a lumpectomy?"

"Very small, almost microscopic."

I thought, Oh, shit, Dr. Hateful is right. He answered my other questions and said if I had more later, he'd be glad to help.

I was on the phone for hours, begging prayers, positive energy or whatever form of support my friends and relatives might have to offer.

At the Haven, I told them I was going back for more surgery. Bob said, "I wish I could go instead of you."

"Thanks, Bob," was all I could say. His kindness overwhelmed me.

As soon as I got on the bus to go back to the hospital, the panic bombed me. I closed my eyes, reached for my inner strength. A beautiful calm took over, which lasted through the night, through the bone scan on Monday and a quick trip to buy a book and some button-up shirts (I had thoughtlessly brought pullovers).

Then I faced Dr. Hateful again. "Your bone scan shows no cancer. That and the complete results from the biopsy indicate we should take your breast and a few lymph nodes."

"Why do you have to take any lymph nodes?" He had told me he wouldn't remove the chest muscle, but I still thought he was being greedy, so I was angry, but I tried to sound polite, for fear of making him angry. If he was going to cut me up, I didn't want to give him any excuse for not doing his best.

"We have to know if the cancer has spread, to decide what further treatment, if any, is needed. I won't do the surgery otherwise." *Self-righteous pig!* No, that insulted the pig.

"So you take a few lymph nodes," I said in my best inoffensive tone. "Then what?"

"If there's cancer in none or one node, no further treatment and you have a thirty to forty percent chance of recurrence." And he continued.

"Can you do it tomorrow?"

"Yes."

I blurred myself through the night and past anesthesia. Whenever the nurses woke me during the twelve hours after the mastectomy, I was in pain; even without moving, I hurt. I couldn't urinate. My first four meals, I had to eat a bit, lie down, eat, lie down, because I was dizzy when I sat up. But I received a cheery bouquet from Roy's son Mike, who was keeping an eye on the Haven while I was gone.

The day after surgery, a nurses' aide came in. "Time to get up and take a walk."

"I still get dizzy every time I sit up and you want me to walk?" General Bitch refused my refusal. I said, "Look, I want me to walk a lot worse than you do I want to go to the lounge so I can have a cigarette."

She smirked. "You have to go all the way to the lobby for that." I wanted to curdle her ears with some of Roy's favorite foul words, but I had to be sensible. She was in control for the moment and I was helpless. The next day, when she ordered my poor whiny roommate out for a walk, I told her we were going to run away. The fantasy appealed to Whiny, so we took off, dragging our portable I.V.'s. General Bitch believed me, "If I have to come looking for you ..."

After we left her behind, we decided to get some big balloons and fly off in them. Whiny wanted a blue one; mine would be red. I asked two cleaning ladies if they wanted to go along. "Sure."

"What color balloon do you want?"

"I'll take a yellow one."

"I'd like orange."

I got through the walk feeling less like falling on my butt than I had the day before, which meant I could walk away from Whiny's sniveling or distract her with wild fantasies. I could walk away from the General, too. That was a delicious thought!

When the sympathetic night nurse came in, I complained about no smoking in the lounge. She pulled a pack of cigarettes out of her picket, "I know what you mean. If somebody smokes in the lounge, I never say anything." Aha! As soon as she left, I grabbed my cigarettes and a styrofoam cup with a little water in it. I didn't turn the light on; I felt just like a college kid again, sneaking a cigarette, but I also felt, "Damn it, I deserve to smoke here! I'm very considerate toward non-smokers. They should return the courtesy!"

At four-thirty Thursday morning, I was wide awake. Roy

was with me, and he was going to see to it that I died of cancer, just like he did! (After sleeping most of the last thirty-six hours, it was no wonder I was wide awake, but I didn't think of that.)

I walked to the nurses' station which was bigger than three patients' rooms. "Do you have any waterbeds in this hospital? I can only lie on my back and that bed is killing me." I wanted to get my mind off Roy.

"No, but we have air mattresses."

"I'd like one, please. And a carton of milk to put me back to sleep."

I did go back to sleep and later in the morning, they decided that since my plumbing was working, they could unhook the IV. What a relief! I was up to a longer walk, so I went down to the lobby for a cigarette. On the way, I passed a sign that said, "Pastoral Office." The next time I went down, I stopped there. "I've just had a mastectomy. I want to talk to someone who can listen to me feel sorry for myself."

Only her name tag showed that she was a nun. Ironic. When I left the convent, I thought I had left nuns behind and there I was searching one out.

Sister Empathy had had cancer, too; she didn't mind if inner strength was the name of my god. She said, "Look to your inner strength to get you through this." She wasn't bothered by Roy's ghost. "It sounds as though you haven't completely dealt with his death." But not one platitude! So I talked and I cried. It seemed that the Church no longer bound nuns' spirits like Chinese women's feet, so that nuns could be real human beings who could feel the pain of others and soothe it.

When I got back to my room, two nurses' aides were putting an air mattress on my bed. Four-inch-square air pockets took turns filling and emptying. When I sat on it, I told Whiny, "It feels like someone is goosing me," which made her laugh.

My brother Joe and his wife sent a basket of fruit; that was practical as well as nice, because I couldn't eat much at meals and was hungry in between. And fresh apples were movers. The fruit, all-bran and prune juice did their work.

Getting out of bed was still slow, but not too painful (I had quickly gone down to aspirin for pain). I was beginning to feel alive again. And Dad was going to be there in a while! I still didn't know if the lymph nodes were clean and I wanted to be able to tell him, so I asked at the nurses' desk. She pulled out my file.

"They're all clean." I grinned, the first real grin since the whole mess had started.

Dad was with me when Dr. Nicely, my plastic surgeon, came in. "When can I go home?"

"When the drainage goes down under ten milliliters."

"But Dad had the same surgery seven years ago and they let him go home even though he wasn't finished draining." I pleaded. Mine was down, but only to forty milliliters.

"In another day or two," he answered.

Friday, I got permission to go out to eat with Dad. I carelessly picked up my purse with my right hand. My arm screamed. Dad didn't notice, though. I wanted him to think I was fine, which I mostly was. It was cold, about five below zero, so I wore my flannel pajamas under my clothes and we set off in high spirits. After a good dinner, we went to his motel and played a game of Rummikub, that he brought for me to give to the men at the Haven. "Dad, what would Mom think about you having a sweet young thing in your motel room?" He looked startled. "I mean me." We laughed.

The drainage was only down to twenty-five, but nothing could bother me. Dad was here and he came through the same operation just fine. His worst problem with it had been when he started up tennis soon after, his left arm couldn't throw the ball up for the serve very well for a few weeks. If he could do it, so could I! And tomorrow, I would go home!

Whoosh, the air went in, whoosh, the air went out of the air mattress. It quickly soothed me to sleep, in spite of my excitement.

By ten o'clock Saturday morning, I had eaten, dressed, checked out and there was Dad to take me home! I was so glad to get out of there and put it all behind me! I had received good care, but the slow parade of walking I.V.'s attached to trudging bodies with pale, pained faces was depressing.

The gray road pointed to freedom, through the sunlit, snowy countryside. We chatted, listened to easy listening radio. I had to reach across with my left hand to open the car door when we stopped for lunch and later for groceries.

At home, Dad brought our things in from the car, while I started a fire in my wood stove. I had to learn how to manage with limited use of my right arm. I'd pull a small chunk of wood from the pile with my left hand and carry it, using my right arm only to balance it. Then I'd shove it into the stove with my left hand, so as not to jerk my tender side. Ten chunks was enough. Lastly I'd stuff in some kindling and light it. I wanted to go right to bed; Dad could stay up a while and load up the stove again. But he came out of the bathroom, "There's no water. The toilet won't flush."

"Oh, no!"

I called the man who had put in the well.

"It's likely frozen in the pipe. Blow a hair dryer at the pipe just inside the house and it'll thaw."

I didn't have a hair dryer. "How long will it take?"

"Only about fifteen or twenty minutes. If that doesn't work, let me know, and I'll come up tomorrow morning."

I told Dad what the well-man had said. "But I don't have a hair dryer. I can get along without water until he comes tomorrow. Right now, all I want to do is crawl into my nice warm water bed."

"But it would be easy. I could crawl under the landing and do it."

"Dad, I don't have a dryer." I didn't feel like calling neighbors to find one and I had a notion of how dirty he'd get if he could slide under the sixteen-inch-high landing. While we unpacked, he persisted. Then my weary brain heard him say, "All we'd have to do is aim the clothes dryer..."

"That's it! We'll disconnect the venting hose where it goes outside and blow that under the landing!"

"What?"

"We'll use the clothes dryer, like you said."

"I meant hair dryer."

"I don't have a hair dryer, but the clothes dryer would

work. The venting hose goes pretty close to the water pipe."

So Dad pulled the hose loose. It was too short, by six feet. We needed a pipe or hose. I looked in the basement catchall closet. Nothing. The sooner we had water, the sooner I could go to bed. Coming to the top of the basement stairs, I spied my vacuum cleaner in the open closet. Aha! We taped cardboard to cover the gap between the six-inch dryer hose and the two-inch vacuum cleaner hose.

"Let's play Rummikub while we wait to see if it works." The excitement of problem-solving had wakened me slightly and I wanted to see if it worked, so I agreed. I knew he didn't care about water for himself. He was being fatherly: if he couldn't cure my cancer, at least he could fix my water.

Forty minutes later, no water. I went to check on our system. The tape had melted off and disconnected the hoses. "You know Dad, if you drink more beer, you could probably pee enough so the toilet would flush without water."

We stuffed the gap with newspapers, checked to see that it held and went back to our game. "Dad, having you here is really great. It reminds me of how you got through the same surgery in fine shape. And if you can do it, so can I!" That was enough. Neither of us wanted to talk about the pain, the fear, the anguish.

At midnight, there was still no water. I'd have to get up at seven thirty to call the well-man. After setting the alarm clock, I snuggled into the warm comfort of my waterbed.

The ringing phone woke me in the morning. Uh oh, no hospital bedside rail to grab hold of so I could pull myself up. I was lying on my back with two pillows under my right side. Before I could figure out how to get up, Dad had answered the phone. Whew! "Maureen, the well man wants directions to get here."

"Go north on seventy-three, past ..."

"Brriinngg ..." The alarm intruded. I tried to sit up. Dad said, "Turn that thing off; I can't hear."

"I'm trying." He was watching from the doorway and seeing my difficulty, came in and turned it off. Finally, I grabbed the covers with my left hand and pulled myself up to sitting. I hated to have him, or anyone, witness my helplessness. I think he was embarrassed, too. So we cheered each other up over breakfast.

The well-man brought five gallons of very hot water, which he poured over the three feet of pipe outside the house and the water ran again.

That afternoon, Dad took some of the guys and me to town to get a Christmas tree. John, as always, picked out the very best one. Dad oversaw getting the tree up. I sat. Tom and Joe brought the Christmas decorations out and the men took turns putting them on, first the lights, then Christmas balls of red, blue and silver, tinsel ropes, knitted red and green stars, crocheted snowflakes and all the rest.

Dad decided I'd be able to manage all right, so he left the next day.

Usually we had evergreen boughs, red ribbons, Christmas cards, Santa Clauses and bells on every table, window and wall, decorations the men had bought or Marion had made or other friends had given us, but I only managed to put up a few that year. I just got too tired over nothing. Bob made a lot of cookies, with Tom helping instead of me. Tom loved licking the beaters, so he was a willing helper.

Our church friends came with gifts and carols and our 4-H kids came with their presents and songs. The smaller kids were fascinated by Rudolf, our caroling reindeer. The grown-up kids liked him, too. When these groups came, the women took charge, so I could just sit back and be glad that my men didn't have to miss Christmas just because I was out of it.

I simplified Christmas dinner. Ham was easier than turkey. Bob made mashed potatoes. Tom opened cans of cranberries and heated up some frozen vegetables. Of course, nothing could stop Bob from making pumpkin pies. All I did was make gravy and direct traffic. I was mildly pleased to see them bustling about the kitchen, mildly unhappy about just watching. Only mildly, though; I didn't have enough energy to get really mad or glad.

I tried to pacify the gods or my body by cutting down on smoking, from a pack and a half to a pack a day. I snacked on raw vegetables at night and I quit drinking coffee, which was easy, since I only drank a cup or two a week.

Life was made of peanut butter, awfully hard to move through. I tried floating: I moved far away from my body and far away from my brain. I totally ignored everything except the bare essentials. I may have rushed a bit on the driving (nine days after surgery) but I hated asking neighbors for the fifteen-minute ride to the Haven, so I shifted with my left hand, like in Ireland, only I had to reach across my body to do it in my own car.

During January, I was mostly cheerful. I reminded myself of what I had learned several years ago in Al-Anon, "What your alcoholic spouse (or life) does to you can be lousy, but what you do to yourself, if you wallow in it, is the destructive part. In other words, spit out the eggshells!" When I felt down in the dumps because I was tired, or when I felt horribly vulnerable (how could cancer hit *me?*) then I'd write to friends, so those near me wouldn't know.

Some of the prescribed exercises were unnecessary. I could still scratch my shoulder blade. But I threw the rope over the door and pulled my right arm up; progress was slow, but pretty steady, until I got it up almost to the top.

Then I decided to try splitting wood. Rather than swing the maul over my head, I'd try dropping a sledge hammer on a wedge after Joe got the wedge stuck in the wood. I split two pieces, using my left hand to lift. Next day, I tried lifting the sledge hammer with my right hand. *Wrong!*

The day after that, I had to go back to the clinic for a "filler" session. Dr. Nicely, my plastic surgeon, had put in a temporary implant when I'd had the mastectomy and six times, he added more fluid to it, to stretch what skin I still had there. When it was stretched enough, he'd take out the temporary implant and put in the permanent one.

When Dr. Nicely lifted my elbow to check the mobility of my arm, I nearly screamed with the pain. "Is that all the movement you have?" He sounded very concerned.

"It was much better, but yesterday, I tried splitting wood and I hurt it."

He was furious. "Why did you do that?"

"Because I like splitting wood." His anger stunned me. I didn't even try to explain how gently I had tried, lifting the sledgehammer only six inches and then letting it drop; I wanted to ease into splitting because when I could do it again, maybe I'd feel more like myself.

I received a letter from Marion.

Dear Rena!

I was so glad to hear from you! And I know you are tough and will come through this in great shape.... Sounds like they did to you about what they did to my Mary and that has been over eight years ago — and I know you will do as well as she did! I won't have it any other way!! ... I know you're feeling better 'cause I've sent you a letter!

As I read it, I smiled. When I reread it, I laughed out loud. A picture jumped into my mind of Marion, all four feet and ten inches of her, growing to about ten feet tall, towering over me and, like a good mother bear, protecting her dear Rena from all harm. Her letter put a magnifying glass on my most precious resource, my inner strength, and helped me to see that I could get through this.

I won little victories: I reached the top of the door; I could raise my elbow above my shoulder.

January 20, 1987

Dear Ellen,

I just received your belated birthday present. Silk long johns!! I don't think I know how to tell you how much I appreciate them. Very practical for Wisconsin. And so luxurious, to have silk caressing this poor chopped-up body of mine!! Of course, it isn't just the present; it's that you took the time to find something for the self that I am today. Ellen, you have a talent for gift-giving and in my condition, I blow everything way out of proportion, so I love the long johns better than any present I ever got!

Last Saturday, I went down to the Cities for a concert of orchestra music. The last number they played was "The Firebird" by Stravinsky. The story the music tells, is that the hero came to a garden where he captured the Firebird, which he released when it promised to rescue him if he ever needed help. Then he saw a group of beautiful maidens, who were under a wicked sorcerer's spell. He fell in love with the princess and had to fight the sorcerer and won with the firebird's help. There I was, in the front row, ten feet from the orchestra. As soon as they started playing, I closed my eyes, let the music flow through me. I started crying. I lived the story, felt every nuance of the music. When the hero fought the sorcerer, I battled with him, because the sorcerer's name was Cancer. I fought hard. And when we destroyed him, I nearly screamed out loud with the triumph. I would beat cancer! What an experience!

Thank you, more than words can say, for the silk. Thanks for being my loving sister.

Love, Maureen

Last night, I talked to Roy (which was maybe a name for a ghost or maybe a name for my own self-destructiveness).

Roy, I hated you for cutting me off instead of letting me help you through your cancer. And I never admitted it. I think the cancer was my hate eating away at me unnoticed. I helped you die and then I talked to you for a few weeks after you died. Until you said you would destroy me and your son. Then I divorced you out of my heart. So my last words to you were fearful and hating. Well, maybe it was my own self-destructiveness talking and not you at all. Death seemed very appealing to me for several months after you died. But I need to stop hating you. I need to get on with my life. I hated you. But I loved you more, and I still do.

Today, I had a letter from Chelle, answering one of my ranting, raving letters. She asked me if I got what I wanted from my relationship with you. That started me thinking. I dug out all the Christmas cards, Valentines, and other cards you gave me. You used to say you loved me, your hugs told me you loved me, and my heart knew it was true. But your cards gave words to the love. I cried as I read them. You gave me love and I gave you love, far more than I would have dreamed possible. With you, I found the courage and help to start the Haven, which is more satisfying and totally right for me than I ever thought a job could be. I watched you grow up and you watched me grow up. In spite of our flaws, when we were together, my love, we were awesome. We were good for each other, Roy, and I am proud of us. I love you. So please take my love and let me be.

Roy yelled, "*No!*"

I kept repeating my message. He kept refusing. My mind wandered; when I came back to him, he agreed to leave me be.

All the loving support from our family and friends gave me strength for my fight with cancer and for settling with Roy. I felt whole again. No doubt I still had some garbage about my cancer to deal with, but after that, it should be small potatoes.

As I recuperated, Bob would say things like, "I still love you," or "You're just as beautiful as ever."

I woke up that morning, hugely mad at the world because I had cancer. I resented the doctor's poking, gawking, machines mapping, outrageous doctor bills — fifteen hundred dollars for one hour of plastic surgery when he put the implant in to "replace" my breast — losing control to appointments, to weakness, to fear of more cancer, more pain, death. Doctors were always right, controlled my treatment and my future. I hated being too tired to put in a normal day's work, too weak and fragile to split wood or play volleyball, having to ask for help, taking four trips to carry what used to take one trip. It messed up my life from all directions!

I was all riled up going to COPE meetings — I shouldn't have to go! That grungy psychologist at the last meeting claimed anger and such emotions are maladjustive. Well, I sure shut him down! At first I tried to make reasonable comments, refuting his claims. Then I got fed up with his bookish prattling. I stood up and yelled, "If I got angry at what you said and killed you, that is maladjusted. If I told you you're full of shit, that's just the plain truth. I am mad about having cancer and I have every right to be. It's a stinking lousy thing to happen. And if you can't understand that, you had better find a different profession!" Maybe he had things to say that the others needed to hear, but if the rest of what he'd planned to say was as unreal as the first part, nobody needed his hogwash.

I also put it to the instigator of forty pages of picayune, detailed paperwork that I had to fill out for the inspector of group homes. After several hours in the Haven office working on that, I went to the kitchen to fix supper.

Looking for garlic, I found two cans of ginger, three cans of poultry seasoning and two cans of garlic powder opened. If I had lost control of my health, by golly, I'd at least have control over the spices! "Bob, why are there two cans of ginger open? And three cans of poultry seasoning?"

"I don't know, dear," he answered calmly.

"Bob, you're supposed to use one up before you start another one. No wonder I've been spending a fortune on spices lately!"

"Yes, sweetie."

"Bob, how can I stay mad at you when you keep being so sweet?" I raged.

"I don't know, honey." His spaniel eyes were round with innocence and affection, which smashed my fury to bits and I burst into laughter. I walked over to him and kissed his cheek. "Bob, I'm sorry I yelled at you. I'm not mad at you. I'm mad at this stupid cancer, and I shouldn't be taking it out on you."

"It's okay." Bless his heart. He could write *the book* on how to treat a woman who's lost a breast to cancer. Only he could barely read.

The next day, we went to Minneapolis to pick up Joe at the airport, coming back from Florida, where he'd been with his daughter's family. I got permission for Bob and Tom to go inside the plane. Later, Bob said, "The cockpit was plumb full of gauges and levers and buttons and switches." We stopped to eat and Bob ordered a whole bucket of chicken, his favorite food. He ate chicken for a week, then our cook fixed chicken. That evening, when we went out to eat, Bob ordered chicken. Joe asked Bob when he was going to start laying eggs. Bob said he couldn't, he wasn't built right. I told him it would save us a lot of money if he would lay eggs, but he never did.

Although I hated doctoring, I chose to have the reconstruction because I wanted to continue to be beautiful. I deserved it. It would be worth the money and the discomfort, maybe not today or tomorrow, but soon. If all went well, they'd finish the new breast (except the nipple) in two weeks and maybe a few weeks after that, I wouldn't have to be so bloody careful and I could work until my muscles complained and not worry about what might happen to my new "breast."

I was very grateful for all the friends who had written and called and been supportive, even if it did lower my IQ (independence quotient). I told myself, "Rena, you are worth all the trouble; you deserve the best care."

But I wanted to split wood, really swing the maul with all my orneriness smashing into the wood. My brain twisted and turned. How could I get rid of all my orneriness when my favorite piss and vinegar outlet was impossible?

The next morning, before I left for the clinic, I put an old glass saucer in a grocery bag and put that into a garbage bag and then in another garbage bag, wrapping each around the saucer many times. Grinning viciously, I went downstairs and smashed it, again and again, on the cement floor. It felt really great, except for the first swing: in my eagerness to smash, I had forgotten and used my right arm. *Wrong*! I switched to my left hand, but the damage was done. I had exchanged a lot of anger for a lot of pain.

Doctor Nicely wasn't mad at me because I couldn't move my arm much, which surprised me. His assistant asked, "Did it help?"

"Yeah." Her grin matched mine. "I don't believe in kicking the dog when things go wrong, but I do like to get rid of the grunge."

"I always beat my wife when I'm mad at life." I looked at him, startled. "No, I'm just kidding, but she's lucky I don't."

"No, *you're* lucky you don't." This was unsettling. Doctor Nicely had been so sympathetic a month ago, when I had babbled on about being tied up in knots over coming to the clinic. But now, after the abuse dumped on my body by the medical profession, he callously joked about wife-beating.

"We're going to be able to get a really good match. I don't

think we'll have to do anything to the other breast at all."
The doctor neatly changed the subject. He had said that just
about every time I'd been there. He'd told me the mess under my arm would improve and the implanted breast would
sag in time. At that point, it had the shape of a very thick
liquid dumped on a flat surface, spreading out willy-nilly. A
blob. But soon it would be beautiful. In one week, they
would put in the permanent implant.

While waiting, I took it out on the wood. I had eased up
to splitting ten chunks, left-handed. I could even use a little
force on the sledge hammer.

The day before the surgery to put in the permanent implant, Dr. Nicely's assistant said, "Check into the hospital
outpatient section at ten tomorrow morning."

"But he said I'd be his first surgery, at eight." He had also
said he'd have me in the hospital for three days, then changed
it to overnight.

"Oh, it has changed." I didn't like it, but there was nothing I could do about it.

That night, in the motel, I couldn't sleep, got up and
wrote a long letter to Marion, lay down, got up, and found an
old Katharine Hepburn movie. At three thirty, I tried to
sleep again. Why was I so uptight? They were just going to
cut a little slit, pull out the temporary implant and put in the
permanent one. And then I'd be beautiful again. I tightened
my foot muscles and relaxed them several times and did the
same for my calf muscles, thigh muscles and on up my body.
One of the "I Can Cope" lecturers had suggested that as a
relaxer. But my body dreaded more surgery and refused to
relax. I slept a little, tightly.

I checked in at ten. Four agitated hours later, they put
me to sleep. I woke up at three. Dr. Nicely came to my room
a few hours later, to look at the results. He grinned and said,
"We really got a good match on this one. You're going to
want a nipple on it."

That evening, a lovely nurses' aide gave me a back rub and
we talked about gardens and splitting wood and stuff. When
she left, I pulled out my old Jobst bra (the ugly harness I had
to wear to keep the new me together) because washing had

softened it; the new one was still stiff and ornery. And I wanted to look at my new breast.

It was ugly! I had expected that the permanent implant would have the shape and size of my other breast, but it was still a flat blob, still two inches higher than my real breast. I was appalled. Either Dr. Nicely was a liar or totally stupid! He'd said it would take a few months for it to settle into its permanent shape, but I knew right then that it would never look anything like my breast. All the anguish and money for a *blob*!

Again, I couldn't sleep, only then anger kept me awake. At two in the morning, a nurse came to take my blood pressure and temperature. Poor woman, she was only doing her job, but I screamed at her. "No, I'm tired of being poked at and gawked at!" She was startled, tried weakly to change my mind and left. If my breast had looked beautiful, as promised, I wouldn't have minded; that would have been worth all the bother. But this monstrosity wasn't worth a hiccup in hell.

At six thirty, another nurse came in. I gave her the same message, more politely, but just as adamantly.

At seven thirty, Dr. Jekyll (formerly Dr. Nicely) came in. I glared at him. "Can I take your blood pressure?"

"No," I spat out. He was the one I was mad at, so I poured on the venom.

"Can I look at the incision?"

"*No*! I'm tired of being pawed and gawked at and all I got out of it was an *ugly blob*! And I'm leaving as soon as I eat breakfast and clean up!"

"How can I discharge you, if you won't let me check to see if you're all right?"

"I don't give a damn if you discharge me or not. I don't give a damn if you take the I.V. needle out or not. If you don't take it out, I will. And I'm leaving."

"It's not good for you to leave without my discharge," he threatened.

I yelled at him, using all the nasty words I learned from Roy and finished with: "You put me through all this pain, expense and anguish and the result is *ugly*!"

"Well, I never promised you it would look like your other breast." That was a lie! "Now, can I just look at it?"

"*No!*" That one word carried all my contempt for him, with plenty of anger, disgust and determination.

Since then, I have seen other women's reconstructed breasts and they were beautiful, so I knew it was possible, but I would never bother trying to get mine looking right.

When I calmed down, a long time later, I thought about my outburst. I was glad I had directed my anger at the one who had caused it and I had told him why I was angry, but I was amazed at the depth of the rage.

Did I overreact? Sure I did; I'd done it before and I'd do it again. I thought back to a haircut I didn't want when I was a kid, to an excessive modesty that threatened to ruin a whole summer, to a jacket Roy left on the couch. Then I laughed, long and deep, because I knew better than to take myself so seriously. I knew I shouldn't bludgeon myself over what's done. I knew, but I was so darn good at it that I really hated to quit.

16

Maureen
Wisconsin
April 1987

Several years ago, I had found Norman Knott's picture of a bear, his symbol of inner strength. A month ago, I had bought a sweatshirt, bright red with a mother bear and two cubs imprinted on it. My energy level hadn't been too great since the surgery, so I wore my strong sweatshirt to Duluth to find a birthday present for Ellen and to see an art exhibit by Dad's cousin's wife, Joan.

The exhibit was in the Duluth Depot Museum, which was a really neat place. After I saw Joan's art (it was quite good), I wandered through the Minnesota displays of Indian artifacts and early white settlers. In the lobby sat a woman surrounded by beautiful handmade quilts. I admired them. She admired my bear sweatshirt and we chatted away. I told her I was looking for something Native American for a present for Ellen.

Following her directions, I came to a large old brick building. Inside, the beautifully refinished wood floors led to a wide wooden staircase straight ahead and intriguing small shops to my right and left. I was drawn to the left one, an arts and crafts place. Paintings, photographs, ceramics, greeting cards... the fawns! A large photograph showed two fawns, lying on the ground, one with its head up, looking curiously at the photographer, the other with its head on the ground, looking bored. I could almost hear the second one thinking, "Mom, why do you always make us do such dumb things?" I went on. I went back to the fawns. Ellen had asked for Native American craft work but I knew she liked deer. So I bought them.

In August, we had canned thirty-six quarts of pickles, thirty-five quarts of tomatoes and thirty quarts of beans; we froze twenty-two quarts of corn and forty pints of zucchini. We sold extras to our friends for money to go to a Twins game. After Labor Day, we started on tomato juice. Whenever we had at least four five-quart pails of ripe tomatoes, I cut the stem end and bad spots out and boiled them for forty minutes. Bob liked to squeeze them through the ricer. I added a bit of salt and garlic powder, boiled them again and poured the juice into jars. Tom and Joe tightened the lids and put them into the canning kettle, where they boiled for two minutes and sat for ten minutes. It was a lot of work, but that juice tasted like summer sunshine in the middle of the winter.

Then we brought in potatoes. Joe dug down with a pitchfork. Tom and Richard sifted through the loosened dirt with their hands and threw potatoes into an ice cream bucket. I sifted through after them to get any they had missed, mostly with my left hand. (Volunteer potatoes every year showed how many we all missed.) John dumped the buckets into the wheelbarrow. "Remember how small the potatoes were the first year? Not even as big as my fist. Now they're five times as big!" Many hills yielded nearly a bucketful. The men bragged, "Wow, look at all of these!" or "Look at this monster!"

We filled the wheelbarrow with potatoes, then pulled up four buckets of carrots and four buckets of onions. Side by side, Joe and Tom pulled the wheelbarrow up to the house and into the east door. Richard, John and I carried the carrots and onions. I laid out newspapers on the floor in an empty bedroom. Tom dumped the wheelbarrow and we spread the potatoes so they would dry. When dry, we would store them in mesh bags in the basement; same with the onions.

In the kitchen, Tom washed the carrots, I cut off the ends and spots and took them to the table; there, Bob, Joe, John, Dan, Art and Richard waited with knives and cutting boards. Thunk, thunk; thunk, thunk, thunk; thunk, thunk. The knives made a merry rhythm slicing through the carrots, accented by an occasional plop as a slice hit the floor or by a loud crunch as someone sampled a piece. When they were sliced, I put them into the kettles of boiling water for three to five minutes. Tom or Joe would then dump them into cold water in the sink. When they were cooled and drained, we'd put them in freezer bags, then into the freezer.

At supper, I sat at the head of the fourteen-foot-long table watching my eight residents demolish four pizzas. Of course I was helping in that noble effort. "Tom and Joe, how about bringing in wood tomorrow? It should be pretty dry since we haven't had any rain for a week."

"Yeah." Joe liked working with wood better than with vegetables. John said, "Me, too."

Dan offered his excuse, "I have to do laundry tomorrow." He would rather work by himself than with the others.

I answered them, "John, of course, you, too. We couldn't manage without you. Yeah, Dan, the laundry comes first." If I let Dan off the hook about helping with wood, he'd probably help; if he didn't, that was all right. "Bob, how about baking some peanut butter chocolate chip cookies for us to snack on while we're working so hard?"

Bob grinned, "Sure." His grin faded. "But I wish I could still help with the wood." His muscular dystrophy slowly, surely deteriorated his body, not as quickly as the doctor thought, but much faster than we wanted it.

Joe answered him, "Bob, you keep our bellies full and we'll keep your butt warm." Then he turned to me, "Rena, when are we going to start cutting wood?" Joe was eager to use his chain saw, now that he could sharpen it right.

"It depends on the weather. I figure we have about two more days canning tomato juice, two more days of bringing in potatoes, onions and carrots. I'd like to finish that first. And we want to get this winter's wood in so it's out of the way for the next bunch. While you're bringing in wood tomorrow, I'll make some vegetable beef soup."

"Good!" We made excellent soup. Those who weren't bringing in wood would cut up five pounds of chuck roast, potatoes, onions, beans, turnips, carrots, rutabagas, zucchini, right from our garden. I'd add some garlic, parsley, beef soup base, salt. It would be a feast fit for a king, or a hard-working crew. "I'd better pick zucchini tomorrow, too. Bob, if there's some small ones, maybe you could make zucchini bread instead of cookies."

"Okay." He loved baking, pies, cookies, quick breads, cakes anything. He liked his place of importance among the other residents as Chief Baker. We all had a sweet tooth.

"And after the garden is emptied, we'll get manure. I think three big pickup loads will do it," I said.

Tom and Joe groaned. They were the Chief Shit Slingers and they knew it. But I had always helped and "Anything Rena can do, we can do better." "This year," I said, "I'll have to let you do all the work, 'cuz my shoulder is still bummed up from that danged surgery." I had tried the prescribed exercises, but gave them up after the implant surgery. I tried doing nothing and the shoulder froze and wouldn't move. I tried physical therapy and a chiropractor. I spent a lot of my insurance company's money, but I wasn't getting anywhere.

"That's okay, we can do it," Tom bragged.

"Thanks, Tom. You guys have all been great getting the work done while I mope around like a decrepit old lady. That's why we went to the Twins' game. I wanted to do something special for you all." Big grins recalled the trip to their first major league baseball game.

"Puckett hit a home run, just for us."

"The game lasted twelve innings, but the Twins finally won."

"We didn't get home until three in the morning!"

Bob's main joy, of course was chicken, "I had chicken twice, on the way down and on the way back! But I didn't get my ball signed."

Joe came back with, "Bob, you'd complain if they hung you with a new rope."

I said, "Bob, I could help you write a letter to the Twins and mail it with the ball, asking them to sign it."

He thought for a moment, "Yeah."

I returned to planning the work. "Joe, one of these days, we'd better change the oil in the van, pickup and car."

"You see," Joe said, "she's never satisfied with the oil I put in. She's always wanting to change it."

I told Dan and Richard, "The corn is all finished. So any time you have some extra ambition, you can pull up the corn stalks. We'll use the stalks to cover the leaves we put on the rose bushes, tulips and daffodils over the winter. They like their leaf and stalk winter blanket."

"You and your flowers!" Bob grumbled. "You can't eat flowers." His Dad had probably told his Mom that.

"Bob, my eyes feast on flowers! Besides, when I get all excited over the hyacinths coming up in January, you always admire them, too." They were planted on the south side of the house, by the furnace room, and popped up every January. Sometimes, they even bloomed. I had thought of moving them to a spot where they would come up later so they would always bloom, but I really liked seeing green in January.

Two weeks later, it was time to cut wood. "Okay, Joe, get out your chain saw. Come on, all you hard-working guys, let's do it! The one-hundred-inch logs, about eight to eighteen inch diameter, were neatly piled, about forty feet long and four feet high; the man who delivered them set them just the way we liked them. I pointed out two logs. "Joe and Tom, get these two straight logs down for skids." They put them at the foot of the pile, perpendicular to it, two feet apart.

"We have room, let's get two more at the ends of the first two." After they had four in place, Joe and Tom rolled seven logs from the pile onto the skids, which kept the logs off the ground, so the chain saw wouldn't be cutting dirt. They placed the logs two feet apart.

"Okay, John, bring the measuring stick over." Joe couldn't remember how long to cut the wood and John was getting a bit old for hard work, so I had Joe cut a broom stick to the length I wanted the wood. Joe got the bright idea to attach that to another piece of handle, at right angles, so John wouldn't have to bend over to hold the stick where it would show Joe where to cut. With the handle, John could also be at a safer distance from the chain saw.

"Tom and Richard, put the big ones that need splitting over here. Put the small ones over there on the poles along the field. We won't have to handle them again until next year, when we take them in the house." Stacking them there made a wind break and kept the snow from piling up in the driveway. "Remember, when you go to pick up the wood Joe has cut, don't get too close to the chain saw. Pretend you're stronger than I am and leave the small ones for me to stack." They laughed.

"Okay, Joe, start it up!" The saw roared into life. Joe cut the end off one log, then the end off the next one and down the line, then came back cutting off the other ends, as indicated by John and the marking stick. Then Joe cut twice more on each piece on the skids. Joe had used a chain saw before he came to the Haven, but not enough to be comfortable cutting the wood while it was stacked, so we worked out our method. As Joe moved down the line, Tom, Richard and I picked up the chunks and stacked them.

With Roy gone, I had to take charge of the wood cutting and splitting and there were huge frustrations until I got it figured out. Then there was the load of wood that was all sandy. It dulled the chain so quickly that Joe spent more time sharpening than cutting. Joe's memory was not good, so now everything was labeled "chain-saw mix" on the gas-oil mixture, "grease for the bar," and so forth.

The saw was sharp that day, and Joe moved carefully from

one log to the next so the first seven logs were quickly cut and stacked. After two batches were done, the pile was a little shorter, so we could lay out ten logs for cutting. When the wood was delivered, he had laid logs crosswise underneath, so we didn't need more skids. When three batches were stacked and the fourth ready on the skids, I called out, "Break time! The zucchini bread will be hot out of the oven by now. Let's go eat!" No arguments about that. Age and caution had kept us from speeding through the woodcutting, but it was going well and the men knew it.

As soon as we opened the kitchen door, the cinnamon smell started our mouths watering. Tom yelled, "Hey, Bob, you got anything for us to eat?" In the TV room, Bob put down his knitting and walked clumsily out to the kitchen.

"The bread just came out of the oven."

I pulled out the knife and cut carefully into the hot loaf. Too hot for thin slices, but that didn't hurt my feelings. "Tom, will you put butter and knives on the table?"

"That's not butter, it's margarine," he teased.

I grinned, "I know, I know, but put it on anyway." I kept a heel for myself. I loved the crunch of the outside and soft inside with the margarine melted right in.

"Bob, this isn't good. It's perfect!" Bob grinned.

I bragged. "What could be better: Joe has his chain saw so sharp, it cuts through the logs like they were butter; John is our expert measuring man; Tom, Richard and I are the masterful stackers; and Bob has made us a wonderful treat for our break time. Even the weather is perfect, sunny and cool but not cold. The only problem is, I can only lift the real little ones. Makes me mad."

Drawn by the noise and the good smell, Art and Jim came out to join the crowd. "Have a piece of bread. I'll go cut some more."

Joe was feeling good about his work. "Rena, I don't know why we have to cut up all that wood. Our work will just go up in smoke!" Then he asked, "Hey, Bob, do you know how to tell if there's an elephant in the refrigerator?"

"Yeah, by the footprints in the Jell-O." Joe doesn't remember that he's told the same jokes dozens of times, but he has such fun telling them that everybody laughs anyway.

"Hey, Joe, did you hear that the department of agriculture is going to outlaw those big round bales of hay?" Tom asked.

"I know, the cows can't get a square meal."

Dan didn't want to miss all the fun, so he came out too. He asked, "Rena, do you know why there are so many Johnsons in the phone book?"

"Sure, 'cuz they all have telephones. Have a piece of zucchini bread, Dan."

"Oh, Bob, bingo is Thursday and it's our turn to bake. What do you want to fix?"

Bob grinned. "Apple pie." Eight men agreed to that.

"Okay, I'll buy apples when we go to town tomorrow." Making apple pie was a delicious tableau. Bob would put on his super-concentrated look as he mixed up and rolled out the crust at the end of the table. Next to him, Tom and Joe traded insults and jokes as they peeled apples. After mixing the flour, margarine, sugar and cinnamon, I cored the apples and passed the pieces to John, Art and Richard to slice. John didn't talk much; he was too busy snitching bites and looking at me with that "Who, me?" look on his face. The others nibbled, but John snitched. If I put a bowl of apples on the table for eating, they'd sit there for weeks. But if I wanted a fat apple pie, I had to buy a dozen extra apples.

"Who's coming for bingo?" asked Art.

"Mary Ellen and Orrin and Ken and Agnes," I said. "Do you want to play charades before bingo?"

They agreed on that, too. Our house rules were that one person would act or draw the word and everybody would guess what it was. We always got very loud and very silly over it.

Dan told the men, "Your clean clothes are out in the living room."

I suggested, "Why don't you guys put your clothes away and then we'll go back to work. The cigarette smoke is as thick as the blarney in here and pretty soon, if we stay here, we'll all pass out for lack of oxygen!"

Even with two rainy days, a Sunday and a town day, we finished cutting the sixteen cords of wood in ten days. Half of it needed splitting. For that we had two splitting mauls, with a sledgehammer and three wedges for the tough ones. Some years, we rented a wood-splitting machine, but we had a good crew that year, so we'd do it by hand, during the winter when it was frozen, easier to split. That's what I would miss most! I *liked* swinging the maul. I'd put all my aggravations on a chunk of wood and split them into bits with the maul.

I had arthritis and a calcium deposit in my shoulder, Doc said. That cut out volleyball, wood-splitting, tennis. No heavy lifting. What a drag! Well, I could stack what they split. And when we finished fall chores, we'd go out to a restaurant and celebrate our good work. It was hard but satisfying. We were providing our own food and heat and making time for important extras, like flowers, sweets and eating out.

As soon as I came into the Haven kitchen, Tom blurted out, "John is dead!"

"He's visiting his brother in Cumberland. He's fine."

"No, his daughter just called. He had a heart attack and died."

I didn't want to believe it, but it was true.

At supper, we talked about John, the seven of us he had left behind. "He was a good man with a hoe." The summer before, he had slowed down a lot. He would hoe for five minutes and rest for ten, but his cheerful presence was always welcome.

Joe said, "He sure liked that measuring stick I made for him."

"He liked throwing horseshoes and playing cards."

"John was in on everything, from doing dishes to flying kites, from working the wood to fishing."

"He always bought sweet rolls when we went to town."

"He loved to eat, especially Bob's Hungarian goulash."

"Remember how, whenever we made apple pie, John always put one piece in his mouth for every one he put in the pie?"

"John was a big Twins' fan. I'm glad he got to go to a game before he died."

When his wife died, John had turned to the bottle for comfort, but the amount of comfort he drank severely threatened his daughter's comfort. After trying everything else, his daughter had brought him to the Haven. He was angry at first, but his easygoing nature came back. He made friends with the dogs and the men and soon found himself drawn into the activities. He had hated bingo at the VA center, because his hearing aid didn't work. Roy had it fixed. I talked John into playing, seating him next to the caller, with his hearing aid facing the caller. He had fun and even won two games. After he forgot his anger, he welcomed his daughter's visits and his young grandchildren.

I said, "He liked buying poinsettias for his daughter for Christmas."

"Don't forget his watermelons! That one was so big, we had to cut it off the vine with a chain saw and haul it up here in the wheelbarrow!" Maybe the after-effects of kissing the Blarney Stone were contagious.

Bob didn't say anything, just sat there looking stunned. John was his best buddy.

I told the men, "The funeral will be Monday at eleven. I'm going and anyone who wants to, can come too." Tom and Joe wanted to go, but not Bob. Later, I told him, "You were John's best buddy. You have to go to say good-bye to him."

"Me and dead bodies just don't get along."

"You don't have to look at the body or go to the cemetery. But you really should go." He went reluctantly.

It was quite a group of men I had there. When Joe had come from the VA center, he was withdrawn. Like everybody else, he did dishes. After Herman left, Joe agreed to cut wood. I bought a small chain saw. It took a while to work out our method for cutting it and it took even longer to teach Joe how to sharpen the saw, because Joe was prickly and could never admit being wrong. I learned how it was done from a chain saw repairman, and wrote out the directions and left them on the workbench, where he sharpened the saw. Without me bothering him, he could read and follow the directions. When he was using a sharp saw, Joe enjoyed the work, partly because it got him out of doing dishes.

Joe and I did a lot of fixing at the Haven. I'd pick his brain and figure out how, and he'd handle the screwdriver or hammer and nails. He mowed the lawn and ran the snow-blower on our long driveway. He loved being useful and said so many times. His biggest problem was hanging on to grudges, but for six years he'd made a good life for himself here.

Dan had changed a lot, too. Mentally ill, he had spent his first year sitting in a chair, chain-smoking until his cigarettes were gone, then bumming them from the others. He was withdrawn into a world which must have been very unpleasant, judging from the scowl on his face. If I told him a joke, he'd laugh, then go right back to his frown. When he first came, I asked him to sweep the basement floor. He pushed the broom around, this way and that, with no sense or direction. I left him alone for a while. Gradually, Dan got better. He could do a good job on the laundry. When the mood hit, Dan would go on a cleaning spree; he'd work for hours scrubbing floors, vacuuming carpets, dusting. He and Joe were our main jokesters. Dan had a much better focus on reality than he had three years ago, but his bad times had intensified, too.

Tom seemed like two people: one was considerate, hard-working and likeable; the other erupted into a mean anger over any little thing. I have seen him sling manure with a rhythm and grace that was a joy to watch. He was the first to offer a guest a cup of coffee. He loved getting dressed up and going out to eat, or going to a Twins' game or to a fishing picnic. He was my assistant grocery shopper, helping me with as many as four carts of groceries. He was my first assistant for canning vegetables. Everybody else sat at the table to chop carrots or snap beans or cut corn off the cob. Tom liked to wet-mop the kitchen floor after everyone else was in bed, especially if there were cookies to nibble on. He had a sizable sweet tooth, about the size of an elephant tusk. Bob and I sometimes made an outrageously rich chocolate bar with marshmallows and a thick fudge frosting. I saw Tom eat an eight-inch by eight-inch chunk of it.

Roy found Art drunk in his car, where he had been living for several months. After Art was sober, Roy took him in at his group home. Art moved to the Haven to cook when Roy went to the hospital for his first cancer surgery. Art liked the Haven because the men weren't drinking like they were at the other place and Art wanted to stay sober. It was okay with Roy, so Art stayed there. His first summer there, Art kept the whole garden weeded by himself. He'd take a hoe out every morning, start at one end and work slowly up and down the rows. By the time he finished, there were enough weeds at the beginning to start over.

Other men and two women have been at the Haven for a short time. A sober, constructive life, in spite of handicaps, didn't suit everyone. Some people, including me, really liked being there. We had it good and we knew it.

A few weeks after John died, we were in town for our weekly shopping. Just before I turned the corner to park and let the men out, I said, "I hope we get a good parking place, so Bob doesn't have to walk far. Hey, John, you're up in Heaven now, help us out, please. Find us a good spot."

Bob looked sour, "He can't hear you."

I turned the corner and there was a space, right in front of the drug store, Bob's first stop.

After that, I asked John's help for many small favors and he always helped. Whenever we had a big problem to face, I'd call on everybody I knew who had died and ask the men to do the same if they felt like it. It sat right with me to do this, and it seemed to work for the men, too, except for Bob. He wanted to believe and to disbelieve, but he never quite made up his mind.

That started me thinking. What did I believe in, since I was no longer a practicing Catholic. I believed what St. Paul said, "We carry this treasure in vessels of clay," which was why the Church was such a mess and why so many Christians acted so rotten. They had too much clay! I believed in the essence of Jesus' message: "Love God and love your neighbor."

I believed in Goddess. Goddess-God probably didn't have a sex, but Goddess seemed more caring than God, and I doubted if it made any difference to Her-Him what we called Her-Him. There was Something bigger than me, and when I connected with the deepest, down-in rightness of myself or of nature, or of beauty, I was a part of that Something and of Everything. And when I acted according to that rightness in myself, I was morally right, which wasn't necessarily by the church's codes. Unfortunately, I didn't always follow my own code. That was my clay.

Heaven felt right to me. So I told Bob when he went to heaven, it would be like a circus, and catching big fish, and baking goodies for other people and being with his mother again. If that wasn't what his heaven would be like, it would be even better, so it was a good picture for him.

In my heaven, of course, my guys and I would keep right on doing what we do so well. My house would only get dirty when I felt like cleaning. When I did a project, I'd know how to use the right tools and the results would be beautiful. I could dance like Mikhail Baryshnikov, sing like Jeanette MacDonald, paint like Norman Knott as well as enjoying their artistry. I would fix and eat tons of delicious food, while watching beautiful sunsets. I'd share these wonderful experiences with great friends.

Above all that I've known on earth that could gloriously continue in heaven, there would be Roy. We'd be right with each other in all the ways there are. As for knowing Goddess in heaven, that was beyond my imagination, but it would surely be better than the frosting on the cake. I'd had some grand moments in this life. In heaven, it would be all splendid, with none of the rotten times.

I still prayed. Only I prayed to John or Aunt Caroline, who died last year, to help me through a tough moment. I felt that they were a part of the Strong and Loving Beyondness. When I experienced a moment of perfection — admiring the fall colors, eating one of Bob's cookies, enjoying the camaraderie and hard work of cutting wood with my guys, helping a dog birth her puppies — by immersing myself in the moment, I glorified Goddess in my joyful acceptance of what she had given me. That was my worship.

My old religion had fit in a recipe box: a recipe for dogma, for morals and so forth. But it was just words in that box and how could words explain anything about that which was beyond us? The words had become vague and shadowy but my faith felt strong.

My dog reminded me of a more urgent reality. Tinker was doing a little dance, feet fidgeting, tail wagging all the way up to her nose, two feet from my recliner where I was enthroned. She watched me expectantly "Okay, okay." I unreclined myself and walked over to the closet while Tinker jumped along beside me, woofing her happiness. I put on my parka and snowmobile boots; I already had on long johns. Tinker bumped me down the stairs. Snapping on her leash would have been a lot easier if she'd stand still. Once in a while, I got impatient with her for getting so rambunctious, though we did this four or five times a day. On my better days, I tried to match her delight in the ordinary.

I opened the door and she rushed out, trying to pull off my arm while I reached back to close the door. The bitterly cold air attacked me, daring me to take a deep breath so it could freeze my insides all the way to my toes.

By the time she dragged me across the driveway, where she watered the snow banked up by the plow, my eyes had adjusted to the darkness of midnight, which was surprisingly light, considering there was no moon. She dragged me out to the road, where she stopped again. I looked up. It was the Northern Lights making it so bright! Through the leafless trees, I could see a milky brightness, so I leaned my head back to look. The lights flashed overhead and even toward the south. Over half the sky lit up with slow splashes of white that would streak out, fade away and then reappear.

As spectacular as it was, Tinker had finished and was ready to walk. I never took a flashlight along, even when it was really dark. That night, not only could I see where the road cut through the woods, but also the snowbank, splotched with dirt, and my dog looking at me, eager to be off, her dark body clearly outlined against the snow.

So off we went, her nose to the ground to see if anything exciting had appeared since she was out before. My feet and her paws crunched the snow, another indication of the cold — no slushy, balmy 35 degrees that night. She stopped, head up, ears perked, as well as long floppy ears could perk. I couldn't hear anything, no wind rustling dry clinging oak leaves, no tree joints cracking their complaints against the cold, no cars or snowmobiles, just silence, silence that begged for an appreciative audience.

We went on to the corner, where my seldom-used road met one even less used, heading north. Here I had a clear view of the lights. Since Tinker had done her duty and explored some, she stood quietly while I gazed at nature's awesome light show. Even though I was warmly dressed, zero degrees was not loitering weather; we headed back. Tinker was patient while I got what I wanted. It seemed to me that I should be more patient while she got what she wanted, like stopping to listen or to sniff.

The next August, Channel 5 TV called from the Cities. It was all set.

"Hey, guys," I announced, "Two social workers are coming tomorrow to see if this would be a good place for them to bring residents, so we've got to clean up around here," I lied. Tom cleaned the bathrooms and Joe vacuumed the carpets. I directed traffic: mop the hall, scrub the kitchen floor, dust the furniture. "Bob, we need some of your molasses cookies for showing off."

We didn't have a noon cook at the time, so I asked our friend, Darlene, to cook, because I'd be far too rattled. "Sure. Why don't you call Bill from the newspaper?" Bill said he'd come. Art had had to move into a nursing home several months ago, so I arranged for him to come, too.

The next morning, at ten, the TV people called to say they were at the airport and they asked me to pick them up. So I told the men that the social workers were lost and I had to go get them. I lied.

A year earlier, Bob had tried to get a baseball autographed at a Twins' game, but he was so slow getting in line that he didn't get any signatures. I had helped him write a letter to mail with the ball, asking for autographs. No answer. In December, Bob and I wrote to channel 5 TV asking for their help. The following August, channel 5 called "We're going to get the autographs, but don't tell Bob because we want it to be a surprise." Well, we had to clean house for TV cameras.

I just lied about why we were cleaning.

I took Bob to the picnic table in the backyard. John Wingate, from the TV station, snuck up behind Bob and the camera recorded his surprise as John presented him his autographed baseball.

John chatted with Bob, for the camera, then we went inside where the camera recorded Bob showing off his prized possession to the other guys. And Bob displayed his other Twins' souvenirs: a coffee mug, a pennant, a miniature bat with Kirby Puckett's signature.

Bill, from the paper, John and his camera man, Darlene and Art stayed for a spaghetti lunch. The men were delighted to be hosting such important people and our guests were delighted to be the cause of our celebration.

On our next trip to town, Bob went into the drugstore, as usual. Every clerk there had seen his picture on the front page of our weekly newspaper. They all congratulated him. Everywhere he went, people commented on his famous baseball. When I picked the men up, Bob had a puzzled, pleased look on his face, as if to say, "All this fuss over me?"

A few weeks later, Bob was on the ten o'clock news. I had called everybody I could think of as soon as I got word when he would be on, and I invited Darlene and her daughter, Christina, over to watch with us. There was Bob on TV! All eyes grabbed our moment of glory. There were Tom and Joe! Ed shouted, "Hey, did you see me?" It was over far too quickly but the men smiled on their way to their bedrooms.

Our friend Beth taped it for us with her VCR. Then she filled the rest of the tape with a home movie about the Haven heroes. She spent a day with us while we showed her how we cut wood, cleaned house, dug up and froze carrots, made zucchini bread, played cards, threw horseshoes, and ate a splendid steak supper to celebrate how great we were.

Watching themselves on TV in this home movie, for the first time or the tenth time, the men loved every minute of it. And Bob, who didn't seem to really realize what was happening at the time he got his ball, said a few weeks later that it was the nicest thing that ever happened to him.

Because my car was rusting out in spots, I had it repainted. It looked good, but it made the van look bad. At supper, I asked the guys if they thought we could paint the van ourselves.

"Sure."

"Shall we paint it red?"

"Yeah."

Joe said, "We could get a patch kit to fix the front part that's rusted through." Then he added, "It would look better if we spray-painted it, instead of using a brush."

"Can you do the painting if I borrow a compressor?"

"Sure."

"I'll see if I can borrow one," I said.

Joe asked, "What do we do about rust spots? If we just paint over them, the rust will just come through again."

After a long "how-to" talk with Chris at the hardware store, I thought I knew what to do. First, we scrubbed the van vigorously. Tom and Joe patched the big hole by the front tire with epoxy and fiberglass cloth. They sanded all the rust spots by hand; then Al and Ed painted the spots with a rust inhibitor. That was as far as we got before town day. It looked ugly, school bus yellow dotted with lots of brownish, blackish blobs. We laughed at our "leopard" and went to town in it anyway.

The next day, I went to the Haven for lunch so we could get an early start on the van. Joe had persuaded our new cook to make pasties. Bob made the pie crusts, and Jeanette peeled and chopped up potatoes, carrots, zucchini, and onions. She fried the hamburger, mixed it with the raw vegetables, put the mixture between pie crusts and baked them.

She left as I was serving it up. A few minutes later, I looked around. Joe had pulled out all the chunks of zucchini and moved them to the far side of his plate. Dan had sorted out the zucchini and the onions (he refused to eat onions unless they were grated; then he didn't recognize them). Tom had a pile of zucchini and carrots (he only ate carrots when they were raw). Bob couldn't chew the carrots because they were still hard (they were supposed to be precooked). Ed and Al didn't want their zucchini either. Every one of them had picked through their pasty and then they enjoyed what was left. I had a hard time not to laugh as I told myself to explain to Jeanette: zucchini and onions must be grated; if the men didn't know they were there, they ate them and the vegetables should be precooked.

After I cleared the table and started Dan and Ed on dishes, Tom, Joe and I went out to work on the van. We taped newspapers over the windows and the bumpers. I had borrowed Ella's compressor; I filled the paint container with fire-engine red paint and turned it over to Joe, who was up on the six-foot stepladder where he could reach the van roof. "Ella said to hold the can about eight inches from the van."

"Okay."

Joe triggered the sprayer and moved it back and forth to cover the area at hand. When he finished, I climbed up to admire his work. "It looks great, Joe!"

After a while, the spray fizzled out, so I called Ella, who told me what to do. Joe unscrewed the paint container and there was enough pressure to splatter paint all over his coveralls. We emptied the paint, ran some turpentine through it and it worked again. We finished the first coat that day and put on a second coat two days later, with only two more red eruptions onto Joe.

"It should have a white stripe," Bob insisted. Joe and Tom agreed. So I got some white paint. We taped to make a clean edge. We had white paint left over, so we sanded and painted the metal bumpers and the wheels. From a distance, where the slightly uneven red paint and the white drips didn't show, the van looked good. Until the doors were opened.

"We'd better paint the inside."

I agreed. Joe wanted battleship gray. Blah. But the others wanted gray, too. I bought paint and a bunch of sponge brushes and gave them to Al, Ed and Bob, who could sit to paint. Two days later, I decorated on the inside around door and window handles with red paint. That perked it up!

"But the seats look terrible!"

I had some royal blue and bright red material at home for making sweatshirts. I took it to the Haven.

"Tom, come out and help me please. I need four hands."

"Sure."

I draped the material over the first bench seat, marked and cut it; then with Tom holding it in place, I pinned it wrong side out to show where it should be sewn. Red for the two front seats and the second bench seat, blue for the first and third bench seats. Kathy said she'd sew them up.

"Who has lots of muscles?" I asked. Joe and Tom came grinning into the kitchen. I directed them, "I need about twenty inch-wide strips torn off this old sheet." Wrinkles betrayed its age; the new sheets were mostly wrinkle-free.

"Hey, Bob, come help me sew," I called.

Bob and I sewed the sheet strips to our blue and red seat covers, so we could tie them in place.

Finally, with the covers on, we all stood back and admired our work. From twenty feet away, the van looked really sharp, red with white trim outside; gray, red and blue inside. For the next few months, everyone who came to the Haven was invited to admire our work: our cook, our bingo friends, Roy's son Mike who was running his father's group home. They were all impressed. Some of them even believed Joe's tale that all the red paint on his coveralls was there because I had sprayed him. Even though it wasn't a professional job, it lasted a lot longer than the paint job I had paid for on my car.

Our "new" van gave me an excuse to invite Tony over to admire our work. Tony liked restoring old cars, so he knew exactly how hard and how successfully we had worked. He praised our work and ignored the imperfections, which really got my men strutting. Tony had lived at the Haven for only a few months, but after he moved into a place of his own, I often invited him back for supper and cards. He was always cheerful, a welcome guest for all of us. He was a paraplegic, with no use of his legs and limited use of his arms.

While deer hunting when he was in high school, Tony had fallen out of a tree stand and broken his neck. After extensive rehabilitation, he found a job and wanted a place to stay where he could get ready to be on his own. So he came to the Haven. I had a wheelchair ramp built, so he could wheel himself out of the house. When he reached his car, which was operated entirely by hand controls, he slid himself across a board and into the car. Then he pulled his wheelchair in and drove off. The ramp ended about three inches off the ground, so I bought a few bags of concrete, which Joe and Tom and I mixed, poured and smoothed, making a sidewalk that was level with the end of the ramp.

Bob's muscular dystrophy relentlessly weakened him, so Tony helped us figure out how to place grab bars in the bathroom that would help both of them.

Tony never talked much, but he laughed at all the jokes the guys told. He enjoyed playing rummy with us, in spite of my peculiar house rules: when I dealt, I stacked the deck. Since I hated to waste the joker, which would happen whenever someone went out before the joker was drawn, I shuffled it with the face cards and shuffled the small cards separately; I put the big cards on top and dealt. I never knew who would get the joker, but it was always played.

His friendly good humor made Tony welcome, but for him to maintain his geniality in spite of what could have been a long bleak future always put our petty gripes into perspective. Tony was an inspiration for all of us.

October 7, 1998

Dear Marion,

I walk out my basement door and look up my driveway, which is a huge Arc de Triomphe. The sides of the arch are dark red leaves of wild blackberry bushes, green weeds and purple wild asters. Above them, a dozen small maple trees burst out in vibrant oranges and scarlets; three large oak trees sport russet leaves; popple leaves show off their golden glow; a few pines add their green to the arch.

Leaves rustle quietly and off to the west, geese honk excitedly about their travel plans. There must be music playing, a galop perhaps, because the wind and sun dance through the trees and chase puffy white clouds across the sky.

Marion, may I have this dance? Join me in spirit and let's galop with the sun and wind, smile at each leaf, fly up to the clouds, admire the view and be glad we have eyes.

Love
Rena

In August, 1988, I had gone to Prairie du Chien for a family reunion, my first. After Mass in Patch Grove at the St. John's Church, which replaced the one my great-great-grandfather had built, we went downstairs for a meal served by the church women. We had roast beef, real mashed potatoes and gravy, green beans and tomatoes right out of someone's garden.

Then we introduced ourselves: "I'm Irene, granddaughter of Maggie and Matthew and these are my children."

"I'm Mary, granddaughter of Charlie and Maureen. This is my husband Jim."

Other than a few first cousins, aunts and uncles, I knew none of the hundred and fifty people here, all descendants of my great-great-grandparents. All these people were my family! I felt the family bond and it was good.

After the introductions, Charles, son of Maureen and Charlie, told us about how our great-great-grandparents had come to Wisconsin and started their farm and built a church and I was hooked. I had written up some family stories for Dad's side of the family and I would do the same for Mom's side.

I liked the people I met. I enjoyed getting to know them, five or ten minutes' worth. But as I talked to Mom's cousins, I looked for the ones with stories to tell. I found several, besides Charles, who lived in Milwaukee and decided to go there when all the fall work was done at the Haven.

In Milwaukee, Charles told many stories and gave me copies of what he had written, copies of old documents, like great-great-grandfather's discharge papers from the Army, back in 1836. He even let me sit in great-great-grandfather's rocking chair, which had passed down through the generations. His generosity overwhelmed me.

Then I met with a few of Mom's cousins, Mary Anne's daughter, Sister Helen and her sister Con, Ro's daughter Agnes and Maggie's daughter Irene, to talk about the "good old days."

Con reminisced, "Oftentimes our cousins stayed overnight in bad weather, because our farm was closer to school. We were enthralled with Colleen's interpretation of Edgar Allen

Poe's tales. John and Bernard would talk and laugh in bed until they were told to be quiet. In the summer, Helen and I loved to have cousin Jennie come because she would play with us. Your mother, Marguerite, and her sister Elizabeth sometimes stayed for a week on their way to Aunt Maggie's. They taught us how to play jacks; monkey up the lamppost was a real accomplishment. A visit to Aunt Maureen's was an overnight trip; the swing in their big willow was a great attraction. They had a high grapevine to climb in the backyard, blackberries to pick in the woods, and flat rocks in the creek made a nice place to wade. Billy had a big dog that scared me when I was little, because it would put its feet on my shoulders and look in my eyes."

Sister Helen recalled, "As a child, my best friends were my cousins and they were many. I counted fifty-four one time. Entertainment was getting together, sometimes singing and dancing, but usually just visiting."

Agnes was not pretty, but when she talked, she glowed, and I knew she had been a captivating university teacher. "When my mother was dying of cancer, every one of her sisters would come and help out, during her last four months. Her brother Johnny came, too. Mother especially loved John, so she asked me to make baking powder biscuits because he liked them. I tried but they were rocks. Mother had a devoted family of brothers and sisters." She reached inside her purse. "Maureen, this might interest you. It's a copy of what I wrote, long ago, about the Priest's room in Uncle Tom and Aunt Lizzie's home."

"Thank you, Agnes."

Irene spoke earnestly, "I recall how my family loved the battery-operated radio we got when I was a child. During the flu epidemic that followed World War I, my mother nursed three very sick children through it. They all lived. After the stock market crash in 1929, banks were closing. When Pa heard there might be a run on our bank, he took a chair and sat in front of the bank. He wasn't one to start the panic, but he wanted his money if there was one. The bank made it." After a pause, she continued, "I worshipped my mother — all of us cousins were close to our mothers and daughters. The women were the strong ones in our family. My mother never voted, never drove a car, still wore long skirts when she died in 1947, but never looked dowdy. All the women were well-dressed and well-read."

I listened, enthralled, to their wonderful stories, trying to take shorthand notes so I wouldn't forget everything. Back at home, I reread Agnes' evocative description of the Priest's room and Charles' delightful story about horse racing; both tell about the early 1900's.

The Priest's Room
(By Ro's daughter Agnes)

Tom and Lizzie, Mother's bachelor uncle and maiden aunt always spent the summer months on the family homestead near Patch Grove, Wisconsin. Uncle Tom wintered in Florida, while Aunt Lizzie lived with her sister Margaret and family in Platteville, Wisconsin.

During the winter months, the house was vacant. The farm was run by a tenant who lived in another house a bit farther down the road. He furnished Aunt Lizzie and Uncle Tom with milk, fresh eggs, and homemade butter.

The homestead was located in a small ravine amid a grove of fragrant pines. On a nearby hill was a cemetery where many of the family were buried. On one corner of the cemetery was a hole which was becoming overgrown with grass and weeds. Mother said the Catholic Church, built by my great-grandfather John, stood on that spot for many years until it was struck by lightning and burned. Later the church was rebuilt in the nearby town of Patch Grove.

When I was a child, I lived on a farm about twelve miles from the Catholic Church in Patch Grove. It was slow tedious travel to Mass as we were among the last families in the county to own an automobile. My Father considered it the devil's own invention.

Many Sundays, Aunt Lizzie invited us to stop on our way home for tea and biscuits. The house always smelled a bit musty as it had been closed for so many months. Papers, books and magazines were scattered on the living room table. Otherwise the house seemed sterile and unused, gave little indication that anyone lived there. Leading from the living room was a bedroom, the door of which always remained closed. One day I asked Mother why. She said it had been used by the priest when he came when the church on the hill was a mission. The priest would come on Saturday to hear confessions and spend the night with the family. Aunt Lizzie never used the bedroom. I was an imaginative child and often wondered about that room. Did the priest perform miracles there? How would it feel to sleep in a bed made holy by a priest? I never found out as the door always remained closed.

Maureen's Son Charlie Remembers Horse Racing

My father's nephew became one of the world's leading jockey's. While riding for Harry Payne Whitney, Frankie won the Brooklyn Handicap on Irish Lad. This was in the early 1900's. Mr. Whitney gave him, as a present, the full brother of Irish Lad. Frankie shipped Royal to my father at Bridgeport and this stallion sired many colts, some of whom became the best race horses in our area.

Royal's finest colt was a mare named Royalette, whose dam was sired by one of our local race winners. We always called Royalette "Star" because she had a star on her forehead. I broke her to ride when she was two years old, in the spring of 1916. We would race like the wind up the bottom land to Jack Hollow, up Jack Hollow to the waterfall and back to the barn. I also rode her on several trips of fifty miles per day to strengthen her endurance. She was easy to handle and was by far the fastest horse I had ridden.

One June day in 1918, when I was fourteen years old, Gypsy Dick, a horse trader, stopped at the farm. He had a small covered wagon in which he lived, like the horse traders used to in those days. The wagon was pulled by two horses with drooping ears. Several other horses were strung out behind the wagon. He asked my Father if he had any horses for trade and we proceeded to the barnyard. He spotted Star immediately and offered some of his horses for her. Pa explained that she was a thoroughbred and was not for sale or trade. Dick then said, "I have a horse that can beat your horse and I'll bet fifty dollars on a quarter mile match race." We looked at his swaybacked horse and accepted his bet. Arrangements were made for the match race two days later on a quarter mile straightaway on the Patch Grove dirt lane.

Word spread quickly around the county and before the race, hundreds of people lined both sides of the lane. Dick went through the crowd making bets. He then insisted on a standing start from a point near the head of the lane facing toward Patch Grove. This was my first race and also Star's first. We had never practiced a standing start, which requires a fast break, like nowadays from mechanical gates. Well, Dick's horse, which he rode, left so fast that he easily beat us by several lengths in the short quarter mile race.

While Dick was collecting his winnings, someone from Boscobel came up and offered to put up one hundred dollars, winner take all, if a rematch would be held at the Boscobel Fairgrounds during the July 4th celebration. Both Pa and Dick accepted and agreed to a side bet in addition to the one hundred dollar purse. Pa insisted on a half mile race to which Dick agreed. Pa also insisted on a running start, which meant that the horses started running from a point about twenty yards from the starting line. If they were not head and head when they reached the starting line, they would be called back.

As July 4th was still several days away, Dick and his horses had time, as did we, to go over to Boscobel — about fifteen miles — and train for a few days. I rode Star from home past the Horace Tyler place to Campbell's Ridge down through the hills to Woodman and then to Boscobel. Gypsy Dick was already at the Fairgrounds when I got there. Both horses were given stalls and provided with hay and oats. People started coming early to watch the horses work out and to make bets with Dick. By that time we knew that Dick's horse was a "ringer." He was a quarter horse and it was said that he had never lost a race. The publicized race brought thousands of people from Grant and Crawford counties, many more than would have normally come for the July 4th celebration. The promoter therefore got plenty in return for his one hundred dollar purse. Dick continued making bets up to the time of the race. Pa made a few side bets also.

I was quite calm when the time came for the race. Star was ready. We got off on the first start and Dick quickly pulled ahead and was leading by a length as we went around the first turn and reached the eighth-mile post. By the time we reached the quarter-mile post, at the middle of the back stretch, Dick was two lengths ahead. At the three-eighths-mile post, I caught him and noticed that his horse's tail had gone up, a sign of tiring. I was slightly ahead as we made the turn and then entering the home stretch I started pulling away and won by three lengths. It was a big day! The thoroughbred could not beat the quarter horse in a quarter mile race, but could easily do so at a half mile. Gypsy Dick should have known this, but he was overconfident because of his victory at Patch Grove Lane.

That was the first of many victories for Star and me. I also raced other horses, until I grew too heavy.

I had just fastened my seat belt on the plane to take me to visit my folks in Florida, when I felt the presence of a great sadness, and the prickles rose from inside me to give my skin goose bumps. I closed my eyes, the better to ignore the flight attendants buzzing in the kitchen behind me.

Even though my sister was already in Florida and I was on a plane, I heard her say, "Mom's dying." Mom had always said, "I want to live until I die," but she had been losing her mind to Alzheimer's disease and alcohol abuse. I still cried, my head in my hands. I turned to Mom mentally, sharing her sorrow. I supposed it was her heart; she'd had problems with it for several years.

Then Mom said, "You're beautiful." I cried harder as I thought of our fifty years of fighting each other, of all the times I so desperately wanted her approval, of all the energy wasted hating myself and her. "Tell them they're beautiful and that I'm proud of them." This was definitely a command to tell my brothers and sister, yet the order lacked the bitchiness and need to control that had always raised my rebellious hackles.

A gentle hand touched my shoulder and a stewardess asked, "Is there anything I can do?" I just shook my head and she went away. Quiet tears wanted to give way to an Irish keening, so I wailed inside myself.

After about an hour, the heaviness diminished and in the second half of my trip, I tried to accept the inevitable.

At the airport, I saw Ellen and thought, "She's alone! Dad must be at the hospital with Mom!" I rushed toward Ellen and blurted out, "How's Mom?"

She looked puzzled by my urgency as she answered, "Well, not too bad if you can overlook her wandering mind."

I couldn't believe it! "She hasn't had a heart attack?"

"No, why?"

I told her about my experience. "It was the strongest and clearest telepathic message I've ever received. I was sure she was in the hospital, dying."

"Dad's in the car, waiting with Mom, so I can tell you how we're planning the estate so that if Dad dies before she does, she'll be taken care of." I didn't hear the details, because I was trying to reconcile the truth of my vision with the present reality. For once, I was grateful that I had to wait for my luggage, as it gave me time to readjust my scrambled feelings.

Mom's greeting was cool. Did she think that Ellen and Joe, who had left that morning, and I were plotting against her? Well, there was something going on behind her back. How could we say, "Mom, you seem to be incompetent, so here's how we'll make sure you're taken care of?" Maybe she sensed it.

But I was really off balance because the caring, approving message I'd received on the plane was followed by such aloof behavior: her cool welcome and then her insistence on watching her TV show. She chose to criticize the women's hair and clothes all through the show rather than talk with us.

When Mom and Dad went to bed, Ellen and I stayed up and talked. She told me, "Mom's getting more confused more often. It's really hard for Dad."

"I know all about alcohol abuse and brain damage, but knowing a bunch of facts doesn't keep me from hurting."

"Yeah."

"Ellen, when did it start? When I was a kid, she'd get

drunk once in a while, but it was no big deal. When did alcohol become her best friend?"

She thought for a moment. "In Africa. When Martin and I went there after our year at boarding schools in Kansas, Mom was part of the social whirl. There weren't very many whites in top jobs like Dad's, so they were high society in Liberia, invited to every party and every party was held together with lots of booze."

"Was she drunk a lot of the time?"

"No, not really. It was more like she was drinking slowly all the time."

"And look at us, the next generation. You and I don't drink much, but we both married alcoholics."

"We both divorced them, too!"

"Was Jerry drinking hard when you met him?"

"I guess he drank a lot, but I never thought he was drunk. The drunkenness didn't show up until after we were married. Roy had quit drinking before you met him, right?"

"Yes, but he hadn't stopped acting like an alcoholic. His favorite hobby was pushing my buttons. He knew every one of them: my pleasure buttons, my mad ones, funny buttons and sad ones. Being married to him was the hardest and best thing I ever did. Hardest because I wanted to love and give and I had to balance that with not letting him walk all over me, because if I had let him, he would have. Allowing bad behavior is encouraging bad behavior. It doesn't help anyone. But he was a better man because of me and I was a better woman because of him, so it was the best thing I ever did."

"Now I see that I didn't have much of a chance with Jerry because his bottle was always between us. Do you think you'll ever marry again?"

"*Not me*! It's just too hard! You know, I always kind of felt like there was pressure: society expected me to get married. Well, I did my duty." I grinned. "Now I can live. How about you?"

Ellen answered, "I feel like I've done my duty, too! But I would still like to find the right man and enjoy a *good* marriage."

Our marriages were both far enough in the past that we

could talk about them easily, if not painlessly. So we talked on, until four in the morning.

The next day, before she left, we had a few moments at the airport. "Ellen, I really appreciate your organizing all the legal stuff for when they die. And I'm so glad we can talk. For a long time, I felt isolated from family. Our closeness the last few years has eased that pain." Our hug was warm, flowing between our hearts.

That afternoon, Dad went out. Mom couldn't find the bathroom that was off the den so I took her in and showed it to her. "I don't mean that one; I know that's there. There used to be one over here, too."

Very gently, I told her, "No, Mom, there wasn't. You're thinking of a different place you lived in. I know it seems real to you, but your mind is playing tricks on you." Then I asked her what she wanted for supper, to get her mind on something else.

That night, we played crazy rummy. It was sad for me to watch the woman who used to win consistently at cards; now her scores were very poor. She replaced a wild card and put it in her hand. Dad said indignantly, "Dear, you can't do that. You have to play it!"

"No, I don't!" Her voice was bitter. I think she knew she was wrong. Her body and mind were dying, but she'd been a fighter all her life and she couldn't quit, just because she was wrong. And Dad had to fight because she was drinking again, after nearly quitting for a few months.

After a few more exchanges, I cried out, "I wish you wouldn't fight! It hurts me!"

Mom turned her anger on me, "We aren't fighting!" She discarded and the game went on. The tension eased.

When Dad went to bed, Mom fixed herself another drink. I said, "Dad wasn't mad about the card game, he was upset over your drinking."

"I'm not an alcoholic, you know!"

"Mom, it really doesn't matter whether you are or not anymore. The point is, drinking will kill you, the way your health is now. And that's a tacky way to go." I put my arm around her to soften the bluntness.

"Well, I can't give up everything!" A terrified child, bewildered by her losses of mind and body begged my understanding, so I hugged her. "I love you, Mom."

It wasn't until the night before I left that I got up the nerve to tell her what I'd been thinking. "Mom, when the time comes, if you should decide to let yourself die, it's okay. It's not that I want you do die. I'd be very sad, but if that's your choice, it's all right."

"Oh, no, I couldn't do that! Your father has worked too hard to keep me alive." She paused, shocked at my suggestion, stood up. "You know, a few years before my mother died, she told me she wanted to die. I was terribly shocked."

"Well, if you choose to live, that's okay, too."

This time, Mom's voice was filled with pain, "I couldn't stand that!" And abruptly, she started toward their bedroom.

"I just mean that whatever you want, I want that for you." Mom didn't answer.

On the plane coming home, I felt how much Mom loved me. I had thought for years that she did her best; all of us kids knew that. And none of us felt loved. I had tried to bridge the gap sometimes, and so had she, but we only caught glimpses of each other. Now her love flooded over me and the fifty-year drought was over.

The following August, Dad wanted a big eightieth birthday party in Watertown, Wisconsin, where he grew up. I drove a longer route to get there, so I could go through Portage. That was the town that grew up around the old-time fur traders' portage between the Fox and the Wisconsin Rivers. It was where Mom's great-grandpa John and his family portaged on their way to settle in Wisconsin in 1833. I asked and found the mile-and-a-half-long road that they had walked so long ago. I drove slowly along Wauona Trail, but I had to pull over to the side. I felt their hard work carrying their belongings, their joy on their way to a new life, their pioneer spirit, their strength. History had been made there, some for the books and some that shaped my life.

Relatives gathered at Watertown from Washington state, San Francisco, Los Angeles, Washington D.C., Atlanta, South

Carolina, Chicago and lots still from Wisconsin. He had agreed to let us decorate the rented hall, so we gathered old photos, tennis rackets, travel posters, a trombone and lots of stuff that reflected his interests. I had even made a large family tree. Ellen, Joe, his wife and kids, Martin, several of our cousins and I decorated. I was delighted to be doing it, as Dad had never been one to let us fuss over him. At two, people started coming and then it was five minutes with these cousins, five minutes with the next bunch.

Three eighty-year old women in Watertown ran a catering business (one of them was Dad's high school classmate) and they did a great job serving up a meal for all eighty of us; they even made Dad's favorite dessert, Schaum Torte, which was a meringue covered with strawberries. Dad's great-nephew, a minister, said grace before we ate.

After our meal, we had "This Is Your Life," where everybody got up and told about Dad's part in their lives. He said he was embarrassed by that, but I think he enjoyed the embarrassment. I knew he liked giving, but I was surprised hearing how well chosen his gifts were: a dress for a niece, a tennis racket to a nephew, encouragement to become an engineer to another nephew, candy for his younger cousins.

Dad hadn't spent much time with any of us who were there, not even his kids, the last thirty years. Yet eighty relatives were there to say, "Thanks for your part in my life." That put my personal Dad in a whole new light. It felt strange to think that of all the hours Dad had lived, very few of them were spent with me; Mom, too, for that matter. Yet what an influence!

I bought a new car, a Toyota, but kept my much-bragged-about 1980 Buick Skylark. The Buick had over 200,000 miles on it, but I'd only had to replace the water pump, the gas tank and the alternator. It was still going strong, but I bought the new one because I could afford it and I didn't know how long my prosperity or my Buick would last. All the men wanted to ride in it at first, but I wouldn't let them smoke in the Toyota, so they soon chose to go back to the Buick.

When the call came from the nursing home that Art had died, it was up to me to make the arrangements. He would be buried in the veterans' cemetery, that was easy enough. I called the pastor at our adopted Lutheran Church. "Pastor Kim, Art has died in the nursing home. He had no family or friends except for us at the Haven and the nursing home, and we want to have a memorial service for him. Even though he wasn't a member of your Church, could you help us out?"

"Of course. Maybe the men would be more comfortable about it all if we held the service right there at the Haven. Then everybody who wants to can speak out and tell Art 'Good-bye' in whatever way they want to."

"Great idea!"

I invited people from the church, people from the nursing home, our 4-H friends. Art was a nice guy, but pretty shy, so I was surprised when about thirty people showed up. Whether they came to say good-bye to Art or to help us say good-bye, it didn't really matter: Art would get a good send-off.

Pastor Kim and her husband, Pastor Arvid, spoke and led us in prayer and then asked if anyone wanted to share a memory of Art.

I spoke. "I visited Art in the hospital, the day before he died. He knew the end was coming. I told him, 'When you get to heaven, Roy will meet you. He'll probably ask what the heck you're doing there. Art answered 'And I'll ask him what the heck *he's* doing there,' and he laughed." That broke the ice and the others talked about him.

Fred commented, "He was always so glad to see us when we came for bingo."

Joe said, "He always kept the coffee made."

"He used to keep the whole garden weeded, all by himself," remembered Tom.

"The last Christmas he was here," said Jinny, the 4-H leader, "he had to be in his room, on oxygen, when we came caroling, so we went into his room and in the hall to sing. I never saw anyone appreciate our music the way he did. He was smiling the whole time we sang."

"He always did his best."

Beth remarked, "When he got so poorly that he needed someone around at night, just in case, Darlene, Mary and I took turns. He was always so cheerful and tried so hard not to be any trouble."

"It was fun seeing him in the Fourth of July parade when he was elected King of the Nursing Home," Al said.

"Remember when we went to the circus and saw him there with the other people from the nursing home?"

Then Tim, a 4-H fellow, turned on a tape of quiet music and read a poem, saying, in Art's name, not to remember him sadly, that he lived on, in the breeze, in a flower, and in other lovely ways.

After that, we served up Bob's spice cake with penuche frosting and ice cream. As we ate, there was a quiet, happy sound to the talk. My men were pleased to have done their duty by Art, even though he wasn't their best buddy. Maybe they recognized that they, too, would get a good farewell when the time came.

Free Twins tickets were getting hard to come by, the cost of tickets was high and some of the men got bored at the baseball games, because there wasn't much to see. But we had over a hundred dollars from our garden produce to spend on a big splurge, their reward for good work.

"Would you guys like to go see the Ice Capades in Duluth this fall instead of a Twins' game?"

Joe's response was immediate, "Yeah!" He liked ice skating on TV. The rest of the men agreed.

"How about the railroad museum? Should we go there, too?" More enthusiasm.

Three fellows from Mike's group home had helped us with our woodcutting and splitting, so we invited them along. We could have all fit into our fine-looking van, but our paint job hadn't made it any easier to drive, so I asked several friends to drive. Polack John, Tom and Bob came in my car. We were less than half an hour on the road, when John asked, "Are we almost there?"

"No, John, we have a long way to go yet."

Five minutes later John said, "I'm hungry. When do we

eat?"

"About another hour, John."

Again he complained, "I'm hungry."

"What are you going to order at the restaurant, John?"

His reply was definite: "Steak sandwich!"

I started singing, "Steak sandwich for John, steak sandwich for John, steak sandwich, steak sandwich, steak sandwich for John," using the melody from a children's song. He laughed. Bob gave me a dirty look, but he didn't complain. The next time John asked how long until we ate, I told him to sing with me. He thought that was fun. The next time, I asked the others what they would eat. Tom thought he'd try chop suey and Bob, of course, would have chicken. So John and I sang all our meals. Next I had him sing old songs with me. Finally we came to the rest area, half way along, where we stopped for the guys to go to the bathroom, have a smoke and stretch their legs. While we stood around smoking, I asked John if he'd sing for Dorothy and Ellery, two of our drivers. "Sure." John looked old, disreputable, a bit of a bum even in his good clothes, but he transformed himself with a huge grin, twinkling eyes, waving arms and shuffling feet as he sang *Down by the Old Mill Stream*. Totally delightful! Refreshed by the attention, a cigarette and a trip to the bathroom, John only asked two more times about how long the trip would take.

I was amazed at the men's interest in the Indian displays and the early settler exhibits at the Old Depot in Duluth, but the big thrill was seeing the old trains. One train had a twenty-foot high, V-shaped snowplow in front of it. *Wow*! The men scrambled up into the cars and engines, passenger cars, and cattle cars. I pushed Bob around in a borrowed wheel chair so he wouldn't get too exhausted.

At the restaurant, John finally had his steak sandwich, which he thoroughly enjoyed. He and the men from Mike's group home seemed were very quiet, almost intimidated by the Chinese restaurant, which was nice, but not luxurious. Maybe they'd never been in such a nice place before.

We arrived at the arena early, to avoid the rush and let the guys have a smoke before they went in, but the wait was worth it. About fifteen minutes after the show started, I turned around to see how the men were enjoying it. The colorful, musical spectacular riveted their attention, grabbed their beauty-starved senses, and delighted them. Good. Then a scantily-costumed woman skated right near us. John yelled out appreciatively, "Damn, she's pretty!" The skater waved in John's direction and everyone around us laughed.

Afterward, we stopped to eat and the men couldn't stop talking about the show. When we started home, everyone was quiet, a tired happy quiet.

When I went to bed, I got all wet. My super-comfortable water bed, Roy's last Christmas present, was leaking again. I slept on the couch.

The next morning, I found the leak and I stuffed towels under the mattress to get the leak above the water level, but I couldn't get it high enough. I tried holding the plastic above the water level while the glue dried, but I couldn't hold it long enough. I went to the garage and took the jack from my car, imagining a terrible howl from the male establishment that protested my unorthodox use of tools. I just grinned. The water mattress rested on angle irons, three of them from side to side slotted into the two going along the sides. I set the jack at the center of the bed and cranked it up, supporting the ends with chunks of wood. Once the hole was jacked up, the glue held.

But when I cranked the jack down, the side angle iron slipped out of two of its slots. I had to jack up the side-to-side angle irons, prop them up, then push the angle iron back into place. When I let the jack down, one slot was in place. A good shove and the other one went down, too. Oh, did I ever brag about how I successfully high-jacked my bed!

Then the electric garage door opener went on the fritz. It opened part way, then stopped. After pushing the button lots of times, it would open all the way or I could disconnect it and open it by hand. Even by hand, it seemed reluctant. I wiped the tracks with paper towels, cleaning off a thick accumulation of greasy dirt; then I sprayed them with lubricant. It worked! Fixing things was fun! Sometimes.

To celebrate getting all the stuff done, I watched *20,000 Leagues Under the Sea,* the 1916 version, which had come in the mail that day. When I was in Prairie du Chien last summer, I read their microfilmed newspapers, looking for more about my family history. I found a 1917 newspaper ad: *20,000 Leagues Under the Sea* was to be shown at Hatch's Opera House. It was the most sensational achievement of its time, promising a million and one strange sights. When I saw the ad, I was sure Mom would have seen it when she was a kid; so when I saw the movie advertised in a video catalog, I had to have it. I received a poor copy, but it was an amazing film with the underwater photography and an exciting story.

Well, I always liked old movies. That dated back to when I was in high school and we finally got a TV. Mom and Dad used to go out sometimes and I would baby-sit. Once in a while, they would stay out pretty late and I would watch television. I fell in love with Douglas Fairbanks, Jr., young John Wayne, Maureen O'Hara, Jeanette MacDonald. We went to movies every now and then, but the TV movies were *much* better, because I was supposed to be in bed.

When Mom and Dad drove in the driveway, the headlights would shine past the window in the dark room where I watched. I would leap up, turn off the TV and run to the back of the house. I had to pass the back door before they came in there, so I was racing the car as it drove up the two-hundred-foot driveway. I rushed down the stairs and into my room, and jumped into bed, heart pounding with the delicious naughtiness of it all, just as the back door opened and they came in.

More than forty years later, I started collecting old movies. John Wayne had lost his appeal, but not my other old favorites. I bought a few new videos, but mostly 1930's. and 1940's. films, musicals, comedies, adventure, romance.

When I was a kid, I used to like them as much for the thrill of getting away with something as I did for the movies themselves. But I had come to see them differently. A few weeks earlier, when I watched *Follow the Fleet* with Fred Astaire and Ginger Rogers, I seemed to be Mom watching her favorite, Fred Astaire. His whole body was so attuned to the music that even his buttons danced. The depression was still hanging on when she saw it and I felt how she loved the elegance, the beautiful music, the splendid dancing. To me, the *Let's Face the Music and Dance* number said it all.

It was ironic. In high school, I had flatly refused to take shorthand as a means to being self-supporting. After rebelling into such independence that I fixed my bed and garage door rather than call a fix-it-man, I enjoyed myself by watching the movies she had loved!

The next day, at the Haven, I started singing, as I often did when I was in a good mood, just a line or two, because that was all I remembered. As usual, Bob complained, "Rena, don't sing!"

"But Bob, aren't you glad I'm feeling so good that I want to sing?"

His sour response was, "Learn to sing first, then sing."

I called to Polack John in the TV room. "Hey, Polack John, will you come sing with me so Bob can't hear me?" John came grinning into the kitchen and we sang first lines to *It's a Long Way to Tipperary, Donkey Serenade, White Cliffs of Dover* and more.

John should have an award. One kitchen wall was devoted to bragging: six framed certificates showed off six perfect inspections, one frame held our first aid cards, and there were eight framed awards. Bob's award was for "Best Baker and Chief Cook," Joe was honored as "Leader of the Outdoor Work," Tom was "Master of the Mop," Jim was the "Most Gentlemanly Gentleman," Ed was "The Holiday Man" and so forth. I signed each one. So, John could be "Best Entertainer." That night at home, I wrote it out. The next day, I put it in a frame and gave it to him, much to his delight, and he hung it with the others.

I had turned on the ten o'clock news so I could catch the weather report. I would stop reading for that. The news was just a carbon copy of every other night, except for changing the names: fighting here, natural disasters there, murders and fires and strikes locally.

I heard "Berlin Wall" and looked up. People were knocking down the Berlin Wall! Impossible! But there they were, screaming, laughing, crying, tearing it down!

When I was in grade school, we prayed every day for the conversion of Russia; it was evil incarnate. The Berlin Wall and the malevolent Iron Curtain separated the free people of the West from the tyrannized people of the USSR. The greedy Russian monster had grown, sometimes rapidly, other years more gradually, all my life.

I cried at the unexpected news. The evil demon was dying! The forty-five-year-old threat of a third world war which would destroy everyone — was that a possibility we didn't have to fear anymore? Could the Russian people finally grow into freedom as we knew it? Only time would tell.

But I realized that an unacknowledged fear I had carried for most of my life, a fear that the diabolical Russian menace would affect my life personally, not just the world way over there, this fear began to crumble, and I felt lighter already.

Dear Leona,

Merry Christmas to you and yours.

Martin has invited us for family Christmas in Atlanta. Now that Mom and I have quit fighting, I have a new reason to dread seeing her: her mind comes and goes and I hate to see her like that.

Our writers' club wrote children's stories and paid to have them printed up. The president of the club was going to order two hundred of them, but grandiose as always, I talked them into five hundred copies. In three weeks, we've already sold nearly half of them. We've had three autographing parties at libraries; hardly anyone showed up, but it was fun anyway. At last, I'm reaping my reward for kissing the Blarney Stone.

I just finished changing the oil in my car and on the first try, I loosened the nut to let the old oil out. I've found that if I jack up the passenger side, crawl under the car and put my foot against the inside of the tire, I can put the wrench on the nut and pull with my hands and push my hands with my knee and it works, but only if I haven't weakened on the last oil change and let a mechanic do it; they all tighten the nut with an electric thingy and then it's very hard to loosen. So, why don't I pay to have it done? Well, it pleases me to be able to do it myself when I'm not feeling overly frustrated about how hard it can be. And I hate paying twenty dollars or so to a mechanic for five minutes of his time, when I earn five dollars an hour for my work.

I do some life-guarding, for lap swimming and for an exercise hour. How did that come about? I took up swimming again after my cancer surgery, because arthritis set in and I finally realized swimming would get me going again. After I swam a year, I decided to try life saving class and did it. And I started guarding sometimes for lap swimming.

But some non-swimming exercisers kept getting in the swimmers' way. They wanted a separate time for water exercise. I knew swimming was the best way to keep my poor old arthritic body going; non-swimmers should get a chance to benefit from the water, too. We sent the word around. Now between ten and twenty sixty- and seventy-year-olds come for exercise time. A physical therapist came and suggested, "Move your arms like this and your legs like that." I wrote down the moves; the women wanted me to read them off. So I do. Then one of them started the others doing square dance moves. Sure. They do Bunny Hop instead of jumping, waltz instead of walk; leg kicking became can-can; a little Hoky Poky for cool down. We exercise vocally, too, talking and singing.

That's an awful lot about me. How about you? Still doing your water exercises? How are your nieces and nephews? Will you be going to Florida this winter?

Have a fine Christmas and a great New Year!

Love, Rena

I was reading the moves for the water exercise group. "Jumping jacks. Row, row, row your boat ..." I led the singing as they jacked. Pat, Marionn and Teresa started singing as the rest of us began the second line. Sister Marcelline, the nun in charge of the singing in the bad old Novitiate days, would be appalled if she heard me, because we weren't singing holy Gregorian chant, I sang mostly in tune and worst of all, we were having fun! I finally realized why I hadn't been able to sing for Sister Marcelline! My then unknown Goddess had refused to let me sing because the old nun couldn't let my heart sing! "Life is but a dream."

"All right, lunge forward," I directed. "I was watching an old Jeanette MacDonald movie last night. She has one of the most beautiful women's voices I've ever heard. Who do you think had or has the best voices?"

"Leontyne Price."

"Frank Sinatra."

"Pavorotti."

"Barbra Streisand."

"Jim Reeves."

"Yeah, his voice is as rich and smooth as French silk pie!"

Cookie said, "Rena." Sister Marcelline must have groaned in her grave if she heard that. We all laughed.

Bob always picked on me when I sang, so I told him what she said. He didn't believe me, though. He didn't believe me when I told him I was perfect, either.

I was guarding for open swimming one Sunday, when suddenly I realized: of the two dozen swimmers, four were black, three were American Indians, three were of Asian descent, and the rest were white. They were playing so naturally, I hadn't noticed what a mixture it was. It had taken far too long for this to occur, but it had happened. I smiled.

Much of the time, the Church got in the way of religion. But sometimes the forms were filled with substance, as they were at Merle's funeral.

Merle was a faith-full active member of the Lutheran Church that adopted the Haven. He and his wife Cookie were Haven friends and Cookie came to water exercise. We'd been to other funerals at their church when our friends Agnes and Orrin died. They were good funerals, personalized, not the old doom and gloom of Catholic funerals forty years ago.

Three of my men went along to say good-bye to their friend. When we got to the church, the parking lot was full, with lots of cars parked along the road. The church was packed, extra chairs along the aisles and flooding over into the entry way. The sadness of hundreds of people weighed heavily.

The minister's eulogy for his good friend was filled with his own grief and punctuated by sniffles from the congregation. Merle's grown children sang several of his favorite hymns. The great sorrow of these people was no surprise. What amazed me was the overwhelming feeling that the love of these mourners for Merle transformed their grief into faith and hope and yet greater love. I felt their faith in God, their belief that Merle was now in heaven, their hope that they would join him later, their common bond of human love strengthening their love of God. I looked up at the ceiling, surprised that the force of their faith and love hadn't lifted the roof right off the church.

It reminded me of the awareness weekends in Austin, where community among us encouraged a vitalized, experiential faith, hope and love. I supposed that wasn't what most people wanted out of religion because if it were, Churches would be a lot different.

Bob was in the hospital. Several months earlier, he'd had swelling in his feet and legs. His doctor put him on water pills, which helped for a while, but when I took him in for his monthly checkup, they were badly swollen again. When the nurse took him away in a wheelchair to the hospital next door to the clinic, I stayed for a word with the doctor.

Trying to be brave, I asked, "How bad is it?"

"You know, I've treated four of his brothers and sisters, who all had the same congestive heart failure brought on by muscular dystrophy."

I nodded.

Very gently, he said, "They all died in their early fifties, and that's how old Bob is."

I took a deep breath. "How long?"

"He'll probably be in serious trouble in six months."

"Okay," I muttered and rushed out to sit in the van, trying to come to grips with the monstrous loss I would have to face. I felt like a Volkswagen smashed by a semi.

I went over to the hospital to tell Bob good-bye. I wasn't going to tell him what the doctor said. Bob was sitting on the edge of the hospital bed, dressed down in a hospital gown. I sat next to him and put my arm around his back.

"What's wrong, Rena?"

"Oh, Bob," I started crying. "Doc says you haven't got too long to live and I can't stand it! You're the best buddy I ever had and I don't want to lose you!"

He patted my knee. He was dying, but he comforted me.

I left to pick up the men, who were in town and told them the doctor thought Bob wouldn't have too long to live. We were quiet all the way home.

When we visited Bob in the hospital, he seemed to perk up some, but when he came back to the Haven, he was totally lifeless. I lost hope. In the past, doctor's predictions about Bob had been wrong, like three years earlier when he had said Bob would be in a wheelchair within a year. Bob used a walker some, but no wheelchair yet, except for big long trips. The latest prognosis seemed dreadfully accurate. I walked through my duties with a ten-ton weight on my heart.

Then I had an idea. "Bob, instead of waiting for your funeral for everybody to say how much they like you, how about if we have a farewell party for you, say, a week from Sunday?"

A little light came into his eyes. "Sure."

I wrote out a note, that since Bob didn't have too long to live, we were going to have a "Bon Voyage" party for him from one to five in the afternoon. I made copies and gave them to our friends from church, to Mike's group home, to waitresses and clerks in town that Bob flirted with, to nurses he knew, to everybody I could think of.

They came. They brought friendship cards, hugs and kisses. They stayed five minutes or half an hour. All afternoon they kept the kitchen full and overflowed into the TV room. Bob wasn't very lively, but he soaked up the affection they brought. He seemed surprised and pleased by all of it.

After that, whenever he was grumpy, I'd say, "Bob, how can you be ornery, when so many people love you?" He'd smile, but he didn't have enough energy to get the smile to his eyes.

A week after the party, I checked over his prescription bottles to see if he needed refills. "This one's okay, need more of that one, what's this? Bob, you have two bottles of Lasix pills. Are you taking pills from both bottles?"

"Yeah."

I called his doctor. Bob had been taking a double dose of his water pills, one from the bottle he had before he went to the hospital, one from the bottle he'd gotten in the hospital. I put one bottle away, so he would take the right dose.

After a week of that, Bob came to life again. I asked him to make cookies for us. I carried all the things to the table, where he sat and measured and mixed, shaped and put them onto the cookie sheets. I couldn't take my eyes off him. He was his old intensely concentrated self, lively as always about his beloved baking.

When he finished, I gave him a big smacking kiss on his cheek. "Bob, guess what? The doctor was wrong again. You are going to live a *long* time."

He grinned and the grin reached his eyes and his ears and even his toes. And so did mine.

I decided on a whim to take the gravel road coming home from the Haven. About a mile down the road, I saw a bear. She had started across the road, but turned around as I approached and chased her cubs up a tree. I stopped the car and turned the engine off. She looked at me and I looked at her. In my mind, I talked quietly to her, "Thank you for letting me see you. I won't hurt you or your cubs. I just want to admire your strength so that I can know my own strength."

We looked at each other for the longest time. Then she called her cubs down and they looked at me curiously, then cavorted after their mother as she ambled across the field. They were almost out of sight over a hill, when she turned around and came back to the tree where she called two more cubs down. The second pair were smaller than the others, but they were all this year's cubs.

The mother bear, strong and caring. Five years earlier, I had seen Norman Knott's picture of a bear, his symbol of inner strength. I'd found some of my own inner strength since then, but I felt a *lot* stronger knowing Bob was all right again.

17

Maureen
Wisconsin,
Fall 1990

I felt murderous. Fortunately there were lots of flies in the house, so I could take it out on them. I swung the swatter wildly at one, probably so I could keep on swinging as it flew around the overhead light.

In July, Mom was doctoring because she hadn't been eating much for a month and Dad was worried. Mom knew it was cancer and the doctors, after three weeks of testing and vague answers finally agreed with her. It was inoperable. They didn't recommend available treatment which would prolong her life, but make her miserable. Mom agreed.

"Hello." Mom answered the phone.

"Hi, Mom, how are you doing?" I asked.

"All right, I guess." Her voice sounded washed-out.

"Say, I watched the best movie last night! *Showboat* with Irene Dunne!"

"Oh, Ben and I saw that when we were courting." She sounded as if she was smiling.

"Did you really?"

"Yes, I remember how surprised I was that he liked it too. He took me to Fred Astaire movies, but he didn't like them much."

"How about Jeanette MacDonald and Nelson Eddy? Remember *Rosemarie*? *Indian Love Call* is one of the most beautiful songs I've ever heard!"

"We saw that one, too," Mom responded.

"I went to Prairie again and read some of the old newspapers. I read that you and Dad, Dave and Colleen went to Black River Falls for a two-day conference. Didn't you have chaperons?"

"I remember that! No, our parents trusted us and they thought the world of Ben and Dave."

"In all the researching I've done, I haven't found much

about your Grandma Annie."

"She was always good to us. She'd give us nickels to go to the movies and she always listened to our stories. But at her wake, my Aunt Maureen lifted me up to kiss her good-bye. That gave me nightmares for a month."

"Tell me about your father."

"I don't want to talk about him!" she answered angrily.

"I know there were very bad times with him. But there must have been *some* good things or funny stories."

"Well," she replied reluctantly, "he made the most awful coffee you ever tasted."

I asked, "Do you think he's in heaven?" No answer. "I think that if he loved you, he is. What do you think?"

Harshly, she spat out, "He had a long time in purgatory first!" Then she softened, "But I guess he made it."

"I've collected a lot of your family stories and now I'm organizing them. It's a mess, but loads of fun. I'll bring you your copy when I come to see you in September."

"I'd like that," she said softly.

"And Mom, I support your decision not to have any treatment. If you change your mind, that's okay, too. It's your body and whatever choice you make, I agree with you."

"Thank you."

"Oh, my dog wants her walk. I'd better go. I'll call you next weekend."

"Good-bye."

We talked often about the "good old days," which kept her mind off her cancer for a few moments and added to my collection of stories. Her cousin Con also shared stories, pictures and newspaper clippings.

All during August, I worked furiously, picking the garden, freezing, and canning during the day. At night, I organized the four-generation story: nine of Mom's cousins telling about their great-grandparents, grandparents, and their nine sets of parents, with a bit about the thirty-two cousins. I had to work quickly so she could read it while she was still well enough to enjoy it.

Organizing the stories was a big job, but typing them was just plain frustrating. My fingers were way out of practice and my typewriter was almost as old as I was. The hyphen seldom worked when I first pushed it; it might mark three spaces later. Sometimes the comma worked right away, sometimes not. The "n" often marked twice. After the first five pages, I could usually type a page with only ten mistakes, but typing and correcting a page took over half an hour.

I felt driven and reluctant and sad. It seemed that when she read the family history, she would die, as if my final tribute gave her permission to let go. Maybe if I slowed down, she would live longer. But I couldn't slow down.

As I put the forty pages of stories and photographs into the folders, I cried. Although I knew editing would have improved it, I felt I had done something important and good. And I knew her end was near.

In September, two days before I was to take Mom her copy, I found out my brother Martin was bringing Mom's sister Mary to visit. He and I generally argued when we got together, so I called him, hoping to call a truce while we were there. We argued on the phone. "We have to egg her on and keep her active."

"Martin, I think we should let her die in peace. I ..."

He interrupted me, "No, we have to keep her going!"

"Martin, you never let me finish what I'm saying!"

"That's because I already know what you're going to say."

"It's very rude!" I gave up.

When I gave Mom her copy of her family history, she didn't have enough energy to get excited, but I felt the rightness of my gift. She sat there, looking through the photographs again and again, pictures of her parents and relatives, people she loved, now dead, people she would soon see again.

Martin and Aunt Mary arrived and after we settled in the living room, Dad said "Let's go out to eat tonight."

I answered, "That would be fine. Or I could fix tuna-noodle casserole." Mom still wouldn't eat meat on Friday. "And Mom wants hoboes for supper tomorrow."

Martin insisted, "I'm going to fix shrimp on the grill tonight."

We managed to decide without a big fight. Martin made

the shrimp on Friday and I made hoboes on Saturday. He didn't want hoboes, so five minutes before they were ready, he took a shower. "Go ahead without me." I ignored his rudeness.

I avoided fighting with Martin, but Aunt Mary's great need for attention bugged me, because I wanted to focus only on Mom.

In spite of the hubbub — Martin was always a center of commotion — I felt close to Mom. Playing bridge while Aunt Mary napped, Mom and I walloped Dad and Martin. I hadn't played much for years, but it seemed I could read Mom's mind when bidding. Time and again, I knew what to do. Early in the bidding, I knew one hand was a misfit, so I passed. Another time, after she answered two spades, I jumped to six no-trump (we made seven). It was good to see her playing well again.

After cards, Mom and I stayed up to talk. I fixed her a drink, emptied her ashtray and sat down across the table from her.

"Thank you, Maureen."

I blurted out, "The one thing I really want to do for you is to make you well, and I can't do that!" I lit up a cigarette. "You see, you have the easy part. We have to stay here and miss you. You'll be up in heaven with your mother, your son David, lots of relatives and friends. You may have some lousy times yet, but when it gets to be too much, you just talk to your mother. She'll bring you home. A lot of people on earth are praying for you; you are very much loved. Our love and prayers will lift you up and their love from heaven will grab hold and pull so it'll be an easy trip."

"I'm not ready yet."

"I know, but when it's time."

"It's good to have you on my side."

"It's good to be there."

We talked some more, so easy with each other. Her voice had lost its vigor, her eyes had no more snap, her body, oh, poor body ... But she had let go of her anger at her alcoholic father, a lifelong force that had kept me and others at a distance.

I was packing to leave, when Martin came into the bedroom. I went to him, reached for a hug. "Take good care of her." I was sobbing.

"I will," he answered gently. We were both surprised.

Then I slipped into the living room, avoiding the dining room, where they were all chatting. Alone, I felt the weight of grief, knew the final parting would come all too soon. Aunt Mary came in and asked, "Are you okay?"

"I'm feeling sad about leaving." She nodded her understanding and left.

Three weeks later, Dad had bad news when I called. My brother Peter had just arrived and Mom hadn't recognized him. I called Joseph. When he and his wife, a nurse, called Dad, Peter asked Marty what to do. "Call a doctor."

It was probably a small stroke. When Mom came out of the hospital, she couldn't walk or get out of bed, but at least she could talk, although it seemed to take longer for her to get her thoughts arranged into words.

Several days later, my brothers, sister and I had our first conference call. I was amazed and saddened by Peter's contribution. He had shut out our family years ago when I had told them of his drug abuse. Now he sounded very knowledgeable about the situation, very cold and detached as he talked at length about Mom's physical condition and Dad's inability to cope. He thought we should deal with it all very objectively and not let our emotions get in the way. No doubt about one thing: Peter was still emotionally constipated.

Two weeks later, I went to help Mom and Dad again; all of us kids were taking turns. This second visit was much easier, because just Mom, Dad and I were there, and much harder, because without all the people around, Mom and Dad argued more. Mom was pretty helpless. I felt good about waiting on her, but I felt rotten that she needed waiting on.

I had suggested to my brothers and sister that we have Mass said in their home, when we all gathered for an early Christmas in November. They had agreed. I told them I would feel right about receiving Communion, even though I was not a practicing Catholic, in a spirit of union with Mom and family and what they did about Communion was up to them. I arranged for a priest to come say the Mass, which gave Mom something to look forward to. I dreaded it though, because if she had deteriorated from September to October, how much worse would she be in November?

Dear Dad,

Just a note to let you know I'm thinking about you, too; all of us kids are. We care very much about you.

A while back, I asked you if you knew how wonderful you are. You said, "That's what people say," as if you didn't really believe it. So I just wonder if you could ever count all the times you've brought a smile to someone's face?

Mom's cousin Maureen has called me several times. When she talks about you, she seems to be smiling. When you met a Puerto Rican in a San Francisco bar and you found out that Mom's cousin Marion taught him English, I know he smiled. When you told us kids that you were ranked second of all Florida tennis players in your age bracket, and months later admitted there were only two players ranked, we not only smiled, we got a great story to make others smile, too. To this day, when my Haven men talk about Christmases past, they remember your helping put up our Christmas tree. When you helped Aunt Adoline with this or that, when you helped other residents at your apartment house, when you showed your slides or played music tapes in a nursing home, ...

The way I figure it, if you put all those smiles end to end, you have a mighty long ticket to heaven, and as you near the end of your life (which I hope is not too near) what is more important than the length of your ticket?

Love,
Maureen

"Hi, Elayne, good to see you." A warm hug welcomed me to my overnight stay near the airport with Marion and her daughter, Elayne. The next day, I would leave for Florida, for our last Christmas celebration with Mom.

"Good to see you, too. Come on in out of the cold. Mother is in the living room." Another warm hug from Marion.

"How are you doing, Rena?"

"Terrible! Absolutely terrible! I talked to Dad last night. He had told his doctor that he was drinking a quart of rum a week. The doctor told him to drink less, so he just finished a quart in four days. Plus all the beer he drinks. Then he said he wanted all Mom's things disposed of while we were there. Since he was *The Boss* now, we had to do things his way. He sounded so cold and mean and bossy. Finally Mom has shown us her loving side, so Dad is showing us another side, too. The worst of it is, after we all go home, if he gets drunk, who's going to take care of Mom? She is so helpless now, she can't even reach a glass of water on her night stand."

"Oh, dear, that is bad."

We were sitting in their cluttery, comfortable living room; the old house had seen many years of caring. "Brother Peter won't be coming. He hasn't been to a family gathering in twelve years. I'm glad he's not coming. I'd like for us to start being family, without all the fighting and jealousy that we usually erupt into and it'll be easier without him, although Mom will be hurt.

"But cousin Ann is coming. She's been planning this trip for months. And Dad never mentioned Ann's plans when we were setting up our early Christmas. Ann has every right to say good-bye to her aunt and it isn't her fault it turned out this way, but she'll just play center stage the whole time and It's Mom who should be the star, not Ann. I wrote her a nasty letter and told her all this, so I wouldn't blow up at her down there and spoil the festivities."

Marion and Elayne listened, nodded, always sympathetic, and never am I wrong in Marion's eyes, even if I know better. "Enough of my self-pity! Here I am with my two favorite people and I'm not even enjoying you, because I'm too busy feeling sorry for myself. Yuck! Elayne, can I help you put supper on?"

"Sure, you can set the table while I make gravy."

"After we eat, let's play Kings in the Corner and if I start whining again, just tell me to shut up and play."

"Sounds good."

Marion and Elayne took me to the airport the next morning. "Thanks for the ride and thanks for listening to me last night. Maybe now I've let off enough steam that I can go down there and make Christmas."

I met Martin in Atlanta. I told him about my fears over Dad's drunkenness. He refused to see it as a problem. I asked him if I should try to switch seats so we could talk on the plane. No.

Brother Joe met us at the Sarasota airport. He didn't see anything to worry about either, because Mom would be dying soon after we left anyway.

At Mom and Dad's, I put out some of the pecan and powdered sugar cookies Bob and I had made, knowing how my brothers enjoyed this Christmas treat. Ann came into the kitchen and told me she'd visit friends Saturday and Sunday so we'd have some time without her. "And while I'm here, I'll just melt into the woodwork." *Ha!* I knew she was trying to be accommodating, but my orneriness was stronger than her thoughtfulness at the moment, so my response was halfhearted.

Mom couldn't inhale enough to light a cigarette, so I'd start one for her when she wanted one, trying not to make a face over the menthol. Mostly she just let it burn out after a puff or two. I went outside to smoke, because smoking bothered Ellen and Frank, and because it was a good excuse to run away every now and then. Ellen followed me out for one of these breaks, asking me if I was okay. "No, I'm not." I told her my fear of Dad's drinking.

"Maureen, what's the worst that could happen if Dad does get drunk after we leave, that he forgets to give her some pills and she dies a few days sooner?"

"No, that's not the worst! Dad is a great guy, but he does have a mean streak and if he gets drunk, she's totally helpless under the control of a drunken man, just like when she was a kid, only then it was her father."

Friday afternoon, while Mom was in the living room, Ellen and Marty sorted out all Mom's clothes and snuck them out. That was what Dad wanted and he was *The Boss.* Later, while she napped, he told us to list what furniture we wanted. He'd move to a small place and didn't want any of it. It felt to me like he wanted to get rid of her. He had been taking good care of her these last months, so my head didn't blame him, but my heart hated him.

That evening, in the dining room, Dad twisted some words around and got all flushed. Martin blurted out, "You're drunk, aren't you?" Everybody laughed. Dad *never* seemed drunk, although he'd been drinking steadily for many years. I went out for a long walk. We were there to take care of Mom so my head knew it was all right for him to be drunk. But I was disgusted with him and afraid for Mom.

Saturday, Father Tim came to say Mass. He brought copies of Christmas hymns so we could all join in. He asked if one of us would read the first lesson. Martin volunteered. Frank would read the second one and Marty would lead the singing.

We started with *Silent Night*. Ellen, seated next to me on the couch, started sobbing and I choked up, too. Joe and Marty kept the singing going until the rest of us could join in. I only looked at Mom once during the Mass; her poor shriveled body gathered energy from the ritual as she sang in a whispery voice. She seemed very peaceful and happy to have her family together for Mass.

After Father Tim walked over to Mom to give her Communion, Joe and Marty stood up to receive. Ellen and I followed and so did Frank and Martin. My eyes watered. For Mom, we showed a solid front, in the way she wanted it most. I was proud of us and pleased that they followed where I led them. When I was in the convent, the novice mistress had taken a survey. She told me nobody in my class wanted anything to do with me. I hadn't thought of that bit of cruelty for years. But my family's response here smiled; even if it was true then, it wasn't true anymore.

Christmas dinner was remarkable in that we all pitched in and nobody fought. Mom was wheeled in, in her wheelchair. She struggled to stay awake and enjoy the good humor we put forth for her benefit. She ate a few bites, but before anyone was finished, she needed to go back to bed.

After her nap, we brought our Christmas presents to their bedroom. After everybody else had left, I stayed with her. She looked peacefully exhausted. I helped her with her

Chapstick and a drink. "Well, Mom, you can sleep with pleasant thoughts tonight. We had a fine Christmas Mass here in your own home, a wonderful dinner, great presents and no fights."

Her eyes lit up as she said, "And everyone went to Communion." She accepted our most important present, our union, our Communion.

"Yes, Mom, because we love you." I sat with her for a while even after she went to sleep.

Ellen, Frank, Martin and I stayed up late to talk. Frank suggested, "Let's stick to our feelings and not get negative toward each other." I was pleasantly surprised because he had always seemed very unemotional to me. He continued: "I don't really know what I feel, or even what I'm supposed to feel." He sounded puzzled and sad.

Martin talked about how he felt after his wife died, a totally unexpected tragedy, from a brain aneurysm. "I hated going back to work, seeing all the guys. They knew Yaja had died and they didn't know what to say and I didn't either. And then I found out I had a whole bunch of garbage left over from Vietnam. When I was over there, I was scared shitless all the time, but I did my job. Then, when I came back home, instead of being treated like a hero, I was scum."

I was practically holding my breath, for fear of interrupting this amazing moment of sharing from my brothers. The talk wandered for a while. Martin returned to his feelings. "The hardest thing for me this trip is seeing Mom so helpless and withered." His voice held pain.

"You've all been here several times the last few months," Frank commented. "You say she has changed. You feel like she loves you. I haven't seen that in these few days; there's been too many people around. The one time I was alone with Mom, trying to think of what to say, Dad came in on us. I don't know if he wanted to protect Mom from me or if he wanted to keep us from getting close."

"Probably both," I said.

Frank went on, "The moment that got to me was at dinner tonight. I looked at Mom and she seemed so vulnerable."

I said: "The hardest part for you is seeing Mom so helpless, Martin and Frank, you saw Mom vulnerable. The worst of it for me is that after fighting Mom for fifty years, we have finally opened up to each other and now I'm going to lose her. All those years wasted!" I put my hands over my face and cried quietly.

After a moment, Martin burst out: "You know, this afternoon at Mass, all those people I thought were so controlled, but they were crying. I couldn't believe my eyes." His voice wobbled.

Later, I commented: "I think Mom, the passionate one, is the glue in our family. Dad has always been the good guy, but Mom held us together. The question is, do we want to be family for each other after she dies or do we just go our separate ways?"

Martin answered: "This family will fall apart when she dies." Ellen and Frank didn't comment.

"I think it's up to us," I said. "If we want to be family, there's no reason we can't be."

Then Ellen advised Frank on how to improve his life and he got mad at her. He had been to personal growth workshops but didn't think the leaders were any closer to experiencing their own truth than he was. He didn't like Ellen's advice any better than theirs. She defended herself and he just kept saying he didn't want her advice. She left, very hurt.

Frank apologized to Martin and me. "I'm sorry, but that was a long time coming."

"Frank and Martin," I said, "it's four-thirty and I'm done in. I'm glad we had a good talk. Martin, I guess you'll be gone by the time I get up. Could I have a good-bye hug?" He gave me a good hug. And so did Frank, the first ever good hug from him.

Ellen woke me in the morning to say good-bye to Frank. As soon as I woke up a bit, I told Ellen, "I'm sorry you were hurt last night. I wish it hadn't happened that way."

"I'll be okay."

"Considering our past, we did pretty well to have only one set-to, and at least Mom and Dad weren't there. I think we put on a wonderful Christmas for Mom. And I appreciate all the organizing you did, getting groceries, cooking and get-

ting rid of Mom's things. I couldn't have done that. Thanks."
We hugged. "Ellen, I think that Mom really appreciated all
of it, too. It seems like Mom used to be a sieve, and no matter
what we did for her, it made no difference, it leaked right
through. But now she seems to have closed up the holes, so
our loving gestures stick. I think she accepts our love."

"What about you? Talk about yourself!" She was angry.

I ignored the anger. "I'm getting to that. I think I'm
closing my holes, too, so that when somebody does something for me, I can feel and accept the caring. I know my
holes aren't completely gone, but they're definitely smaller."

The rest of Sunday was calm in between good-byes; the
hard part was over.

Monday morning, the hospice worker came to give Mom
her bath. When the helper came out of Mom's room, I said,
"You asked Mom if she had any hallucinations and she said
no, but last night she saw a man in her room. I told her that
her mind was playing tricks on her, then I changed the subject and she let it go."

She handed me a sheet of paper about the signs of imminent death and said gently, "You'll notice she has many of
these indications now," and she touched my arm to comfort
me. I could only nod. I didn't want Mom to suffer but I sure
didn't want her dead either.

While Dad and I ate lunch, I confronted him quietly about
his drinking. "Dad, it really bothers me that you've been
drinking so much."

His reply was angry. "Well, it's none of your business, but
I need to drink to put up with all this."

"But how can you take care of Mom if you're drunk?"

"I've been taking care of her for three years now. That's
enough, I don't want to talk about it any more. You don't
know how hard it's been, so I'll drink all I want to and you
can't stop me!"

Later, I was fussing over Mom when Dad brought in Linda,
a friend of Frank's, who had just come. She stood on one side
of Mom's bed, I stood on the other side. After a weak hello to
Linda, Mom looked at me and said, "It won't be long now,
will it." Not a question, a statement.

I wished Linda wasn't there, but Mom wanted reassurance. I knelt beside the bed and held her hand. "No, Mom, it won't be long. Pretty soon, when you're ready, your mother will come for you. And the Blessed Virgin. And Grandma Annie. I think your mother will tell you she is very proud of you. And there will be a grand reception for you in heaven. You'll get to dance with Fred Astaire and play the violin with Yehudi Menuhin. All your fondest dreams will be real. Your body won't be a bother any more. Heaven will be more glorious than the best moments you've had on earth, with none of the lousy times." Tears ran down my face, but my voice was calm and comforting. "We'll miss you something terrible, but at least we'll know you've got it made." The peace in her face showed me that I was saying the right things. "Should we pray together?" Mom nodded. "Hail Mary, full of grace, ... " "Remember, oh most gracious Virgin Mary, that never was it known, that anyone who fled to thy protection ... was left unaided ..." When we finished, I squeezed her hand and left.

Wet-faced, too, Linda followed me out and said, "I wish I could have talked like that to my father before he died. But I didn't know the words and then suddenly he was gone."

I said, "I need a long walk."

"Do you want me to come with you?"

"No. Thanks, but I'd like to be alone."

"Okay."

Bless her heart, Elayne met me at the airport, with a good long hug. As we walked to the baggage claim, I jabbered about the very painful, sometimes positive experience. Marion had waited in the car and she invited me to Red Lobster and to stay overnight with them.

I replied, "For years, I've come back from a trip with no one to meet me. It was lonely. Now after a very difficult week, you pamper me by meeting me at the airport, offering me my favorite dinner and a bed for the night. That feels good and warm." After a moment I added, "I'd like to eat with you and then go home. I've been in an emotional hurricane and I want to crawl into my cave and hide for a while, even from my friends."

"Of course, we understand."

"Thanks."

It took a while, but I did come to realize that my anger at Ann and Dad was not about what they did; it was about running away from the nearness of Mom's death.

I was sitting in my recliner, when my wandering mind felt terror, anguish, horrible pain. I recognized that it was Mom dying. It only lasted a moment. I looked with my heart, and saw the fear was gone. I was smiling peacefully. Yes, she had won over. Whatever heaven was, she liked it. I sat there for quite a while, savoring the glorious feeling she shared with me. She died three days later. I didn't understand how I experienced her death before it happened, but I did.

When she answered the phone, I said, "Pastor Kim, this is Rena. Since my mother died, I'm afraid I've been cutting off the men at the Haven. We need to have a memorial service, so they can help me say good-bye to her."

"Yes, Rena, just a minute. I'll get Pastor Arvid on the other line." She called her husband.

"What I'd like is an informal service, like what we had for Art at the Haven. I hope it's all right for me to ask this when I'm not a member of your church." I needed help and they were the right kind of people to turn to.

"We'd be glad to," she said. "It fits our ministry to your group home."

The following Saturday afternoon, Marion and Elayne drove over a hundred miles for the service. Our friends, Fred and Joan brought flowers and Dorothy and Ellery brought a cake. When we were all seated in the TV room at the Haven, Marion was right beside me. I wished my one obnoxious resident hadn't joined us and I wondered how Dorothy's young grandson would take it.

I took a deep wobbly breath and my voice jerked out, "Last night, I wanted to call off this service, because then I wouldn't have to say good-bye to Mom and then maybe she wouldn't be dead." And besides, part of me hated for anyone to see me all torn up and vulnerable. The youngster echoed my pain with a loud wail, so his grandma took him in her arms to comfort him. Our two springer spaniels had calmed down after the arrival of all the company, but they heard my grief, too, and they jumped on my lap to comfort me.

Petting the dogs, I plunged ahead. "Instead, I played all my weepy music and I cried. At first, I was afraid to cry, fearing that all my losses these past five years would flood out and drown me. But you were coming to help, so it would be all right. Thank you for coming."

I nodded to pastor Kim and she talked about the birth of Christ in a short, appropriate sermon.

Then I talked. "Mom's father was an alcoholic, which caused her a lot of unhappiness as a child. She became an alcoholic, too, but waited until her six kids were mostly grown up before she let the bottle take over her life. Even before then, she was always fighting with Dad and us kids. Two and a half years ago, her mind started going bad. Last July, the doctors found that she had inoperable cancer. She finally forgave her father and let go most of the other garbage she'd been hanging on to for years."

I went on. "Incredibly, her mind cleared up. We took turns visiting Mom and Dad and found that she let us get close to her. She concentrated all her failing energy to let us feel her love for us. Once she let her love show, I knew it had been there all along, but for most of my life, I hadn't felt it, and I had ached for it all those years." My voice was calmer so the boy and the dogs settled down. I continued: "I know that if I've really let her love into my heart, I haven't lost it and I'll be all right. I am very proud of Mom for making her peace with everybody. But I miss her. Now, let's read from the Bible. As it describes wisdom, I think it also describes Mom." The hardest part over, I reached for Marion's hand; she squeezed and held on.

I asked Joe to read. "'For within her is a spirit intelligent, unique, subtle, active, irresistible; she pervades and permeates all things. She is a breath of the power of God. She is a reflection of the eternal light.'"

"'In each generation,'" Dorothy said, "'she passes into holy souls; she makes them friends of God and prophets; she is indeed more splendid than the sun, she outshines all the constellations .'"

I read, "'She it was I loved and searched for from my youth. I therefore determined to take her to share my life, knowing she would be my counselor in prosperity, my comfort in cares and sorrows. By means of her, immortality shall be mine; I shall leave an everlasting memory to my successors.' In Mom's last months, being with her was to feel the truth of Saint John's words." I nodded to Ed.

He read, "'My dear, let us love one another, since love is begotten by God and everyone who loves is begotten by God and knows God. God is love and anyone who lives in love lives in God.'"

"And to misquote St. Paul ... " I said and looked at Marion.

She added her part: "'As for you, Marguerite, your life has been poured away and the time has come for you to be gone. You have fought the good fight to the end; you have run the race to the finish!' So now you receive your reward, to fly with the angels, to dance with Fred Astaire, to play the violin with Yehudi Menuhin. No matter how gloriously we imagine your dearest dreams coming true, we know heaven is all that and more. And in due time, we'll join you there, knowing our love is the tiniest glimpse of what heaven is all about."

Out of the corner of my eye, I could see Marion raise a hanky to her eyes. When her son died a year ago, she told me she was all out of tears. I guess she saved a few for me, bless her heart. She was still squeezing my hand and though my fingers were fast asleep, I didn't want her to let go.

Then Pastor Kim and Pastor Arvid sang a hymn and he played his guitar. After that, Pastor Kim talked about losing her mother a year earlier, sharing her tears with us; Joe, Joan, and Tom told about their losses. We said a "Hail Mary" because that was Mom's favorite prayer. And we sang Christmas carols for Mom's first Christmas in heaven.

"And now let's eat," I blurted out. Pastor Arvid made it sound more dignified. "Yes, now that we have fed our souls, let's feed our bodies."

Out in the kitchen, I intended to busy myself with serv-

ing the cake and ice cream, but found myself hugging my
friends. I was like a dry sponge, soaking up their warmth. I
told Pastor Kim, "Thank you," and her hug assured me she
understood how much more I meant than the usual "thank
you" for a small courtesy.

We chatted cheerfully as we ate and hugged again when it
was time to go.

When I got up the next morning, I realized I felt fifty
pounds lighter. At the Haven, I told the men, "Thanks for
your help yesterday. I feel much better after sharing the farewell to Mom with my friends." Later, Bob and I were playing
cards at the kitchen table. Ed, who can behave inappropriately
sometimes, came out and said, "So you feel a lot better today?"

"Yep, I do."

"That's good!"

In ten minutes, he was back again, "So you figure your
mother is dancing with Fred Astaire?"

"Yep."

"That's good!"

So even Ed understood. That was *good*!

Back at home after our family memorial service for Mom
in December, I was getting ready for bed when I clearly heard
Mom's voice say, "Well done, Maureen." I was deeply touched
that she acknowledged me, but the emotional turmoil caught
up with me anyway. Relief that she was finally and completely all right, grief over losing her and a thousand other
emotions roiled my stomach, and my stomach rebelled.

After a week on dry toast and 7-Up, I went to the doctor
and told him how upset my stomach had been since Mom's
memorial service. He noticed my pathetic-moose sweatshirt.
"I'm trying to laugh at myself."

"That's good." He prescribed a month's worth of Tagamet
so I could make Christmas for my guys at the Haven. I really
felt like crawling in a hole and pulling it in after me, but that
wasn't practical. The Tagamet worked, but I was still up and
down. Sometimes I missed her terribly. Another night, I felt
Mom's love had finally freed me, and all of us, to be whatever

we wanted to be. Long ago, I could always think, "If Mom wants it, I don't!" or "I'm a mess because Mom was a mess. How could I succeed if she couldn't?"

One night I thought, she poisoned us by a lifetime of bitterness. She had a deprived childhood, but Mom was a very successful woman. She wanted money and she got it. She wanted to travel and she lived in a dozen foreign countries and traveled in many more. At the end, she wanted love and we all offered our best. And yet, she poisoned us. Because she *never*, until the last few months, seemed to enjoy getting what she wanted. All her life, she fiercely hung on to the garbage in her life: her anger at her father, her anger at the priest who thought she'd never get another chance to marry, the wrong things her kids did, the squalor of the countries she lived in.

Yet at the end, she let go of her bitterness and anger. Did I want to wait until I was dying before I let go of the poison? Is the poison what I want to accept of her heritage?

I wondered how much mothering Grandma Cece gave Mom. Her mom died when Cece was young, so Cece raised her brothers and sisters. With her own children, was Cece sometimes too busy earning money for food and clothes to spend much time mothering them? If Cece didn't mother Mom, how could Mom mother us?

A few years ago, I told Ellen that I thought Mom raised us to be independent because her father, a binge alcoholic, was probably an emotional yo-yo: very gentle when sober, very mean when drunk. I didn't particularly think there was physical abuse, but he was not to be depended on, *no-how*. Maybe Mom thought we'd be better off at a distance, where we couldn't get hurt so badly. But as she was dying, Mom saw that "at a distance" was a very lonely place. So she pulled herself together to tell us that.

Her father's alcoholism poisoned her even as he loved her in his weak way, but the poison wasn't enough to kill the strength and love in her, only enough to hide it. If it didn't kill her loving strength, why should I let it kill mine?

On New Year's Day, I watched the Vienna Philharmonic concert on TV. When they played the "Blue Danube Waltz"

I saw Mom dancing with Fred Astaire. I cried at the joy and beauty I felt. Death seemed very attractive, because exquisitely beautiful and splendid moments on earth were so few and so short, but heaven would be forever glorious.

Dear Frank,

I feel closer to you after our hard times together when Mom was dying. So it's high time I told you thanks. However, it will take a long Irish tale to get to why I'm thanking you.

After my cancer surgery, my right arm didn't work. After a year of exercises, physical therapy, doctoring, and a chiropractor, my neck got real nasty, too. A chiropractor fixed my neck. Doc said my shoulder was arthritic, the wear and tear kind. Nothing else had helped, so I took up swimming.

I started with six laps, fifty meters each, swimming slowly and awkwardly on my back, cuz my arm wouldn't work right, taking long breathers at each end of the pool. I kept it up, four times a week for a year and finally decided to go for fifty miles, like the other lap swimmers were doing; it took me over five months, but I did it. Another swimmer asked me if I was going to take the Life Saving course that spring; then I could be in the lifeguard rotation when the regular guards were on vacation.

My arm and neck worked pretty well, but tipping my head back to breathe in the breast stroke aggravated my neck. I couldn't do the crawl much because I couldn't breathe without getting water up my nose. It should be simple, breathe in and out of my mouth, but it just didn't work. I told the teacher about these problems and she said, "Okay, do what you can."

When I was a kid, I had to take Beginning Swimming and Intermediate Swimming twice before I passed them. I took Advanced Swimming and Junior Life Saving. When I took Senior Life Saving, you were a "victim" for the test. The first time I "rescued" you, you fought so hard that I had to hold you with both arms, so you wouldn't get away, instead of using one arm for swimming. The second time, you grabbed my wrist (as ordered) and I got out of that and all of a sudden, you grabbed me around the neck (not in the orders!). So I went under (as we were supposed to) and got loose and dragged you in again. I was so mad at you by the time I got you to shallow water, I dumped you and stalked to the beach. One of the kids asked, "Did you see how he scored you? You got a four! That's the best he's given anyone! Well, I was really proud of that, but not proud enough to stop being mad.

Anyhow, there I was, half a century old, taking Life Saving again. One of the lap swimmers, a seventy-year-old man was taking the course for the first time.

The first class, we had to jump in without letting our heads go under water. Most heads went under the first time, but not mine! That felt good! There were a lot of new things in the course, but I did fine.

On the test, I lost points for not swimming the full two laps of crawl or breast stroke, but I earned perfect scores on most of the rescues. I passed easily; so did the seventy-year-old. I had been really depressed for a long time, what with my divorce, Roy's death, my cancer and all. I hadn't realized how rotten I'd been feeling until I felt so good about passing Life Saving and swimming fifty miles.

That winter, I guarded a few times. I felt really important, just like a silly teenager. Life guarding was a high status job back when I was a teen, and I had finally achieved it, at age fifty.

But the word was out: insurance companies demanded that all guards have lifeguard class, by January. Well, I knew I'd never pass that because, among other things, I'd have to swim twenty-five meters, using the crawl, in eighteen seconds. Bob, who is a strong seventy-two year-old lap swimmer, worked for months before he could do it.

Marva, who would teach the class, was guarding for lap swimming one day. "All right," I said, "as long as you have your stopwatch here, time me, so I'll know it's way beyond me."

"Nineteen and one-tenth second." Botheration! That meant I could probably do it. So I went to the first class. Afterwards, she timed me again. Nineteen and a half seconds, reasonable after three hours of class. I first tried to go the whole way without breathing, but that didn't work, so I settled on three breaths. Scissor-kicking when I breathed usually gave me air, not water. She timed me at lap swimming; a noseful of water slowed me to twenty seconds.

Inspection was coming up at the Haven so I could only try one more time. Bob told me to eat beans the night before because jet propulsion would help. So I rested up the day before, ate half a can of beans that night and the rest with breakfast.

Here was my last chance. I did a racing dive, stroked as fast as I could, first breath, "Don't slow down, Rena," second breath, "Keep going, Rena," third breath, "Almost there, faster Rena!" I passed the finish mark and stood up.

"Seventeen and one tenth second!" The lap swimmers heard her and cheered; I was amazed and VERY proud of myself. The course itself was easy.

(To this day, Bob believes I farted my way to victory. He is so proud of helping me, I'll never tell him otherwise. Actually, beans are a good source of energy, so in a way they did propel me.)

Anyway, whenever I needed to bolster my ego among the strong young swimmers in Life Saving or Lifeguard class, I'd tell about bringing in my big brother all those years ago. If I could bring him in then, I could do it again now.

Yes, I got long-winded. It must be from all that swimming. But a good story deserves a little wind. Well, thanks for the memory of bringing you in. I earned the good score, but after all these years, thanks for giving it to me. (In those days, I couldn't hear a compliment from you.)

I'm still on an emotional roller coaster over Mom's death, but I'm keeping up the swimming. Hope you're getting through it all.

Love
Maureen

It was a gorgeous day for early March. I checked the temperature, 54 degrees, and grabbed my jacket to walk Tinker. I leashed her and out we went. Fortunately, with all the melting, the ashes I'd spread out for better traction were on top again, so her mad dash out the door didn't land me flat on my face. Across the road, potty stop. Then up the road. My heart was happy, my wide-open jacket flapped, Tinker pranced along the top of the snowbank as I walked beside it. Tinker usually strains at the leash so hard she can barely breathe but she stopped and looked at me. I laughed. Ten feet farther, she looked at me again and I laughed again.

The road still had a lot of sloppy snow, but the few bare spots were getting bigger. Except where the snow plow had spattered dirt, the snow was white and the sun sparkled off the snow in tiny flashes of rainbow colors. There were puddles of water in every low spot. I heard a couple of geese honking and the pussy willows were out.

Partly what made me so receptive to the promise of spring that day, was what happened the day before at our writers' club; each member read something she had written, so I read my short story about Grandma Cece, where she goes to her mother-in-law to cry on her shoulder about Art who is a non-providing, alcoholic husband, and Cece and Annie end up making sugar cookies.

Well, I choked up a little reading the first part, because I'd done some crying myself. I kept my eyes on the paper, but I noticed a few hands went up to a few faces to wipe off tears. When I read the fun part, I heard chuckles and when I finished, there were many compliments.

At home, I heard Mom say, "Well done, Maureen." Mom shared my accomplishment, which blew it magnificently out of proportion into a glorious triumph! "Thanks, Mom!"

That night, I dreamt I visited my childhood home. On what had been the screened-in porch, there was a lovely jungle of plants, all the way to the ceiling. The front door was a beautiful, dark oak. As I went into the living room, I was delighted with how nicely it had been fixed up, comfortably old-fashioned with lovely furniture that looked easy to sit in. Muted floral wallpaper warmed the walls. The kitchen felt right for homemade bread and cookies.

The house was one and a half stories. The upstairs had had an open archway between the two large bedrooms where my brothers and sister and I slept. Now walls and doors divided the space into four small, cozy bedrooms. The small bathroom was remodeled, too, green and peach so now it would be a neat little hideaway for reading a book, instead of a place to get in and out of as quickly as possible.

I opened the little door at the far end of the bathroom which led to the attic. The center of the attic, maybe twenty by twenty feet, had had a floor; on the sides, where the roof sloped down to the floor, and at the far end were just joists, and under them, the living room ceiling. Clothes racks and boxes cluttered up the attic.

In my dream, the whole attic was much larger. The floored area had been made into a dormitory, with six beds and dressers, very homey looking and the unfloored area was lowered several feet so on three sides, around the dormitory, were sitting areas with easy chairs, lamps and bookcases. I was especially pleased with the attic, in my dream, because it had been an unused room.

When I woke up, I smiled. The house was me. Each part of the house was a satisfying delight, but particularly the attic, which had never been used, except for storage. The attic was my group home, which was the fruit of my heritage. It had ripened as I accepted and embraced the loving strength I had received from my fore-mothers, ordinary women who lived ordinary lives extraordinarily well, as I had discovered when I had gathered family stories from Mom and her relatives, searching for yet another undeveloped aspect of my Self.

My heritage from my mother came from a long line of strong, caring women. Her father's alcoholism made it very difficult for her to pass on the caring part, but in the end, she let down her barriers and I had searched long enough to finally be able to see who she was and that she did love me very much.

The dream told me that at last my whole house was in order. And this Self, which I could finally like, which I had struggled to put together, this Self wasn't my creation after all. This Self had come from my ancestors. Thanks Maggie, Annie, Cece, Marguerite and all the rest of you. Now, my attic was a well-used room.